Kane

Blood Moon

ALSO BY STEVE GANNON

STEPPING STONES

GLOW

A SONG FOR THE ASKING

KANE

ALLISON

L.A. SNIPER

INFIDEL

Kane

Blood Moon

Steve Gannon

A
KANE
NOVEL

Kane: *Blood Moon*

Library of Congress Cataloging-in-Publication Data
Gannon, Steve.
Kane: Blood Moon / Steve Gannon.
p.   cm.
ISBN: 978-0-9979152-6-6

Printed in the United States of America
10 9 8 7 6 5 4 3 2 1

Again, for Susan—muse, kayak coach, and love of my life

And as always, for Dex

Magpie

One for sorrow,
Two for mirth
Three for a funeral,
Four for birth
Five for heaven
Six for hell
Seven for the devil, his own self

~ Michael Aislabie Denham's *Proverbs and Popular Sayings of the Seasons*, 1846

Kane

Blood Moon

Prologue
Geology Seminar

She was stunning.

Watching her hurrying to class, he felt a rush of anticipation. He fought against it. For the next few hours he needed to maintain complete and absolute control.

There would be time enough later for what was to come.

Careful not to follow too closely, he kept her just in view, watching as she made her way through the Murphy Sculpture Garden. Then, pretending to be talking on his cellphone, he trailed her past the Law School building farther south. Glancing briefly at the ornate brick structure as he passed, he smiled to himself, recalling having presented several law lectures there years back.

A second-year graduate student, she was currently enrolled in UCLA's Earth, Planetary, and Space Sciences Department. With her parents picking up the tab, she was working on a Master of Science degree in geology. On two previous occasions he had followed her to her Friday night geology seminar.

This evening would be the last.

From weeks of social media research, he knew much about her. He knew she was twenty-three years old, the daughter of a police captain, and that she had a younger sister who was almost as beautiful as she. He knew she lived off-campus in an apartment on Gayley Avenue, and that she was taking a six-week summer geology course to complete several missing units. He also knew that upon completion of her studies, she planned to work as a petroleum geologist—knocking down a respectable six-figure salary.

More to the point, he knew where she parked her car, a late-model Toyota 4Runner. He had positioned his van adjacent to it in the parking structure.

As she passed the Schoenberg Music Building, he increased his pace. She was nearing her destination, and he wanted to make certain she was safely ensconced in her classroom before returning to his van.

Minutes later, as her tall, slim figure disappeared through the geology building doors, he smiled again, thinking of the next time they would meet.

Everything was ready.

There was nothing to do now but wait.

Chapter 1
Taken

Ella Snead hated being late.

As she rushed back to her car—a backpack crammed with notes and textbooks slung over one shoulder—she glanced at her watch, mentally cursing whoever had barred Parking Structure 2 to graduate student use. Although her hard-won UCLA parking pass still granted access to Parking Structures 3, 4, and 7, they were a half-mile farther from the geology building than Lot 2. Worse, Lots 4 and 7 were two-level buildings and usually always full—especially on nights when an event like Homecoming, Bruin Family Weekend, or a basketball game was scheduled.

Which left Parking Structure 3. Sure, Lot 3 was huge, but it was also all the way up on Hilgard and Sunset—a *mile* farther from her geology classrooms. Ella glanced again at her watch. Her seminar had run late, and she was supposed to meet friends for dinner in Santa Monica. There was no way she was going to make it on time.

As she passed Parking Structure 2, she sighed in frustration, noting that several floors of the seven-level building appeared vacant. "It isn't fair," she said aloud, increasing her pace.

For one, Ella told herself, UCLA was an R1 institution—meaning that a significant portion of university funding came from research grants. And graduate students, most of whom worked later hours than their faculty contemporaries, were the nonpaid workhorses who brought in much of that money. Bottom line, graduate students shouldn't have to trudge all the way across campus just to get to their cars . . . especially late at night.

Twenty minutes later, upon reaching Lot 3, Ella had nearly decided to pen a scathing letter of complaint—assuming she could determine where to send it. Is so, maybe she could get one of her law-school friends to help. She knew several whom the recent Lot 2 change had inconvenienced, although to be accurate, law students had a considerably shorter journey to Lot 3 than did she.

Upon reaching her 4Runner, Ella sighed again. Although plenty of empty slots on her level still remained, a careless student had parked a van right next to her car, leaving little space between them.

Probably some frat guy late for a Friday night beer-bust, she thought irritably.

Ella hesitated. Then, after glancing around and seeing no one present, she unslung her backpack. Removing her keys from a side pouch, she began squeezing between her Toyota and the van, deciding there was still enough room to slip into her driver's side door.

As she inched forward, the van's cargo door suddenly slid open.

"Sorry, did I park too close?" said a tall, dark-haired man, stepping out behind her.

Startled, Ella dropped her backpack, feeling the first tendrils of alarm. "A little," she mumbled, bending to retrieve it. "But I think I can manage."

"Here, let me help," the man offered, pushing something into her back.

An excruciating shock coursed through Ella's body.

She screamed in pain. Her torso twisted, beginning to convulse.

An instant later her legs gave out.

A gloved hand clamped across her mouth, muffling her cries.

And still the pain continued, wave upon wave of electrical current coursing through her limbs.

Strong arms dragged her into the van.

Seconds later she felt a needle stab, then a burning sensation in her arm.

Her hands were forced behind her, her wrists quickly lashed. Her ankles were secured as well.

It may have been only seconds; it may have been a minute. But by the time the pain finally eased, Ella was barely able to speak.

This can't be happening, she thought.

Heart racing in terror, she gazed up at her abductor with horror-filled eyes. "Why?" she managed to sob.

The man didn't respond. Instead, he slapped a strip of tape across her mouth.

She couldn't get any air.

Don't panic. Breathe through your nose . . .

Ella strained against her bonds, her eyes traveling the interior of the van, searching for a way out.

An extension ladder was bungeed to the wall behind her.

Below that, a metal container—the lid open, holes in the top.

Something lay sprawled on the floor beside her, covered with a tarp.

A body?

Adding to Ella's terror, a paralyzing lethargy had taken command of her limbs.

She could barely hold up her head.

The shot he'd given her?

The hazy realization occurred that if she were ever to escape, that time was now.

She had to fight.

But by then it was too late.

Chapter 2
Jacob's Ladder

Have you ever been somewhere and suddenly realized you were utterly out of your element? You're at a party, say. Everyone there has a Ph.D., and they all want to discuss their dissertations. Or a friend has convinced you to attend one of his drum-circle "therapy sessions," and now the presiding shaman wants you to share.

Like that.

In my case, I was at a world-class kayaking competition being held on some of the most dangerous whitewater in North America, and I didn't know one end of a kayak from the other. Fortunately, I wasn't competing.

But a good friend of mine, Special Agent Sara Taylor, was.

Considering that I owed her my life, I was there that afternoon to support Taylor in any way I could. Still, as I glanced around, I felt isolated, surrounded by strangers, and completely out of place.

"When will Sara be taking her first run?" asked my youngest son, Nate, yelling to be heard over the roar of the river behind us.

Turning, I was struck by how much my youngest had matured over the past several years. He would be turning seventeen the following day and now stood well over six feet tall. If he kept growing, I thought absently, he would wind up being as big as I am, maybe bigger.

Unfortunately, the resemblance between us didn't end there. Although Nate was street-smart, athletically gifted, and strong, he also had a dark side. Of all my children, Nate's teenage years had been the hardest—not only for him, but for the rest of our family as well. Impulsive, loyal to a fault, quick to both laughter and anger, his moods as transparent as crystal, Nate, God help him, was the most like me.

"That's Agent Taylor to you, Nate," I said. "And to answer your question, I'm not certain when she'll be taking her first run.

Soon, I would think. She placed second last year, so she's seeded in the top five."

At FBI Special Agent Taylor's request, Nate and I had accompanied my friend to Banks, Idaho, to watch her compete in the elite division of the North Fork Championship. Taylor's race was an invitation-only event in which a field of twenty-five expert kayakers from around the world would compete on class-five whitewater that was beyond the ability of most, with Taylor being one of only two female entrants in a field primarily dominated by men. Making the competition especially dangerous, the previous winter had been an extreme snow season for Idaho, and the North Fork of the Payette River was running at record levels. The water had claimed lives earlier in the year, and several competitors had taken one look at the turbulent course and quickly resigned from the race.

As near as I could estimate, about six or seven hundred kayaking enthusiasts were gathered there that sunny Saturday afternoon to watch the competition. Although barely 1:00 p.m., the temperature had already risen into the mid-eighties, with sandals, T-shirts, and swimsuits seeming the order of the day. Flanking a procession of parked cars, a fleet of kayaking kiosks, shade canopies, and food stands lined the roadside bank of the river, their colorful presence lending a festive atmosphere to the event, despite the obvious danger involved.

"The lineup lists Taylor's last name as Blackadar," Nate observed. "Shouldn't I be calling her Agent Blackadar?"

"'Taylor' was her married name," I explained. "She still uses that for work at the Bureau. Her granddad was a kayaking pioneer. There's some history there, so she goes by 'Blackadar' when she competes."

"Well, whatever she calls herself, she's awesome, huh?"

I realized I was being tested. "She's a *friend*, Nate. I'm not looking for anyone to replace your mom."

My wife, Catheryn, mother of our four children and the only woman I have ever truly loved, had been killed by a sniper's bullet the previous year. Although eight months had passed in the

17

interim, her loss was still as keen as if it had happened yesterday, wounding our entire family, every one of us, beyond repair.

And her death was because of me.

Nate lowered his gaze. "I know," he said. Then, brightening, "Sara—I mean, Agent Taylor—said that after the race she would get me into a hard-shell kayak and teach me to paddle. We're still sticking around, right?"

I nodded. "All week, assuming you don't drown," I answered with a smile.

Following the conclusion of a problematic murder investigation the previous spring, I had taken some time off from work to decide what to do with the rest of my life. Although I had recently resumed my position as the D-III supervising detective for the West Los Angeles LAPD homicide unit, I still had plenty of accumulated vacation days, and I intended to use them.

"Are you going to join us on the river? Agent Taylor said there are lots of easy sections we could do."

"Maybe," I answered uncertainly. "Although I'm not sure there's a kayak out there that will fit me," I added, being considerably larger than most of the boaters I had seen on the river.

"C'mon, Dad." Nate coaxed. "Agent Taylor said you could squeeze into a Zet Director or maybe a Jackson Nirvana, whatever they are."

"We'll see," I replied, realizing that like it or not, I would probably be joining my son on the river.

In the wake of Catheryn's death, Nate had experienced a deep depression that nearly ended in tragedy. Our family had come together in support, and although Nate was being treated with antidepressants and attending weekly therapy sessions, we were all still concerned about him. As kayaking was the first thing in which he had shown any interest in quite some time, I wanted to nurture that interest in any way I could, even if it meant cramming myself into a tippy kayak and heading down some cold, choppy river—probably upside down.

Nate peered over my shoulder. "Hey, isn't that Agent Taylor's boat up there on the ramp?"

18

I glanced behind me at the boat launch—a long, curving structure with a "Red Bull" banner hung on the side. The end of the ramp had been extended out over the river, about a hundred yards up-current from the first rapid. As Nate had noted, Taylor's red kayak was now perched on top, second in line behind another competitor's.

"That's her," I said. "Let's climb down the bank for a better look."

Together, Nate and I scrambled down a granite-strewn embankment to a boulder just feet above the swollen river. That close to the water, it was impossible to hear anything but the roar of the rapids, and Nate and I gave up on conversation and simply watched.

Shortly afterward, the competition got underway.

Downstream from the launch ramp, the race began in earnest at a rapid called Jacob's Ladder—or to locals, simply Jake's—continuing through a dangerous series of drops known as Golf Course. Increasing the course difficulties, tubular PVC gates had been hung above the water, their placement forcing boaters to take the most challenging lines, with significant penalties imposed for missing or even touching a gate.

Taylor was the second competitor off the ramp. I held my breath as I watched her kayak fly off the end, splashing to the raging river ten feet below. She somehow managed to angle her boat in the air, landing on an edge that quickly turned her downstream, gaining a few precious seconds. Several strong strokes brought her to the initiation of Jacob's Ladder, at which point she disappeared beneath the roiling water.

My hands suddenly turned clammy.

An instant later Taylor reappeared, her white helmet barely visible above the churning foam. She powered through a standing wave, flew off its crest, and paddled hard to make the initial series of gates. Again she edged, putting her craft on a seemingly impossible angle to complete the move.

The crowd around us began cheering at her approach. Mouths agape, Nate and I watched as Taylor negotiated an unpredictable, chaotic feature that I later learned was called Taffy Puller—a curling, pencil-sharpener wave that proved the downfall of many contestants who followed.

A quick series of strokes brought her to the second set of gates. Taylor ducked to avoid clipping one of the plastic tubes as she passed, braced with her paddle, slipped her boat sideways, and reentered the violent main current. Moments later she flashed around a bend and was gone, vanishing behind a copse of pines.

Nate and I sat in stunned silence. Actually, even if my son had been able to hear me above the roar of the river, I don't think I could have found words to express my surprise and admiration for the athleticism I had just witnessed.

From the awed look on Nate's face, I knew he felt the same.

Forty-five minutes later, following the first round of competitors, a break was called in the race to give contestants a chance to rest before the commencement of the second half. So far there had been no serious injuries. No one had been forced to swim either, which despite the presence of safety boaters along the shoreline, was always a dangerous occurrence on the North Fork.

While Nate and I were waiting for the second round to begin, we returned to the road to look for Taylor. Shuttle vehicles had been stationed downstream to ferry boats and contestants back to the starting ramp, but Taylor had yet to return. Upon reaching the top of the embankment, Nate turned to me, astonishment at the extraordinary event we had just watched still shining in his eyes. "Holy shit," he said.

"You can say that again," I agreed.

Nate grinned. "Holy shit."

Peering downstream, I spotted Taylor's white helmet among a group of contestants, with grins and high-fives getting shared all around. Watching, I was struck by the support the boaters were showing for one another, and I could see why Nate wanted a piece of the sport—although I hoped that his kayaking involvement, were he to pursue his interest, would never take him onto the waters of the North Fork.

I was about to suggest that we get something to eat when my cellphone rang. I glanced at the screen.

It read: "No Caller ID."

I decided to take the call anyway. "Dan Kane," I said, catching Nate's attention and pointing toward a kiosk selling hotdogs.

"Detective Kane?"

"Who's calling?"

"Let's play."

"Who is this?" I asked.

But by then, the line had gone dead.

"Everything okay?" asked Nate.

"Crank call," I said, repocketing my phone. "C'mon, let's go grab some grub."

But despite my assurance to Nate, something about the call bothered me. I was almost certain that voice-changing software had been used.

Why?

Nate and I downed a couple hotdogs apiece, washing them down with a Coke. Afterward, still disturbed by the call, I decided to get a *57 Verizon trace. But as I withdrew my phone to do so, it rang again.

"Listen, pal," I said without checking the screen. "I don't know how you got my cellphone number, but—"

"Dan, this is Lieutenant Long."

Nelson Long was my boss at the West L.A. station, as well as being one of few members of the LAPD brass whom I trusted. "Sorry, Lieutenant. Thought you were someone else."

"I need you back here," said Long, as usual cutting to the chase.

"I'm on vacation."

"You're a homicide investigator, Dan. You're always on call."

"Tomorrow is Nate's birthday."

"I know, and I'm sorry, but something's come up. The body of a young woman was discovered on UCLA campus this morning. Deluca has taken lead on the investigation so far, but the press is already all over it, and it's going to be a mess. An

21

expedited postmortem exam is scheduled for tomorrow morning. We need you back here ASAP."

Glancing at Nate, I felt a sense of unease at the prospect of handling what would undoubtedly become another high-profile murder case. My job had endangered my family more than once, and I didn't want a repeat. Nevertheless, I was also drawn by the possibility of losing myself, if only temporarily, in a new investigation. Deciding that if things got personal, as they had in the past, I could always back away.

"I'll catch a plane back this afternoon," I said.

Nate had been listening. He looked away as I disconnected. "You have to leave?" he said, unable to hide his disappointment.

Days earlier, Taylor, Nate, and I had driven together to Idaho. With two of Taylor's kayaks strapped to the roof of my Suburban, stopping only for food and gas, we had made it to the Payette River in record time. Currently, we were camped in a beautiful forested area overlooking the South Fork of the Payette. I was bunking on a foam pad in the back of the Suburban; Nate and Taylor were sleeping in tents. Despite our bucolic setup, our rustic camping was significantly improved by the presence of clean bathrooms and showers, a Subway franchise, and several excellent restaurants within few minutes' drive. It was a kid's paradise, and I knew Nate didn't want to leave.

In answer to his question, I nodded. "Sorry, Nate. If you want, you can stay up here with Taylor and come home later, as planned."

Nate looked doubtful. "Really?"

"Really. No reason your vacation should be ruined because of me. I'll regret missing your birthday tomorrow, though. Maybe we can do something special when you get back?"

"I'd like that, Dad."

"Then consider it done." I hesitated, wanting to say more. "I'm proud of you," I finally managed. "You know that, right?"

Nate looked away. "With all that's happened, I'm not sure why."

"None of what happened was your fault. That was entirely because of me. No one else."

"You can't take all the blame, Dad—especially when it comes to me. You remember what Ali says about mental illness, right?"

Nate was referring to his older sister, Allison, who usually had some smartass comment to make about nearly everything. "Yeah, she claims mental illness is hereditary," I laughed. "You inherit it from your kids." Then, in an effort to turn the conversation, "Speaking of which, your mom had something to say about children, too."

"Not to have them?"

I smiled. "Some would agree with you on that. But no, your mother had other ideas on the subject."

"Okay, what did Mom say about kids?" Nate asked, returning my smile.

"Your mom thought having children is a gift you give yourself."

Nate's smile faded. "Huh," he mused.

"And the longer I'm around, the more I tend to agree with her." Then, placing my hands on Nate's shoulders and holding his gaze, I repeated, "I'm proud of you, Nate. Not only for being a great son, but also for the way you've handled some really hard things—things that would have devastated more than a few adults, let alone someone your age. Anyway, I guess what I'm trying to say is, happy birthday. I'm sorry I won't be here tomorrow to help you celebrate, but I hope it's a good one."

Chapter 3
It Goes to a Hundred

Ella Snead woke to a pounding headache and the astringent smell of Lysol.

For a moment she had no idea where she was. Adding to her confusion, something was fastened around her neck.

Ella opened her eyes. With the exception of a dim glow coming from somewhere above her, she was immersed in total darkness.

She lay for several seconds without moving, trying to clear her mind.

Then the horror came flooding back.

Oh, God, where am I?

With a groan, Ella raised a hand to her throat. Searching with her fingers, she explored whatever was encircling her neck. It felt like a nylon strap, with a rectangular box attached to one side.

A dog collar? Jesus. Get it off!

Ella fumbled at the buckle fastener, her fingers scrabbling at the webbing. Below her chin she found what felt like a small padlock.

Fighting panic, she sat up. A rough fabric lay beneath her. A woolen blanket, maybe. And a pillow.

A bed?

In addition to the throbbing in her temples, Ella's lower back was on fire. Reaching behind her, she felt a pair of raised welts just above the line of her underwear.

From his shocking device?

Carefully, she eased her legs off the bed, finding the floor with her feet.

Now what?

A harsh light suddenly came on.

Squinting into the glare, Ella quickly scanned her surroundings. She was on a small bed in the corner of a rectangular, windowless room. To her left and behind her, concrete walls formed three sides of the chamber. To her right, the thick metal bars of an iron door formed the fourth.

Ella's breath caught in her throat.

On the other side of the bars, her abductor sat lounging in a chair, an arm's length from her bed.

Hairs rose on the back of her neck.

How long had he been watching?

"Why are you . . . why are you doing this?" Ella stammered.

The man stared, his expression displaying nothing. Slowly, he cocked his head, as if he were inspecting an insect.

"My parents have money," Ella pleaded, trying to keep her voice from quavering. "I promise I won't tell."

The man shifted. As if considering Ella's proposal, he leaned forward, forming a steeple with his fingers.

Ella had only glimpsed the man briefly during his attack. Now she regarded him carefully, hoping for an explanation. He was tall and appeared to be in his early forties. He was also strikingly handsome, with thick black hair that came to a widow's peak in front, and a muscular, athletic torso. Despite his movie-star appearance, Ella shuddered as she looked into his eyes, seeing nothing behind them but cold, endless darkness.

"Please," Ella begged, suddenly close to tears. "Just . . . let me go. I won't tell."

The man raised a hand. In it, he held a small device. He pressed a button.

A tone sounded from Ella's collar.

Her hand went to her throat. "What was that?"

"A warning. No more lies."

Ella fell silent. Unable to meet the man's gaze, she again glanced around her prison. In the light of an industrial ceiling fixture, she noted a steel sink mounted on the back wall. A preformed plastic tub and shower stall sat beside it, a cabinet and a toilet nearby. On the ceiling, near the light, was an exhaust fan and what appeared to be a webcam. She also noticed that her bed was bolted to the floor.

"You will bathe when your light is first turned on, and you will keep your cell clean and presentable at all times," the man instructed, his voice devoid of even the smallest trace of compassion.

Again regarding her captor, Ella suddenly had the impression that despite his handsome face, it was as if he were wearing a mask, a façade of mimicked human expression that hid something unspeakable beneath.

"You will find a supply of dry food, makeup, and toiletry items in the cabinet by the sink," the man continued. "You may occasionally receive a hot meal. Each day you will place all trash and uneaten food in a plastic bag and set it outside the bars. Near the cabinet is a composting toilet, which requires following directions on the lid. Drinking water is available at the sink. Do you understand everything so far?"

"Please let me go," Ella sobbed, lowering her head.

"Do you understand?" the man repeated.

"Yes. I . . . I understand."

"In addition, you will wear any garments I may provide, and you will follow any instructions I give—immediately and without question. Again, do you understand?"

Ella nodded.

"Out loud."

"I understand."

Raising her chin, Ella risked another look at her captor. He was sitting in a small alcove, walled off from her prison by the bars of the cell door. A portal with an archery-slit window and a deadbolt lock was set in the wall behind him. Photography lights stood nearby, along with articles of camera equipment. There was also a cabinet, similar to the one in her cell. Behind the photography lights was a chest refrigerator, with ropes and pulleys mounted above it. An industrial handcart was leaned against a nearby wall, close to a metal storage box with holes drilled in the top.

With a shiver, Ella realized she had probably been transported in that very box.

The man stood. "Remove your blouse and skirt."

Ella shook her head. "No, please . . ."

The man scowled. Pressing a button on his device, he delivered a brutal electrical shock to Ella's throat.

Ella screamed, clutching at her collar.

Though the shock lasted less than a second, it was cruelly convincing.

"Stop," Ella pleaded. "No more."

"Remove your blouse and skirt," the man repeated.

As Ella began undressing, the man brought his remote control close to the bars. A display on its face read, "10."

"It goes to a hundred," said the man. "Don't make me use it again."

Later, as she lay alone in the darkness, Ella recalled the photographic equipment she had seen outside her cell. Were it not for her initial confusion, she would have known earlier.

Now, she did.

She had seen news accounts of a kidnapper whom the media were calling The Magpie, and she had seen the online photos he had posted of his victims. She now knew who had taken her, and what was to be her fate.

And with that knowledge coiling in her mind—scathing in its hideous, unalterable consequence—Ella screamed, screamed, muffling her cries with her fists, her eyes welling hot, bitter tears, her heart filled with desolation and hopelessness and abject, bottomless despair.

Chapter 4
Autopsy

After catching a last-minute flight home from Boise, I grabbed a cab at LAX, made a quick stop at the West L.A. station, and returned home to my house in Malibu.

The next morning, following a few hours of sleep, I drove Catheryn's Volvo to the Los Angeles County Coroner's office on North Mission. Being Sunday, traffic was light most of the way in. Arriving early, I spent some time in the Volvo reviewing the case, perusing a thick, three-ringed binder known in LAPD vernacular as a murder book.

The murder book, which against departmental regulations I had borrowed from the station the previous evening, would eventually contain all records and files pertinent to the UCLA homicide investigation—autopsy findings, field-interview summaries, detailed measurements of the dumpsite, and so on—although at the moment the only records present were Deluca's death report, his preliminary entries in the crime report, and several photographs. Although over the course of my career I had seen more than my share of human cruelty, I found those photos difficult to view.

Thirty minutes later I attended a Class A postmortem exam of the remains of the unidentified young woman whose nightgown-clad corpse had been found on UCLA campus—her body hung from a stand of bamboo in the Mildred E. Mathias Botanical Garden—her long, wet hair clinging to her scalp, a ritualistic application of makeup painting her face.

The official coroner's report, including a toxicology screen for the presence of drugs and toxins, would not be available for days, but the initial findings were consistent with a cause-of-death diagnosis of carotid obstruction and asphyxiation by strangulation, with carotid bruises on internal tissues demonstrated at autopsy. Although the hyoid bone in her throat was still intact, petechial lesions—burst capillaries on her face and the conjunctiva of her eyes indicative of strangulation—were also noted.

Livor mortis, a port-wine staining of the skin caused by pooling of blood in the lowest portions of a body after death, was present on the young woman's back and buttocks. Because livor mortis becomes fixed and unchangeable within a few hours of death, the purplish markings indicated that the body had been moved postmortem and placed in a different position. From this I concluded that the Botanical Garden probably hadn't been the murder site, merely the place where the body had been dumped.

Additional observations by the forensic pathologist included the presence of ligature marks on the woman's wrists and ankles. Tissue bruising indicated that these lesions had occurred premortem, as opposed to a number of postmortem injuries to the chest, legs, and forearms caused by her body having been hung with wire—again suggesting that the young woman had been murdered elsewhere.

Other findings included a two-inch encirclement of roughened skin on the neck, a lesion not considered as having been caused by ligature, but rather by the prolonged presence of some sort of collar. Within the "collar mark," fresh burns on one side of the throat were present, along with additional burns in various stages of healing. Puncture wounds were found on the woman's back. I had seen similar injuries during a departmental Taser demonstration, left after the Taser's electrical barbs were removed from an unhappy volunteer's skin.

Genital tearing and bruising, along with the presence of a spermicidal lubricant, indicated that the young woman had been raped premortem, but the possibility of postmortem penetration was not discounted. Because of the spermicidal gel, it was likely that the assailant had used a condom, making the presence of semen doubtful.

In a case such as this in which rape is suspected, the coroner's investigator had undoubtedly taken DNA swabs at the scene. Nevertheless, at my direction, a second set of swabs were procured from the victim's mouth, vagina, and anus. Swabs were also taken from the carotid areas of the neck, in the hope the killer might have left trace DNA during the act of strangulation.

The presence of soap under the victim's nails and the damp condition of her hair suggested that the killer had washed her body after death, making the procurement of skin evidence— touch DNA, fibers, hairs, semen, latent fingerprints, and so on— unlikely. We ran the tests anyway.

Although I realized we were undoubtedly duplicating efforts made at the UCLA site, because I had not been present at that time, I had additional photographs and fingerprints taken as well, along with dental radiographs to assist in identifying the body.

The killer had been extremely careful, implying that this wasn't his first murder. From the photos, it was also clear that he liked what he was doing, and that he possessed more than a passing knowledge of police procedures.

Bottom line, I had a bad feeling that this was just the beginning, and it was going to get worse.

Chapter 5
Botanical Garden

Following the autopsy, I took the 10 Freeway back across town, unsettled by what I had learned. Traffic continued to be light, and twenty minutes later I turned north on the 405 Freeway, exiting via the Westwood off-ramp. Upon arriving in Westwood I planned to meet my partner, Detective Paul Deluca, at the UCLA Mildred E. Mathias Botanical Garden. Before proceeding any further with the investigation, I wanted to get Deluca's take on the case.

Still thinking about the autopsy, I descended onto Wilshire Boulevard and headed toward UCLA. Before arriving, however, I received an unexpected call from my daughter. Even before picking up, I knew what she wanted.

"Please tell me you're covering the UCLA murder," Allison blurted, getting right to the point. Despite the rush of city noise outside the car, I could hear the excitement in her voice.

Although Catheryn's Volvo had Bluetooth capability, I had never liked using a car stereo for conversation, so instead I switched my iPhone to speaker and placed it on the dashboard. "What makes you think I'm back from Idaho?" I replied, avoiding giving her an answer.

Allison was a newscaster for CBS2/KCAL9. She had recently moved up to an anchor position on CBS News at 6, her meteoric rise at the network mostly due to brains, talent, and perseverance. Nevertheless, at least part of her ascent up the media food chain was thanks to her ability to worm information out of her police-detective father, who would be me. When it came to my job, Allison and I had butted heads over the issue of access in the past, and more than once.

"Grandma Dorothy told me you were back," Ali replied, her tone indicating that I should have known.

Catheryn's mother, Dorothy, had driven down from Santa Barbara and been staying at our Malibu beach house for the past several weeks. Despite being a brand-new mother, Allison had returned to work shortly after giving birth, and Dorothy was helping to care for my granddaughter, Katie.

"C'mon, Dad," Allison begged. "Lauren says this story is going to go national," she added, referring to the Los Angeles CBS bureau chief, Lauren Van Owen. "Talk to me."

"What do you want to talk about?" I asked, attempting to delay the inevitable.

"Dad . . ."

"Look, Ali, I just got back to town. I don't have anything to tell you. And even if I did, I'm not in a sharing mood."

"Okay. I understand. But let me point out something here, in case you've forgotten. We worked well together on the Infidel investigation. Granted, I got a promotion, but you got something, too. Never hurts to have a friend in the media, remember?"

"I remember," I said, begrudging the point.

"So I'm simply suggesting the same arrangement as before. Anything you can tell me without compromising your case will be held in strictest confidence. Then, when I have your permission to use it, I'll attribute whatever you give me to 'unnamed sources in the department.' What do you say?"

"What do I say? I say I can't believe I raised such a pushy daughter."

"Runs in the family, Pop."

As much as I hated to admit it, Allison was right about having a friend in the media. I thought for a moment, deciding there were a few items that would undoubtedly be revealed at a press conference later that day. "Okay, maybe there are a couple things I can give you," I said. "But they had better not come back to bite me later."

"Don't worry," Ali assured me, something in her manner reminding me of a cheetah spotting a limp. "And thanks. Like Lauren said, I have a feeling this story is going to go ballistic."

"It's not a *story*, Ali. We're talking about the murder of a young girl."

"Sorry. You know what I mean. This *investigation* has all the earmarks of turning into a media frenzy, and I want to get in on the ground floor."

"Okay," I said. "I can tell you this: The autopsy of an unidentified woman was performed this morning at the L.A. County Coroner's office. The preliminary cause of death will be listed as carotid obstruction and asphyxiation by strangulation. The examination results will also indicate that the victim was probably not murdered in UCLA's Botanical Garden, but that her body was placed there at some later time."

"Anything else?"

"Not at the moment. By the way, the information I just gave you will probably be revealed at a press conference later today, so feel free to use it now."

"I owe you, Dad."

"And I intend to collect."

"Anytime. One last question. Was there any indication that the victim had been held for some period of time before her murder?"

"Why would you ask that?" I hedged, recalling the partially healed burns on the woman's neck.

"Just a long shot—trying to connect the UCLA murder with another story. Never mind. Hey, are you going to make it to dinner at the beach tonight? My hardworking husband Mike is still shooting on location, but I'm bringing Katie, and Grandma Dorothy said she's fixing something special," Allison coaxed. "Travis is flying home from New York today, too."

"First I've heard of it. But unless something comes up, I'll be there," I replied. "Seeing my granddaughter is always a treat. Travis, too," I added, referring to my oldest son, who was enrolled in a music program at Juilliard. I hadn't seen Trav in months, and I was looking forward to catching up.

"Excellent," said Allison. "See you there."

Shortly after hanging up, I arrived at the UCLA Botanical Garden, a steep canyon preserve situated on the southeast corner of campus. Its lush acres contained diverse plants and trees from around the world, along with several ponds and a stream trailing down the center. Not surprisingly, a fleet of mobile news vans were parked on the street outside, with reporters doing stand-ups in front of the garden's south entrance. A crowd of onlookers had gathered on the sidewalk nearby, and I noticed LAPD patrolmen in their midst taking statements.

As the garden grounds were still under investigation, yellow crime-scene tape was strung across the corner of Hilgard and Le Conte Avenues, blocking the garden gate. Upon arriving I pulled into a red zone, parking behind an LAPD cruiser. As I exited my car, I noticed Deluca's vehicle across the street, also parked in the red.

"Detective Kane!" shouted a reporter as I started across the pavement. "Any update on the murder?"

At this, the rest of the pack turned my way.

"No comment," I replied, heading for the safety of the crime-scene tape.

"Have you identified the victim?" another reporter called.

I kept walking. "No comment," I repeated.

One of the journalists stepped in front of me, blocking my way. "C'mon, Kane, give me something," she begged, thrusting a microphone in my face.

"What part of 'no comment' didn't you understand, Lois?" I asked, recognizing her from an earlier case.

Although startled by being called by name, the reporter persisted. "Considering the way the body was displayed, could this be the work of The Magpie?"

Her question was something I hadn't considered. I knew that a serial killer whom the press had nicknamed The Magpie was currently active in the Pacific Northwest. Upon discarding the body of a victim, one of the killer's signature behaviors was the immediate kidnapping of another woman from the same area, hence the name. Like magpies and their larger crow cousins, the killer was leaving a shiny object—in this case the corpse of a previous victim—in place of another young woman he stole. But as far as I knew, no one had been kidnapped at UCLA.

Encouraged by my hesitation, Lois pushed on. "Does this mean The Magpie has taken another victim?"

"The Magpie?" I said, beginning to lose my temper. "I have never been able to fathom why you news people insist on coming up with some cutesy-pie name for every dirtbag who commits this kind of crime. The Magpie? Really? As far as I'm concerned, whoever killed that young woman and hung her up in there like garbage is bottom-feeding scum—and I intend to see he gets exactly what he deserves."

"And what is that?" asked Lois, still thrusting her microphone in my face.

I pushed past, having had enough. "Use your imagination," I muttered.

Ignoring a continued barrage of questions, I finally managed to duck under the crime-tape barrier. On the other side I joined Deluca, who was conferring with a patrol officer keeping an official record known as a crime scene log, recording the name of each person entering the garden. At my approach, Deluca looked up and grinned. "Hey, *paisano*. Been making friends with our brothers and sisters in the media out there?"

"Hardly."

"Roger that. Know what they call a busload of reporters heading over a cliff?"

Having heard it before, I smiled. "A good start," I replied, displaying my ID to the officer manning the crime scene log. As he began entering my name, rank, and shield number into his record, I turned back to Deluca. "By the way, I grabbed the murder book from the station last night. I'll get it back later."

Deluca nodded. "You read it?"

"I did. Now I want you to run it down for me."

"Sure." Deluca rubbed his chin, which already displayed a dark, five-o'clock shadow that routinely made an appearance on his face well before noon, no matter how closely he shaved. "We got a call yesterday from the UCLA police informing us that the body of a young woman had been found in the Botanical Garden," he continued. "I spoke with a Lieutenant Greenly, who commands the university's Investigative Division. He was more than happy to let LAPD take over, as they aren't really set up to handle a murder investigation. Banowski and I rolled on it, arriving here around eleven."

"Who found the body?"

"A couple of art students. Came down to sketch some plants or whatever. The garden opens at nine a.m. on weekends, but no one had been in the area till then. We interviewed the students. Nothing much there. You see the pictures?"

"Yeah," I answered. The photos in the murder book had showed the victim hung with wire from stalks of bamboo, as if on display. The weight of her body had dislocated both her shoulders, reminding me of a painting I had once seen, *The Crucifixion of Saint Andrew*, by Caravaggio.

"Grim," said Deluca. "Whoever did that doesn't deserve to be breathing the same air as the rest of us."

I nodded. Death penalty opponents could often argue a good case until they saw something like that, after which they began to have doubts.

Glancing across the street, I noted several additional mobile news vans setting up on Hilgard. A media frenzy was developing, and I had been in that situation before. In a murder investigation, a news blitz was usually a no-win situation for everyone, especially the police. As such, I was still unsure whether I wanted to continue working the case, considering that my past involvement in high-profile investigations had sometimes ended badly. On the other hand, I had become progressively angry at the callous manner in which the young woman had been killed and discarded like trash. "This is going to be a mess," I noted.

"No doubt about it, *paisano*."

I took a deep breath, deciding to put off a decision as whether to continue the case. For now, I resolved to set aside my misgivings and concentrate on elements of the investigation. "Who came out from SID?" I asked, referring to the LAPD's Scientific Investigation Division criminalist responsible for the collection and preservation of all trace evidence taken from the scene. Although SID had recently split into two new bureaus— the Technical Investigation Division (TID), and the Forensic Science Division (FSD)—most investigators, like me, found it impossible to keep up with changing departmental acronyms and still used the old ones.

"Frank Tremmel," answered Deluca.

"Good. Did Art Walters from the coroner's office work the case, by any chance?"

"Yep. Everyone sent out their first-string."

"Excellent," I said. I had worked with both Tremmel and Walters on previous investigations, and I knew their skills to be topnotch.

"According to liver temp and the state of rigor, Walters estimated the time of death at somewhere between midnight Thursday and four a.m. Friday—although he hedged the timeframe because the body had been moved," Deluca went on, referring to his notebook. "In any case, the garden usually closes at five p.m., so we're assuming the killer dumped the body sometime after that, probably at night."

"Dumped? More like *displayed*."

"Yeah. Sick bastard's obviously looking for attention. Anyway, we've been canvassing for witnesses since yesterday. With all the sororities and student housing across the street, not to mention campus buildings overlooking the garden, it's a huge area to cover. UCLA police are assisting. We had some guys detailed over from Pacific Division as well. So far no results."

I looked up, spotting a number of UCLA structures topping a rise to the west, most with a view of the garden. "So the question is, how did our guy get in here without being seen?" I wondered aloud.

"Here's how I have it figured," said Deluca. "We found what looked like fresh tire marks on the curb at the corner of Le Conte and Hilgard. In addition to a couple of maintenance gates, there are only three entrances into the garden—two up on the ridge off Tiverton Drive, and the third down here on Le Conte. All the gate locks were intact except for a padlock here on the south entrance, which was missing. We're assuming our guy jumped the curb, cut the lock, and drove in, concealing his vehicle deeper in the garden."

"Makes sense," I said. "Late at night, if he timed it right, no one would notice. And once he was in, he would have all the time he needed to hang the body and do whatever else he did in there. Anyone find the lock?"

Deluca shook his head. "Maybe he took it with him. Anyway, I had SID take casts and photos of fresh tire tracks in the dirt. I checked with the groundskeepers. The tire impressions were wider than their maintenance vehicles' wheelbase. No other motorized vehicles are supposed to be in here, so the tracks might be from the killer."

"Think we can get a make on the tires?"

"Maybe. SID is currently working with the FBI on that.

"Anything else?"

Deluca thought a moment, then shrugged. "That's about it."

"Well, good work, Deluca."

"Thanks. Too bad it doesn't amount to shit."

"It's still early."

"Yeah."

"Let's take a look at the dumpsite," I suggested, deciding that Deluca was probably right in his assessment. Usually homicides were solved quickly or not at all. Given the situation, our first line of investigation would be based on the premise that the killer knew his victim, although to date even authorities didn't know who she was. Assuming we were able to identify her, forensic evidence gathered at autopsy and at the dumpsite would only prove useful once we had a suspect. And aside from checking friends, family, boyfriends, and so on, the most likely way to obtain said suspect was via a witness, informant, or a confession that could be verified with physical evidence. I had a feeling none of those would be forthcoming.

I followed Deluca though an open gate into the garden. Making our way down a dirt path, we proceeded deeper into the grounds, along the way passing a glass-covered bulletin board with a schematic outline of the area. "Where are we headed?" I asked, pausing to peer at the display.

Deluca placed a thick finger on the glass. "Right here, where the stream ends in a pond," he said, indicating a spot on the map between the gymnosperms and the Malaysian rhododendrons.

We set out again, a thicket of palms and man-sized ferns closing in on all sides. The path quickly narrowed, soon becoming too constricted for a vehicle. "The guy must have carried her in from here," I reasoned. "Has to be fairly strong."

"Right," Deluca agreed. "The bamboo patch is right around the bend."

Just then my cellphone rang. I checked the caller. It was Taylor.

"Hey, Taylor. How did the race go?" I asked, letting Deluca get a few paces ahead.

"I took third," she replied. "Not bad, considering my lack of preparation."

"Congratulations." Then, sensing something in her voice, "Everything okay?"

"Something came up," said Taylor. "I've been ordered back to work."

"Why?"

"I don't know. I'm flying home this afternoon. We need to talk about Nate."

After receiving Lieutenant Long's summons, I had driven directly to the Boise airport, accompanied by Nate. Afterward my son had returned to the river in my Suburban, with the plan being for him to remain in Idaho with Taylor, after which the two of them would drive my car back to Los Angeles.

"He's going to be disappointed," I said.

"I know. Look, if it's okay with you, I've arranged for Nate to spend the rest of the week up here with friends at Cascade Raft & Kayak. It's a family-owned operation on the Payette, just down from Banks. They have a kids' kayak camp and have agreed to let Nate join in—food and housing included. He would start tomorrow."

"I don't know, Taylor."

"It's a first-class operation, and Nate would absolutely love it. Plus they promised to put him on a plane and send him home when the clinic is over."

"What about my car?"

"An agent at the Boise field office will drive it back. You should have it by tomorrow night. Here, talk with Nate."

A moment later Nate came on the line. "Dad, I really want to do this," he said. "Can I?"

I hesitated.

"Please?"

"Sure, kid," I finally agreed. "Just don't drown, okay?"

"Don't worry. Sara . . . I mean, Agent Taylor, told me that her friends, the Longs, are some of the most experienced river rescuers out there. Not that I'll need rescuing."

"If you say so," I laughed. "Okay, I'll cancel your counseling session with Dr. Berns on Wednesday, but you'll need to keep your regular appointment the following week."

"No problem, Dad. And . . . thanks."

I had continued to walk during Taylor's call, trailing a few steps behind Deluca. Upon disconnecting, I joined my partner beside a small pool. From there the dirt path circled around a grove of waist-high ferns, just inside a thicket of bamboo.

"He wired her up over there," said Deluca, pointing to a stand of bamboo with shoots as thick as a man's wrist. I noticed that visitors had scratched graffiti into some of the green stems: "I love Toni," "JW + SS," and the like. I also noted several marks on the shafts made by the wire used to bind the woman's arms and legs to the stalks.

As I stood trying to match the idyllic setting with the horror I had seen in the murder-book photos, my cellphone rang again. This time the display read: "No Caller ID."

"Kane," I said, accepting the call.

"I'm pleased to see you've accepted my invitation, Detective Kane," said an electronically modified voice.

I felt a chill. "Who is this?"

A long silence.

Then the caller spoke again.

"Let's play."

Chapter 6
Prisoner

Although awake for hours, Ella had been afraid to move. Suddenly the overhead light came on, once more illuminating her prison in a harsh, unforgiving glare. Ella rolled over, fighting a wave of nausea that had gripped her since awakening. Squinting into the light, she peered up at the webcam on the ceiling, wondering whether the man was watching.

When first regaining consciousness, muddled and confused from the drugs he had given her, she'd had no idea how much time had elapsed in the interim. Later, when her mind began to clear, she had taken a tentative inventory with her hands, groping in the darkness. Her clothes were missing, replaced by what felt like a nightgown. She was still sore from the attack in the parking structure, but not between her legs. She didn't think he had sexually assaulted her. She would have known.

Or would she?

His hateful collar still encircled her neck. After his initial demonstration, the man had used it a second time when she'd refused to take a cup of pills he had thrust through the bars.

His second shock had been worse than the first.

Afterward, the man's drugs had rendered her nearly comatose, unable to mount even the slightest resistance. Strangely, she had remained conscious throughout—at least during most of it—as if she were *outside* her body, watching what was happening from afar.

Though her memory was fuzzy, she remembered being undressed, and makeup being applied, and being positioned in various positions and poses while he worked with his cameras. She thought he might have removed her collar, but she wasn't certain.

And throughout, emotionally numbed by the drugs he had given her, it had seemed as if everything were happening to someone else.

Later she had slept.

Now Ella shook her head, trying to focus. She was forgetting something.

Oh, God, he told me to shower as soon as the light came on. What will happen if I don't?

It was a risk Ella was unwilling to take. With a final glance at the webcam, she swung her legs off the bed and hurried to the shower, again wondering whether he was watching.

She also wondered whether he had turned on the light.

Or was it was a timer?

It was something she needed to find out.

Leaning into the fiberglass enclosure, Ella twisted the handle. Then, reaching down, she tested the water flowing from a spout lower down. The temperature took a few moments to warm. When it did, she stripped off her nightgown and stepped into the tub.

Bath or shower?

Shower.

Get this over as quickly as possible.

Ella closed the shower curtain and lowered her head beneath a nozzle higher up, letting a warm stream of water flow over her neck and shoulders.

Suddenly she remembered her electric collar.

Heart pounding, Ella pulled her head from beneath the spray and fumbled at the shower handle. By the time she managed to turn it off, however, she realized she hadn't been shocked.

Thank God for that.

After quickly finishing her shower, Ella stepped from the enclosure and glanced around her prison. Atop the sink was a towel, along with her clothes from the previous day. Wasting no time, she dried herself and dressed, determined to cover up before he returned. Afterward she inspected her face in a polished metal mirror above the sink, discovering that her lips had been painted with cherry-red lipstick. Angrily, she wiped her mouth with the towel.

Next she continued a survey of her cell, hoping to find something, *anything*, that might help her escape. As he had said, the cabinet contained a cache of granola bars and a selection of cosmetics, deodorant, toothbrushes and toothpaste, a box of tampons, a hairbrush, plastic trash bags, and several rolls of toilet paper.

Ella's stomach rumbled. Realizing she hadn't eaten since yesterday, she unwrapped a granola bar and ate it as she proceeded with her search.

A self-contained toilet sat beside the cabinet. On the front, a label above the seat read, "Sun-Mar Excel." A low stool sat at the base, blocking a pullout drawer at the bottom. From the rear of the assembly, a two-inch vent pipe ran to a hole in the ceiling. To her relief, Ella also noticed a privacy curtain.

He doesn't want to watch me on the toilet.

Is that something I can use?

Inspecting the toilet more closely, Ella discovered a pullout handle near the seat, along with directions for rotating some sort of internal drum. Next she slid aside the stepstool and withdrew the bottom drawer. Inside was a layer of dry, darkish material—presumably the final product from whatever composting process was involved. Surprisingly, there was no odor that she could detect.

The final object in her cell was the bed—a thin mattress, a single pillow, and several woolen blankets—the bedding atop a plywood platform supported by a stout metal frame.

There seemed to be nothing she could use to escape, let alone fashion into a weapon.

Not giving up, Ella peered beneath the bed. Near the front of the platform, close to the metal edge where it was difficult to see, someone had scratched something in the plywood.

Lying on her back, Ella scooted underneath. Now she could read the writing. A name: Alexa Kiel. And beside the woman's name, tally marks—four vertical scratches and a final diagonal in each cluster. There were five such groupings, with an additional two slashes at the end.

Twenty-seven days.

Ella brought a fist to her mouth. It appeared that another woman had been held captive here. She had remained alive for twenty-seven days.

How long will I have?

Tears welled in Ella's eyes. With a surge of determination, she fought against them.

Crying won't help. There has to be a way. Something . . .

Wiping her eyes, Ella came to a decision.

I will not die in here, she promised herself.

I will obey him, seduce him, do anything he wants.

And when the time comes . . . I will kill him.

I don't know how, but I will.

The sound of footsteps announced his arrival.

The glass window in the outside door darkened as he twisted the deadbolt. Moments later he stepped inside, tucking a key on a chain beneath his shirt.

Today he was smartly dressed—suit coat, slacks, a dress shirt open at the collar. His black hair had been neatly combed. Regarding his features, Ella was again struck by how much he resembled a fashion model—at least when he was wearing his human façade.

Unfortunately, she had seen him with it off.

"Good morning, Ella," he said, moving to her prison door as smoothly as a dancer. He smiled, as if greeting a friend, but the smile never touched his eyes. "I brought you some breakfast. Egg McMuffins, I think they're called. Yum. If you behave, you may have them later," he added, setting a Styrofoam container with McDonald's markings on the floor outside her cell, just out of reach.

"Is it morning? How long have I been here?"

The man glanced at his watch. "Actually, it's a bit past noon. And don't worry about the days. They will pass soon enough."

"What do you want?"

The man sat in his armchair, once more steepling his fingers. He peered at her thorough the bars, as if considering. "I thought we might chat a bit today, get to know each other before you take your medicine," he replied.

At the mention of medicine, Ella's heart fell.

"To start, tell me about your father."

"He's a police captain, and he's going to find you. You had better let me go right now."

"I think not." The man rocked back in his chair, touching his fingers to his lips. "Tell me about your policeman father, Captain William Snead. Did Captain Snead or someone like him sexually molest you when you were younger?"

"What? Why would you . . ."

"Answer the question," the man instructed, reaching for something on the arm of his chair. With a chill, Ella realized it was his remote control.

"No."

"No?" The man hovered his thumb over the control.

"No! I mean, no—I was never molested," Ella corrected.

"Ah." The man shook his head. "I find it hard to believe that a young woman as beautiful as you managed to avoid some sort of childhood sexual abuse. Maybe at the hands of an uncle, or a favorite teacher? Someone you trusted?"

When Ella remained silent, the man continued. "The statistics are staggering. The prevalence of childhood sexual abuse in the United States is close to *twenty-five percent*, and that's for all female children—not just the unusually adorable little girls like the one I'm certain you were. Several studies put that figure at over a third, by the way—especially in countries like China and India."

"I was never molested," Ella repeated.

"Again, I find that hard to believe, but we'll let it go for now."

"I'm telling the truth. Now, tit for tat," Ella suggested, deciding to take a chance. "I answered your question. You answer mine. Is the ceiling light on a timer, or do you turn it on?"

"Interesting choice of words," the man mused. "But this is not a negotiation. Nevertheless, I'll answer your question, as I can see why you might want to know. The light is indeed on a timer. I can also turn it on at will."

"Thank you," said Ella, hoping to set a precedent.

The man nodded. "Now it's time to take your medicine."

"You don't have to drug me."

45

"Oh, but I do," said the man, standing. He crossed to the alcove cabinet and returned, offering her several colorful tablets in a paper cup. "Fill the cup with water from the sink and come back. I want to watch you swallow."

"You don't need those pills," Ella pleaded. "They make me sick. I'll . . . I'll do whatever you want."

"I know you will. And what I want is for you to take your medicine," the man replied, his expression tightening. "Right now."

Lowering her head, Ella took the cup.

"And don't think you can trick me by hiding the pills under your tongue," the man warned, as he had the day before. "If you do, I'll know."

Chapter 7
Beach House

U pon leaving UCLA, I returned to the West L.A. station, checked in with Lieutenant Long, caught up on paperwork that had accumulated in my absence, and spent the rest of the afternoon thinking about the case. Toward the end of my shift, I finally heard from Verizon regarding a *57 trace on the call I had received in the garden. At the time I had thought the caller must have been somewhere nearby—watching from the crowd across the street, or observing from one of the buildings overlooking the garden. Otherwise, how had he known I was present?

I had instructed Deluca to take photos of the crowd across the street. In addition, I contacted the UCLA police and had them check for suspicious individuals in nearby buildings. Their search proved fruitless, and I didn't expect much from Deluca's cellphone photos, either—but one never knew.

Regarding my *57 trace, it turned out that the voice-altered call had been made from an untraceable burner phone, with cell-tower triangulation placing the origin at a mall in Orange County.

Had the timing of the killer's call simply been a coincidence?

Maybe. But when it came to a murder investigation, I didn't base explanations on coincidence.

Later, after identifying myself as a police officer and jumping through a few legal hoops, I'd had Verizon place a trap-and-trace device on my phone. In the future, the trap-and-trace would reveal a caller's phone number and all routing information necessary to ID the source location. It could not, by law, include the contents of whatever conversation I might have, so afterward I visited the iTunes store and downloaded a recording app to my phone as well.

Someone, possibly the killer, wanted to stay in touch.

The next time he called, I planned to oblige.

I returned to my home in Malibu later that evening, taking Pacific Coast Highway north to Las Flores Beach. After parking on a shoulder of PCH outside my house, I pried myself from the confines of Catheryn's Volvo, hoping my larger Suburban showed up soon.

From the impression often given in film, many think that Malibu is exclusively populated by movie stars, Academy-award winning film producers, A-list television personalities, and trust-fund millionaires. Granted, there are plenty of those, but there are also lots of the rest of us—normal, hardworking individuals who prize residing in an area that's beautiful, close to the city, and relatively smog-free, and who are willing to put up with coastal traffic, brushfires, mudslides, floods, and storm surf to live there.

Years back Grandma Dorothy had grown up in Malibu, spending summers at her family's getaway beach cottage. The ancient house had been built in the early thirties on a small cove at the mouth of Las Flores Canyon, situated near the northernmost crescent of Santa Monica Bay. At the time, the ramshackle structure had been a Gilligan's Island-type bungalow, its termite-ridden timbers seemingly supported by little more than beach cane and bougainvillea.

Dorothy had eventually inherited the property, and when Catheryn and I were married, she had deeded it to us as a wedding present. In years to come, it was there that we had raised our four children, with porches walled in and bootlegged additions tacked on to accommodate our growing family.

On a night that had nearly taken all our lives, our rustic home had burned to the sand. We eventually rebuilt on new piers and pilings, and our new house was solid, better than ever. Nevertheless, we all still missed the rickety, tumbledown structure that for years had been the cornerstone of our lives.

"Something sure smells good," I called into the house as I pushed through the front door, making an effort to put aside the problems of my job, at least for the moment. As usual, inside the entry I was greeted enthusiastically by our family dog, a yellow Labrador retriever named Callie.

"That's gotta be me, Pop," Allison's voice floated back. "Just took a shower."

I smiled, regarding my daughter as I stepped into the kitchen, with Callie at my heels. Although Allison had been a tomboy when growing up, she—like her mother—could look absolutely stunning without much fuss. Also like Catheryn, and to Ali's credit as well, I had never seen her unfairly use her appearance to get her way.

"We're having jambalaya," Grandma Dorothy announced from the stove, where she was stirring something in a large pot. "And it's dinner you're smelling," she continued, shooting Allison a good-natured look of admonishment. "Not Allison's recent shower."

"Whatever it is, it smells great," I repeated, noticing that my oldest, Travis, and his girlfriend, McKenzie, were also present. I smiled and hugged them both. Then, stepping back, "Trav, great to see you. And McKenzie, a big welcome to you, too."

"Thanks, Mr. Kane."

"Yeah, thanks, Dad," said Travis. Tall and lean, with fine features and an economy of grace not inherited from me, Travis would be starting his third year of graduate study at Juilliard that fall. Along with a talent for composition and conducting, he was a concert-level pianist, and as such he had difficult choices to make regarding his future. Though I wanted to help, those were decisions for which I was totally unqualified to offer advice, as Trav's musical abilities were also gifts not inherited from me, but from his mother—who before her death had been offered the position of principal cellist for the LA Philharmonic.

"It's great to be home, Mr. Kane, if only for a few weeks," said McKenzie, taking Trav's hand. With a smile, Travis circled her with an arm and pulled her close.

Watching the two of them, I noticed that although McKenzie had always been a head-turner, she had recently changed in some way I couldn't quite define. Though she still parted her long, dark hair in the center, framing her intelligent amber eyes and high cheekbones, there was something different about her. A moment later I had it. Always a bit on the shy side, McKenzie now carried

49

herself with an air of confidence that sometimes came with maturity. It suited her.

"Jeez, get a room, lovebirds," Allison groused. "And to think you used to be my best friend, Mac. Have you no taste in men?"

"Shouldn't you be checking on your daughter, Ali?" laughed McKenzie, who, like the rest of us, had long ago grown inured to Allison's teasing.

"Katie is sleeping peacefully in Grandma's room, thank you very much," Ali replied. "Let's not do anything to wake her. Please."

"You're saying I can't visit my own granddaughter?" I asked. "I haven't seen her in a week."

"Later, Dad. After dinner, okay? Let her sleep for now."

"Speaking of dinner, the jambalaya is almost ready," said Dorothy. "Can we get the table set?"

"Inside or out?" asked Travis.

"Let's eat on the deck," I suggested. "It's still light out, and it's a nice evening."

Minutes later, after Travis and McKenzie had shuttled plates, napkins, and silverware downstairs to our redwood deck, we assembled at a picnic table overlooking the beach. Callie lay on the planks nearby, as usual picking a strategic spot from which she could keep an eye on the food.

After Dorothy finished saying grace—invoking a blessing for friends, family, and all our loved ones who were no longer with us—everyone dug in, serving up generous portions of the rice, shrimp, smoked sausage, and chicken creation that Grandma had flavored with just the right amount of Cajun seasoning and cayenne pepper. With the addition of warm sourdough bread and a fresh salad that Allison had prepared, it proved a perfect meal. Although I had enjoyed my time with Taylor and Nate at the river, I was happy to be home.

"Good grub, Grandma," Travis said between bites. "Makes me forget any thoughts of becoming a vegetarian."

"We humans didn't claw our way to the top of the food chain to be vegetarians," I noted sagely.

"Thanks for that tiny bit of wisdom, Pop," Allison laughed.

"Mmm, this is absolutely delicious, Mrs. Erickson," said McKenzie.

"Thank you, McKenzie. And please call me Dorothy." Then, after glancing at Travis, she returned her attention to McKenzie. "You're nearly family now, right?"

This was the type of question that normally would have gone right over my head. I was aware, however, that Dorothy didn't approve of Travis and McKenzie's sharing an apartment in New York. And in Dorothy's opinion, neither would have Catheryn. Although Dorothy would never volunteer her opinion on that issue unless asked, I also knew that if Trav and McKenzie were to continue their current living arrangement, Dorothy wanted to see them married—and the sooner, the better.

McKenzie blushed, not missing the implication of Dorothy's query. "Yes, ma'am," she said, turning to Travis for help. "At least I feel that I am."

Oblivious of the feminine undercurrents coursing at the table, Travis nodded and continued shoveling down jambalaya.

"How's work at the agency going, Mac?" Allison jumped in, attempting to save her friend further grief.

"Great," McKenzie replied with a grateful smile. "I've already made inroads at several major publishers, plus I have three new books in the works, including yours—if you would ever finish your edits."

Upon graduating from college, McKenzie had taken a position as a literary agent at a New York firm, in large part to remain close to Travis. In addition to being an up-and-coming journalist at CBS, my daughter was also a talented writer, and Mac was currently representing Ali's second novel—an as-yet untitled exposé based on Allison's experiences as a fledgling journalist. My daughter's new book focused on the kidnapping/murder of a young Hollywood starlet named Sharon French, loosely mirroring a case I had investigated some years back. With Ali's misuse of inside information repeatedly causing friction between us back then, it had been a difficult time for us both, with a measure of mistrust and hard feeling between us still remaining.

"Yeah, well . . . as for finishing my novel, I'm still trying to figure out how to publish it without torpedoing my career at CBS," Allison replied.

"Just get it done, Ali. We'll figure out where to go from there."

"Yes, ma'am," Allison replied, shooting her friend a sloppy salute.

"I don't make an appearance in this new book of yours, do I?" I asked. Allison's debut novel, a story in which I had been portrayed as a less than sympathetic father, had been published the previous year. Making matters worse, during a blizzard of media attention following a recent investigation, my face had been plastered on every news rag, magazine, and TV screen across the country. Spurred by interest in the case, sales of Ali's initial novel had skyrocketed. To be fair, I deserved most of the criticism leveled at me in that first book, but I was wary of a repeat.

"Don't worry, Pop," Allison replied with a grin. "Everyone on the planet already knows you're not perfect, but who is? I myself have been accused of being condescending," she confessed, glancing at her brother across the table. "That means I talk down to people, Trav."

"Thanks for the clarification," Travis laughed.

"Is Nate still in Idaho?" McKenzie ventured, sending our freewheeling discussion in another direction.

"He is," I replied. "When I got recalled to work, Nate decided to remain up at the Payette River with Agent Taylor and learn to kayak."

"You're kidding. You left Nate up there in the woods with this, uh, *friend* of yours?" Allison demanded, raising an eyebrow.

"Nate wants to learn to paddle, and Taylor signed him up for a weeklong kayak clinic with some friends of hers. Anything wrong with that?"

"Whatever," said Allison.

"You have a problem with Taylor, Ali?"

"No problem," Allison replied, her tone indicating otherwise.

"Well, I miss Nate," said Travis.

"We all do," said Dorothy. "But after all that's happened, he deserves to have some fun.

"No argument there," Allison sighed. "I just . . . worry about him."

"Nate is going to be fine," I said, willing it to be true.

"Anyway," Travis continued, "when Nate gets back, I was thinking—"

"I wondered what that grinding noise was," Allison interrupted.

"I was thinking that when Nate gets back," Travis pushed on, ignoring Allison's gibe, "we should throw a family get-together. A barbeque or something."

"A barbeque next week sounds good," I agreed.

"Mike should be back from his shoot by then, too," said Allison.

"How's that going? Mike's the second-unit director of photography on this one?"

Allison nodded. "It's a big step up for Mike, and things are going great. In fact, they're going to wrap ahead of schedule, which is almost unheard of on a feature film."

"Excellent news," I said. "When he gets back, at least there will be someone else to help Grandma with your daughter."

Allison looked away. "Katie is doing just fine. Maybe I should have taken more time off before returning to work, but that's not how things are in the news business."

"Lord knows I love taking care of Katie," Dorothy interjected. "But it certainly wouldn't hurt for you to spend a little more time with your daughter."

"Katie is fine," Allison repeated, lowering her head in a stubborn gesture that reminded me of her mother. "Let's talk about something else. How's the new investigation of yours going, Pop? One of our reporters saw you this morning at UCLA."

"I don't think we should discuss Dan's work at the table," said Dorothy.

"Okay, let's talk about the news," Allison persisted. "Anyone see the photos The Magpie has been posting on the internet?"

Then, turning to me, "Do you think he has anything to do with your UCLA case, Dad?"

"Allison," Dorothy warned. "Enough."

"I agree with Grandma," I said, disturbed by Allison's question.

"Fine," said Allison, again lowering her head.

A feeling of dread began expanding in the pit of my stomach. That was the second time someone had suggested that the body in the Botanical Garden was the work of The Magpie—a serial killer who, as far as I knew, was operating exclusively in the Pacific Northwest.

I needed to see those online photos.

Unfortunately, I was fearful of what they would show.

****

Later that evening, after Allison had departed with Katie and Travis and McKenzie were upstairs cleaning up after dinner, Dorothy and I retired to our outdoor swing. By then the sun had dropped behind Point Dume to the west, lighting the horizon in shades of orange and gold. We sat awhile without speaking, gazing out over the sand and enjoying the last light of the day. The tide was out, and mounds of seaweed, driftwood, and crab hulls littered the beach to the water's edge. I also noted that a southern swell had started to build offshore, presaging heavy surf for the next few days.

Dorothy finally broke the silence. "We haven't had much time to talk since you returned, Dan. How are you doing?"

I shrugged. "Okay, I guess. A lot on my mind."

"The new investigation that Ali mentioned?"

"Yeah, that. And Nate, of course."

"Nate is going to be okay. He's made a lot of progress over the past month. It's the new case that's bothering you, isn't it?"

"Dorothy, I can't really discuss—"

"I don't need details," she interrupted. "Just tell me why you're so upset."

"You noticed, huh?"

"You're not that hard to read, Dan. Talk to me."

I hesitated. "Okay," I said. "I'm worried the UCLA case is going to turn into another high-profile media frenzy."

"And in the past, that's exactly the type of investigation that has cost our family dearly."

I remained silent.

"Dan, we've talked about this before. Catheryn's death wasn't your fault."

"Everyone keeps telling me that," I replied. "And on some level, I believe it, but . . . I don't feel it inside. If it weren't for my job, Catheryn would still be alive, and that will never change.

"And now, as much as you would like to forget her loss and bury yourself in work, you don't want something like that to happen again."

"No, I don't."

"Dan, there's more involved here than your guilt over Catheryn. Don't you see how your withdrawal is affecting everyone around you?"

"I don't want to talk about this right now, Dorothy."

"You may not, but *I* do. I hate to see you so sad."

"What about you?" I demanded. "After all that's happened, can you honestly say *you're* happy?"

Dorothy hesitated. "Am I happy? Mostly, I suppose," she said, turning to face me. "But life isn't about being happy and having everything go perfectly. That's just a dream. The truth is, life doesn't always go perfectly, and no one will always be happy."

When I didn't reply, Dorothy asked, "Do you remember what you said at Ali's wedding reception?"

Though surprised by her question, I thought back, bringing my wedding toast to mind. "I reminded everyone that we are all going to experience tragedy and loss before we exit this world, and that all of us are going to be hurt, and get sick, and feel pain, and lose people we love."

"Sounds almost word-for-word," Dorothy observed. "I keep forgetting that memory of yours."

I looked away. "It's a curse more often than a gift."

"What else did you say that evening?"

"Dorothy . . ."

"What else did you say?"

I shrugged. "I concluded by pointing out that sad fact was exactly what made cherishing moments like Mike and Ali's wedding so important, because moments like that made our lives truly worth living."

"Do you believe those words?"

"I did at the time. Now I'm not so sure."

"You have to believe in life, Dan. Despite all our family has lost, my faith helps me do that. I know you have doubts when it comes to religion, so you'll have to find another way. But find that way, Dan."

"I'm not sure I can."

"You have to. Pain and loss are part of being alive; that's simply the way things are. The important thing is to find hope and meaning and possibly even joy in life, even when things go wrong. Maybe *especially* when things go wrong."

"Where'd you get that, your knitting circle?" I shot back, regretting my words the instant they cleared my lips.

Tears started in Dorothy's eyes, but she didn't look away, even for an instant. "Catheryn was your wife and the mother of your children, but she was my daughter as well," she said. "I loved her, too."

"I'm sorry," I apologized, seeing in Dorothy's eyes the same courage and resolve that had been Catheryn's. And as Dorothy held my gaze, I also realized the ultimate source of Catheryn's strength. "I didn't mean that," I mumbled.

"I know you didn't," Dorothy said gently. "Listen, Dan. I realize you're worried about endangering our family again with this new case. Let me ask you something. Are you doing what you truly want to do in life?"

I didn't answer.

"All right, I'll ask an easier question," Dorothy pushed on. "How many promises have you made over the course of your lifetime? Not promises like, 'I promise to take out the trash,' or 'I promise to get a haircut.' I mean *important* promises."

"Where are you going with this, Dorothy?"

"I have a point, and it's this: How many of those promises have you broken?"

Unprepared for her question, I found myself taking an unexpected moral inventory, my thoughts traveling back over years of broken vows.

When Catheryn and I had married, I vowed always to be faithful. Shamefully, it was a promise I had broken.

When our first son, Thomas, was born, I had promised to be the best father possible. Another broken promise, a betrayal that had ultimately cost the life of our firstborn.

After Tommy's death I had attacked my family in a drunken rage of anger and self-pity, later promising to somehow make everything all right. Although I hadn't touched alcohol since, life moves on, and some things can never be mended.

And years later at Catheryn's funeral, upon accepting responsibility for my wife's death, I had pledged to never again disappoint those I loved. To my shame, I was uncertain whether I had done everything to keep that vow.

And later still, on a night when Nate had attempted to take his own life, I had promised to accompany my son on every step of his road to recovery, and that I would never again betray his trust. Although I hadn't outright broken that one, I wasn't certain I had done everything possible to keep it, either.

And worst of all, Catheryn—whom I had promised to love and protect—gone because of me.

Not much cause for pride.

"Dan, I didn't mean to put you on the spot," Dorothy continued, sensing my discomfort. "I know you would never break an important promise. I was just trying to make the point that you're an honorable man."

I started to object, but she silenced me with a raise of her hand. "I know that at times you have doubts about yourself . . . but *I* don't. Otherwise I would have never let you marry my daughter. So what I want from you now is another promise, and it's one I want you to keep."

"What?" I asked numbly.

"I want you to promise to take a long, hard look at yourself, and to make an honest assessment of what is truly important in your life. Then I want you to decide what you want to do with your remaining time on Earth . . . and commit to it," she replied, her eyes never leaving mine. "Will you promise to do that?"

I hesitated. Finally, with a sigh, I nodded.

"Say it," she said.

I hesitated a moment more.

"Say it."

"I promise," I replied at last.

Dorothy smiled. "Good. I'm going to hold you to it."

Just then my cellphone rang. I checked the screen. The call was from Lieutenant Long.

I listened on the phone for less than a minute. "What?" Dorothy asked as I disconnected, seeing something in my expression.

"That was my boss. I'm wanted downtown at headquarters."

"Now?"

I nodded, not certain what was going on myself. "Right now."

Chapter 8
Evening News

One hundred and forty miles to the south, in the San Diego residential enclave of Rancho Bernardo, Dr. Erich Krüger poured himself a generous portion of Macallan single malt Scotch. Cut-crystal tumbler in hand, he retired to his living room and turned on a flat-screen TV that took up most of one wall. Settling back in a leather armchair, he lifted a remote control and flipped through the channels, finally settling on CBS Evening News.

Dr. Krüger relaxed as the news report began, feeling a sense of satisfaction and accomplishment.

It had been a good day.

The UCLA murder story came on after station break, following a national news roundup. As Brent Preston, a blond, self-assured network anchor launched into his report, Dr. Krüger leaned forward, listening intently.

"A sixth victim has been discovered in The Magpie murders, this time in Los Angeles," Mr. Preston began. "The body of a young woman was found early yesterday in the UCLA Botanical Garden. Early this evening, a photograph of her corpse appeared on the internet, with the label "Miss June" written across the bottom. This latest victim joins five of the killer's previous 'calendar' murders, one for each month. Here with more from Los Angeles is CBS correspondent Allison Kane."

The scene shifted to another news desk, this one presumably in Los Angeles. A strikingly attractive newscaster with a mane of reddish-auburn hair and pale green eyes assumed the reporting reins—her presence, in Dr. Krüger's opinion, a definite improvement over that of Mr. Preston.

"Thanks, Brent," said the female correspondent. "This morning LAPD detectives returned to UCLA to continue their investigation of this gruesome killing. In the past, The Magpie has always kidnapped a new victim near the dumpsite of his previous kill. As yet, however, no one has been reported missing from the area."

Dr. Krüger took a sip of Scotch, wondering whether he had made a mistake in the choice of his latest acquisition. Allison Kane certainly seemed worthy. Actually, more than worthy. But then again, given the contentious history between her father and Captain William Snead—a history widely reported in the national media—his current selection of a female guest made the game much more stimulating.

The scene shifted again, this time to a crowded street with the UCLA Botanical Garden in the background. A large, rough-looking man with flinty eyes and unforgiving lines in his face was wading through a throng of reporters, ignoring questions from all sides. Dr. Krüger recognized him immediately, over the past months having seen the man's image in numerous news reports.

"Considering the way the body was displayed, could this be the work of The Magpie?" a female reported shouted, thrusting a microphone in the detective's face.

Kane hesitated, seeming caught off-guard by the question. Sensing an opening, the reporter followed up with another. "Does this mean The Magpie has taken another victim?"

"The Magpie?" said Kane, his eyes hardening. "I have never been able to fathom why you news people insist on coming up with some cutesy-pie name for every dirtbag who commits this kind of crime. The Magpie? Really? As far as I'm concerned, whoever killed that young woman and hung her up in there like garbage is bottom-feeding scum, and I intend to see he gets exactly what he deserves."

"And what's that?" asked the reporter.

"Use your imagination," said Kane, pushing past.

Dr. Krüger's expression tightened. Eyes narrowing like gunsights, he downed a gulp of Scotch and stabbed the TV control, sending the screen to darkness.

Bottom-feeding scum?

Things weren't supposed to go like that.

Dr. Krüger finished his drink in one long swallow. Then, lips compressed in a bloodless slash, he strode to his bar.

Another drink?

No.

Video gaming?

No, again.

Something better . . .

Leaving his tumbler on the bar, Dr. Krüger strode to his den. Sitting at his desk, he booted up his computer, logging on to a private, password-protected server that hosted his webcam streams. Scrolling down, he selected a feed labeled: "IR/Playpen."

Ella was awake in her cell, stumbling around in the darkness, her hands outstretched, helpless, as beautiful as ever.

Not for the first time, Dr. Krüger felt the urge to take her immediately.

Unfortunately, that would spoil the game.

No, he would put off taking his pleasure.

Nevertheless, the cravings were becoming unbearable.

Granted, he would force himself to wait . . . but not much longer.

Soon.

Chapter 9
A Visit with the Chief

The LAPD police administration building, a ten-story, 500,000 square-foot behemoth of stone and glass colloquially known as PAB, had replaced the aging Parker Center—the LAPD's former headquarters—in 2009. Occupying an entire city block and surrounded by some of the city's most iconic architecture, PAB serves as the center for the department's four command bureaus and its twenty-one wide-ranging patrol divisions. In addition to the core building, a civic plaza, a public auditorium, a police memorial, and several terraced gardens surround the central structure—design elements intended to suggest a "nature-based experience," as well as symbolizing the department's new era of openness and connection with the city. Unfortunately, I had yet to experience much of the latter. The administration of the LAPD through the offices of the mayor, the police commission, and the city council had always been rooted in the world of politics, and upon passing through PAB's front doors, I knew to expect more of the same.

After leaving Catheryn's Volvo in a parking structure on West First Street, I walked a short distance back to police headquarters, working out the kinks in my legs. My thighs had started cramping while driving Catheryn's considerably smaller vehicle, and I once again hoped my Suburban showed up soon.

Upon arriving at PAB, I hung my shield on my jacket pocket and proceeded to a reception desk near the rear of the lobby. "Detective Kane," I said to a female duty officer stationed behind the counter. "Here to see Chief Ingram."

"Yes, sir." The duty officer glanced at my creds, found my name on a roster, and issued me a temporary visitor's ID. From there I took an elevator to Chief Charlie Ingram's tenth-floor suite. I still hadn't figured out why I had been summoned, especially at that late hour, but I suspected it had to do with the UCLA murder. Whatever the case, I knew I'd find out soon enough.

I had met Chief Ingram on more than one occasion, and in each instance I had found him to be reasonably intelligent, occasionally charming, and as honest as one could expect any senior administrator to be. Unfortunately, he and I had failed to see eye-to-eye several times in the past, and the results had not been pleasant. Thanks to my successful conclusion of a recent investigation, I was once more in the chief's good graces—at least for the moment—and it was a situation I wanted to continue.

After stepping from the elevator, I proceeded down a broad, well-lit hallway to Ingram's tenth-floor office. A secretary there led me past several spacious rooms and a darkened conference area to the chief's private suite. As I entered Ingram's inner sanctum, he glanced up from his desk, pausing in a conversation with Assistant Chief Owen Strickland.

Smiling, Ingram rose to shake my hand. "Dan, glad you could join us," he said.

"Didn't know it was optional," I replied. Ingram's grasp was firm and dry, and he held my eyes for a moment before resuming his seat. Like many individuals in positions of power, he had a gift for making one feel special. On the other hand, I had seen him do the exact opposite, and more than once.

"Detective Kane," said Assistant Chief Strickland, not offering to shake. "I think you know everyone here," he went on, regarding me with a look of ill-concealed distaste.

Realizing that Strickland and I still had issues to resolve, I glanced at the somber group assembled in the room. Against a far wall I spotted the broad, friendly face of my boss, Lieutenant Nelson Long. As an African-American, Long had earned every promotion and commendation he'd received on his rise up the LAPD ranks, and I was glad to see him present. He was talking with Captain Lincoln, commander of the West L.A. division. Both were standing with Deputy Chief Jon Chow from West Bureau, the operations unit charged with oversight of six LAPD divisions, including mine. All three officers in my immediate chain of command nodded in my direction without comment, doing nothing to lessen my curiosity.

Also present was FBI Assistant Director in Charge Alan Shepherd. ADIC Shepherd was accompanied by a handful of agents, many of whom I recognized from the Los Angeles field office. A few nodded my way as well.

To my surprise, Special Agent Sara Taylor was also standing with the Bureau group, her unexpected presence lighting the room like a shaft of sunlight breaking through the clouds. Taylor had on a white blouse, dark slacks, and a matching jacket that accented her slim figure. Prior to the NFC kayak race, she had cut her mid-length blond hair even shorter—claiming that her hair was the last thing she wanted to fuss with when competing. On Taylor, like everything else, short hair looked great.

Catching Taylor's attention, I shot her a puzzled glance. She lifted her shoulders in a shrug, indicating that she had no idea why we were there, either. I was about to cross the room to join her when Captain William Snead, my departmental nemesis, strode in. I groaned inwardly. Snead and I had problems going back to patrol days. Since then I had served under him on two task-force investigations, and I had vowed there would never be a third.

"Sorry I'm late," Snead mumbled. He seemed distracted, his pale, hatchet-thin face even more pinched than normal.

"No problem, Bill," said Ingram. "It's understandable." Then, glancing around the room, "I think we're all here. Owen, you want to get things rolling?"

"Yes, sir," said Assistant Chief Strickland. "I'm sure you are all aware that a photo of the UCLA murder victim was just posted on the internet. Is there anyone here who hasn't seen it?"

"I haven't," I said.

Several others spoke up as well.

Strickland moved to Ingram's desk, hit a few keys on a laptop, and turned the screen so everyone could see. The room fell silent. As I had feared, the computer display showed the corpse of a young woman wired to a thicket of bamboo. I recognized some of the graffiti carved into the stalks, confirming the location.

Although the image had been shot at night, I also noted that the young woman's nightgown-clad body appeared to have been expertly lit—with professional key, fill, and hair lighting sources illuminating the scene. Across the bottom of the photo, in bold, block letters, the killer had added the words, "Miss June."

Strickland adjusted the cursor, scrolling through five similarly disturbing photos, all showing murdered women in grotesque, suggestive poses. Looking closer, I noticed that they all had burn marks on their throats, lesions similar to the ones I had seen that morning at autopsy.

"The Magpie victims," someone commented.

"Correct," said Strickland. "His sixth showed up yesterday on UCLA campus. She has been identified as Sandy Stafford of Seattle, Washington. Ms. Stafford disappeared three weeks ago from University Village, a shopping mall just north of Seattle. Her parents recognized the photo and called it in."

"Damn," said one of the FBI agents. "That's how her parents found out?"

"That's how they found out," said Ingram.

"I thought that dirtbag was only active up north," I said. "What's he doing in Los Angeles?"

"Developing new hunting grounds, maybe," offered Shepherd.

"The point is," said Ingram, "we don't want a repeat of that situation down here, and when I address the media at a press conference tomorrow morning, I want to assure them that is *not* going to happen."

From accounts in the news, I knew that over the past five months a string of serial killings had terrorized the cities of San Francisco, Portland, and Seattle. Unable to make headway on the case, authorities in all three cities had suffered increasingly harsh criticism in the media. I suspected that Chief Ingram, Mayor Fitzpatrick, and every other Los Angeles politician with skin in the game would attempt to get ahead of the curve on this. Which, of course, would make conducting the investigation even more problematic.

"I'm going to keep it simple," Ingram continued, glancing around the room. "I want this guy shut down, and I want it done as quickly as possible—using any and all available resources. Unfortunately, our situation cuts across numerous jurisdictional boundaries, so I called everyone here tonight in the hope of avoiding organizational SNAFUs. Ideas on that?"

When no one replied, Ingram turned to Shepherd. "Director Shepherd, thank you for being here tonight. Any suggestions from your end would be appreciated."

Shepherd, whose perennially youthful appearance belied a razor-sharp mind and a talent for organization, thought a moment before responding. "First of all, although this latest killing does seem to be the work of the so-called Magpie, one of his signature behaviors is the immediate kidnapping of another victim," he said. "I wasn't aware that another woman had been taken."

Ingram glanced at Snead, then returned his gaze to Shepherd. "We just confirmed that. We haven't released it yet to the press."

"Was she abducted from UCLA?" asked Shepherd, seeming surprised.

Ingram nodded. "A parking structure."

"Okay, then it seems our unsub has chosen to operate in new territory," Shepherd continued, referring in Bureau-speak to the killer as an unknown subject. If nothing else, "unsub" was a designation I preferred to the nickname bestowed by the media.

"In the course of investigating his five previous murders, the Bureau has been working with local law enforcement agencies in Northern California, Portland, and Seattle," Shepherd went on. "Concerning this latest murder, our L.A. field office would be willing to continue that same arrangement with LAPD."

"LAPD assumes lead on the UCLA killing; the Bureau places its resources at our disposal, coordinates with other law-enforcement agencies, and serves as a clearing house for information?" suggested Ingram.

"That framework works for us," Shepherd replied.

"And we share credit when this is over?"

Shepherd considered a moment. "As long as we have an agent detailed to your investigation," he said. "Special Agent

Taylor has previously worked with Detective Kane. Would her presence as a Bureau liaison be acceptable?"

I glanced at Taylor, finally realizing the reason for her presence.

"It would," said Ingram. "Let's move on. What do we know about our man so far?"

Shepherd rubbed his chin. "Not much, I'm afraid. To date he has left almost no forensic evidence. It even appears he's bathing his victims before dumping them, meticulously removing all possible trace evidence—fingerprints, fingernail scrapings, touch DNA, hair and fibers, and so on."

"The unsub seems to know a lot about police procedure," volunteered one of the agents standing with Shepherd. "Could he be a cop?"

"We're not going to start chasing our own tails on that," Ingram declared. "Not yet, anyway. The media would have a field day."

"Good point," Shepherd agreed.

"So what *do* we know so far?" Ingram pressed. "Aside from the fact that he's not leaving much forensic evidence."

Again, Shepherd thought a moment. "As I said, one of our unsub's signatures is that he abducts a new victim after dumping his current kill," he replied. "Following that, he holds her for several weeks before raping and strangling her. So far the longest he has kept any victim alive is twenty-seven days."

"You might have your order reversed on that," I broke in.

"What do you mean?" asked Shepherd.

"For one, the women he's murdering have all been unusually attractive, so it's probably safe to conclude that he isn't selecting his victims at random."

"Right," Shepherd agreed. "Our psychological profile indicates he's been stalking his victims—possibly for months before they're abducted. So?"

"So I think our guy is kidnapping his next victim *before* he dumps his last. Otherwise, if something were to go wrong with the abduction and his latest body had already turned up, everyone in the area would be on full alert—spoiling his little game. I think he's abducting his next victim *first*."

"Good point, although I'm not certain how it helps," said Shepherd.

"You never know," I said. "Also, I have a feeling this scumbag is strangling his victims and *then* raping them. Maybe repeatedly."

"On what are you basing that?"

"A hunch. I've seen it before."

"We don't conduct investigations based on hunches," Strickland interrupted.

"Then call it experience," I shot back, tiring of Strickland's antagonism. "You have something to say to me, Assistant Chief Strickland?"

For once Ingram didn't intervene. "That's correct, Detective Kane," Strickland replied, his face darkening. "In my opinion, considering your insubordinate behavior on the Infidel investigation, you should have been summarily dismissed from the force. You are here simply because—"

"—because if it hadn't been for Kane, those psychos would still be cutting off people's heads," Taylor broke in. "Instead of criticizing Kane, Assistant Chief Strickland, you should be kissing his butt."

Everyone turned toward Taylor, staring in surprise.

"Excuse me?" said Strickland.

"She said something like that at a Bureau briefing, too," one of the FBI agents mumbled.

"What did you just say to me, Agent Taylor?" Strickland demanded.

"You heard me," said Taylor, not backing down. "If it hadn't been for Kane's so-called insubordination, LAPD would have two black eyes on the Infidel case right now, instead of just one. The Bureau, too," she added with a glance at Shepherd.

Bright spots appeared on Strickland's cheeks. "It was pure, dumb luck that Kane managed to—"

"My dad used to say, 'The harder you work, the luckier you get,'" Taylor interrupted again.

"Is that so? Well, aphorisms aside, Agent Taylor, I don't think you appreciate your position here," Strickland warned. "You worked with Kane on the Infidel investigation, so as far as I'm concerned, you are skating on thin ice as well. Let me spell things out for you. Your job here tonight is to take orders and keep your mouth shut."

"That may be," Taylor shot back, her temper flaring. "But I don't take orders from you."

During this exchange I had been trying to signal Taylor to silence. Unable to get her attention, I glanced at Chief Ingram, who had remained uncharacteristically quiet. To my surprise, I noticed a fleeting smile cross his lips.

"But you do take orders from me, Special Agent Taylor," Shepherd intervened.

"Yes, sir," said Taylor, lowering her gaze.

"Let's get back on topic," Shepherd suggested. "We were in the process of discussing our unsub." Turning, he addressed a lean, tough-looking individual whose granite-hard eyes and close-cropped hair spoke of a military background. "Special Agent in Charge Gibbs, you're as up-to-date as anyone on the Bureau's efforts on this case. Do you have anything to add?"

SAC Gibbs placed his hands behind his back and stood at parade rest. "Yes, sir," he replied. "In addition to interviewing family, friends, and coworkers of the murdered women, Bureau teams have been researching any means by which our unsub may have initially made contact. Phone records and social media sites—Facebook, Instagram, Twitter accounts, and the like—are being scrutinized. We have also been trying to establish any connection, however minimal, between the victims. So far we've come up empty on all fronts."

"Any luck running down the source of the online photos?" asked Ingram.

"No, sir," said Gibbs. "He's been posting his pictures using TOR and uploading to a European social network. To date the best we have been able to do is to trace the original uploads to public Wi-Fi sites in Portland, Seattle, and San Francisco. We're currently watching those locations. So far no repeats."

I had experienced this problem before. TOR, or The Onion Router, was a hidden-service-protocol network that allows someone to upload a photo or video in New York, for instance, and have the post show up as originating from someplace else, say Moscow, with a different IP address. Uploading to an overseas social network compounded the problem. "Any video surveillance at those Wi-Fi sites?" I asked.

Gibbs shook his head. "We've added some webcams of our own, but none was previously present at any of the sites. The guy is being careful."

"Can't you take down the photos?" asked someone else.

"We tried. As soon as they show up, his pictures are immediately reposted on other worldwide websites. We take one down; three more pop up someplace else." Gibbs paused to collect his thoughts. "On the plus side," he continued, "we have made progress developing a database of anyone who has purchased a dog training collar during the past twelve months—either online or from a west coast retailer."

"You mean a shock collar?" asked Snead, who until then had remained silent.

"Correct," said Gibbs. "The shape, size, and location of burns on the subjects' throats indicate that the killer is using some sort of shocking device to maintain control of his victims. We think it's a dog collar."

Snead paled.

"A couple of other things to note," Gibbs went on. "Like Kane said, we don't think the unsub is choosing victims at random. More likely he's stalking them, so we've been investigating that aspect as well. Several leads have turned up, but nothing definitive. Another thing: Toxicology exams on the victims showed the presence of a combination of date-rape drugs. We've been trying to run down the source of those drugs, so far without success. Last, with the discovery of each new body, the current victim's family has received a typed communication from the killer. Plain, 20 lb. copy paper, Hewlett Packard printer, double-spaced, 12 point Times New Roman. Untraceable unless we find the printer. By the way, we've withheld that last descriptor from the press, as it has been helpful in disproving a surprising number of confessions that have come in on our tip line. You will probably experience that issue as well."

"What did the letters say?" asked Snead.

"Just insults designed to inflict pain on family members," Gibbs replied. "In his communications, the unsub claims that each young woman he's taken is a filthy slut—a willing participant in early childhood sexual abuse, giving hand- and blowjobs at fourteen, screwing at fifteen—that kind of thing."

"Sick bastard," someone noted.

"Let's move on," Ingram suggested, turning to me. "Kane, you're lead investigator on the UCLA murder, correct?"

Before I could answer, Snead jumped in. "Chief, this is going to be a high-profile case, to say the least. HSS normally handles those situations," he said, referring to the Homicide Special Section of the LAPD's Robbery Homicide Division, a section under Snead's command. HSS detectives are an elite group of investigators who routinely cover the city's most difficult, high-profile cases. As such, The Magpie investigation was clearly within their jurisdiction.

"I have no problem with HSS taking lead," I offered.

Ingram scowled. "We're not running a democracy," he said, shooting Snead a look of irritation. "Here's how things are going to go," he went on, his tone leaving no room for discussion. "Kane will assume lead on the UCLA investigation. HSS will collaborate with the Bureau in an FBI/LAPD interagency effort. Together, we will bring this case to a rapid resolution. And make no mistake, we *will* end this quickly. If not, heads will roll."

"Will I be reporting to Captain Snead?" I asked. "Because I *do* have a problem with that."

"Your job is to do what you're told," Strickland warned, his tone echoing his earlier altercation with Taylor.

"Careful, Assistant Chief Strickland," I said. "I might have to sic Agent Taylor on you."

At that, Lieutenant Long and several agents with Shepherd laughed aloud. Even Ingram cracked another smile. For his part, Strickland looked ready to explode. "Kane, I swear to God," he said, "one more word out of you and I will personally see that you are—"

"Let's get back on topic, Owen," Ingram broke in. "We all want the same thing here, right?" Then, to me, "To answer your question, Detective Kane, you will be reporting directly to your supervisor, Lieutenant Long, and to me. No one else. Per protocol, Lieutenant Long and Captain Lincoln will pass information up the command chain through Deputy Chief Chow, so you will have as much personal autonomy as possible. Except as necessary, you will *not* be attending FBI or HSS briefings. Although this arrangement might entail a risk of duplicating work, daily updates to my office should keep that at a minimum."

Again, Snead started to object. Ingram silenced him with a peremptory raise of a hand. "Bill, we both know why it has to be this way. You too, Owen," he said, glancing at Strickland. "We discussed this."

Strickland glared at the floor.

"Yes, sir," Snead mumbled.

"Kane, what do you have on the UCLA murder so far?" Ingram continued, returning his attention to me.

"A couple of things," I replied. "But first, will someone please enlighten me on this mutt's nickname? The Magpie? I did some research. The notion that magpies steal shiny objects and leave something in their place is complete fiction—based on an old Rossini opera."

"When did the facts ever influence the media?" someone muttered.

"Good point," I agreed, deciding to let it go. "Anyway, regarding the UCLA murder, at autopsy we found a pair of barb wounds on Ms. Stafford's lower back. I've seen marks like that before. I think they came from a Taser."

"So in addition to a shock collar, our guy is using a Taser to control his victims?" Taylor broke in, speaking for the first time since her reprimand from Shepherd.

"I think he did with the UCLA woman," I answered. "I haven't seen reports on the other murders, so I can't speak to that.

Whatever the case, maybe we should take a look at Taser purchases."

"Good idea," agreed Ingram. "Anything else?"

"I have a feeling this guy is looking for his fifteen minutes of fame," I went on. "Maybe we can use that."

"Maybe," said Shepherd. "Assuming that is the case. What makes you think he's motivated by a desire for recognition?"

"For one, the photos he's been posting on the internet. For another, he phoned me."

At that, all heads turned in my direction.

"Twice," I said. "The first time was in Idaho. I didn't realize then what was going on."

"What did he say?" asked Snead.

"He said, 'Detective Kane? Let's play.' There was something off about his voice, like it had been electronically altered."

"Let's play?" said one of the agents. "The guy thinks this is some kind of game?"

"Wouldn't be the first time," I replied. "He also could be trying to prove he's smarter than we are. I've seen that, too."

Ingram leaned forward. "You said, 'twice.' When did you receive your second call?"

"At UCLA, in the Botanical Garden. Same electronically altered voice. This time he said, 'I'm pleased to see you've accepted my invitation, Detective Kane. Let's play.' I got a *57 trace on that one. The call originated from a burner phone in Orange County."

"So where does that leave us?" asked Ingram.

"His calls suggest several investigative approaches," I reasoned. "For one, how did he get my cellphone number? We should look into that. For another, I contacted Verizon and had a trap-and-trace placed on my phone. I also downloaded a recording app. If he calls again and I get a sample of his voice, maybe we can figure out what kind of device he's using, then reverse the process and hear his actual voice. Along those lines, maybe we could develop a database of voice-altering software purchasers and compare it to, say, the dog-collar list. Or to a catalogue of Taser purchasers, if we go in that direction."

I noticed Shepherd writing in a notebook. "Anything else?" he asked, glancing up.

"It might be helpful to have our current forensic team investigate any future Magpie killings, along with reviewing all past cases to date."

At the mention of future murders, an uneasy silence settled over the room.

After a long moment, Ingram glanced at his watch. "Okay, let's call it for tonight," he sighed, signaling an end to the meeting. "Thank you all for coming in."

As people began filing out, I stopped at Ingram's desk. "Chief, could I have a word?" I asked quietly. "I have some concerns."

Ingram looked up. "I thought you might, and I appreciate your not bringing them up during the meeting. Let's step outside. Mind if I smoke?"

I shook my head.

Ingram opened a desk drawer and withdrew a cigar from an engraved wooden box. "Cuban Partagás," he informed me, clipping an end of the cigar with a silver cutter. "I have a friend who gets them wholesale."

Exiting a sliding-glass door, I followed Ingram out to a triangular terrace overlooking West First Street, with City Hall looming in the background. Not for the first time, I was struck by the proximity of police headquarters to Los Angeles's seat of political power, concluding that the juxtaposition of the two buildings was more than mere coincidence.

"We were out here once before, you and I," Ingram observed, lighting his cigar.

Although I had never smoked, I found myself enjoying the dark, earthy aroma of Ingram's Partagás. "Yes, sir. The Infidel investigation," I said, moving to the railing and gazing out over the lights of the city.

"At that time, I asked you to be a team player," Ingram went on, taking a deep puff on his cigar. "Despite what happened on the Infidel case, I'm asking you again."

"Why me? By all rights, this investigation should go to HSS."

"Several reasons. For one, I want someone on the investigation who can think outside the box. Despite stomping on a lot of toes, fostering an atmosphere of insubordination, and pissing off almost everyone in the process, you're that someone."

"Thanks, Chief—I think," I said with a grin. "You said several reasons. What else?"

"We'll talk about that later. For now, I realize you have reservations about taking this case. It's the risk posed to your family by another high-profile investigation, right?"

"Yes, sir."

"Considering what has happened in the past, that's a reasonable concern," Ingram conceded. "Nevertheless, in light of the cellphone calls you mentioned receiving, it must have occurred to you that you've drawn the attention of a dangerous killer. As a result, your family may *already* be in danger.

"Yes, sir," I repeated, a hollow sensation expanding in the pit of my stomach.

Ingram was right, which presented a dilemma: I could withdraw from the investigation, put in for early retirement, and hope for the best; or I could work the case and depend on LAPD to protect my family, should that become necessary. Unfortunately, police protection for my family hadn't worked out well in the past.

Bottom line, neither option looked appealing.

"I know that you think we dropped the ball when guarding you and your family during the Infidel investigation." Ingram continued. "I assure you, that won't happen again."

Dropped the ball? I thought to myself. Painting a bulls-eye on my back would have described it better. "How about keeping my name out of the media this time?" I suggested.

"Of course, at least as much as possible. Look, Dan, you were made to do this kind of work. So do it. As I said earlier, you will have as much autonomy as possible, and I'll have your back. Are you in?"

I hesitated, again considering the possibility of simply walking away. "Can I think about it?"

Ingram's sunny demeanor abruptly clouded over. "I'll need an answer by tomorrow morning."

"Yes, sir."

After leaving Ingram on the terrace to finish his Partagás, I encountered SAC Gibbs and Taylor in the hallway. From the tension in the air, it looked like Gibbs had just finished a categorical chewing-out of Taylor, who for her part was attempting to look chastised and nearly succeeding.

Both glanced up as I approached, and I heard Taylor mumble, "It won't happen again, sir."

Apparently satisfied, Gibbs turned on his heel and started toward the elevators.

Joining Taylor, I watched as Gibbs stepped into an empty elevator cab. When the door had closed behind him, I said, "That probably wasn't such a hot idea sticking up for me in the meeting, Taylor. But . . . thanks."

"Someone had to say something."

"Maybe, but you probably didn't do your career much good."

"Probably not," Taylor agreed. Then, brightening, "So— we're working together again. Part-time, anyway."

"Maybe. I haven't decided yet about taking the case. Lot of things involved."

"Considering what happened last time, I don't blame you. When will you know?"

"Ingram wants a decision by tomorrow morning."

"Keep me in the loop, okay?"

"You'll be the first to know," I promised. "Or at least the second," I added. Then, changing the subject, "Nate and I were completely blown away watching you at the kayak championship. I had no idea."

"Thanks," Taylor replied, a flush rising to her cheeks.

"And I appreciate your arranging for Nate to take that clinic," I went on. "He's totally excited about learning to paddle."

"Nate's a great kid. I really like him."

"Me, too."

"Speaking of which, I'd be happy to pick up him at LAX when he gets back."

"Not necessary, Taylor. I can manage, assuming my Suburban ever shows up."

"I just talked with the agent who's driving it down. You'll have it later tonight. And I would love to pick up Nate, really. I want to talk with him about his clinic."

I shrugged. "Okay. I'm sure he would like to see you again, too."

Taylor grinned. "Assuming he hasn't drowned by then."

"Yeah, assuming that," I laughed.

We rode the elevator to the lobby without speaking. Standing beside Taylor in the confined cab, I was acutely conscious of her presence. Deciding she was undoubtedly the best thing about the chief's meeting that night, I stepped out with her to the ground floor. To my surprise, I found Captain Snead there waiting.

"May I have a word with you, Detective Kane?" he asked, glancing at Taylor. "In private?"

"I'll talk with you tomorrow," said Taylor, starting for the door. "Good night, Captain Snead."

Seeming preoccupied, Snead nodded. "Good night."

I watched as Taylor strode confidently across the lobby, wondering what Captain Snead wanted to discuss.

For years Snead had made no secret of his animosity toward me, with his hatred dating back to patrol days. One year out of training, when Snead and I were both brand-new P-II patrol officers, Snead had been booking a wino who was so far gone that he decided to relieve himself right there in the station. Unfortunately, he wound up pissing on Snead's leg. Snead started using his baton on the rummy, at which point I had intervened. Furious, Snead had made the mistake of throwing a punch at me. I wouldn't call what happened next a fight, as I only hit him once. Snead was unconscious after that, and for the next six weeks he had to drink milkshakes through a straw. Since then we'd had numerous confrontations—mostly involving Snead's determined efforts to get me booted off the force.

Now, although curious regarding Snead's presence, I said nothing, letting the silence between us grow.

Snead shifted from foot to foot. Finally he spoke. "I owe you an apology."

"I don't think I heard you correctly," I replied, unable to hide my surprise.

"I never offered my condolences to you and your family when Catheryn was killed. Despite the bad blood between us, I was wrong not to do so. I'm sorry for your loss, Kane. I truly am. And I regret not saying something sooner."

"I . . . well, thanks," I said, completely caught off guard.

"I also regret not having said something to you earlier when you lost your son, Thomas. That had to be a terrible time for you."

"It was."

"The job has cost you a lot."

"Is that what this is about?" I said. "Because if it is, you don't have to worry about my taking your HSS investigation. I just had a talk with the chief, and I'm going to inform him tomorrow that I won't be working the case. And if that means putting in for early retirement, so be it."

Snead looked upset. "That's not it," he said. "I got a call from the killer yesterday, too."

"What did he say?"

"Same thing he said to you. 'Let's play.'"

"You need to get a trap-and-trace on your line," I advised. "Get a recording app on your phone, too. If you receive another—"

Snead raised a hand. "Already done."

"Then what . . .?"

Snead hesitated. "My daughter, Ella, disappeared on Friday night," he said. "From a UCLA parking structure."

I felt the hairs rise on the back of my neck. "The same night the killer dumped a body in the Botanical Garden."

Snead nodded. "Campus police found Ella's backpack and car keys on the pavement beside her vehicle. No one has seen or heard from her since."

"I'm sorry, Bill. Maybe there's another explanation?"

Snead shook his head. "She was supposed to meet friends for dinner. When she didn't show up, they called everywhere. She's gone. And I think *he* has her."

"That's why Ingram didn't want HSS taking lead on the investigation," I said, things starting to fall in place. "I'm surprised he's allowing you to be involved at all."

"I insisted."

"I understand, but—"

"I'm on the investigation, Kane. End of discussion."

"Okay."

"We haven't disclosed my daughter's kidnapping to the press yet. When we do, the media will go ballistic."

"Roger that. You and me, our past disagreements reported in the media, your daughter being kidnapped. This isn't a coincidence."

"Departmental rivals—one whose child is abducted, the other who has to find her before it's too late. That's why that twisted bastard called you, right? And it's why he called me. It's some kind of sick game he wants us to play."

"Probably." I felt a chill, realizing that the killer could have just as easily abducted Allison.

Snead regarded me intently. "I have no right to ask anything of you, but I need a favor. I want you to take the case."

"That's the last thing I'd have expected to hear from you."

"You and I are on opposite sides of the fence on almost everything," Snead agreed. "Except for this. I don't approve of your methods, but you do get results. I can't overlook any resource that might save Ella."

I glanced away. "Bill, I'm sorry, but—"

"Please, Kane. I'm begging you. It's my daughter."

I hesitated. If I investigated what would certainly become a high-profile case, I might be putting those I loved at risk, as I had in the past. Nevertheless, my family could already be in danger, as Ingram had pointed out.

In any case, time was running out for Ella Snead. And given the circumstance, Allison could be next.

I hesitated a moment more, then came a decision. Though uncertain where it would lead, I turned to Snead. "Will you be seeing Chief Ingram in the morning?"

"I will, but—"

"Give him a message for me."

"What?"

"Tell him I'm in."

Chapter 10
Storm Surf

Following a restless night's sleep, I arose the next morning before dawn.

Still thinking about the UCLA murder, I wondered once again whether I had made a mistake by agreeing to Ingram's strongly worded request. Of one thing I *was* certain: I wanted to find whoever had killed Sandy Stafford of Seattle and hung her in the Botanical Garden like a side of beef.

And when I did, I hoped he resisted.

Moving quietly so as not to wake the rest of the household, I pulled on a T-shirt and a pair of swimming trunks, grabbed my swim fins and surfing wetsuit, and headed for the beach. With a yawn, Callie roused herself from her corner bed and followed me out—as usual ready for whatever activity I had planned, regardless of the hour.

As I had expected, yesterday's four- to five-foot southern swell had continued to build overnight. In the dim light, I could make out a ghostly progression of gigantic waves lining up offshore, with monstrous ten- to twelve-foot gray-green breakers slamming the sand and vibrating the deck beneath my feet. Prudently electing to skip my customary morning swim, I instead exercised on the deck for the next forty minutes, completing a regimen of push-ups, sit-ups, bar chins, and dips. By the time I paused to face the dawn, a sheen of sweat covered my arms and chest, and my breath was coming hard.

As my breathing slowed and my blood-thickened muscles began to relax, I turned to regard our house, checking to see whether anyone else had risen. To my disappointment, the windows all remained dark. Nevertheless, I smiled as I inspected the glass and timber structure that had replaced our former home. Although lacking the ramshackle appeal of our previous dwelling, it more than made up for any lack of rustic charm with new foundation piers, larger windows and bedrooms, upgraded plumbing and wiring, expanded decks, and a new seawall that would stand for decades.

Upon rebuilding after the fire, Catheryn had insisted we replace a number of palms that had been consumed in the blaze, as well as replanting several beds of beach cane, flowering bougainvillea, and aloe. All had flourished, their presence once more seeming to root our home to the sand upon which it sat.

As I stood enjoying the first weak rays of the sun, I noticed a group of terns scuttling along the water's edge, racing to avoid the upsurge as they pecked out their morning breakfast. Above, I could hear the press of traffic on Pacific Coast Highway beginning to build. Later, driving would slow, with bumper-to-bumper traffic more often the norm than not, but for the moment the morning belonged to the birds, and Callie, and me.

"How 'bout it, girl?" I said, leaning down to stroke Callie's sleek head. "Ready for a swim?" With a feeling of regret, I noticed the first signs of gray beginning to show on her muzzle.

Callie looked up, her intelligent golden eyes clearly conveying the words, "Are you nuts?"

"C'mon, girl," I coaxed, pulling on my surfing wetsuit and grabbing my swim fins. "At least let's go take a look."

I still had time before I had to leave for work, and I was reconsidering my decision to skip my morning swim. I liked to finish whatever I started, in this case my workout. Having spent years on the beach, I was a strong swimmer and an experienced bodysurfer. Nevertheless, I had categorically forbidden my children to enter big surf alone, ever. Going out in the massive waves would be violating my own rule.

Reluctantly, Callie followed me across the seawall to a sandy berm near the water's edge. There she stopped and sat. Refusing to proceed further, she watched me with sad, wistful eyes.

"It's okay, girl," I said. "Just kidding about the swim. That surf is way too big for you. Maybe for me, too."

As the sun began lighting a sliver of eastern sky, I stood at the water's edge, swim fins at my side. Enveloped in roar and mist, I stared out at the angry Pacific, awed by its power. I remained there for several minutes, studying the waves. At one point I thought I noticed a pause in the sets. Given hope, I moved down the sand to an outflowing riptide and donned my fins. Taking a deep breath, I dived in.

I am still unsure why I did it. Maybe I was trying to forget the pressures and uncertainties of the new investigation, replacing the dangers involved in working a high-profile case with more immediate ones that I knew how to handle—or at least I hoped I did. Whatever the case, I was committed. Caught in the rip, and there would be no turning back.

The outflowing current carried me quickly to a smaller inside break. Lifting my head, I saw an eight-foot wall of foam boiling toward me. After a hurried gulp of air, I scratched for the bottom, submerging an instant before the hissing foam enveloped me. Realizing the worst was yet to come, I emerged on the backside and continued swimming, beginning to think I had made a mistake. The waves were a lot bigger than they had looked from shore.

And I still had to get past the outside break.

Pausing to tread water, I checked the oncoming waves. Getting past the break of a five-foot set was one thing; making it out through twelve-foot surf was another. My stomach sank as I saw a fourteen-footer approaching, an angry plume of spray flying from its crest.

I had to reach deeper water.

Lowering my head, I kicked for all I was worth, my arms and legs driving me toward the advancing surge. In shallow water, being caught inside a breaking wave that large could mean a broken shoulder, a snapped neck, or being knocked unconscious—all of which could prove fatal.

The riptide continued ferrying me seaward. Combined with my strokes, I thought the outrushing current would be enough to shuttle me past the mountainous wall of water before it curled.

I was wrong.

I wasn't going to make it.

Dive!

Taking another hurried breath, I submerged again, pulling for the safety of the bottom. As I descended, I felt the mass of the wave moving over me, trying to drag me back. Thankful I had taken time to don my fins, I kicked with all my strength. Heart pounding, hands scrabbling against the sand, I fought against the terrible sucking power of the wave, its force diminished by my depth but still strong enough to drag me back into its maw.

Red haze dimmed my vision. I couldn't stay down much longer.

And still the wave pulled at me, unwilling to release its grip. Lungs burning, thighs cramping, I forced myself to stay down several more seconds, waiting for the wave to pass.

For a sickening instant I thought I wouldn't make it.

Somehow I did.

After what seemed a lifetime, I resurfaced, only to find another monstrous swell approaching. Taking a gasping breath, I dived again, still riding the riptide. Progressively sucked seaward by the outrushing flow, I repeated this again, and again— eventually fighting my way past the break of even the largest waves.

I was safe . . . for the moment.

A dozen lateral strokes carried me out of the rip. There I tread water to catch my breath, feeling the power of each passing swell lift and lower me on its journey to the shore.

Finally recovered enough to continue, I set out again, swimming to a raft that neighbors and I had anchored offshore some years back. As usual, a spattering of bird droppings layered its ten-by-ten surface. Deciding to forgo cleaning the poop and climbing aboard to rest, I continued swimming westward against a long-shore current, breathing on my right to avoid a chopping spray from seaward.

Twenty minutes later, upon arriving at a rocky point marking the western terminus of Las Flores Beach, I paused about two hundred yards from shore. Then, breathing on the opposite side, I set out on my return.

Several times on the trip back I found myself drifting too close to shore, with the swells forcing me to retreat to deeper water. During that time I also noticed that the waves were continuing to build, and I began to worry about returning to shore. It had never been my intention to surf any of the larger waves. Instead, I had planned to wait for a pause in the swells, then swim to the inside break and ride a smaller wave back to shore.

Upon returning to the raft, I again tread water, hoping for a pause in the sets. Minutes passed. With a feeling of apprehension, I began to realize that my original plan was not to be. If anything, the waves were increasing in size, with no pause in between. To make matters worse, despite my wetsuit, I was getting cold.

As I waited, hoping I hadn't made a foolish error by entering the waves that morning, my thoughts returned to The Magpie case, and to the obscenity the killer had left on display in the Botanical Garden. With a growing sense of unease, I realized that like the treacherous water in which I was now immersed, I was at the mercy of unpredictable tides and currents on the new investigation, and any misstep could send my life spinning in ways I was unable to predict. With an effort of will, I forced myself to concentrate on my present situation, deciding to worry about the investigation later—assuming I made it to shore.

Shivering, I glanced over my shoulder. With dismay, I saw one of the largest waves of the day bearing down on me with the unrelenting fury of an avalanche. I had two choices: Turn and sprint for deeper water, or take my chances and ride it in.

Praying I wasn't making another bad decision, I chose the latter.

Heart in my throat, I waited, gauging the oncoming giant's approach. Thrust skyward by the ocean floor, it continued to rise, higher . . . higher . . .

At the last instant, as I sensed the first sucking rush of the oncoming surge, I turned and raced for shore. Legs churning, arms slashing the water in a strong series of strokes, I felt the wave rise beneath me.

If I went over the falls, a drop to the shallows could prove fatal.

Don't think about that.
Swim!
Several final kicks . . . and I was in.

Right arm extended, I plummeted down the curling face, a glitter of spray flying into my eyes. Arching my back, I cut left before bottoming out. I felt myself slowing . . . then rising again on the nearly vertical wall.

And again I dropped. Accelerating into another turn at the bottom, I cut free of the wave just before it closed out. Emerging on the backside, I gulped a breath of air, lowered my head, and kicked for the sand, hoping to avoid a pounding by the following swell.

Somehow surviving a battering from the next several sets, I made it to the inside break. Nearly exhausted, I struggled to keep my head above the foam. Shortly afterward, with a flood of relief, I managed to catch a smaller wave, riding it most of the way to shore.

Teeth chattering, I stripped off my fins and waded through waist-deep water to the beach, still fighting the outrushing surge. When I arrived in the shallows, Callie bounded into the backwash, greeting me with unabashed canine joy.

As for me, I had never been happier to be anywhere in my life. Still shivering, I headed back to the house, unexpectedly recalling my promise to Dorothy. To my surprise, I found myself looking forward to the challenges of the new investigation, and protecting those I loved, and getting on with my life—hoping those issues were not mutually exclusive.

Following a cold shower on the deck, I toweled myself dry, went upstairs and fed Callie, and brewed a pot of coffee. The house was still quiet, and I decided to let everyone sleep. Steaming mug of java in hand, I returned to my bedroom and dressed. Then, moving to my gun safe in the corner, I entered the combination and removed my service weapon, a Glock .45 ACP model 21. Strapping on my shoulder rig, I headed for the front door.

On the street outside, I found that my Suburban had arrived sometime during the night. The keys were on the floor. Happy to be driving my larger vehicle once again, I pulled onto Pacific Coast Highway during a lull in traffic, making a mental note to thank the Boise agent who had made the delivery.

Traffic was light, and on the way into town I placed a call to Nate. As the phone began ringing on his end, I switched my iPhone to speaker and placed it on the seat beside me.

"Hello?" Nate answered, sounding sleepy. "Dad?"

"None other. Hope I didn't wake you."

"It's time I got up anyway," Nate yawned. "Everything okay?"

"All's good on my end. How about you?" I replied, deciding not to mention my ill-advised venture into the surf that morning, a lapse in judgment that still worried me. Now that the flush of surviving the gigantic waves had started to fade, I once more wondered whether taking the case would turn out to be a dangerous mistake in my professional life as well.

"Great on my end, too," said Nate, starting to wake up. "I like Agent Taylor's friends at the rafting company. I can't wait to get on the river."

"Stay upright in your boat, okay?"

"I'll try. Tom and Chad said I'll be learning an Eskimo roll, just in case."

"Tom and Chad?"

"Cascade Raft family members, and two of the best kayak instructors anywhere. Anyway, Agent Taylor says my surfing experience should make me a natural."

"I suppose kayaking can't be much more dangerous than surfing."

"Well, there *are* rocks in the river, which makes things a little different," Nate laughed. "Don't worry, Dad. I'll be fine."

"See that you are. By the way, Taylor will be picking you up at LAX when you get back."

"Cool."

"And next Wednesday we'll resume your regular appointments with Dr. Berns."

"I haven't forgotten, Dad. Gotta run."

"Okay. Stay safe, kid."

After disconnecting, I glanced at my watch. I still had thirty minutes before the start of my shift. Instead of turning left on West Channel Road, I continued east on Pacific Coast Highway toward Santa Monica. Before arriving at the station, there was a friend I wanted to see, and maybe pick his brain.

Chapter 11
Photo Shoot

In the silence of her prison, groggy from the drugs she had taken the day before, Ella Snead lay on her bed, as still as death. The overhead light had come on earlier. As ordered, she had showered and dressed. Afterward she had taken advantage of the light to explore her cell further, this time discovering a cabinet drawer filled with women's clothes of various sizes—skirts, blouses, underclothes, sweaters, slacks—all freshly laundered.

Had he purchased her a variety of clothes, not knowing her measurements? Or were they simply leftovers from previous captives? Either way, Ella decided to wash her own garments in the sink and hang them in the shower to dry.

Later she had returned to bed, dreading the man's arrival.

Now what? she wondered, trying to quiet her trembling hands by clasping them tightly in her lap.

Will he visit again today?

Of the previous day, she remembered little. She vaguely recalled being undressed and photographed in different poses—sometimes in nightgowns and frilly underwear, sometimes without. And again, throughout it all, it had seemed as if she were watching herself from afar. One thing she *did* remember clearly. After entering her cell, he had removed her collar.

And maybe that could help.

Minutes later, the sound of footsteps announced his presence. As the man entered the chamber outside her cell, Ella once more saw him tucking a key inside his shirt. "Good morning," he said, setting another McDonald's box on the floor before seating himself in his chair.

Ella glanced at the McDonald's carton. The one he'd brought previously had contained egg and bacon sandwiches, which she had thrown up shortly after wolfing them down. She had to be more careful. She needed to maintain her strength, and the granola bars in the cabinet weren't going to be enough.

"Did you sleep well?"

Sensing that her terror somehow fed her captor, Ella fought to hide it. "No."

"I myself slept rather well."

"How nice for you."

His face darkened. "Sarcasm doesn't become you, Ella," he warned, lifting his remote control. "Nor does incivility. Will an attitude adjustment be necessary?"

Ella looked away, unable to meet his gaze. "Please, just let me go and I won't tell any—"

He shocked her.

This time the electrical surge was worse than before.

Ella screamed. "You son of a bitch, let me out of here!"

He shocked her again.

And again.

"No more," Ella begged, weeping.

"That's entirely up to you."

"What do you want? Is it sex?"

The man stared through the bars, his face expressionless.

"Because I'll do whatever you want," Ella said, lowering her eyes. "Anything."

The man shook his head. "No, no, no. We were making such progress before you ruined things with your tawdry offer of sex."

"I . . . I'm sorry," Ella backtracked, realizing she had made a mistake.

The man remained silent, as if considering. Then, "I accept your apology," he said.

"Thank you," Ella replied, attempting to sound sincere. Taking a deep breath, she glanced at the ceiling. "Can you watch me on that webcam whenever you want? Even with the light turned off?"

"Of course. It's an infrared device. Everything is recorded for later viewing as well."

Being the daughter of a police captain, Ella was familiar with surveillance equipment. From the faint glow emanating from around the webcam lens, she already knew it was an infrared device, able to track her in the dark. She hoped the man didn't realize that once her vision had adjusted, the feeble red light allowed her to navigate her darkened prison. She couldn't see everything, but enough.

"Could you leave the light on?" Ella begged. "Please? At least during the day. It's horrible to be in complete darkness and not see anything at all," she added, testing her theory.

"That's a privilege you must earn," the man replied.

"If this isn't about sex, why are you doing it?" Ella asked again, taking a different tack.

"Because I can," the man replied.

"You're sick."

"There are many who would agree. Were I able to experience even the tiniest bit of shame or remorse, which—unlike most of the puppets currently populating our planet, I don't—things might be different. On the contrary, I *like* what I'm doing. We're nothing in the grand scheme of things, nothing but dust, so what possible difference could anything I do now make in, say, fifty years? A hundred? A thousand? So as long as I don't get caught, why shouldn't I do whatever I want?"

"You're sick," Ella repeated.

"And you think you're tough. Am I right, Ella? Are you tough?"

Ella didn't answer.

"I'll tell you what, tough little Ella. I'm going to reward you for your candor. You may have several additional hours of light each day, starting this morning."

Although Ella's heart leapt, she remained silent.

"But now it's time for you to take your medicine," the man continued. "And the next time we meet, I want to hear all about your lovely sister, Julie."

Though appalled that he knew her younger sister's name, Ella still remained silent.

She had the beginnings of a plan, and anything she said might spoil it.

Chapter 12
Hank Dexter

After disconnecting with Nate on the drive into town, I next called Taylor, informing her that I would be working The Magpie investigation and arranging to meet her later that afternoon to compare notes. Last, I called an old friend, Hank Dexter, telling him to expect me.

Upon arriving in Santa Monica, I pulled to a stop on West Pico, parking in front of a store with a neon sign above the door that read: Hank's Radio and TV. Hank's shop hadn't opened yet, so I rapped on the storefront window. Moments later Hank peered at me through the glass, his weathered face lighting in a grin. With a wave, he motioned me to the front door.

"A pleasure to see you again, Dan," said my elderly friend as I entered, regarding me over a pair of antique, wire-rimmed glasses.

"You, too, Hank."

After ushering me in, Hank locked the door behind us. Glancing around, I noticed stacks of unopened shipping boxes near the entrance, rack upon rack of stereos and computers to the right, shelves jammed with ham radio equipment, microphones, and speakers to the left, and an armada of flat-screen televisions plastering the far wall. "Business looks good," I observed.

"Can't complain," Hank agreed.

Years back I had worked a drive-by shooting in which Hank's teenaged son, Mitchell, had been present in a crowd indiscriminately sprayed with gang-retaliation gunfire. Mitchell had been struck in the spine and wound up riding a wheelchair. Over the course of the investigation, Hank and I became friends, and we still stayed in touch.

"How's Mitch?"

Hank smiled again. "Couldn't be better. He and Milli just made me a grandfather twice over—this time with a baby girl, Elizabeth. She came two weeks early, but she's healthy as a horse."

"That's wonderful news, Hank," I said, remembering how delighted I had been holding my own granddaughter for the first time. "Please extend my congratulations."

"Will do." Hank regarded me curiously. "I'm assuming there's more to your visit this morning than catching up on old times. What's up?"

I shoved my hands into my pockets, trying to decide how much to say. I trusted Hank, but I didn't want to put him in a compromising position. "I'm working a case in which some dirtbag has been sending us voice-altered messages," I replied. "I'm hoping we can use that somehow. What do you know about voice-masking techniques?"

Hank shrugged. "I'm not an expert on voice changers, but I can probably fill in a few blanks. Let's head back to my workbench. Want some coffee?"

"Thanks, already had my dose for the day," I said, following Hank deeper into the store. After Hank had poured himself a mug of black coffee, we ducked under a counter and made our way to a brightly lit service area in the rear. Hank moved a piece of disassembled electronic equipment from his workbench, set down his mug, and dropped into a well-worn armchair.

"We're talking about software, right?" I said, perching on a nearby stool. "Not hardware?"

Hank nodded. "For the most part. There are a few dedicated hardware systems still out there, but voice masking nowadays is mostly done with software run on any generic computer. Most laptops have plenty of computing power to do the job."

I thought a moment. "Okay, so here's what I want to know. First, is it possible to reverse the voice-masking process and revert to the original sound? And second, is there any way to tell what kind of software someone is using?"

"So you can track it to a particular purchaser?"

"Something like that."

Hank rubbed his chin. "Hmmm. Okay, let's start with your first question, which will help understand the issues involved with your second."

"Just keep it simple, okay?"

"Of course," Hank sniffed, looking disappointed. "To start, the most basic form of sound modification is to speed up or slow down a recording of something—like playing an old LP record faster on the stereo turntable. In that case you're speeding up time, which raises the sound frequency, or pitch."

"And you wind up with something sounding like Alvin and the Chipmunks' *Christmas Song*."

"Right. Getting back to the original pitch simply requires slowing down the recording, which is way too easy to be useful as a masking technique. I only mention it to make the point that unlike altering a recording, a good voice changer has to be able to operate in *real time*—and do so without speeding up or slowing down the underlying speech."

"Changing the pitch without changing the speed."

Hank nodded. "Correct. That's where things get complicated."

"How about skipping the complexities?"

"I'll do my best," Hank agreed, again looking disappointed. "But there are a few geeky principles you need to grasp to understand what comes next."

"Go ahead," I said, deciding to shut up and listen.

"Okay," Hank continued, removing his glasses and pinching the bridge of his nose. "There are several ways to achieve our real-time goal of changing the pitch without changing the underlying speed. One is a technique that converts a sound stream into its Fourier transform spectrum. The resultant frequency values are then modified in some way, after which an inverse mathematical function is used to convert the altered spectrum back to audio."

"You're losing me, Hank."

"Sorry, but bear with me. Another technique involves layering numerous audio samples, or 'grains,'—each no more that around ten milliseconds or so. By time-compressing or time-expanding each 'grain' and dropping segments of them back into the original, live-microphone frequency, you have the basis of a real-time pitch shifter. There are other methods as well, some of them proprietary."

"Are any of those techniques reversible?"

"Depends," Hank hedged. "If you know the *exact* software, and the *exact* settings—maybe."

"Maybe?"

"Along with the complexities I just mentioned, it's also possible to add randomizing parameters," Hank explained. "With them, for example, a man's voice can be made to sound like to a woman's, or a child's, or a space monster's. If you don't know how that original modification was achieved, there's no way to reverse it."

"Damn," I said, beginning to lose hope.

"There *is* some good news," Hank went on. "For one, it's difficult to mask someone's speech patterns. Most people have a distinctive way that words come out of their mouth—rhythm, inflection, repetition, and so on—which can help make identification possible. For another, each of the voice-masking algorithms I mentioned has its own earmarks—sampling rates, noise distribution, harmonic addition ratios, and so on."

My attention picked up. "So it might be possible to determine what software was used?"

"It would be difficult, but possible," Hank agreed. "There are hundreds of voice-changing systems out there, from inexpensive software packages with a dozen generic presets, to algorithms with almost unlimited capabilities. By the way, the music industry has been using pitch-altering 'Auto-Tune' software for years—cleaning up missed notes, as well as using it for effect in songs like *Believe*."

I nodded, recalling Cher's hit from the nineties. "But it's possible?"

"Theoretically. Of course, you would need a sample of the altered voice to start with."

"I'm working on that."

"Well, if there's anything I can do to help, don't hesitate to ask."

"Thanks, Hank. I might just do that." Then, glancing at my watch, "In the meantime, I have to get to work."

"There *is* one thing that's puzzling," Hank mused.

"What?"

"If your suspect wanted to send you a voice message without getting caught, why resort to using complicated software when there's a much simpler method—one that's completely untraceable?"

"And that is?"

"Why didn't he just type out his message and use text-to-speech to send it?"

Chapter 13
Squad Room

Deluca was already at work in the squad room when I arrived. So was Lieutenant Long. Deluca was sitting hunched at his second-floor desk, with Long peering over his shoulder. Both glanced up as I hit the top of the stairs.

I crossed the crowded room, heading for Deluca's workstation. On my way over Deluca shot me a chin nod, then returned his attention to a file on his desktop. "Lab work on Sandy Stafford," he explained when I arrived.

"And?" I asked.

"Blood and urine analysis showed the presence of Ketamine and GHB," Long replied.

I knew that Ketamine and GHB were both commonly abused street drugs taken to achieve euphoria and increased sexual drive. Ketamine was a veterinarian anesthetic with hypnotic, stimulant, and hallucinogenic properties; GHB, or gamma hydroxybutyrate, was a depressant.

Both were often referred to as "date rape" drugs. I also knew that Ketamine and GHB both belonged to a dissociative class of hallucinogens capable of disconnecting communication between brain and body—producing a state in which one could be aware of what was happening but unable to move. Mixing the two drugs was particularly dangerous, rendering a user susceptible to blackouts and amnesia, even coma.

"So besides imprisoning his victims, he's drugging them as well," I noted.

"Right. Increased histamine in the ligature marks on Stafford's wrists and ankles indicates they were made before the time of death," Deluca continued. "Same with the vaginal injuries."

"Anything else?"

Deluca nodded, checking his notebook. "A match came back on the tire tracks we found at the Botanical Garden. Bridgestone

All-Season Duelers. P215/70R16. Made for SUVs and commercial utility vans. Could come in handy."

"If we find the vehicle for comparison," I agreed. I hesitated and then continued, informing them that Captain Snead's daughter, Ella, had been kidnapped from UCLA on the same night that the body of our victim had been dumped in the garden. I watched as their amazement changed from shock to concern as they did the addition.

"This has to be horrible for Captain Snead and his family," said Long. "How is he holding up?"

"Not well," I answered, recalling the look of desolation in Snead's eyes the previous evening.

"Damn," Long said softly.

We all fell silent.

"Not a random abduction," Deluca finally muttered.

"No, it's not," I agreed, again realizing it could just as easily have been Allison. "I'm not certain what it means, but the killer's choice of victims was not a coincidence."

Once more, we all fell silent.

"After Ingram's meeting last night, it's safe to assume that you two will be on this full-time," Long sighed at last. "Let's head back to my office and start reassigning pending investigations. Afterward we can figure out what to do on the UCLA case. Kane, you have any ideas on that?"

"A few," I said, following Long to his office at the back of the squad room.

For the next hour, working at a table in Long's office, the three of us reviewed our open West L.A. homicide cases, discussing ways to shift responsibility to other squad detectives, many of whom were already overloaded. Working from memory, I gave status evaluations and detailed breakdowns of all current investigations, along with scheduled court appearances and personnel allocations for the following weeks. Once we had established a tentative plan for our open-case reassignments, Deluca and I returned to the squad room to tie up administrative loose ends with John Banowski, another homicide detective.

Banowski, who would be shouldering a significant portion of my D-III oversight responsibilities while Deluca and I were off the regular duty roster, was a thick-necked individual with a wrestler's going-to-fat-physique and a thinning, crew-cut hairstyle that probably hadn't changed much since high school. As Deluca pulled over a chair from an adjacent desk, Banowski settled his bearlike body on the corner of my workstation. There, for the next forty minutes, we went over our outstanding cases, file by file.

When we finished, Banowski shook his head. "Lotta work for the rest of the squad to pick up while you and Deluca are sidelined on The Magpie investigation," he sighed, levering his bulky frame from my desk.

"You can handle the added responsibility, John," I said. "Plus it'll look good in your personnel folder."

"Whatever," Banowski grumbled, heading back to his own workstation. "Just bag that asshole so we can get back to normal around here."

Until then, Deluca hadn't queried me about last night's meeting in Ingram's office, and I hadn't volunteered. I was happy being back at work, and I didn't want to spoil things by revisiting the politics involved in the case—figuring they would come up soon enough. As it turned out, I didn't have long to wait.

As if on cue, Captain Snead appeared at the top of the stairs.

"Damn, trouble just arrived," said Deluca.

Spotting us across the room, Snead began threading his way back. "Kane, Deluca," he said upon arriving.

"Captain Snead," I replied. "What brings you down here?"

"You know damn well why I'm here," said Snead. Then, glancing at Deluca, "Give us a minute, Detective."

"Sure," said Deluca, giving Snead a look of sympathy. Then, returning to his desk, he busied himself by aimlessly riffling through paperwork.

"Actually, I *don't* know why you're here," I said once Deluca had departed. "Don't you have a task force to run?"

"Despite what Chief Ingram told you last night, I'm here to straighten out any misconceptions you might have regarding not reporting to me on the investigation," Snead informed me. "I need to know every move you make."

"Not going to happen."

"Damn it, Kane! You can't—"

"I realize we're talking about your daughter," I interrupted. "And I can imagine how you must feel. I'm not saying we can't work together, or that you won't be in the loop. I'm just not taking orders from you. Too many cooks in the kitchen. If you have a problem with that, take it up with Ingram."

At that, Snead seemed to deflate. "I just can't bear to think about what he's doing to her," he said quietly.

"I know. Look, let's talk this through and see how we can best use our resources," I suggested.

Snead nodded, pulling over a chair from an empty workstation.

I signaled Deluca to return. After Paul had seated himself across from Snead, I continued, again addressing Snead. "Here's how I see things. As I said last night, it's no coincidence that you and I find ourselves in this together. Thanks to media coverage on the Infidel case, whoever took Ella knows our history. He kidnapped the daughter of an LAPD captain to get as much media attention as possible, and he abducted her from my patrol area to make certain I'd catch the case. His phone calls tell me he wants me in the forefront of the investigation—probably because he assumes you and I will wind up on opposite sides of the fence."

"You're saying this is some kind of game for him?" said Deluca.

"Looks that way. The question is, can we use that?"

We all paused in thought.

Not coming up with anything, I pushed ahead. "Okay, Captain Snead, I agree with your not revealing Ella's abduction, at least for the moment, but let's keep that possibility in mind. For now, there *are* a few things we can do."

"Like what?" asked Snead.

"For one, we just got the tox report back on Sandy Stafford. It showed the presence of Ketamine and GHB in her system. Both are considered date-rape drugs, like those used on the previous victims. We might try locating the source."

"Most so-called recreational drugs are gang-distributed," Deluca observed. "We could check Los Angeles clubs, bars, rave scenes—looking for anyone who's recently bought both. We should make sure the feds are following up on that aspect in the previous murders, too."

"Good idea," said Snead. "I have contacts in the gang units. I'll look into date-rape drug purchases around L.A. What else?"

I thought a moment. "How did he get my cellphone number? Or yours?"

"Someone in the department?" suggested Deluca. "Someone who knows you both?"

"That would be a fairly short list, but we should check," I said. "We could also find out whether this mutt called anyone else during his previous murders. If that's the case, our man may have hacked into his victims' social media sites—Facebook, WhatsApp, Messenger, and any phone apps that are out there."

"I have a Facebook account," Snead noted doubtfully. "I don't use any of those others."

"No, but your daughter probably did," Deluca pointed out. "And when she added her contacts to Messenger, for instance, your cellphone number may have been included. Messenger then matched your cell number or your email address to known Facebook users, and bingo, you're in there—whether you are Facebook friends with any of those people or not."

"Let's ask the Bureau to have their nerds check on that," I suggested. "The feds are already researching Sandy Stafford's Facebook friend requests, along with comparing her social media sites to those of previous victims. Having them look into the possibility of a phone hack would dovetail in." Then, moving on, I turned to Deluca. "How's the UCLA canvass for witnesses going?"

Deluca shook his head. "We're still searching for anyone who might have seen the killer entering the garden. Along those lines, I set up a meeting with UCPD to discuss campus security cameras," he replied. "We're supposed to get together this morning at UCLA with Lieutenant Greenly."

"Good work, Paul," I said. Then, to Snead, "Speaking of security cameras, we have a reasonably accurate timeframe on the murder. How about checking traffic cams in the area? If nothing else, we should have a shot of the killer leaving the site, no matter which direction he went. We'll have footage of ten thousand other commuters as well, but we could compare our findings with traffic cam footage from the killer's other dumpsites—maybe come up with a shot of the guy leaving another location."

"And maybe even get a license number," added Deluca.

"I'll have my team look into that, too," agreed Snead. "Anything else?"

"The killer used voice-changing software both times he called me," I said.

"Same with me," said Snead.

"If we can get a recording of his voice the next time he calls, we might be able to identify the masking software he's using," I suggested, deciding not to mention that I had already started looking into that. "You're ready to record him if he calls again, right?"

Snead nodded. "I am, but so far he hasn't actually said anything incriminating. You realize that with the exception of criminal activity, California requires two-party consent for voice recording, right? It could present a problem."

I knew Snead was bringing up a "fruit of the poisonous tree" legal issue—an evidentiary doctrine stating that any illegally obtained evidence was inadmissible in court, as was everything else resulting from the original illegal search.

"That dirtbag will never see the inside of a courtroom," Deluca predicted.

"You may be right, Paul," I agreed. "But if we do get a recording of the killer's voice, let's be careful about how we submit it as evidence. Granted, there is no expectation of privacy for someone using the phone in the commission of a crime. Even so, given how careful this guy has been with what he's said so far, both Captain Snead and I should get warrants on our cellphones to ensure there's absolutely no room for a motion to suppress, if we get the case to court. Suspenders *and* a belt. You understand what I'm saying here?"

Snead and Deluca both nodded. "I'll get it done today," said Snead.

"Okay," I finished, making a mental note to do the same. Then, glancing at my watch, "Deluca, you and I need to get over to UCLA and talk with this Lieutenant Greenly." Rising, I added, "Captain Snead, thanks for stopping by."

Snead stood as well. As he did, I regarded him closely. He looked exhausted, almost shell-shocked, as if he hadn't slept in days.

"One more thing, Captain."

"Yes?"

"A lot of capable people are doing everything possible to locate your daughter," I said quietly. "We'll do our best to find her . . . no matter what."

Chapter 14
Getting Warmer

The UCLA police department is one of ten University of California patrol agencies—each with statewide jurisdiction over campuses and properties owned by the UC Regents, each with its own sworn officers and police chief. I knew a number of LAPD officers who had gone to work for UCPD, so upon bulling my way through a crowd of reporters still clogging the Botanical Garden's south entrance, I wasn't surprised to find an old friend there waiting.

"Dan, it's been too long," said Tony Choi, a colleague who had recently retired from the Beverly Hills PD to take over as UCLA chief of police. "Glad to see you're still upright," he added, his round, tanned face splitting in a grin.

"Me, too," I chuckled, shaking Tony's hand. Tony was standing inside the yellow perimeter tape, accompanied by a uniformed UCPD officer. Nearby, an LAPD patrolman was still keeping the crime-scene log, as the garden grounds continued to remain sealed. I also noticed that across the street reporters were busy doing follow-up reports—probably enumerating all the things they didn't know and hadn't learned since yesterday.

"This is Scott Greenly," Choi continued, indicating the intense, whip-thin man beside him. "Lieutenant Greenly heads up our Investigations Division. His detectives did the initial workup on the murder, so he should be able to answer any questions you may have."

"Good to meet you, Greenly," I said, shaking his hand. "My partner, Paul Deluca," I added as Deluca, who had a court appearance later that afternoon and had driven over in his own car, ducked under the tape.

"Pleasure," said Deluca, shaking hands with both Greenly and Choi. "Wish it were under different circumstances."

"I hear you," said Greenly.

"Dan, I have an appointment at the Law School, but please call if there's anything I can do to help," said Choi, checking his watch. "And let's grab dinner sometime and catch up."

"Sounds good, Tony."

After Choi had departed, I turned to Greenly. "Let's talk about campus security cams that might have caught a shot of the killer, or possibly his vehicle," I suggested.

"My guys have been working that angle since we found the body," Greenly replied. "So far, nothing. The problem is, UCPD doesn't have a campus-wide security system. There are cameras scattered around in unrelated networks, but none in the Botanical Garden."

"So where are they?" asked Deluca.

"Mostly where there are concentrations of students," Greenly explained. "Over 150 security cams are in our on-campus housing areas, primarily to prevent theft. 200 or so watch over the UCLA Associated Students Store—again to prevent theft. Like I said, there are various departments using security cameras, but—"

"—no centralized monitoring," I finished.

"Correct. Nevertheless, we have been checking security-camera networks one-by-one and reviewing footage for the time in question. So far we've been concentrating on the south end of campus, particularly in the vicinity of the Botanical Garden. Nothing so far."

"Any surveillance in the parking areas?"

Greenly shook his head. "You're referring to the young woman who was abducted from Parking Structure 3?"

"Right. A grad student named Ella Snead. By the way, we haven't released that to the media yet."

"We don't talk to the press, so don't worry," Greenly assured me. "As for the parking structure, we may not have cameras, but we do keep a record of anyone using a credit card to pay for parking. Would that information be helpful?"

"Absolutely. Can you fax us those records?" Deluca jumped in, withdrawing his wallet and handing Greenly a business card.

"Consider it done," said Greenly. "You can also pay for parking by phone using our Parkmobile system, or register your vehicle for payment, or get a quarterly permit. I'll include those items in the report as well. Regrettably, our self-service pay stations also take cash, so your guy might not be on any of those lists."

"Damn," said Deluca.

"Let's get back to the security cams," I suggested. "We figure Ella was returning from class when she went missing. Could you look up her class schedule for that evening and check any cameras that might have caught her walking to and from Parking Structure 3?"

"And maybe get a shot of someone following her?" said Greenly, realizing where I was going. "We're on it."

"How about taking a look at the parking structure?" suggested Deluca.

"Sure," said Greenly. "It's about a mile from here. Where's your car?"

"Law School lot."

Greenly glanced at the ridge behind us. "I'm parked closer, up on Tiverton. C'mon, I'll run you guys over to Lot 3."

"You, go, Paul," I said, deciding there probably wasn't much to see at Parking Structure 3. "I'll check on our canvass across the street and meet you back here when you're done."

As Deluca and Greenly started off, I ducked under the perimeter tape and headed toward a knot of onlookers near the news vans. Noticing several patrol officers working the edges of the crowd, I approached one of the patrolmen. "Got a minute?" I said, flashing my credentials.

"Yes, sir," the young patrolman replied, nearly snapping to attention. From his spit-shined shoes, razor-creased uniform, and freshly shaven face, I concluded that he was probably still in his probationary "boot" year on the force.

"Relax," I said, noting that his nameplate read, "Olsen."

"Yes, sir."

"I'm not going to bite, Olsen," I continued. "At least not just yet. Where's your field training officer?"

"That's my TO over there talking with the Asian woman," said Olsen, pointing across the crowd. "Want me to get him?"

"No, I want to talk to you," I said, leading him away from a cluster of curious reporters. "How's the canvass going?"

"Fine, sir."

"Meaning you haven't turned up squat."

Olsen reddened. "Uh, that would be correct, sir."

"Nobody suspicious in this crowd of concerned citizens?" I asked, still wondering how the killer had known to phone me when I entered the garden.

"No, sir, nobody suspicious," said Olsen, smiling at my sarcasm. "Not that I've noticed, anyway. Everyone's just curious about what happened."

"What are you telling them?"

"Not a damn thing, sir."

"Keep it that way," I said, deciding that Olsen was doing a good job and a word to his sergeant was in order. "Carry on."

"Yes, sir."

I returned to the garden's entrance and ducked back under the tape, still puzzled by the timing of yesterday's call. As I saw it, there were two possibilities: One, an accomplice had been watching from the street or a nearby building. Or two, the killer's perfectly timed phone call had been a coincidence. I had trouble believing the latter, but it was something I still needed to consider.

Then another thought occurred. I pulled my iPhone from my pocket, hit the "settings" button, and selected "Wi-Fi." Seconds later my screen displayed several dozen Wi-Fi networks in the vicinity, all requiring passwords. I shook my head, deciding there were too many to investigate on my own.

Instead, I called Taylor.

She picked up on the third ring. "What's up, Kane? I thought we weren't going to compare notes until later."

"We weren't, but something's come up. I'm at the Botanical Garden. What are the chances of getting someone from your CART unit down here to meet me?" I asked, referring to the

Bureau's Computer Analysis Response Team. "It may be a little out of the norm for your Bureau techs, but it's important."

"If it's important, no problem. What do you need?"

"I need to locate a Wi-Fi router."

Twenty minutes later, Deluca and Greenly rejoined me at the garden's south gate. Greenly departed shortly afterward, promising to stay in touch. Taylor arrived shortly after that, accompanied by a man I recognized from the FBI's CART unit, having worked with him on another case. He was carrying several pieces of electronic equipment, including a radio antenna that looked like a fish backbone—with progressively shorter metal tubes fastened like ribs to a central connecting spine.

"Thanks for coming, Taylor," I said. Then, turning to the technician, "Arturo, good to see you again."

"You too, Detective," said Arturo.

"Paul, how's it going?" said Taylor, extending a hand to Deluca.

"Can't complain," said Deluca, taking her hand. "Banowski sends his best."

"Back at him. How's he doing? Still trying to lose weight?"

"Uh-huh. Now he's even hitting the gym. He's so proud of his rock-hard abs, he's protecting them with an extra layer of fat."

"Sounds about right," Taylor laughed.

"By the way, Kane told me about your kayak competition," Deluca went on. "Third place in a world-class event. Who knew you were a jock? Anyway, congratulations."

"Thanks," Taylor replied, looking pleased.

As Deluca and Taylor were talking, I noticed a purplish discoloration on Taylor's neck. "Go a couple rounds with someone?" I broke in, not having recalled seeing the bruise the previous evening.

"What?" said Taylor. Then, a hand going to her throat, "Oh, that. I, uh, tangled with a rock at the competition," she mumbled. "So tell me about this Wi-Fi router you want to locate."

"And what's with the TV antenna?" Deluca chimed in, glancing at Arturo's oddly shaped apparatus.

"It's a Yagi directional antenna," Arturo explained. "It's tuned to detect Wi-Fi frequencies, not television signals."

"Huh?" said Deluca, still looking puzzled.

"I've been wondering how the killer managed to phone me at exactly the right moment yesterday, just as we arrived at the dumpsite," I explained. "When his call turned out to be from Orange County, I thought maybe he had an accomplice who tipped him off. Then another possibility occurred."

Taylor jumped in. "You think our unsub may have set up a surveillance camera?" she asked, slipping into Bureau-speak.

I shrugged. "It's been done before. Here, check it out." I withdrew my phone and brought up the display showing Wi-Fi networks in the area. "I need to know how many of these have a view of the garden."

"No problem," said Arturo. "But first, maybe we can narrow things down a bit. Where were you *exactly* when you got your call?"

I glanced at the foliage behind me. "At the dumpsite."

"Then let's begin there."

After logging in with the patrolman keeping the crime-scene record, we proceeded single-file down the winding footpath into the garden, arriving minutes later at the bamboo thicket where the killer had hung Sandy Stafford's corpse.

"I was standing about here," I said, gazing up at the bamboo.

"This may have been a mistake," said Arturo, after running a cable from his antenna to a compact receiver he had brought with him. "There's no line-of-sight from the street to this part of the garden. Well, at least we can start by getting some basic directions."

After adjusting a knob on his receiver, Arturo swung his antenna across the garden, starting at the bamboo and turning in a full circle. "We'll need a reading from a second location to actually pinpoint each router," he said, walking a dozen yards down the path. Then, still checking his receiver, he began another rotation. "Hmmm . . . that's odd."

"What?" I asked.

"Every available Wi-Fi network is east of here, probably in buildings on Hilgard," Arturo answered, turning in the opposite direction. "Except for one. And it's close."

Just then my cellphone rang.

I checked the screen: "No Caller ID."

I raised a hand for silence, activating my recording app at the same time. All eyes turned toward me as I answered the call.

"Hello, Detective Kane," said a voice that sounded all too familiar. "I see you've brought friends."

I remained silent. If possible, I didn't want my voice on the recording, or any extraneous noises, either. Nevertheless, I motioned for Arturo to keep searching.

"Cat got your tongue, Detective?"

Walking quietly, I trailed behind Arturo. Antenna out front, he moved into a patch of ferns.

"Oh, I understand. You're recording this, aren't you? Of course you are."

I continued to remain silent, signaling for the others to stay where they were.

Pointing his antenna up the slope, Arturo crossed a small stream. I followed, climbing a bank covered with some kind of flowering shrub.

"Getting warmer, Detective."

Arturo froze upon arriving at a dirt path higher up. Glancing back at me, he pointed to a copse of conifers farther up the slope. About twelve feet above the ground, fastened to the trunk of a tall cedar, I could just make out the lens of a webcam. The device was cleverly hidden in branches, the lens poking from a small gray box.

"Ah—you've found me."

At that moment, I'm not certain what I felt. There was a rush of excitement, but along with it came a nagging suspicion that something was wrong. It all seemed too easy—as if we had been *meant* to find the killer's webcam.

"Congratulations, Detective Kane," said the digitally modified voice. "We have made contact, you and I. Nevertheless, if you think Edmund's paltry principle will assist in your niggling investigation, you're sadly mistaken."

With that, the line went dead.

Chapter 15
Starbucks

D r. Erich Krüger removed his AirPods, powered down his prepaid cellphone, and took a final sip of coffee, leaving the cup half full. Allowing himself a small smile of satisfaction, he stored his wireless earphones and returned them to his briefcase.

All in all, he decided, things were progressing well.

Reclining in the front seat of his Mercedes-Benz S-Class sedan, Dr. Krüger continued watching the sylvan scene on his laptop, tracking Kane and his gaggle of assistants through the Botanical Garden. Revisiting the UCLA site, if only in cyberspace, reminded Dr. Krüger of the exquisite experience he had enjoyed on Friday night.

And from there, his thoughts naturally turned to his latest acquisition.

Did he have time to visit?

Outside, traffic on Camino Del Mar was beginning to pick up. Dr. Krüger glanced at his watch. He had been in the seaside city of Encinitas checking on his next calendar girl, Miss August, when he had received a motion-activated alert from the UCLA webcam. Unfortunately, he was still thirty minutes from home. Complicating matters, he had a consultation appointment scheduled for noon that day at his Rancho Bernardo office, precluding any thought of paying a visit to his current guest—at least for the moment.

Regretfully, a session with Ella would have to wait.

Dr. Krüger shut down his webcam software, exited his voice-masking program, and closed his computer. After disconnecting the burner phone, he placed everything in his briefcase—with the exception of the cellphone, of course. That would have to go.

Leaning across the passenger seat, Dr. Krüger opened the glove box and withdrew a monogrammed silk handkerchief, using it to remove any stray fingerprints he might have left on the phone. Then, briefly stepping from his car, he placed the cheap cellphone on the asphalt and splintered it beneath his heel. Next, the shattered device went into his half-full Starbucks cup, the plastic top secured in place. Again using the handkerchief to remove any remaining fingerprints, he placed everything into a clean paper bag. Later, the bag and its contents would be deposited in a trash receptacle several blocks distant.

Attention to detail was a habit Dr. Krüger had embraced long ago. What might seem an insignificant detail could make the difference between freedom and incarceration, and Dr. Krüger intended never to be caught.

Dr. Krüger started his car and exited the Starbucks lot. As he pulled onto Camino Del Mar, he allowed himself another brief smile, deciding that things were progressing better than well.

Better than well, indeed.

Just as planned.

Chapter 16
Bombshelter Bistro

O ur CART team will want to take a look at that webcam,
Kane," said Taylor, digging into her Cobb salad. "Mmm,
this is delicious," she continued. "And we'll need a copy of that
phone recording, too."

Upon discovering the killer's webcam, I had called
criminalist Frank Tremmel from SID back to the site. Using a
ladder, Tremmel and an assistant had removed the surveillance
device, along with taking photos and plaster casts of several
indentations at the base of the tree—presumably left by the
killer's ladder. Afterward, for the first time feeling guardedly
optimistic about the investigation, we had elected to grab lunch at
the UCLA Bombshelter Bistro—a student hangout on a pleasant,
tree-lined terrace just north of the Botanical Garden.

"Don't worry, Taylor. As soon as SID is done, I'll make sure
your guys get a look at the webcam," I assured her, finishing the
last of my turkey sandwich. Rocking back in my chair, I glanced
around the food court. Behind us, a scattering of students had
gathered beneath a vine-covered pergola—some working on
laptops, others having a bite to eat between classes—none near
enough to overhear our conversation.

"And the phone recording?" Taylor persisted, reaching for
her iced tea. As she did, her jacket sleeve rode up, exposing
another bruise—this one on her wrist.

"Kayaking must be more of a contact sport than I thought," I
noted.

"Sometimes," Taylor replied, noticing my glance. "Don't try
to change the subject," she went on, pulling down her sleeve.
"What about your phone recording of the killer's voice?"

Deluca, who had ordered short ribs, julienne vegetables, and
potatoes, wiped his fingers on a paper napkin. "Speaking of that
recording, we need to discuss some 'fruit of the poisonous tree'
issues here, Taylor," he said, starting on another rib. "California
requires two-party consent for phone recordings."

While waiting for Tremmel to arrive, I had checked my trap-and-trace on killer's call, establishing that the transmission had originated from an untraceable phone in San Diego. By then, Arturo had departed to return to the CART unit in West L.A., and the three of us had listened to the recording in private. Several times, in fact—so we all knew what was involved.

"There is no expectation of privacy in the commission of a felony," Taylor pointed out. "Besides, the federal requirement for voice recordings is single-party consent. You consented, didn't you, Kane?"

"That's not the point," I replied. "I haven't had time to get a warrant for recording the killer's voice, and if this gets to court in California, I don't want to take even the slightest chance of the case getting kicked on a technicality. Don't forget, even though he's masking his voice, the guy hasn't actually admitted to the commission of any crime. The privacy issue may not apply."

"Then what are you suggesting?"

"I'm not suggesting anything. I'm simply saying that I'll be happy to send the Bureau a copy of the *voicemail* that the killer just left on my cellphone."

"Voicemail, huh?" said Taylor, clearly unhappy with my solution.

"Works for me," said Deluca.

Taylor shrugged. "If it comes out . . ."

"Then we're back to the poisonous tree issue, which we're trying to avoid," I said. "Are you good with this or not?"

Taylor hesitated. "You'll have to delete the part where the killer mentions your conversation being recorded."

"I don't remember his saying anything like that," I replied, deciding to take the recording to Hank Dexter for some judicious modification before anyone else heard it.

"Fine," said Taylor, her tone saying otherwise.

"The killer mentioned something about 'Edmund's paltry principle.' Who the hell is Edmund?" asked Deluca. "And more to the point, who uses words like paltry?"

"I'm not sure what's up with the killer's stilted vocabulary, but he was referring to Dr. Edmund Locard," I replied.

"Edmund Locard? Who's that?" asked Taylor.

"Locard was a pioneer in forensic science, best known for his famous 'exchange principle,'" I explained. "It may seem obvious now, but early in the 20th century it was an entirely new way of thinking about trace evidence and crime investigation," I continued, bringing a textbook description to mind. "Simply put, Locard's exchange principle states that when two objects come in contact with one another, especially during a violent action constituting a crime, each will take something from the other, as well as leaving something behind. Or put more simply, 'Every contact leaves a trace.'"

Taylor regarded me curiously. "How do you happen to know that?"

"Forensic Science 101," said Deluca, accustomed to my occasional displays of memory. "Kane never forgets anything."

"Not exactly true," I said. "I'm forgetting *something* here. I'm not exactly certain what, but . . ."

"Whatever it is, you'll think of it if it's important," advised Taylor. "In any case, this confirms something about the killer. He's versed in forensics."

"Unfortunately," I agreed, still unable to shake the feeling I was missing something.

"We learned another thing about our unsub today," Taylor went on.

"What?" asked Deluca.

"He's probably driving a van, or maybe a pickup truck."

"Huh? Oh, because of the ladder," said Deluca. "Good one, Taylor."

"Thanks. So where do we go from here?"

"For one, we can check the killer's other dumpsites and see whether he left surveillance equipment at any of those," I suggested. "As we're talking about multiple locations across several state lines, the Bureau should probably handle that."

"Done," said Taylor.

"We can also investigate recent purchases of surveillance gear, once we establish the type and make of the equipment he left here," I went on. "The webcam is probably motion-activated, with an online archival site recording the live feed," I reasoned, having used that type of surveillance setup myself. "We could investigate that aspect as well, maybe develop a webcam and archival-site database to compare with our other lists—canine training-collar purchases, or anyone who's recently bought a Taser, for instance."

"How about checking to see if this hump has made other calls?" Deluca jumped in. "To the families of previous victims, or to other investigators? Maybe he said something we can use."

"I don't recall any mention of other calls in our files," said Taylor. "But I'll check."

"It may not be possible, but now that we have a sample of the killer's modified voice, maybe we can reverse the altering process and determine what he actually sounds like," I suggested, deciding not to mention my visit to Hank. "We could also try to trace his voice-changing software to a particular program.

"Develop a list of software purchasers?" mused Taylor. "Could work."

"Maybe. Anyway, I'll deliver a copy of our guy's voicemail to the Bureau ASAP," I promised. "I'll get a copy to our SID guys as well—see who comes up with something useful first."

Deluca finished the last of his meal, wiped his sauce-covered fingers on his rumpled napkin, and turned to Taylor. "On another subject, I heard you defended Kane at Chief Ingram's meeting last night," he said, regarding Taylor with a look of admiration. "Took guts."

"Stupidity is more like it," said Taylor. "What's up with Assistant Chief Strickland, anyway? He acts like he has a corncob stuck up his . . . stuck up somewhere."

"Long story," I said. "I'll tell you sometime."

"Can't wait."

"Damn, a guy could get used to this place," Deluca interjected, leaning back in his chair and watching as a pair of long-legged coeds strolled past.

"Jeez, they're half your age, Deluca," said Taylor.

"So?"

"So you're a married man."

"A guy shouldn't have to give up on his dreams just 'cause he's married," Deluca countered.

Taylor stared in disbelief.

"He's jerking your chain, Taylor," I chuckled. "Deluca has been happily married for as long as I've known him."

"Actually, I haven't said a word to my wife in almost a month," Deluca revealed with a sad shrug. Then, checking his watch, "Damn, I have to go. Court appearance."

"I thought you and Molly were getting along," I said.

"We are," Deluca replied, rising from the table. "I just didn't want to interrupt her."

"Paul, you are such a pig," Taylor laughed.

"Thanks. Love you, too," Deluca said, grinning. "Later."

As Taylor and I watched Deluca depart, I felt the atmosphere between us shift, as it had the previous evening in the elevator. It wasn't a bad change, but it wasn't something I could put my finger on, either. I could tell that Taylor sensed it, too. She had visited the beach house a few times, but on each of those occasions there always had been others present. I wondered whether the unease between us was because the last time we were actually alone together, she had killed a man to save my life.

Taylor broke the silence. "Hear anything from Nate?" she asked, tipping back the last of her iced tea.

"I talked with him this morning. He's excited about his kayak clinic. Thanks again for setting that up."

Taylor lowered her gaze. "Nate's had a hard time, losing his mom and all. I'm happy to do anything I can to help."

Again, we both fell silent.

This time, I spoke first. "Can I ask you something?"

"Depends. What?"

"It's none of my business, but what's with the bruises?"

Taylor looked away. "I told you, I clipped a rock during the competition—"

"I know what you told me," I broke in. "Now I'm going to tell you something about me. I don't know how, but I can always tell when someone isn't telling the truth. Always. And right now, you're not."

"Well, you're right about one thing," Taylor shot back. "It's none of your business."

"Sorry," I apologized, surprised by her vehemence.

Again, Taylor looked away—this time seeming embarrassed. "Sorry if I overreacted."

"No problem. It's just, well, if there's anything I can do . . ."

"I'm a big girl, Kane. I can take care of myself."

"Okay," I sighed. "Message received."

Chapter 17
Ella

L et's talk a bit before we get started," said the man, settling himself in his armchair. "Do you still maintain you weren't sexually abused as a child, as you claimed earlier?"

Sitting on the edge of her bed, Ella felt a chill, recognizing the hunger in the man's eyes. She nodded, fingering the collar circling her neck. "I wasn't abused."

"Fine. Then let's discuss some of your early sexual experiences instead."

"You tell me something first" said Ella, attempting to sound submissive. "

"This isn't an exchange," the man warned, lifting his remote control. "I ask the questions. I thought you understood."

"No, wait! I understand. I . . . do. I just thought you could tell me what kind of pills you've been giving me. Where's the harm in that?"

"That's not the point," the man replied, still fingering his control. "Nevertheless, as you said, where's the harm? You like the drugs you've been taking, don't you?"

For the past several days, upon recovering from the man's pills, Ella had suffered bouts of nausea, followed by headaches, dizziness, and blurred vision. On the upside, she seemed to be developing a tolerance as well. "Yes," she lied, forcing herself to meet the man's gaze.

"I thought so," said the man, his handsome face creasing in a grin.

Ella felt another chill. Despite his smile, the man's eyes had remained as impenetrable as marbles.

"To answer your question, you've been enjoying a combination of party drugs," the man informed her. "I find their street names enlightening. 'Cat Valium,' or 'Special K,' or just plain 'K' describes one; the other goes by 'G,' or 'G-riffic,' or sometimes 'Grievous Bodily Harm,' which is probably closer to the truth."

Ella remained silent, clinging to her small victory. Having grown up in a police household, she was familiar with the substances the man had named. Their pharmaceutical descriptions were Ketamine and GHB. In addition to being popular at all-night "rave" parties, both were both considered date-rape drugs that, in addition to producing a state of euphoria, could cause disorientation and amnesia. Of the two, GHB was the most physically addictive, but dependence on either could develop following prolonged use.

And tolerance could develop as well.

On the second day of her captivity, while exploring the drawer of castoff clothing, Ella had found a belt. Afterward she had squirmed beneath her bed, hoping the man wasn't watching on his webcam. Using the belt-buckle prong, she had added her name below that of Alexa Kiel—presumably one of the man's previous victims—scratching it into the underside of the plywood. As had Alexa, she then began tallying her days, at least as nearly as she could figure. Counting the mark she had placed there that morning, seven gouges followed her name. How many more would there be before the man's pills lost their paralyzing effect?

More to the point, she thought, *by then will I still have the strength to escape?*

The man glanced at his watch. "Unfortunately, we'll have to save the exploration of your early sexual encounters for another time," he announced, rising from his chair. After crossing to the alcove cabinet, he returned to her cell door and thrust a cup of pills through the bars.

Early in her captivity, Ella had been puzzled by several things. For one, why was the man taking pictures of her? Upon reviving after her first "photo session" and finding herself clothed in a revealing nightgown, she had assumed the man was using his pictures for masturbatory purposes—maybe keeping them in some sort of sick souvenir scrapbook. Sensing a question about that would anger him, especially after his reaction when she had offered him sex, she had refrained from asking.

Nevertheless, that didn't explain why the man was so interested in discussing her sex life. What possible difference could humiliating her in that way make to him?

As Ella moved to the bars to accept the man's proffered cup of pills, she risked another look into his eyes. Unguarded, his mimicked human mask had slipped. And in that instant, Ella realized the reason for his interrogation.

He was toying with her, as a cat torments a mouse . . . just before killing it.

Chapter 18
Exchange Principle

The following Monday evening, as I sat on our swing gazing at the setting sun, I chewed over The Magpie case in my mind. Although we were only a week into it, things were already showing signs of stagnation, with investigators progressively being forced to revisit ground already covered. In addition to my own work on the case, I had spent considerable time researching the FBI's earlier efforts, hoping to find something in a previous murder that might prove helpful.

I had found nothing.

I had also scoured the Bureau's Violent Criminal Apprehension Program report, as well as studying a psychological profile compiled by their Behavioral Analysis Unit-2—which, like their VICAP unit, had recently become part of the National Center for the Analysis of Violent Crime. In true Bureau fashion, NCAVC was itself now part of the FBI's Critical Incident Respond Group, or CIRG. Bewildered by the Fed's alphabetic complexity, I decided that the more things changed with the Bureau's acronyms, the more they remained the same.

For again, I found nothing.

And as much as I tried to tell myself otherwise, I realized that unless something changed soon, we were going to have to wait for the killer to do it again . . . and hope he made a mistake.

On Wednesday, following our discovery of the webcam, I had paid another visit to Hank Dexter. Concerned with "fruit of the poisonous tree" issues, I had requested Hank's assistance. Without asking questions, my friend had removed the initial portion of the killer's message, leaving only his final, voice-masked declaration: "Congratulations, Detective Kane. We have made contact, you and I. Nevertheless, if you think Edmund's paltry principle will assist in your niggling investigation, you're sadly mistaken."

At my direction, Hank had also checked for the presence of any revealing background sounds, finding none.

Afterward I had forwarded the killer's supposed voicemail to Taylor at the Bureau, as well as sending it to Snead's investigative team via my daily report to Chief Ingram. I also left a copy of the modified recording with Hank. My hope was that with Hank and two topnotch agencies working the problem, someone would be able to identify the killer's voice-altering software. To date a number of programs had been ruled out, but we still hadn't discovered which digital masking tool he was using.

On a positive note, a search of earlier dumpsites had turned up two additional webcams—one near Seattle, another at a San Francisco site. Both surveillance devices had been cleverly concealed some distance from the bodies, and both proved identical to the webcam we found at the Botanical Garden.

As hoped, SID had quickly identified the surveillance systems' component parts. Mounted inside compact, weatherproof enclosures, the killer's cameras turned out to be battery-powered IP webcams with night vision capability. The killer had added an untraceable data sim card, a burner phone, a wireless Wi-Fi router, and a backup battery to complete each setup—everything available online for under $250 per network. It was decided that the batteries, burner phones, and sim cards were too common to trace, but a database of webcam and router purchasers might prove useful. Investigating those areas had fallen to the Bureau, whose online resources extended further than LAPD's. Currently, a comparison of our growing webcam/router database to our other lists had proved unproductive.

Along similar lines, IP addresses had been extracted from each of the killer's routers, but ascertaining a physical location for his archiving server had hit a brick wall, as had attempting to pierce his hidden-service protocol TOR network.

Bureau and LAPD investigators were still generating a catalogue of anyone who had recently purchased a dog-training collar or a Taser device. Snead's contacts in the gang unit were inquiring about Ketamine and GHB sales, particularly to the same client. Unfortunately, recreational drugs are widely available and easy to buy, and that line of investigation had petered out, too. FBI researchers were combing through victims' social media sites searching for correlating contacts, friend requests, and online interests. Along with our own cyber searches, I had heard from Taylor that the Bureau was even reaching out to an unnamed government agency, hoping for assistance in determining how the killer had acquired my cellphone number, as well as Snead's. It was possible that Messenger or some other phone app had been breached, but the hacker had yet to be found.

I was also in regular contact with Lieutenant Greenly, who was keeping me apprised of any pertinent UCLA surveillance footage that turned up. Like our other lines of investigation, efforts on the campus security-cam front had proved negative.

Last, working on the theory that the killer was stalking his victims, Deluca and I had worked through the weekend interviewing Ella Snead's friends, teachers, classmates, residents in her off-campus apartment building, and anyone else who might have been able to shed light on her disappearance. Although there were still a number of individuals left to contact, to date no one had noticed anything out of the ordinary.

Bottom line, shoe leather was hitting the ground, reports were being generated, databases were ballooning—and everyone was coming up empty.

Making matters worse, on Friday the killer had posted an online photo of Ella. The shot had been taken through what appeared to be the bars of a prison cell. The photo showed Ella asleep on a small, rumpled bed beside a concrete wall. Little else of the cell was included in the picture, but enough of Ella's face had been visible for the media to quickly identify her as the daughter of LAPD Captain William Snead.

As expected, that particular revelation inspired a renewed wave of media interest. Additional press conferences followed, each making the investigation more problematic. Along those same lines, I had been ducking calls from Allison all week, and I wasn't looking forward to her questions later that evening at dinner.

One positive development had come in at week's end. Working on the theory that the killer was driving a van, examination of Caltrans traffic-cam footage had turned up a white, 2004 Chevrolet Astro cargo van merging onto the 405 Freeway on Saturday morning, entering via a Sunset Boulevard on-ramp at 1:23 a.m. The van's license plates belonged on a 2015 Toyota Highlander, not the van. A Portland traffic cam showed a similar van leaving the vicinity of a second dumpsite—on that occasion displaying different stolen plates.

Chevy Astro vans were a common vehicle, with thousands on the streets of Southern California at any given time. Nevertheless, a "Be-On-The-Lookout" BOLO notice had been issued to all LAPD patrols, with an additional statewide advisory that anyone stopping a white Astro van use extreme caution.

Not much, but something.

"How's the barbeque coming, Dan?" Dorothy called down from the kitchen.

I slid off the swing and checked the grill. "Nearly done," I answered, flipping a line of breasts and applying a further slathering of sauce.

"Allison is almost finished feeding your granddaughter, so we can eat before long," Dorothy called back. "I'll put on the corn."

"Yell when it's ready," I replied, closing the barbeque lid and returning to the swing.

Travis and McKenzie were upstairs helping Dorothy with dinner preparations. I had invited my ex-partner, Arnie, to join us, but he'd had previous plans with his girlfriend, Stacy. Ali's husband, Mike, was on location again, so it would just be the five of us at the table. Six, if you counted Katie, although after nursing, Allison usually left her daughter asleep in the bedroom.

"Hey, Pop. What's new?" asked Allison, appearing at the bottom of the stairs.

"Not much," I answered glumly.

Allison joined me on the swing, giving it a push with her foot to set it in motion. "Huh. That's strange," she said. "Considering the way you've been avoiding my calls, I would have guessed you've been really busy on The Magpie case."

"Ali, I don't have anything to tell you about the investigation. On or off the record."

Over the past week Allison had been delivering a series of CBS news reports on the case. Unlike many of her media colleagues, she had refrained from leveling accusations at investigating agencies—no one is safe in his or her own home, police are ignoring rising crime in middle-class neighborhoods, and so on—and I was grateful for that. Nevertheless, I simply didn't have anything to give her.

"And that's because you haven't made any progress?" Allison persisted.

"You don't really expect me to answer that, do you?"

"Not really, Pop. Just making conversation. By the way, how long have you known it was Captain Snead's daughter who was abducted?"

"From the beginning."

"It's not a coincidence, is it? The kidnapping of Snead's daughter; your being the lead investigator on the case. The killer is playing some kind of game with you and Snead, isn't he?"

I nodded. "With Ella Snead caught in the middle."

"God, that's awful. I've always thought that people like Snead were the reason for middle fingers, but this has to be devastating for him and his family. I feel so sorry for them."

"Me, too," I agreed, my mood sinking.

After my first discussion with Snead at PAB, I had asked Allison to leave town until the case was closed, explaining that I had attracted the attention of a psychopath who might want to target our family, especially her. Predictably, she had refused, assuring me that she would take precautions. Nevertheless, now that she knew the full situation, I decided to try again. "Ali, maybe the time has come time for you and Katie to visit Mike on location. Just till this is over."

"We already talked about that. I'm not slinking out of town every time you're involved in a high-profile case."

"But—"

"I'm not leaving," Allison interrupted. "Let's move on. Are you going to find Ella before . . ."

"I don't know, Ali," I sighed, realizing I wasn't going to convince her. "I'm sure as hell going to try."

"I know you are, Dad. And I meant what I said before. If there's anything I can do to help, let me know."

"Thanks. While we're on the subject, please extend my thanks to Lauren for not running a countdown on the abduction."

It had been eleven days since Ella's disappearance. The longest any of the killer's victims had survived was twenty-seven days, and Ella's time was running out. In a ghoulish attempt to grab attention, many in the media, including several national news networks, were running a daily register of Ella's remaining days.

"Dinner's ready," Dorothy's voice sounded from above. "Come and get it, you two."

"You don't have to call me twice," said Allison, hopping from the swing. "Need me to carry anything up, Pop?"

"No, I've got it handled."

After forking the sizzling chicken onto a wooden platter, I headed upstairs, checked on a sleeping Katie, and joined everyone at the kitchen table. By then Dorothy had carried over the rest of our meal: corn on the cob, baked beans, sourdough bread, and a fresh green salad.

"I'm starving," said Travis, spearing a chicken breast and reaching for the corn.

"Grace first," said Dorothy.

"Uh, right," Travis mumbled.

We all joined hands as Grandma Dorothy said grace, as usual invoking a blessing for family, friends, and all our loved ones who were no longer present. As I listened with one ear, I gazed out our kitchen window, letting my mind drift. Absently, I noticed that a full moon had risen over Santa Monica, lighting the waves in a ghostly silver glow.

"Amen," said Dorothy, finishing a particularly long blessing that evening.

"Amen," we all echoed, reaching for the serving bowls.

"Damn, Dorothy," I observed as I forked a piece of chicken and ladled a mound of beans onto my plate. "Your dinner benedictions are getting longer and longer. We're liable to waste away one of these days waiting for your final 'amen.'"

"Oh, hush, Dan," she said. "A little religion won't hurt you."

"Yeah, Dad. Mom used to say that, too," noted Allison, dishing up a serving of salad and passing the bowl to McKenzie.

At the mention of Catheryn, an uncomfortable silence ensued. Finally Travis spoke. "Is Nate getting home tonight?"

"He is," I answered. "Agent Taylor is picking him up from LAX."

"That would be your *friend*, Agent Taylor?" said Allison, her expression tightening.

"What are you implying, Ali?" I asked, not missing her tone.

"Nothing. Just asking for clarification."

"Then you're right. Taylor is a friend. A good friend. Plus I owe her my life. That's all there is to it—not that it's any of your business."

"Actually, it *is* my business," Allison countered, not backing down. "Considering what Nate is going through, it's *all* our business."

"What do you mean by that?"

"Just what I said. I think your *friend*, Special Agent Taylor, is using Nate to get closer to you. It's obvious that Nate is trying to fill a void left by Mom's death, and—"

"That's not the way things are," I interrupted. "Taylor isn't going to do anything to hurt Nate. Subject closed."

"Yeah, well—"

"Subject closed, Ali."

"Fine," said Allison, her expression indicating that the subject was anything but closed.

Another uncomfortable silence followed, during which Dorothy pinned me with a look I couldn't quite decipher. Finally turning back to Allison, Dorothy asked, "How is Mike's new film progressing?"

"Okay, I guess," Allison replied with a shrug. "I just wish my wayward husband would stay home once in a while and help with Katie. Give you a break, Grandma."

"I adore spending time with my granddaughter," Dorothy replied. "I really do, but don't you think your job might be interfering—"

"We've been over this," Allison broke in.

"I know, but . . ."

"Mom had to choose between kids and a career, and she chose being a mom—at least until we were older. Bottom line, she wound up regretting that decision."

"That's not true. Catheryn loved being a mother," said Dorothy.

"I agree," I added.

"You would," Allison replied angrily.

"Jeez, sis. This isn't like you," said Travis. "What's up?"

"Sorry, Trav. I'm trying to have an adult conversation here," Allison shot back. "Can I ignore you later?"

Travis laughed. "I'm going to miss you, Ali," he said, shaking his head.

"Why? Going somewhere?"

"Actually, we are," McKenzie intervened. "I have to get back to New York and sell that book of yours, and Trav needs to rehearse for a performance he has booked in August. You knew that, Ali. We're leaving next week."

"Do you need a ride to the airport?" I asked.

"Thanks, Dad, but we have to return our rental car to LAX anyway," said Travis.

"Darn," said Allison, unable to hide her disappointment. "I didn't realize you guys were leaving so soon. Will you be back for my birthday? We could celebrate Nate's belated birthday then, too. Dadzilla said he'd throw us a beach party, just like old times."

"In August? Maybe," Travis answered, glancing at McKenzie.

"Please try to come back," said Allison. "I'm sorry if I seem a little, uh, irritable tonight. I'm, I don't know . . ."

Just then I heard the front door open. "I'm back!" Nate called into the house. "What's for dinner?"

"Unfortunately, dinner is pretty much history," I informed my son as he trooped into the kitchen, followed by Taylor.

"We *do* still have dessert," I went on, standing to give Nate a hug.

"Vanilla Häagen-Dazs with fresh peaches and peach preserves," Dorothy added temptingly.

"Works for me," said Nate, accepting hugs from Travis and Ali as well. "Everyone knows Agent Taylor here, right?" he continued, plucking a final piece of chicken from the platter.

"I don't," said McKenzie, rising to shake Taylor's hand. "McKenzie Wallace."

"Sara Taylor. A pleasure to meet you, McKenzie," said Taylor. Then, to Allison, "Good to see you again, Allison."

Allison nodded without extending her hand. "You, too, Sara."

"Would you like to stay for dessert?" asked Dorothy. "We have plenty."

Taylor glanced at her watch. "Thanks, but I really should get back—"

"Please stay," Nate implored. "Grandma says there's plenty."

"Yeah, Taylor," I added. "Stick around. A couple extra calories won't kill you."

Taylor glanced at Allison, then back at Dorothy. "Thanks, but I don't want to impose."

"You're not," Dorothy reassured her. "We'd love for you to join us."

Taylor hesitated, and for a brief moment I sensed a subtle female undercurrent flowing in the room, an invisible web of feminine interaction that, as a man, I had long ago given up attempting to plumb.

"Please," Nate begged. "You can tell everybody what I learned on the river."

"Okay," Taylor finally agreed. "Thanks, Dorothy. I'll stay for a few minutes."

"Great," said Nate, pulling over a chair for Taylor and taking a seat beside her.

As McKenzie began helping Dorothy dish up dessert, Allison turned to Nate. "So what did you learn up there? Besides not drowning, of course."

"Well, for one thing, I learned you're only half as smart when you're upside down in a kayak," Nate laughed.

"My friend, Chad Long, says your brother's a natural," added Taylor. "Nate's comfortable in the water, maybe from surfing, which is really important. Plus he has great butt-balance."

"Great butt-balance, huh?" said Allison. "I'm so proud of you, Nate."

"I can't wait to go again," said Nate, ignoring Allison's gibe. "Will you take me sometime, Agent Taylor?"

"Sure," said Taylor. "There's great kayaking up on the Kern River, not too far from here. The water should still be running through August this year, and there are a couple sections you could handle for sure."

By then Dorothy and McKenzie had placed dessert bowls in front of everyone, and the table momentarily fell silent as everyone dug in.

Nate finished first. "Hey, anyone know why you can't trust atoms?" he asked, pushing away his bowl.

"Why, Nate?" asked Dorothy.

Nate grinned. "Because they make up everything."

"Good one," laughed Travis.

"Yeah, Nate. It's gratifying to see that your jokes have finally progressed to eighth-grade level," Allison added with a smile.

"I disagree, sis," Nate chuckled. "That one had science in it, which at least qualifies as high-school humor." Then, yawning, he announced that he was going to bed. "Big day. 'Night, everyone," he said, giving Taylor a hug.

After Nate had departed, Allison turned to Taylor. "You certainly seem to have made a big impression on my younger brother," she noted coldly.

"I hope it's a good one," Taylor replied. "Nate's a great kid."

"Yes. He is."

"Is there something you want to say to me, Allison?"

"Not just now, Sara."

"Please don't mind my daughter," I stepped in, giving Allison a look of warning. "She's having trouble with her manners tonight."

"Yeah, don't mind me," echoed Allison, her tone less than apologetic.

Taylor shrugged and rose from the table. "I have to be going anyway. Thanks for dessert, Dorothy. It was delicious."

I rose as well, shooting Allison another look of irritation. "Let's head downstairs for a sec, Taylor. There's something I want to discuss."

Taylor nodded. "Okay. But I do have to get going."

"It will just take a minute."

Followed by Callie, who never missed an opportunity to join a family member on the beach, I led Taylor to the deck outside. Overhead, the moon hung majestic in the sky, and we stood there for a moment gazing out at the shimmering ocean. "I can't get over how beautiful it is here," said Taylor. "And so close to the city."

"Catheryn loved it here, too," I agreed. Upstairs, I could still hear Trav and Allison talking at the table.

"Let's take a walk," I suggested. Without awaiting Taylor's response, I pulled off my shoes and socks and started toward the water. After a moment's hesitation, Taylor kicked off her sandals and followed me out onto the sand.

Led by Callie, Taylor and I picked our way through a littering of kelp and driftwood to the ocean. Then, keeping to the firm sand at the water's edge, we started toward the lights of Santa Monica.

"What did you want to talk about?" asked Taylor.

"The investigation," I replied, absently sweeping my gaze over an unbroken line of homes paralleling the beach. A number of them still had lights burning inside, providing an intimate glimpse through unshuttered windows of other families, other secrets, other lives. I wondered whether any of them were as complex and confusing as mine. Somehow, I suspected that they were.

"What about the investigation?" Taylor prodded.

"I didn't want to talk in front of Allison, but things have nearly ground to a halt on my end," I said.

"Ours, too. What are we going to do? Wait for him to do it again?"

"I don't know, Taylor. I still feel like I'm missing something. I just don't know what."

"Like I said, if it's important, it will come to you."

Upon reaching a string of condos marking the eastern terminus of Las Flores Beach, we turned back, retracing our footprints in the sand. By then Callie had found a chunk of driftwood and in true retriever fashion, kept insisting I throw it for her.

"Is the investigation really what you wanted to discuss?" asked Taylor.

"Not really," I admitted. "Actually, I wanted to apologize for Allison's behavior."

"Not necessary, Kane."

"Yeah, it is. Despite her spikey personality, Ali has a good heart. Unfortunately, she's always been a little overprotective of her younger brother."

"She thinks I pose a threat to Nate? How? By taking him kayaking?"

"She thinks you're using Nate to get closer to me."

"What? Jesus, Kane, you just lost your wife. Does Allison really think I would—"

"She's not thinking, Taylor. At least not clearly. She thinks Nate is trying to fill a void left by Catheryn's death, and she's worried you'll harm him even more."

"You don't think that, do you?"

"No."

"Because I would never do anything to hurt your son. Ever."

"I know that. But Ali is . . . look, there's something I haven't told you."

"What?"

I took a deep breath and continued. "After Catheryn's death, Nate became seriously depressed. Not, 'I'm sad' depressed. *Clinically* depressed. Do you understand what I'm saying?"

Taylor nodded.

"Nate hid his illness from everyone," I went on. "At least most of the time—and none of us did anything about it. Then one night last winter, he stole my pistol and tried to take his own life. I barely got there in time to stop him."

"Oh, my God. I . . . I didn't know."

"We're getting him the best possible care. He's taking meds and seeing a counselor, and he's going to be fine. I'm sure of it. But . . . Allison can't help being big-sister protective of him."

"I understand," Taylor said quietly.

By then we had nearly returned to the house. Taylor turned toward me. "Thanks for telling me about Nate. Now I want to apologize for something. I'm sorry for being such a bitch the other day when you asked about my bruises."

"I was out of line. You don't have to apologize—"

"I want to," Taylor interrupted. "You were right in thinking that something was wrong. I was just too ashamed to admit it."

"Who hurt you?"

Taylor looked away. "My ex-husband visited the other night."

"Mark."

Taylor regarded me curiously. "How do you know his name?"

"You told me," I replied, referring to a meeting I'd had with Taylor during an earlier case several months back. "At the Scotch 'n' Sirloin."

"I don't remember," said Taylor. "I do recall having a bit too much to drink that night," she added, seeming embarrassed. "What did I say?"

I thought back, bringing our conversation to mind. "You said you grew up in Salmon, Idaho, and got married at eighteen, right out of high school. You worked as a secretary to put your husband Mark through college and law school. Later you returned to college yourself, then attended Chapman Law. Upon graduating, you joined Mark at a law firm in Burbank. When your marriage imploded, you took some time off, did some thinking, and decided you needed a change. You applied to the FBI and were accepted."

Taylor shook her head. "You're a strange guy, Kane."

"So I've been told."

Taylor hesitated, then pushed on. "I should have known that Mark and I would never work as a couple. I'm a Sagittarius, and he's an asshole."

"I hear you," I chuckled.

"What I didn't say at the Scotch 'n' Sirloin was the reason our marriage imploded."

"He's a batterer."

Taylor nodded. "At first it was just an occasional slap. But as time went on, things got worse. Afterward he would always say he was sorry, promising it would never happen again. Several times he even cried and brought me flowers, and everything would get back to normal. Then the cycle would start all over, getting worse each time."

"And you accepted his apologies."

"I loved him, and he wasn't always violent. And when he was, I thought it was my fault. I was sick, Kane. Pitiful, huh?"

During my patrol days, I had seen my share of domestic violence. Although I knew a few LAPD field officers who still considered family disputes to be low-priority calls, I had learned to take them seriously, as a significant number eventually resulted in homicide. Of the thousands of women murdered nationwide each year, almost a third die at the hands of husbands and boyfriends. I also knew that there were various reasons—emotional, economic, religious, even hostage-like syndromes—that caused women to remain in abusive relationships.

"Were you afraid to leave?" I asked.

Taylor nodded. "I felt trapped. Trapped and scared. I thought that if I tried to get out, his violence would escalate. I . . . I felt worse than trapped. I felt helpless. He told me if I left him, he would hurt me in every way possible. I was afraid he might kill me."

"You didn't report any of this?"

"No. Everyone adored Mark. People thought he was the perfect, loving husband. I didn't think anyone would believe me—not even the police."

"I'm sorry, Taylor. What finally happened?"

"During my last visit to an emergency room, an attending physician didn't buy my story. He called the police. Although I stuck to my fabricated version of what had happened, Mark flew into a rage when we got home."

"What did you do?"

"I left. I didn't take anything. I just got in my car and drove. I wound up staying with my sister, Jeannie, in Detroit. I got some counseling while I was there, which opened my eyes to what was going on. Afterward I got a three-year domestic violence restraining order against Mark. Once the DVRO was in place, I filed for divorce."

"Good. "

"And aside from several court appearances during our divorce, I never saw Mark again," Taylor finished. "Until Sunday night."

"After our meeting with Ingram?"

Taylor nodded. "When I got home, he was waiting on my doorstep. He said his law firm had opened a second office in Santa Monica, and that we would be seeing a lot more of each other."

"What about the restraining order?"

"Expired. I never renewed it. After all those years, I thought everything was over."

"What happened next?"

"He'd been drinking. He insisted on coming inside."

"And you let him?"

"I was terrified, Kane. I know it doesn't make sense, but all the old fears came flooding back. PTSD, maybe. Whatever the case, I was in the nightmare again, powerless, worse than ever. He told me he had repurchased his gun collection from his brother—weapons that had been taken from him per my original restraining order. When I told him to get out, he grabbed me, knocked me down, punched a hole in my wall. And I didn't do anything. I'm so ashamed of myself . . ."

"You didn't do anything wrong, Taylor."

"I didn't do anything right, either. Instead of standing up to him, I ran outside when I had the chance. He was gone when I returned, but I know he's coming back.

"I swear, I'm going to make your ex-husband wish he had never—"

"No," Taylor interrupted. "This is something I have to handle myself. And I will."

"But—"

"I *need* to handle this, Kane. On my own. Do you understand?"

"Not really. But okay, if that's what you want. Just know that if there's anything I can do, I'm here."

"I know," said Taylor. "I'm sorry I'm such a mess," she went on, her voice breaking. "I'm so disappointed in myself. And I'm embarrassed to be so weak. The sad thing is, part of me believed I didn't deserve any better."

"From where I stand, I don't see anything you need to be embarrassed about," I said gently. "You deserve the best, Sara. As for being weak, that's bull. You're a strong, capable woman—one that any guy would be lucky to have."

Taylor smiled sadly. "Glad you think so."

During our conversation, Callie had continued to prod me with her piece of driftwood, attempting to get me to play. Finally taking pity on her, I grabbed the stick and tossed it up toward the beach house, keeping her clear of the water. As she bounded off, I noticed Allison standing outside on our deck.

Taylor saw her, too. "Give me a minute with your daughter, okay?" she said.

"Sure."

"And thanks for listening to my sorry tale," Taylor added as Callie returned, tail wagging, stick in her mouth. "I'll see you tomorrow."

I threw the stick again for Callie, watching as Taylor stepped over the seawall and joined Allison on the deck. Their figures were silhouetted in light from the house, and although I couldn't hear their conversation, I could tell from their body language that their exchange didn't begin well.

Ignoring Callie's prodding, I watched the two women. Before long Allison stiffened and headed for the stairs. Then she turned and said something. I had seen my daughter act that way before, and I knew that whatever her reply, it was spiteful. Taylor shook her head and continued talking.

Allison crossed her arms and looked away, but she kept listening.

And Taylor kept talking.

Minutes passed.

And then something changed.

Little by little, Allison unfolded her arms. Taylor stepped closer and placed a hand on Allison's forearm. Allison shook it off. After a moment Taylor raised her hands to Allison's shoulders, forcing my daughter to meet her gaze.

Long seconds went by.

And then to my astonishment, my prickly, sarcastic, irritable, petulant, immensely talented, deeply sensitive daughter lowered her head and moved into Taylor's arms, accepting her embrace.

Allison and Taylor remained joined for several seconds, their figures backlit against the house. Then, releasing Allison, Taylor turned for the stairs and departed, not looking back.

As Taylor disappeared into the house, I stood indecisively, wondering what had just happened. After a final stick-toss for Callie, I joined Allison on the deck. At my approach, I saw her wipe her eyes with the back of her hand.

"Everything okay?" I asked.

"Everything's fine," she mumbled.

"What did you and Taylor just talk about?"

"Nothing. Just . . . girl stuff."

"If you say so."

"I say so."

"Well, in that case, I'm going inside. Cold out here."

"I'll join you. And Dad?"

"What?"

"I love you. You know that, right?"

"I do, Ali," I replied, now more confused that ever. "I love you, too."

Later that evening, I was unable to sleep. As I lay in bed staring at the ceiling, I reviewed the events of the day, revisiting them in my mind. I was still puzzled by what had passed between Allison and Taylor, but whatever it was, I took it to be a positive turn of events. I was also happy that Nate seemed to be climbing out of the pit of depression that had nearly ended his life—even if it meant risking his neck in a kayak.

As for Taylor's domestic abuse, I hadn't yet decided what to do. Taylor wanted to handle the problem herself, and I understood that—at least from an empowerment point of view. Nevertheless, I wasn't certain I could just stand by and do nothing.

Which brought me back to the investigation.

I had been minimizing things when I'd told Taylor that the case was grinding to a halt. The truth was, the investigation had *already* ground to a halt. We had nothing to go on. We needed something new, and waiting for the killer to do it again was an option I was unwilling to accept. Making matters worse, I still couldn't shake the feeling I was missing something.

Taylor had claimed that if it were important, it would come to me. Although I had discounted her advice at the time, I didn't have a better idea.

Maybe it was time to try a different approach.

As I lay in bed, I let my mind drift, working the edges of the case. It was an investigative technique I had used before, a method akin to not looking directly at something in the dark.

On a hunch, I reviewed my last phone conversation with the killer. "Congratulations, Detective Kane," he had said. "We have made contact, you and I. Nevertheless, if you think Edmund's paltry principle will assist in your niggling investigation, you're sadly mistaken." I had been puzzled by the killer's use of the words "paltry" and "niggling." As Deluca had pointed out, who talks like that?

And suddenly I had it.

I had seen those words before. I had read them in a book.

A textbook.

And not just any textbook.

Although I easily brought up the passage in my mind's eye, I rose from bed and went to my bookcase to make certain. On a middle shelf, my fingers found the textbook in question: *Forensic Science: Cases and Materials on Criminal Investigation*, by Dr. Erich Krüger. I scanned the pages, locating the section I wanted on page sixty-seven.

A chill shivered up my spine as I read the words: "Initially dismissed by 20th century critics as a niggling, paltry addition to the field of forensics, Edmund Locard's exchange principle has since proved an indispensible tool in scientific crime analysis."

Niggling. Paltry.

All along, I had felt we needed something new to pry open the case.

Well, I had just found something new.

But what did it mean?

Chapter 19
Something New

I met Deluca at the West L.A. station the next morning. At my request, Taylor skipped her FBI briefing and joined us in the squad room as well.

"Damn, Kane," said Taylor upon arriving. "You look like hell."

"Been up all night," I sighed, rubbing a hand across my face.

"You're not all that great looking even on a *good* day," Deluca observed with a grin. "And this isn't one of them."

Taylor dragged over a chair, joining Deluca at my desk. "You find something?"

"Yeah, *paisano*. What's up?" asked Deluca.

I reached for my copy of *Forensic Science: Cases and Materials on Criminal Investigation*, which I had brought with me from the house. "Remember the killer's message, the one he left on my phone?"

Deluca nodded. "Who can forget?"

"At the time, I got the impression there was something familiar about his choice of words," I said. "I finally figured out what." I opened the textbook. Taylor and Deluca moved closer, reading the passage I had marked on page sixty-seven.

"Huh. 'Niggling' and 'paltry,'" said Taylor, regarding me with amazement. "You *recalled* seeing those words together somewhere and tracked down the source?"

I nodded.

"So what does it mean?" asked Deluca, still staring at the book.

"A couple possibilities come to mind," I replied. "Either the killer has read this textbook and inadvertently parroted those words, or—"

"—he did it on purpose, 'cause he's screwing with us," Deluca finished.

"I think it's more likely that he made an unconscious slip, but either way, at some point our man came in contact with this book," I reasoned.

Taylor leaned forward, something in her intensity reminding me of a hunting dog on scent. After her near breakdown the preceding evening, I was pleased to see the change. "How can we use this?" she asked.

"It's a long shot, but we could assemble a list of anyone who has bought Krüger's text and compare it to our other databases— dog-collar and surveillance-webcam purchasers, say," I suggested. "Or maybe the voice-altering database, if we ever figure out what software he's using."

"CART is making progress on that," said Taylor. "There aren't *that* many masking programs. Our techs say they'll crack it."

"Let me know when they do." Reminding myself to place a call to Hank and see how he was doing, I rocked back in my chair and rolled my neck, working out some kinks. "Anyway, I googled the author, Dr. Erich Krüger," I continued. "Krüger taught forensics at the School of Criminal Justice and Criminalistics at California State University, Los Angeles. After that he was involved in developing a graduate criminalistics course at UC Irvine. Later he retired from academia to join the private sector, but while teaching at both universities he made routine use of his own textbook. A list of students who were enrolled in his courses could be our first step."

"Without a warrant, that's going to be tough," Deluca pointed out. "I've run into this before. Per the federal Family Educational Rights and Privacy Act, schools don't just hand out student names."

I thought a moment. "So let's take a run at it from another direction. Lots of teachers keep class records. Maybe this Dr. Krüger did, too."

"What else did you find out about Krüger?" asked Taylor.

"You're thinking maybe we should take a look at him, too?" said Deluca.

"Maybe. He wrote the book. What do you think, Kane?"

Steve Gannon

"I ran Dr. Krüger's name through the system. He came back clean—no arrests, warrants, or convictions—but at this point I'm not ruling out anyone," I answered. "We need to talk with Krüger about getting a list of students. We can get a feel for him when we visit."

"I'll see whether the Bureau can turn up anything on him," Taylor offered.

"Good idea."

"Is Krüger a medical doctor?" asked Deluca.

"Dr. Krüger has a Ph.D.," I replied. "He graduated with a law degree from Stanford, then earned a doctorate in Criminology, Law and Society at UC Irvine. After writing his forensics text and teaching at Cal State, he returned to UCI, becoming one of the youngest full professors in the history of the university."

"And now he's consulting?"

I nodded. "Has an office near San Diego. He provides expert-witness testimony for anyone who can afford his services."

"Okay, so along with checking out Dr. Krüger as a possible suspect, we're looking for a forensic student who's used Krüger's book, maybe while being enrolled at UC Irvine or Cal State," said Deluca. "We might also widen the net to include anyone who's purchased Krüger's textbook, either at a bookstore or online. Lotta ground to cover. How do you want to handle it?"

I thought a moment. "Paul, you and I will hit UCI and Cal State to see what we can shake loose. Taylor, your Bureau creds give statewide authority, so you and I will visit Dr. Krüger in San Diego. Call his office and set up an appointment. And don't say what it's about. In fact, give the impression we want to hire his services."

"I'm on it," said Taylor. "What about textbook sales?"

"The Bureau should probably take the internet transactions on that, as they have a longer online reach. LAPD can check college bookstores and local retailers."

"If I remember correctly, Cal State's criminalistics school is located in the Hertzberg-Davis Forensic Science Center," Deluca interjected, referring to an East L.A. regional crime lab that provided investigative services to LAPD and the Los Angeles

144

Sheriff's Department. "As the nation's largest municipal crime lab, it employs over 400 forensic specialists."

"You remember correctly," I groaned, my sense of optimism beginning to plummet as I realized where Deluca was going. "You think we should take a look at them, too."

"We have to. We know our guy is versed in forensics and police procedures, and they all have access to Krüger's book."

"I'll suggest it to Ingram, but he won't like investigating our own. And neither will Snead. You realize the can of worms we would be opening—especially if the media got wind of it."

"I hate to say it," Taylor noted glumly, "but we should probably have the Bureau contact local authorities in Portland and Seattle and do the same."

With that we all fell silent, realizing the difficult task before us. What had begun as an apparent break in the case had abruptly morphed into a complex, potentially impossible undertaking.

"Okay," I said, rising from my desk. "Maybe we'll get lucky. Let's get to it."

Chapter 20
Dr. Berns

Deluca and I worked through the remainder of Tuesday and all of Wednesday morning visiting Cal State and UCI, as well as several other Los Angeles colleges using Krüger's textbook. As Deluca had predicted, all refused to provide the names of any students, past or present, without student permission.

On another front, Taylor's call to Dr. Krüger's office had been transferred to an answering service, which informed her that Dr. Krüger was out of town testifying on a case and would be unavailable until early the following week. Also frustrating, Snead had summarily vetoed our request that HSS detectives take a look at Hertzberg-Davis employees, saying he simply didn't have the resources—especially considering the number of credible tip-line leads that had yet to be investigated. Not surprisingly, Ingram had backed him up. Snead did agree to have his team run a perfunctory check for any suspicious activity in the lab ranks, which I suppose was something.

Wednesday afternoon, frustrated by our lack of progress, I took some time off to drive Nate to his counseling appointment in Orange County. Nate was being treated by a psychiatrist friend of mine, Dr. Sidney Berns, who was employed in the Department of Psychiatry and Human Behavior at the University of California, Irvine School of Medicine. Along with his private practice, Dr. Berns regularly served as an expert witness for the Orange County District Attorney's office. Like many police officers, I held deep-rooted misgivings regarding the psychiatric profession, but I had worked with Berns on several criminal cases and had come to respect his opinion. I trusted him as well.

More important, Nate trusted him, too.

Following an exasperating ninety minutes navigating freeway traffic to Orange County, we arrived at Bern's office at the UCI Neuropsychiatric Center. Leaving my Suburban in a lot across from the white, three-story building, I waited in an outpatient reception room during Nate's session with Dr. Berns.

Fifty minutes later Nate returned to the waiting room, accompanied by Dr. Berns. Berns, a tall, slim man with arresting, pale-blue eyes and a gray-streaked ponytail, smiled when he saw me.

"How's it going, Sid?" I said, rising to shake his hand. "Everything still good with Nate?"

"Nate is doing fine," said Berns. "Actually, we plan to start tapering his meds before long, which will be a big step forward."

"Glad to hear it," I said. I had been deeply shaken by my son's depression and the danger it entailed. Even though Nate seemed back to his old self, Dr. Berns's reassurance came as a relief. "Thank you again for all your help," I added. "I'm grateful beyond words. You know that."

"You're welcome," said Berns. Then, "Take care of yourself, Nate. You, too, Dan. I'll see you both next week."

"We'll be here," said Nate.

"Sid, I know you're busy, but do you have a moment?" I asked.

"For you, of course," said Berns, glancing at his watch. "I have to be in court by three, but I'm free till then. Let's talk in my office."

Leaving Nate watching TV in the reception room, I followed Berns through a residents' lounge to a spartan, eight-by-twelve workspace with a single window looking out on a cement patio. Waving me to a chair, Berns slid behind a desk littered with files, paperwork, and a framed photo of his wife. Conspicuous by its absence was his normally overflowing ashtray.

"Finally kicked the habit?" I observed. "Good for you, Sid."

"Took a while," Berns said sheepishly. He pulled up a sleeve, exposing a nicotine patch on his upper arm. "I'm still on the patch, but I'm over the worst of it."

"I'm sure your wife is delighted."

"That's an understatement," Berns agreed, rolling down his sleeve. "What did you want to talk about? I meant it when I said Nate is doing great."

"I know you did, Sid, and again, I'm truly grateful for your help."

"What, then?"

I hesitated, trying to decide where to start. "I need to ask about an investigation," I began.

"Anything I can do to help, you know that."

"You've heard about The Magpie murders?"

Berns nodded. "And his most recent abduction? I feel terrible for Captain Snead and his family. I haven't seen your name in the papers, but I take it you're working the case."

"I'm one of many. There's a massive effort underway to bring this guy down."

"And you're not having any luck."

"No, we're not," I admitted.

"I'm not surprised."

"Why do you say that?"

"A number of reasons. For one, you are clearly dealing with a dangerous psychopath."

"Aren't they all? Dangerous, I mean."

"Not always," Berns replied. "At least not from a criminal aspect. It's estimated that around one percent of our population exhibits a broad constellation of psychopathic traits, but most individuals in that category never resort to violence."

"One percent, huh? Well, this guy is certainly in the violent section of that one percent."

"Granted. As such, you are dealing with someone who feels no guilt, empathy, or remorse, making his motivations difficult to anticipate, let alone comprehend. One thing is certain: Hard as it is to imagine, he *likes* what he's doing. By the way, in my opinion your killer was born that way, although some in my profession think environmental factors might also play a part in the development of his antisocial personality disorder."

"Really? Antisocial personality disorder? Seems a bit of an understatement."

"That's the most recent DSM-5 definition," Berns explained, referring to the Diagnostic and Statistical Manual of Mental Disorders. "And I agree. Monster would be a better description."

"No argument there."

"Anyway, your killer is intelligent, organized, and murdering strangers for no other reason than exerting control over them and achieving sexual gratification, which compounds the difficulty of finding him. When it comes to his ultimate motivation, however, make no mistake. This isn't really about sex for him. It's about control. Your monster sees everyone around him, particularly young women, as pawns to be used in any way he wants."

Berns paused for a moment, then continued. "From what I've seen to date in the news, your man has a highly developed ritual and is well into his killing cycle. I would expect he is carefully planning his activities to ensure he won't be caught. As I said, finding him will be difficult, maybe even impossible. I hate to be negative, but if you do catch him, luck will probably play a part."

I scowled, unwilling to accept Berns's pessimistic assessment. "Luck, huh? Well, I hope you're wrong. Look, I've read the Bureau's profile on the killer. According to the FBI analysis, he's a white male, mid-twenties to early forties, high intelligence, incidents of animal torture, playing with fire, childhood abuse, and so on. As you pointed out, he's motivated by control and sexual gratification. I understand all that, but I'm just not getting a feel for the guy. Is there anything else you can tell me?"

"Hmm. I can't be too certain without seeing the case reports, but a couple of things do come to mind. For one, he's undoubtedly an accomplished liar. He mimics human emotions he doesn't feel, as if he's wearing a mask—displaying a human face that hides the monster within. Outwardly he can seem charismatic and charming, but inside he feels none of the emotions he's imitating." Berns rubbed his chin. "For another, this isn't the first time he's done this."

"Yeah, he started in January—"

"No, that's not what I mean. From the complexity of his current murders, I think his first human killings started long ago. He probably hid his earlier crimes, but now the situation has changed. Now he wants recognition. These latest murders are a new game for him—a killing cycle in which he's challenging authorities to stop him and reveling in publicity at the same time."

"You think he wants to be stopped?"

"Just the opposite. He wants to prove his superiority over everyone, *especially* the police." Berns regarded me closely. "In addition to demonstrating a desire for notoriety, his taking Captain Snead's daughter suggests that he wants to challenge authorities directly. He's making it personal."

I nodded, again thinking of the danger to Allison and the rest of my family. "After the news coverage on the Infidel case, it's no secret that Snead and I are enemies. By abducting Snead's daughter in Westwood, the killer made certain I would catch the case."

"He's amusing himself by forcing you and Captain Snead to work together."

"Which could also be putting my family in the crosshairs again."

"I'm afraid you may be right."

We both fell silent.

Finally I continued. "Anything else?"

Berns nodded. "The strangulation aspect."

"What about it?"

"From what I've also read in the papers, your killer is strangling his victims. Strangulation, especially manual strangulation, is a signature behavior with which your man exerts power and control over young women."

I was familiar with the subject, over the course of my career having investigated a number of strangulation murders. Manual strangulation was the most common method employed during intimate-partner violence, although occasionally ligatures like scarves and belts were used as well.

"A signature behavior like that usually persists," Berns continued. "It's part of his ritual."

"He gets off on it."

"Right. Strangulation is a form of torture that has been likened to drowning, so your man is obviously a sadist, possibly a necrosadist. As such, he may need to see his victims die—or at least know they are *going* to die—to achieve sexual gratification."

"And this signature behavior of his, the strangulation of his victims, is something he may have been doing all along? Even during his earlier murders?"

"I'd bet on it."

Another avenue had just opened up. "Thanks, Sid. I appreciate your help," I said, rising to leave.

"A couple of other observations before you go," said Berns. "Even though your killer is posting monthly pictures of his victims, I don't think he's on a true lunar cycle."

"He's simply creating some kind of perverted calendar."

"Correct. He's not delusional, as might be suggested by a lunar cycle. He knows *exactly* what he's doing. He may also be saving souvenirs—clothes, rings, photos—items to help him savor his kills and recapture the pleasure of his acts. That may prove useful, if you ever find him. And watch for anyone who seems just a little *too* helpful on the tip lines."

"We're doing that," I said. "Thanks again, Sid."

"Anytime."

As I turned to leave, another thought occurred. "On a different subject, are you familiar with UCI's Department of Criminology, Law and Society?"

"It's not part of the School of Medicine, but we sometimes interface with them, particularly concerning forensic matters. Why do you ask?"

"I need to talk with someone who used to work there, a Dr. Erich Krüger. Ever hear of him?"

"Of course. His textbook on forensics and criminal investigation is standard reading for anyone in the field."

"Ever meet him?"

"No, but from what I've heard, he was a departmental star for years. Brilliant mind, youngest full professor, prolific writer, and so on. It was a shock to everyone in his department when he left."

"Any dirt on the guy?"

Berns regarded me quizzically. "Not really. I heard he came from a wealthy family. I also heard that like many intellectual giants, he has a huge, narcissistic ego, and he wasn't well liked by his students. Otherwise, I don't have any personal knowledge of the man."

"Okay, Sid. I appreciate your input. See you next week."

"Right. And Dan? I hope you catch this guy. As I said, he likes what he's doing, and he's going to keep doing it until he's stopped."

On the return drive to West L.A., Nate, able to nap in the most trying of circumstances, quickly fell asleep. Unlike our drive to Berns's office during which we had talked almost nonstop, I found myself on my own. Navigating on autopilot, I let my mind drift, mulling over my conversation with Berns. One thing he'd said had caught my attention: The killer had done this before.

And he had probably strangled his earlier victims as well.

I wasn't certain where that would lead, but I intended to find out.

And I knew right where to start.

Jeroen Aken, a detective friend of mine, worked in LAPD's Cold Case Homicide Special Section—one of the five sections included in Robbery-Homicide Division. Like Snead's HSS unit, CCSS detectives worked under Robbery-Homicide command, being tasked with investigating open, "cold-case" murders that had remained unsolved for over five years, and that were no longer being actively investigated by other detectives.

Aken and I had come up through the Academy together. Despite being a capable investigator, Aken was also one of the few detectives on the force who, over the course of his career, had managed to get into more trouble with the LAPD brass than I had. Well, maybe not more, but at least as much. In any case, Aken was a good friend, and I knew I could depend on him for a favor. I had just made a mental note to call him when my cellphone rang.

It was Taylor.

"We found him," she said as soon as I picked up.

"Who?"

"The Magpie. We found him, Kane," she repeated. "An emergency meeting has been called. You need to be here at the Bureau field office by five."

"I'm stuck on a freeway in Orange County."

"I don't care if you're stuck on the moon. Get back here now."

Chapter 21
Emergency Meeting

After phoning Dorothy to arrange a ride home for Nate, I dropped my son at the West L.A. station and headed directly to the Bureau's Los Angeles field office on Wilshire.

At a few minutes before five, I arrived at the Wilshire Federal Building—an aging, seventeen-story monolith whose top five floors house the FBI's Los Angeles headquarters. Taylor met me at the main entrance and whisked me through security. A visitor's ID clipped to my jacket, we then rode a high-speed elevator to the Command and Tactical Operations Center on the sixteenth floor.

I had spent time in CTOC as a police liaison on a previous case, and as I trailed Taylor into the brightly lit suite of interconnected rooms, I noticed that not much had changed in the interim, with banks of computer workstations in CTOC's two command centers, marked OPS1 and OPS2, still fully manned. After making our way past a control room farther in, we entered a conference area crowded with Bureau agents and LAPD officers, many of whom I recognized.

With the exception of Chief Ingram, all the major players from our initial PAB meeting were present—Assistant Director Shepherd, SAC Gibbs, Assistant Chief Strickland, Captain Snead, and my immediate superiors Lieutenant Long, Captain Lincoln, and West Bureau Deputy Chief Chow—along with Deluca and Taylor and at least a dozen special agents. And me.

As Taylor and I stepped inside, I could feel a sense of excitement coursing through the room, as palpable as an electric current. I glanced at Taylor, who despite my prodding on our elevator ride had remained silent. She shook her head again, as if to say I would find out soon enough.

Noting our arrival, Special Agent in Charge Gibbs glanced at his watch. Then, stepping to the front of the assembly, he took a position near a wall covered with TV screens, clocks displaying the time in international cities, and a world map. "We're all here now, so everyone grab a seat and we'll get the briefing underway," he said, raising his voice to be heard. Once everyone had found a place, Gibbs paused to let the room settle, his ramrod-straight spine and no-nonsense manner again reminding me of a gunnery sergeant, or possibly a master chief petty officer. "In the spirit of cooperation between FBI agents and LAPD investigators," he continued, "we are here to discuss recent developments in The Magpie investigation."

"What recent developments?" interrupted Strickland. "This is the first I've heard of any recent developments. Why wasn't LAPD kept in the loop on this?"

"You were," said Gibbs. "In an attempt to identify the unsub's voice-masking software, both of our agencies have been analyzing the voicemail he left for Detective Kane. Our techs simply came up with an ID first."

"And?" said Strickland.

"The software he's using is a high-end digital tool made by a French company," Gibbs explained, ignoring Strickland's ill humor. "Flux Ircam Trax V3, to be exact. Using proprietary technology, Flux software can modify almost any sound characteristic—age, breath elements, even the gender of a speaker."

As Strickland had already broken protocol and turned the meeting into a free-for-all, I decided to speak up. "And you cross-referenced Flux purchasers to one of our other databases?"

Gibbs nodded. "We got a hit when comparing the Flux database to our list of webcam purchases. Payments for both were made on a Visa debit card linked to a Wells Fargo checking account in Newport Beach."

"And the name on that account is fictitious," I guessed. Although most banks require a social security number and other forms of identification when opening an account, in an era of identity theft, a few hours of internet research made those items surprisingly easy to acquire.

"Correct," said Gibbs. "Using bogus ID, our unsub set up the account six years ago. He made two initial cash deposits of nine thousand dollars each, then had his bank statements sent to a private mailbox in Laguna. The name and social security number on the account belong to a California resident living in Bakersfield—a Mr. James Goodall—who was unaware that someone was using his identity."

"Any prints on the registration materials?" asked an agent near the front.

Gibbs shook his head. "With the exception of the cash deposits, our unsub did everything online. Same for the postal service."

"Bank security cameras?" asked Deluca.

"Unfortunately, no. He never used an ATM, so no photos there, either."

"Did you subpoena the bank records?" asked Taylor.

"We did," Gibbs answered. "Most recently, the debit card in question was used for the online purchase of six Belkin wireless netcams—identical to those found at the dumpsites. But here's the interesting thing. Three years ago the card was also used to pay for a land lease on an agricultural parcel in Trabuco Canyon."

"Trabuco Canyon. That's in Orange County, somewhere near Rancho Santa Margarita?" I broke in.

"Correct," said Gibbs. "Trabuco Canyon is an unincorporated community in the foothills of the Santa Ana Mountains. Anyway, after leasing the land, our unsub used the card to purchase a forty-foot metal storage container and bury it on the property— supposedly as a bomb shelter."

"And you think he might be holding his victims there," concluded Snead, speaking for the first time.

"We do. Confidence on that is high on that for a number of reasons," Gibbs explained. "For one, the Wells Fargo card was also used to pay for a number of modifications to the container, including the fabrication of an interior compartment, welding improvements, a ventilation fan, electrical and plumbing facilities, and so on. We contacted several of the contractors involved. All work was done according to faxed plans and paid for with the same debit card. A few of the contractors actually talked with our unsub on the phone, but no one ever met him."

"Did you get copies of the plans?" I asked.

"In some cases, yes," Gibbs replied. "They show dimensions for an interior partition, specifications for plumbing and electrical additions, and so on. They're available on a table in back."

"So where do we go from here?" asked Strickland.

"We're bringing the Orange County Sheriff's Department in on this," Gibbs replied. "They have agreed to assist LAPD and the Bureau in any way possible. At the moment they have an unmarked car in Trabuco Canyon, with eyes watching the site. Here's a shot of the property."

Gibbs nodded to someone in the back. Moments later the overhead lights dimmed and a screen behind Gibbs sprang to life, showing a rural hillside with a weed-choked meadow at its base. At one end of the field was what looked like a ten-by-ten storage shed. A tubular, plastic water tank and a rack of solar panels sat nearby. Otherwise, the lot looked deserted.

"We're assuming the storage container is buried beneath the shed, but we haven't confirmed that as yet," Gibbs noted.

"Any surveillance devices?" asked Mason Vaughn, another agent whom I recognized from an earlier case. "The unsub's, I mean."

"Good point," said Gibbs. "The OC sheriffs haven't noticed any surveillance webcams, but given past experience with the unsub, that doesn't mean they're not there. There is no indication that our unsub is there at this time, either. If we go in with a warrant and he's not present, we may wind up back at square one."

"You're not suggesting we just sit around and wait for him to show up?" Snead interjected. "There's more at stake here than an arrest."

Like everyone in the room, I knew that Snead was concerned with the survival of his daughter, and I didn't blame him. There were some who thought that because of the family situation, Snead shouldn't be involved in the case at all. Early on, however, Snead had made it clear that he would take part in any action we launched in Trabuco Canyon, and his participation wasn't up for discussion. And I didn't blame him for that, either.

On the other hand, I could also understand Gibbs's hesitation to go in before we knew the full situation. With no links to the killer other than what we had so far, there was a good chance that if we tipped our hand without catching him, he would disappear like a puff of smoke—only to resurface somewhere else.

A heated discussion ensued, with all sides weighing in. In the hope the killer showed up soon, the Bureau was unanimous in recommending a twenty-four hour stakeout before moving in. Strickland remained neutral, although I could tell he sided with the Bureau. Snead, on the other hand, was adamant in demanding that we go in immediately and free his daughter.

In the end, I suggested a compromise. "We go in now, disable any surveillance devices we find, and rescue Ella—assuming she's there," I began. "After that we—"

"What do you mean, *assuming* she's there?" Snead demanded. "This whole line of investigation was your idea. Now you're saying you don't even think she's there?"

"I'm not sure *what* I'm saying," I replied. "But things seem a little too . . . easy. For one, Ella's online photo showed a concrete wall in her cell. This is a metal storage container. I have a bad feeling about this."

"Once again, Kane," Strickland broke in, "we are not running the investigation based on your *feelings*."

At this rebuke, a number of special agents glanced away, including Gibbs. "Maybe we should," someone mumbled in the back.

"What was that?" Strickland demanded, glaring at a several SAs near the rear.

No one responded.

After a moment I continued, ignoring a renewed scowl from Strickland. "Anyway, whether we find Ella or not, if our guy isn't present, we establish airtight surveillance on the site. And when he does show up, he's ours."

There was an unspoken sense in the room that Snead was liable to attempt a rescue ASAP, regardless of whatever we decided. And like me, no one blamed him. As a result, my suggestion was eventually accepted on all sides. A team composed of Bureau agents, Snead's HSS detectives, West L.A. investigators including Deluca and me, and a team of LAPD special weapons and tactics operators would go in. LAPD and SWAT would take the lead; FBI agents and Orange County Sheriff's Department officers would provide support.

We would free Ella. And if the killer weren't present, we would button down the site and wait for him to arrive.

Simple.

It was a good plan.

Nevertheless, I couldn't ignore the feeling that something was wrong.

Chapter 22
SWAT

Following the Bureau briefing, our combined forces caravanned to Orange County, arriving at Trabuco Canyon just before dark. By then Snead's detectives had obtained a search warrant and Metro's D Platoon SWAT van was en route, just a few minutes out.

Once everyone had arrived, including Metro's SWAT operators, we convened at the mouth of the canyon, establishing an incident command post in a parking lot behind a rustic general store. As we gathered behind the market, I noticed that in addition to SWAT, Metro had sent their on-staff doctor and another team member I whom recognized as a hostage negotiator.

I hoped neither would be necessary.

Assembling near SWAT's black, Lenco BEAR armored vehicle, I joined Captain Snead, SWAT commander Lieutenant James York, Special Agent in Charge Gibbs, and Sergeant George Lyons—the officer who managed York's ten-man squad—to confer with OC Sheriff's personnel already onsite. As the ranking LAPD officer present, Snead assumed field command. It was agreed, however, that once the green light was given for SWAT to breach, Lieutenant York would be calling the shots.

By then the moon had risen, illuminating the landscape in an eerie, ghostly glow. Everyone was nervous. Things were proceeding according to plan, but we all knew from experience that once the operation got underway, anything could happen.

As Snead, York, and Lyons were reviewing the entry plan, a Sheriff's cruiser pulled to stop beside the SWAT van. After killing the engine, Lieutenant Huff, an officer I knew from a previous task force, eased his wiry frame from behind the wheel. "Hey, Kane," he said, noticing me as he exited. "Should have known you'd be in on this."

"How's it going, Ken?" I said. "Glad to see you finally lost the wimpy moustache."

"Screw you," Huff chuckled, passing a hand across his clean-shaven face. "Who's this?" he asked, regarding Taylor, who had ridden to Orange County with Deluca and me.

"Agent Taylor, Lieutenant Huff," I said, making the introduction.

"Pleasure," said Huff, taking Taylor's hand.

"Lieutenant Huff," Snead called from the SWAT van, breaking off a discussion with York. "An update, please."

Reluctantly releasing Taylor's hand, Huff glanced in Snead's direction and nodded. As we all walked over to join Snead, Taylor asked me quietly, "Jeez, Kane, do you know everyone in this town?"

"Only the ones worth knowing," I replied.

"What do we have so far, Lieutenant Huff?" Snead asked upon our arrival.

"Well, for starters, the property in question is located a couple miles up the canyon," Huff replied. "The main road in, Trabuco Oaks Drive, eventually loops around and returns as Hickley Canyon Road. Your lot is close to where the road doubles back. Part of the site is wooded; the rest is grass and weeds. We have two teams covering the area. There's a storage shed at the east end, with a padlocked door and what looks like a water tank and a rack of solar panels nearby. We still haven't spotted any external surveillance devices. We don't think any are present, at least not outside."

"Any movement in the shed?" I asked.

Huff shook his head. "Nothing. We have a blockade down the road, ready to question anyone going in or out of the area. So far everything has been quiet."

"Neighbors notice unusual traffic in the area?" asked Deluca.

Again, Huff shook his head. "Mostly vacant land up there. Only a couple of residents. No one remembers seeing any strangers."

"Maybe he drives in at night," suggested Snead.

"Maybe," said Huff, looking doubtful.

Turning to York, Snead glanced at his watch. "Ready to roll, Lieutenant?"

York straightened. "Yes, sir."

"Then let's do it."

Driving separate cars, our forces followed Huff's cruiser and the SWAT van up Trabuco Canyon, passing expansive, tree-lined estates, horse corrals, and a checkpoint manned by two Sheriff's Department's black-and-whites. As the area became more wooded, the paved road narrowed and turned to dirt. Another half-mile up, we pulled to a stop several hundred yards from the site.

Although I tried, I couldn't spot either of the Sheriff's surveillance units. I could, however, make out a prefabricated storage shed on the eastern edge of the meadow. In the moonlight, the one-story structure appeared to be abandoned. Gazing at it, I wondered whether Ella Snead was inside. If she were, I couldn't imagine how lost and forsaken she must feel.

After watching the shed for several minutes, Snead turned to York. "It's all yours, Lieutenant," he said. "Please bring her back safely."

The plan was for York's ten-man SWAT squad to split into two five-man elements. It was also decided to use a stealthy initial approach, followed by a dynamic breach to effect the rescue.

Listening in on SWAT's tactical frequency, Taylor, Deluca, and I watched as the black-clad operators composing the first five-man SWAT element approached the shed, moving down from the trees in single file. Upon reaching the shed, the operators spread out and encircled the perimeter walls. Next, a team member deployed an Opti-wand—a small, infrared camera mounted atop a telescoping rod, with a fiber-optic video output linked to the operator's heads-up helmet display. Without exposing himself, the officer raised the camera to a side window, mirroring the interior of the shed. On the other side of the structure, I saw another operator do the same.

Upon receiving a go-ahead from the first group, the second SWAT element emerged from the trees and rushed the shed, Heckler & Koch MP5s in hand.

The padlock on the shed door quickly gave way to a bolt cutter. Moving as one, the breach team then assembled in a tight, five-man stack. The first man in the stack cracked the door. The second man tossed in a flashbang stun grenade.

Following a deafening explosion, the breaching unit went in hot and heavy, clearing the interior of the shed.

The shed was empty. No surveillance devices inside.

A search discovered a trapdoor in the floor, concealed beneath a rug. A dark, cavernous space lay below.

The buried storage container.

After additional Opti-wand mirroring and a second flashbang grenade, the second unit breached the space below, again meeting no resistance. Two members of the initial SWAT element guarded the trapdoor from above; the remaining three operators of the first element secured the shed's perimeter.

At that point Snead, York, and Gibbs entered the shed, followed by Taylor, Deluca, and me.

"Is she down there?" Snead called through the hole in the floor.

"We haven't located her yet," a voice floated up. "There's a walled-off partition and another padlocked door. We're checking it now."

Suddenly lights came on down below, illuminating the buried container in a sickly reddish glow.

"What the hell?" mumbled one of the operators.

"Motion detector," said someone else.

Kneeling, I peered into the hatchway. A steel ladder led down, accessing a rectangular space with ribbed metal walls and enough headroom for a man to stand. A sink and toilet were fastened to the rear wall. I also noted sprinkler heads mounted on the ceiling.

Snead started to push past, intending to join the team below. I stopped him. "There are already enough guys down there, Captain," I said. "Let them do their job."

Snead started to argue. He stopped when one of the SWAT operators appeared at the base of the ladder. "We cut the lock on the walled-off section," he said. "Nobody's there."

"He moved her?" said Snead. "We're too late?"

"No, sir," said the operator. "It looks like nobody's *ever* been there."

"Then what—"

"Lyons, get your men out, " I yelled down. "Don't touch anything else. Just get your guys out now."

Angrily, Snead again tried to push past. "Kane, what the hell are you—"

And then everything went terribly, horribly wrong.

I heard a metallic click, like an electrical relay snapping shut.

To a sudden blare of dissonant music, the space below abruptly came alive.

The red light brightened. A ventilation fan began gusting air into the lower chamber, venting out the trap door. Inexplicably, the ceiling sprinklers in the storage container activated, showering everything in the chamber with a rain of liquid. The toilet and sink began overflowing as well.

But it wasn't water raining down from the sprinkler heads, soaking the SWAT officers caught below.

It was gasoline.

Propelled by some concealed mechanism, a horizontal metal plate began ratcheting across the opening in the floor.

"Get out!" I yelled again, grabbing the plate and attempting to stop its advance.

Deluca and Taylor joined me, struggling to hold back the metal barrier. Gasoline vapors were wafting up, filling the shed with fumes. One of the SWAT operators jammed his MP5 across the hatch.

The other SWAT officer present in the shed leaned into the hole. "Team evacuate!" he shouted. "Evacuate!"

Suddenly the gasoline ignited.

One SWAT member made it out.

Assisted by his teammate from above, he squirmed through the opening, engulfed in flame. Snead, Taylor, and Deluca dragged him outside. The operator's fire-retardant Nomex gloves and his protective balaclava would help, but I knew he would never again be the same.

With a surge of horror, I saw the stock of the MP5 beginning to buckle.

I fought to hold back the hatch.

The second SWAT officer up the ladder wasn't as fortunate as the first. As he thrust his shoulders through the fiery opening, the MP5's polymer gunstock shattered.

The plate snapped shut, crushing the man's chest.

With the trapped officer now blocking the opening, any chance of escape for his teammates was gone. Choking on billows of smoke, I pulled off my coat and wrapped my hands in my jacket, trying for some protection from the flames. Straining for all I was worth, I placed a foot on either side of the opening and pulled, wincing at the heartrending cries echoing from below.

The SWAT officers in the shed joined me, struggling to open the hatch.

Mixing with the squeal of music and the roar of the inferno, a cacophony of screams sounded from the container below.

Frantic fingers scrabbled at the opening, fighting to escape.

And I could do nothing.

I felt a hand on my shoulder.

Deluca.

"We have to go," he said.

By then, flames had engulfed several sections of the shed.

I glanced at the SWAT officers. "One more try."

They nodded.

Eyes burning, muscles straining, we fought to retract the hatch.

And failed.

"Dan, it's time," said Deluca, pulling me to my feet.

Deluca and I stumbled out, followed by the two SWAT officers, emerging from the smoke seconds before the shed burst into flame.

Although I tried not to, as we left I glanced back at the officer trapped in the hatchway. My heart broke as I saw his eyes following us out. Mercifully, I think he died of suffocation before the blaze consumed him.

At least I wanted to believe so.

Stunned, we gathered in the moonlit field, all of us who remained.

Silent in our shock, we watched as fire engulfed the shed, knowing the obscenity that lay beneath. And as the pyre lurched and settled, sending a storm of sparks spinning into the night sky, Taylor moved to stand beside me. Wordlessly, she took my hand. Turning toward her, I saw in her eyes a glitter of tears, and in her face, illuminated by the blaze, her horror at the immense, hideous cruelty of the mind that had devised such a trap.

Deluca joined us.

For once my partner had nothing to say.

Nor did I.

I was angry.

I had made a fatal error, and men had paid for it with their lives.

The killer had meant for us to discover his voice-changing software. He had wanted us to match that discovery to his bogus checking account. He had left a trail for us to follow . . . all the way to a deadly trap set long, long ago.

And I had bought it all, all of it—hook, line, and sinker.

The killer had been planning this moment for years.

With a surge of shame, I realized he had been one step ahead of us the entire time.

I had underestimated him.

Staring into the fire, I made a silent vow.

I would not repeat that mistake.

Chapter 23
Prison Shank

Crouched at the base of her prison toilet, Ella Snead toiled in the darkness, fashioning a weapon.

Although the light in her cell had been extinguished hours earlier, Ella had drawn the privacy curtain around the toilet anyway, hoping her captor wasn't watching. She was fairly sure he couldn't see what she was doing, but she also knew that if she remained in there too long, he might grow suspicious. He had told her his video feed was being archived, so she couldn't assume that simply because he wasn't watching at the moment, he might not view the recorded footage later.

Suddenly she heard a noise.

She froze.

Oh, God, is he coming?

Heart in her throat, she waited, not moving a muscle.

Seconds passed.

Nothing.

Ella finally unclenched her fists, deciding that the darkness must be playing tricks on her. When her heart finally slowed, she took a deep breath and resumed her labor.

Several days earlier when the light had been on, Ella had managed to slide back her toilet a few inches, exposing the concrete floor beneath. When she finished working that night, she would reposition the toilet, covering the marks she had scraped on the floor. Her nascent weapon would then go into the drawer at the bottom of the toilet, concealed beneath a layer of compost. It was the one place she was confident the man wouldn't look.

Pausing to check her progress, Ella used her fingers to test the dagger she was crafting. Her makeshift "prison shank"—a toothbrush whose fat end she was tapering to a point—was taking longer to complete than she'd hoped.

She had first started grinding the red plastic handle against the floor beneath her bed. It had seemed the perfect place for her to work, as the cramped confines beneath her cot were out of webcam view. In addition, should the man happen to check, her time there could be explained by the growing tally of scratches she had cut into the plywood. So far she had made twelve gouges with her belt-buckle prong—two groups of five, and two more—adding her marks below the twenty-seven that her prison's former occupant had totaled.

Ella suspected that her crude reckoning of time was something her captor had already discovered. Maybe it even amused him. Unfortunately, the red toothbrush handle left telltale marks on the floor, which was something he might also notice and *not* find amusing.

Does he search my prison? she wondered.

Probably, she decided.

It was a risk she could not afford to take.

Ella hadn't seen her captor in days, which was puzzling. As near as she could tell, he had visited daily in the past. Had something happened to him?

After his last appearance, he had left an extra stash of granola bars in the cabinet.

Was he planning to be gone?

At first, that possibility had seemed attractive.

Then another thought occurred.

What if he never comes back?

With a shrug, Ella had decided that starving might be preferable to whatever fate her captor had in mind.

Using her fingers, Ella adjusted a wad of clothing she had crammed beneath her dog collar, protecting her throat. She had no illusions that the flimsy insulation would offer much protection should the man discover what she was doing. He would simply turn up the voltage on his device, or do something worse. Nevertheless, although she had avoided wearing the cloth insulation whenever he visited, it made her feel less vulnerable when she was sharpening her weapon.

It didn't make sense, but she did it anyway.

Clenching her teeth in determination, Ella resumed her work, all the while considering how best to conceal the dagger on her person when the time came to use it. Of one thing she was certain: She needed to stay focused and strong to make that a possibility.

And she would.

She had no choice.

Best case scenario, she would somehow tempt the man into having sex with her. Then, at the right moment, she would strike. After her earlier experience offering the man sex, however, Ella considered that prospect unlikely.

There was also a chance she would develop a tolerance to the man's drugs—assuming he didn't increase her dosage—enabling her to fake unconsciousness and catch him unaware. But as time went on, that possibility seemed to be becoming less likely as well.

Worst case scenario, she could jam a wad of clothing under her collar, refuse to take his pills, and wait for him to enter her cell. Maybe she could surprise him, stab him—where?

The throat.

Or the chest.

Or maybe his eyes.

Whatever happened, Ella knew from listening to her father's prison stories that the important thing in a stabbing was to keep stabbing. One hole in someone isn't enough.

Can I do that?

Grimly, Ella lowered her head and continued sharpening her weapon, deciding that if given the chance, she would stab her captor without hesitation.

And she would keep stabbing until he was dead.

For again, she had no choice.

Chapter 24
Blood Moon

Iow could this have happened?" Chief Ingram demanded. No one replied.

I glanced around at the faces in Ingram's office. We had lost four men the previous evening, and the mood there the following morning was grim. Making matters worse, the killer had posted a video of the carnage.

"Until now, in its more than five-decade history, do you know how many SWAT officers have been lost in the line of duty?" Ingram continued angrily. "One," he answered, not waiting for a response. "And last night we lost *four*? So I ask again, how could this have happened?"

Again, no one replied.

Assistant Chief Strickland finally spoke up. "How about you, Kane? You were lead investigator on the UCLA murder, and you always seem to have something to say. Who screwed the pooch?"

Every eye in the room turned toward me. Uncertain how to respond, I stared at my hands, which Metro's doctor had dressed at the scene with gauze and hydrogel. Singed by the blaze, my eyelashes and eyebrows were also missing, along with a fair portion of my hair. Bottom line, I looked like shit, and I felt like it, too.

"I did," I said at last. "I should have seen it coming."

"What do you mean by that?" Strickland snapped.

"It was all a little too easy," I replied. "Discovering the webcams, running down the voice-altering software, finding the fake credit card. The guy set us up. I should have seen it coming."

"To be fair, The Magpie's recent behavior constitutes a significant alteration in his modus operandi," interjected Director Shepherd, who was also present that morning with SAC Gibbs and Taylor. "No one at the Bureau anticipated his change in M.O., either."

"I never should have green-lighted the breach without first securing that hatch," added Lieutenant York, Metro's SWAT commander. "I'm as much to blame as anyone."

"The plate that trapped your men was concealed beneath the floor. There was no way for you to have known," I pointed out, realizing that, like me, everyone felt responsible.

"That may be, but it still shouldn't have happened," said York.

"None of this should have happened," said Ingram. "There will be plenty of blame to spread around later. Let's move on. How is Lyons doing?"

Sergeant Lyons, who had led the storage-container breech, had been the only officer to make it out of the firetrap alive.

"I talked with a doctor at the UCI burn center this morning," York replied. "Lyons is still in intensive care, but he's going to pull through."

"I'm relieved to hear that," said Ingram. Then turning to me, "What do we know about the firetrap?"

Following the arrival of Engine 45 from Rancho Santa Margarita, the blaze had eventually been extinguished and the bodies of our men recovered. Since then investigators had been sifting through the rubble.

"We don't have all the results yet," I answered. "We do know that the gasoline accelerant was stored in an above-ground water tank. The fuel was gravity-fed to a sink, toilet, and sprinkler heads inside the metal container. A ventilation fan and an electrically powered barrier plate were probably activated when SWAT opened a door down below. We think the killer sparked the blaze with a phone call."

"And he knew to do that because . . ."

I shrugged. "He evidently had a webcam concealed in the underground container, the same one he used to record the fire. Probably got a webcam alert when our guys entered the space below the shack."

At my mention of the killer's video, the room fell silent.

The internet post chronicling the deaths of our men, a loss the media were now calling "The Blood Moon Murders," had quickly gone viral. Although it had only been hours, the horrific video had already garnered millions of worldwide views. Like me, most officers in the room had watched it, if only because we felt we had to.

Once.

I would never watch it again.

"What's with the weird music?" asked one of Snead's detectives. "You know, in the killer's video?"

"The eerie music, if you can even call it that, is from a video game," replied Gibbs. "*The Legend of Zelda: Breath of the Wild*. My son plays it. At one point in the game the sky glows, the air fills with burning embers, and the moon rises red—a blood moon—like during a lunar eclipse. According to my kid, the ascent of the blood moon is accompanied by a respawn of all your enemies."

"Zelda, huh? Anything to investigate there?" asked Taylor.

Gibbs shook his head. "We started down that road and quickly gave up. Too many gamers out there."

"So where does that leave us?" asked Lieutenant Long, posing the question on all our minds.

"Director Shepherd?" said Ingram.

Looking dejected, Shepherd turned toward Gibbs. "Gibbs, you want to run it down?"

"Yes, sir," said Gibbs, taking a moment to collect his thoughts before continuing. Then, "Working with Captain Snead's unit, we are still compiling databases of anyone recently making an online or retail purchase of a dog training collar, a Taser device, or the forensic textbook in question—*Forensic Science: Cases and Materials on Criminal Investigation*. So far no correlations."

"After what just happened, how do we know those parameters aren't just more red herrings?" asked Strickland.

"We don't," said Gibbs. "We still have to follow up."

"I agree," said Ingram. "Please continue, SAC Gibbs."

"Yes, sir. Working on the theory that our unsub is stalking his victims, our CART techs have been combing through social media sites, looking for any commonality—friend requests, contacts, and so on. So far nothing there, either.

"In addition, we have reached out to a sister agency in the hope of determining how the unsub obtained Captain Snead's and Detective Kane's cellphone numbers," Gibbs continued. "That agency is also cooperating in an attempt to pierce the hidden-service-protocol network that our unsub is using to post his photos and videos. The best we've been able to do so far is to locate his upload sites. By the way, his latest video was posted at a Starbucks in Arizona.

"Last, our field offices in Portland, Seattle, and San Francisco are working with locals to interview witnesses, search for stalkers, and vet any forensic experts who might be involved in the murders." Gibbs shook his head. "In summary, we're coming up cold on all fronts."

Ingram turned to Snead. "Bill, what do you have?"

"Not much," Snead replied. "Our contacts in the gang unit came up with a list of Ketamine/GHB purchasers, none of whom panned out. The fact is, an anonymous purchase of the date-rape drugs in question is impossible to track. Our canvass for a witness or informant has hit a brick wall. We're still hoping to determine who opened the fake checking account in Orange County, but we're not hopeful. We're also assembling a retail-purchase list of anyone buying the forensics textbook Kane came up with, but that could be a false trail as well."

"Like the voice-altering software and the surveillance webcams," said Ingram. "Any thoughts on that, Kane?"

"I honestly don't know, Chief," I said, beginning to doubt those lines of investigation as well. Nevertheless, although Deluca and I had struck out requesting a list of forensic students from various universities, I made a mental note to visit the textbook's author. "I still think we should follow up, like Gibbs said."

"Do that," said Ingram, turning back to Snead. "Anything to add?"

Snead had seemed shell-shocked the previous evening when his daughter hadn't been found, and from his appearance, he hadn't slept since. "Again, not much, except that following the killer's latest video, our tip line has been ringing nonstop," he said. "We have a BOLO alert out on the killer's Chevy Astro van, if it *is* his van. Maybe we'll get lucky."

Again the room fell silent, every investigator present thinking the same thing: Time was running out, and our efforts had been reduced to grasping at straws and hoping to get lucky.

Ingram turned to me. "Sum up your efforts to date, Detective Kane," he ordered, sounding exasperated. "And skip any bullshit about what you've done so far that *hasn't* worked. Tell me what you're doing right now that will."

"I do have one possibility," I ventured, wondering how to present it.

"Are you going to make us guess?" demanded Strickland.

"No, I was just . . . anyway, our problem is that we're not certain which of our leads may have been intentionally left by the killer. We don't know what to trust."

Several investigators nodded, including Gibbs.

"Based on the complexity of the killer's M.O., it's likely he started his activities a lot earlier," I reasoned. "Back then he was probably strangling his victims, too."

"And in the past he might not have been as careful as he is now?" Taylor jumped in, anticipating where I was going.

"Right. So we look at unsolved strangulation murders— especially those involving abduction—and see where that leads us. Maybe he made a mistake earlier in his career. If nothing else, we can be fairly certain that anything we turn up won't be a false lead."

"Seems a bit oblique," Strickland noted doubtfully.

"Maybe. But unless someone has a better idea, I think we should pursue it," said Shepherd. "I can have our northern field offices work with locals in the Portland/Seattle area on that. Maybe extend it to the western states."

"Thanks, Alan," said Ingram. "I'll bring Robbery-Homicide's cold case section in on it as well." Then, with a glance around the room, "Anything else?"

When no one spoke, Ingram pushed on. "Fine," he said. "For those of you living on another planet, there's a press conference downstairs in a few minutes. Mayor Fitzpatrick will be making a statement, after which Director Shepherd and I will have the pleasure of addressing our friends in the media."

A number of detectives smiled grimly. As the investigation had dragged on, many in the media were now accusing Los Angeles authorities of incompetence—blaming elected officials, police administrators, and investigators alike. Sparked by worldwide horror at the "Blood Moon" video, what had begun as a national news story had become an international disgrace, with the mood in the press turning ever more toxic.

The eyes of the world were upon us—not that I cared.

I had one thing in mind, and it wasn't looking good in the press. The killer had reaped the recognition he so obviously desired. I wanted to make certain he got everything else he deserved as well.

"Director Shepherd and I will be heading downstairs shortly," Ingram continued. "I'm not certain how we are going to explain last night's events, but when we do, I want everyone here present. I also want Assistant Chief Strickland, Captain Snead, Lieutenant York, and Detective Kane standing up there on the podium with me. Understood?"

We all nodded.

"A memorial for our murdered SWAT members has been scheduled at the Crenshaw Christian FaithDome. It will be held on Sunday of next week," Ingram concluded, glancing around the room. "I will be announcing the memorial service at the end of the news briefing. Needless to say, we will *all* attend that event as well."

Again, everyone nodded.

Ingram checked his watch. "Okay. It's time to close ranks, go downstairs, and face the music."

Chapter 25
Disturbing Call

"Miss me, Ella?"

As near as she could estimate, it was Ella's seventeenth day in the man's prison. It had also been five days since she had last seen her captor, a time during which she had suffered the nauseating symptoms of drug withdrawal. Adding to her misery, her stash of granola bars had run out two mornings earlier.

"Where were you?" she asked, avoiding his question. Not meeting his gaze, she swung her bare legs from beneath the covers and sat on the edge of her bed.

"A business trip. You are not the only concern occupying my time. Here, I've brought you something," he coaxed, setting a McDonald's carton on the floor. "Sausage and Egg McMuffins. I hear they're yummy."

For some reason, the man seemed uncharacteristically elated. Ella eyed the McDonald's box, feeling her stomach rumble with hunger.

"You know the rules," the man warned. "You get your treat, but only if you behave."

"Behave? What else can I do in here besides behave?" Ella demanded, scratching at a rash that was developing under her collar.

"Careful, Ella. Someone might get the impression you don't respect me."

Ella lowered her gaze, forcing herself to remain calm. Upon hearing his approach, she had barely managed to hide her weapon in the compost drawer, yank the protective clothing from beneath her collar, and return to her bed in time—slipping under the covers just before he entered.

Ella's makeshift dagger was almost ready. She couldn't afford to have him discover it now. If he did, she was certain her captor would consider her turning a toothbrush into a weapon somewhat less than good behavior. "Fine," she mumbled, attempting to appear chastised. "What do you want me to do?"

"Hmmm," the man mused, toying with his remote control. "So many options, so little time. I know. Let's continue delving into your early sexual experiences."

"Why?" Ella asked, although she already knew the answer. "Haven't you humiliated me enough?"

"I ask the questions," came the reply, accompanied by a paralyzing bolt of electricity.

Ella screamed, clutching at her throat. "No, please! I'll . . . I'll do whatever you want."

"I know you will. And what I want *right now* is for you to do as I say."

"I will," Ella said softly.

"Speak up."

"I'll do whatever you say," Ella replied, raising her voice.

"Good." As the man rocked back in his armchair, Ella realized she had never loathed anyone as much in her entire life. Suddenly she heard a buzzing. The man withdrew a cellphone from his pocket and checked the screen.

Looking irritated, the man answered the call, listening intently. Moments later his face turned pale. Without explanation, he withdrew the key from beneath his shirt and started for the exit.

"I need to eat!" Ella called after him, realizing he was about to leave. "Please!"

Without a glance in her direction, the man kicked the McDonald's carton closer to her cell door, spilling its contents on the floor.

****

Climbing the stairs outside Ella's prison, Dr. Krüger wondered how a day that had started off so well could have quickly turned so bad.

Life wasn't fair.

On Wednesday he had spent a satisfying afternoon in a Phoenix courthouse, defending a guilty client and making a fool of an inexperienced prosecuting attorney. Even better, later that evening at his motel he had received an alert from the webcam concealed in his underground storage container. Someone had entered the Trabuco Canyon trap.

Dr. Krüger had watched the SWAT intruders on his laptop, waiting for the perfect moment to touch off the blaze. And to his satisfaction, everything had gone as planned. After posting a video of the conflagration, he had spent additional satisfying hours the next morning watching LAPD authorities squirm through a press conference. Topping it all off, the remainder of the court case had gone well. Thanks to his testimony, the defendant was as good as free, although everyone in court knew he was guilty. And on Sunday, after collecting a hefty fee for his services, Dr. Krüger had flown home to a large Scotch and a warm bed.

Monday morning had promised to be another glorious day, starting with a visit to his latest acquisition, Ella Snead. Although Ella was beginning to grow tiresome, as they all did in the end, she still had a few pleasures to surrender before her demise.

Then, delivered to him on his answering service, a message: *Detective Daniel Kane will be arriving at your office within the hour.*

Krüger reexamined his actions, wondering where he had gone wrong.

The webcam purchases?
The checking account?
The firetrap?

The last time Dr. Krüger had felt this unsure of himself was on an evening long past, on a night when he had lost control with that troublesome graduate student. Her death had been her own fault, of course. She had asked for it. And although blame had been shifted and everything had eventually worked out, his nearly being caught had been something he vowed would never happen again.

Yet years later, here was an LAPD detective knocking at his door.

Dr. Krüger paused to analyze the situation.

The police couldn't know for certain, he decided.

Otherwise, they would already have him in custody, rather than calling to make an appointment. Nevertheless, somehow Detective Kane's investigation had led him to his threshold.

How had Kane managed to get so close?

And more important, what did he want?

Chapter 26
Dr. Krüger

The following Monday morning, Taylor and I departed for San Diego at a little after 9:00 a.m., giving freeway traffic a chance to settle. Although by then the bandages were off my hands, my palms were still scabbed, and I asked Taylor to drive us down in her Bureau vehicle, a Ford Crown Vic.

On the way there in her "Bucar," Taylor wanted to talk about Trabuco Canyon. I didn't. As a result, she talked; I listened. Like me, Taylor was deeply disturbed by what had happened and wasn't sleeping because of it. Also like me, she felt that the loss of our men was somehow her fault. Though it didn't make sense, I guess when horrible things happen, there's always plenty of guilt to go around.

Upon arriving in Rancho Bernardo, we located Dr. Krüger's office in a smartly landscaped corporate area hosting a number of upscale tenants, among them Hewlett-Packard, Nokia, and Sony. After checking the address, I pointed toward a sleek, one-story building on the perimeter of the complex. "That's it over there," I said.

Taylor nodded, parking her Crown Vic beside a Mercedes-Benz S-Class sedan.

Deluca and I had hit a dead end compiling a database of university students who had used Krüger's textbook. Without a warrant, the institutions in question simply wouldn't divulge that information. I hoped Dr. Krüger would be more accommodating.

As we exited her car, Taylor asked, "Have you decided how you want to do this?"

Nearing San Diego, Taylor and I had talked about the best way to conduct the interview with Dr. Krüger, not coming to a decision. Clearly, Krüger could be a suspect. After all, he had written the textbook in question. On the other hand, lots of people had read it. In addition, like my initial search, Taylor's subsequent Bureau report on Dr. Krüger hadn't turned up anything of a criminal nature, and after the mistake we had made in Trabuco Canyon, I didn't want to jump to conclusions.

"Depends on how cooperative this Dr. Krüger decides to be," I answered after a moment's thought. "Let's play it by ear."

As we approached Dr. Krüger's building, I wondered whether the connection to his forensic textbook would turn out to be another dead end, in which case our trip to Rancho Bernardo would be one more futile effort. Attempting to remain positive, I turned my thoughts to the single bright spot in our investigation—one that couldn't be a red herring, and therefore one that might actually pan out.

Following Thursday's press conference, I had taken advantage of my visitor's badge to head back up to PAB's sixth floor. Passing the Detectives Bureau's office and a DB conference room along the way, I eventually found my friend, Detective Jeroen Aken, slouched behind a desk in Robbery-Homicide's Cold Case Special Section.

Aken, wiry and fit even though his hair had started to gray, grinned when he saw me. "Kane," he said. "You're looking even bigger and uglier than I remembered. Good to see you."

"You, too, Jerry," I replied with a smile. "Forgive my not offering to shake," I said as he rose and extended a hand, giving him a fist-bump instead.

Aken regarded my singed face and burned hands. "I heard what happened last night," he said. "I'm sorry, Dan. That was a terrible loss. And again, I was so sorry to hear about Catheryn. You doing okay?"

I lifted my shoulders. "One day at a time. You know how it is."

"Yeah."

"How about you? Still living in Hollywood Hills?"

"I am. My daughter is there with me now, too."

"Must be nice."

"It is . . . mostly," Aken laughed. "You know kids." Then, after pulling over a chair for me, he slumped back into his own seat. "What happened in Trabuco Canyon must have been . . . tough," he went on. "I can't imagine. You getting counseling?"

Over the years, LAPD had increasingly mandated compulsory counseling and "general training updates" for any officer discharging a weapon in the line of duty. Technically, the loss of our SWAT members didn't apply. Nevertheless, the department had offered voluntary psychiatric sessions to everyone involved—either in-house or with a private therapist. As far as I knew, no one had taken them up on the offer, as seeking counseling for anyone on the job was a complicated matter. Officers were supposed to be able to withstand hardship, and failure to do so could show a lack of professionalism and emotional control—possibly indicating a mental disorder that could relate to one's fitness for duty, as well as any expectation of privacy.

"I'm good," I said.

"Right. You're here about The Magpie case?" said Aken, changing the subject.

"How did you know?"

"Word's out. Our lieutenant got a call from Ingram's office. CCSS is to extend every courtesy to West L.A. on The Magpie investigation, and so on. Needless to say, I'll be happy to help. What do you need?"

Wearily, I dropped into the chair Aken had provided, realizing that finding the killer had become a priority for the entire department. At the news briefing Ingram had announced a citywide tactical alert, meaning officers could be held over on their shifts for as long as necessary. Unfortunately, I also realized that throwing men and money at an investigation didn't necessarily bring results.

"Here's the situation," I began. "Between you and me, we have zip on this dirtbag. He seems to be knowledgeable regarding forensics and police procedures, so he isn't giving us much to work with. Worse, he's left several false trails, and we're beginning to doubt ourselves on just about everything. The one thing we're fairly certain of is that he probably started his killings much earlier.

"And maybe he made a few mistakes back then," Aken concluded. "So with that in mind, you want to review cold cases and maybe find something that could help with your current investigation?"

"I know it's a long shot, but right now it's the best we have.

Aken regarded me doubtfully. "From what I've heard, your guy has been active in the Portland/Seattle area. Los Angeles is new territory for him. Our RHD cold cases will only cover LA."

"The feds will work with out-of-town PDs on everything else," I explained. "Nevertheless, I have a hunch our guy is local. He knows the area here too well. If we turn up an old killing of his, I think it will be from somewhere around L.A."

"Okay, what search parameters do you want to include?"

"Female victims, manual strangulation, possible abductions. We should also look for the use of a Taser or something similar, especially if a kidnapping was involved. Our guy has been feeding his victims Ketamine and GHB, so let's put drugs on the list, too."

"What about timeframe? Cold cases start five years back."

"Let's begin there and work our way back."

Aken nodded. "I'll need a few hours to tie up some loose ends, after which I'll start doing research. Shall we meet here tomorrow?"

"Sounds good, Jerry. And thanks."

But after spending all of Friday and the rest of the weekend with Aken and Deluca and Taylor sifting through CCSS files, I had begun to question that line of investigation as well. Granted, there were plenty of open strangulation murders. Not surprisingly, however, most of the cold cases we examined displayed the earmarks of unsolved domestic violence, not the work of a serial killer. Time was running out, and we had yet to find anything we could tie to our current investigation.

Now, as Taylor and I pushed through a pair of thick glass doors into Dr. Krüger's reception area, I realized that unless something broke soon, finding Snead's daughter in time was becoming more and more unlikely.

"May I help you?" asked a young receptionist, smiling at us from behind a polished mahogany counter.

"We're here to see Dr. Krüger," I said, flashing my shield.

Although the receptionist seemed momentarily flustered, she quickly recovered. "Yes, officer," she said, checking her schedule. "Do you have an appointment?"

"Don't need one. We're here on official business. Please tell Dr. Krüger we're waiting."

"Yes, sir," she said, lifting a multi-line phone and pressing a lighted button. As she began speaking softly into the handset, I glanced at Taylor. She shrugged, indicating she had no idea where this was headed, either.

Moments later a door opened across the room. A tall, dark-haired man with a tennis-court tan and a muscular, health-club physique stepped into the reception area, skirting a brace of potted palms on his way in. "Detective Kane?" he said, smiling pleasantly.

I nodded.

"I'm Dr. Krüger," the strikingly handsome man informed me. "My answering service told me you would be arriving, but they didn't mention a time. My apologies for keeping you waiting."

"Actually, we've been trying to contact you since last Tuesday."

"Sorry. I was in Arizona testifying at a murder trial." Then, smiling at Taylor, "And you are?"

"Special Agent Taylor," she replied, smiling back.

"May I see some identification, please? Actually, I would like to see credentials from both of you," said Dr. Krüger, his smile fading as he returned his gaze to me.

I held up my ID. Dr. Krüger gave it a cursory glance. "LAPD. Aren't you a bit out of your area, Detective Kane? Off the reservation, I think it's called?"

"He may be, but I'm not," said Taylor, withdrawing her Bureau credentials. "And Detective Kane is with me."

Dr. Krüger spent considerably more time inspecting Taylor's identification, grasping the edge of her credential case and trailing his thumb across her photograph. I also noticed that when Taylor refused to relinquish her ID during his inspection, he made a point of touching her hand. "Detective Daniel Kane and Special Agent Sara Ann Taylor," he said, his eyes lingering on

Taylor. "Let's retire to my office. I assume you want to discuss The Magpie investigation," he added, turning to hold the door open for Taylor.

"Why would you assume that?" I asked, following Taylor in.

"I recognize you from Thursday's televised briefing at police headquarters," Dr. Krüger explained. "You were hard to miss, standing on the podium behind Chief Ingram, considerably taller than everyone else."

We followed Dr. Krüger down a short hallway to his private office. Again he held the door for Taylor, then closed it firmly after I had stepped inside.

The interior of Dr. Krüger's office continued the polished mahogany theme from the reception area—raised paneling, crown molding, chair-rail millwork, antique desk—reminding me of something one might see at an exclusive men's club. Dr. Krüger settled himself in a regal leather armchair behind his desk, waving us to a pair of lesser seats in front. "How may I assist you?" he asked.

Taylor sat. I remained standing. "You're right about one thing, Dr. Krüger," I began. My initial impression of Dr. Krüger was that something seemed not quite right about him. In addition, he had written the textbook in question, but that didn't make him a killer. As his name hadn't shown up on any of our burgeoning databases, I decided not to jump to conclusions. Setting aside my suspicions for the moment, I continued. "We're here to get your cooperation on The Magpie investigation. But first I'm going to reveal some details of the case that haven't been disclosed to the media. I need your assurance that anything I say will remain confidential."

"Of course," said Dr. Krüger. "By the way, after what happened to your SWAT officers, doesn't the media's puerile nickname for the killer seem a bit . . . ridiculous? I mean, a bird?"

"I couldn't agree more," I said, pushing on. "We believe the killer has an understanding of forensics and police procedures, and he's using that knowledge to avoid leaving evidence. We also have reason to believe that he has read your textbook on the subject."

Krüger steepled his fingers. Ignoring me, he looked thoughtfully at Taylor. "Hmmm. And what reason leads authorities to believe he's read my book, Special Agent Taylor—as you seem to be the only one present with proper credentials."

Deciding to make use of Krüger's interest in Taylor, I remained silent, letting her continue the interview. "Well, your textbook *is* the definitive work on the subject," she answered. "Our thinking is that anyone with a knowledge of forensics must be familiar with your book."

Krüger nodded, seeming satisfied with Taylor's flattery.

"We're compiling a list of anyone who has purchased or read your textbook," Taylor continued smoothly. "Unfortunately, the institutions at which you taught—Cal State and UCI—have refused to turn over a roster of their forensic students. We're hoping you might have kept a record."

"Actually, Sara, I have a complete listing of all my students over the years," said Dr. Krüger, for some reason seeming amused. "Without a warrant, however, I am bound by the same regulations that I'm certain both universities quoted in their refusals."

"That's going to be unfortunate for you," I broke in, deciding the moment had come to apply some pressure.

Dr. Krüger turned to me, his dark eyes hardening. "Why is that?"

"Because if the media were to find out that the renowned Dr. Erich Krüger, celebrated criminalist and expert-witness consultant, had refused to assist authorities in The Magpie investigation, your lucrative consulting business might just dry up and blow away—along with your so-called reputation."

"Are you threatening me?"

It was my turn to smile. "Not at all, Dr. Krüger. I'm just pointing out how things might look to the uninformed. As for the press getting wind of your refusal to assist in a life-and-death situation, well . . . I can just about guarantee it. You know how nosy those reporters are."

Dr. Krüger stared at me. Oddly, I had the feeling I was missing something. I can usually get a "read" on someone. From

Dr. Krüger, I was getting nothing. Along with that, my bullshit meter was suddenly pegged in the red.

"We need that list, Dr. Krüger," Taylor intervened.

Dr. Krüger hesitated. "If I were to provide a record of my students, and I'm only saying *if*, would my cooperation be held in confidence?"

"Absolutely," Taylor agreed. "When can we get those names?"

Dr. Krüger paused a moment more. "I suppose I could fax you a list sometime tomorrow."

"We need it this afternoon," I said, sliding my business card across his desk. "Here's the number."

Dr. Krüger picked up my card. "Agreed, as long as you keep my name out of things." Then, rising, "Now, I think it's time for you both to leave. I'll walk you out."

In the parking lot, Dr. Krüger's mood seemed to improve. Once more ignoring me, he took Taylor's hand. "It has been a pleasure meeting you, Special Agent Sara Taylor," he said, turning up the wattage on his picture-perfect smile. "I hope our paths cross again sometime soon."

With that, Dr. Krüger used a remote control to unlock the black Mercedes parked beside Taylor's Crown Vic. With a final smile at Taylor, he slid behind the wheel and exited the lot, not looking back.

Taylor raised a hand to her hair, watching as Dr. Krüger drove away. "That was, uh, interesting," she said. "And we're getting his list."

"Yeah, we're getting his list," I agreed, once more sensing that something was *off* about Dr. Krüger. Throughout our interview he acted strangely smug, even when I'd pressed him on the subject of his students. Again, that didn't make him a killer. Nevertheless, until proved otherwise, I decided to continue considering him a possible suspect.

****

As he wheeled onto Camino Del Norte and headed east, Dr. Krüger reviewed his meeting with Detective Kane. Learning that Kane and his lovely partner merely wanted information regarding his forensic students had been reassuring. Granted, Dr. Krüger's text *was* the definitive work on the subject, as Agent Taylor had so charmingly pointed out. Still, there had to be more to it.

But what?

Of one thing Dr. Krüger was certain: He didn't like Detective Kane, not one bit. Something about the dangerous-looking Irish cop reminded him of his own father, and of the violent, father-son relationship that had ended just days before Dr. Krüger's fifteenth birthday. And with that unexpected connection, Dr. Krüger's thoughts traveled far into the past, all the way back to the day that had changed everything.

He had been planning the act for almost a year. His experiments with neighborhood dogs and cats had proved instructive, but the time had come for more. Determined to escalate his activities without getting caught, he had risen to the challenge, spending weeks immersed in research on the subject of murder. Dr. Krüger smiled, realizing that his decision to end his father's routine beatings and occasional sexual abuse had undoubtedly played a seminal role in his later forensic career.

It had been a cold, gray Saturday in November. His father, a university professor, had been working at home in the den, two-finger typing some academic correspondence. As usual, his mother was busy that day at her volunteer thrift-store job in San Diego and wouldn't be returning until later that evening.

Young Erich Krüger had departed the house early that afternoon wearing a coat, a hat, and a pair of leather gloves. He had ridden his bike to a local theatre, where he had purchased a ticket for a classic noir film he had already seen. After pointedly conversing with an usher selling popcorn, he had viewed the first twenty minutes of the movie, waiting until the woman on the screen had been dutifully stabbed in the shower. Then, heart pounding with excitement, he had slipped out a side exit and returned home.

He had stashed his bike and entered the rear of the house, making certain no one noted his arrival. He removed his hat and coat, but kept on his gloves. Silently, he crept to his parents' bedroom and withdrew his father's automatic pistol from a bedside stand. After checking the magazine and chambering a round, he made his way back to the den.

Although surprised to see him, his father had simply grunted and continued his typing. As young Erich pretended to gaze at his father's correspondence, he reached behind his back and retrieved the gun tucked in his belt. He brought up the weapon and pressed the muzzle to his father's temple.

His father flinched. "What the fu—"

Young Erich pulled the trigger.

The explosion was deafening.

His father slumped in his chair, blood spurting from his temple—once, twice . . . then slowing to a dribble.

Next young Erich placed the pistol in his father's right hand and forced his finger against the trigger. Pointing at a wall, he then fired the weapon several more times. In the course of his research, he had learned that someone working up the nerve to end his or her life with a gun often fired test shots. More to the point, young Erich wanted to ensure the presence of gunshot residue on his father's hand, should anyone decide to check.

He let the pistol fall to the floor. Leaving the weapon where it lay, he reached across his father's limp body to the typewriter, withdrawing the bloodstained letter that the late Professor Krüger had been writing. Setting it aside, Erich cranked in a new sheet. After inspecting his father's lifeless hands to make certain no blood was present, he pressed the tips of his index fingers to the proper keys, typing out a final missive.

Professor Krüger's suicide note was short but convincing.

It simply read, "I'm sorry."

Briefly, after burning his father's stained correspondence, young Erich exited the house to dispose of his clothes, shoes, and gloves—making certain they would never be found. A painstaking scrubbing in the shower followed, after which he "returned" from the theater to discover his father's body—making certain, of course, to retain his ticket stub.

Later, the findings of a coroner's investigation proved almost as short as Professor Krüger's suicide note: Professor Krüger had been moody and depressed, and in a final act of desperation, he had taken his own life.

Simple.

Young Erich was thrilled at how easy it had been. None of his meticulous precautions had proved necessary, but it never hurt to be careful. And after that, he knew he would have to be very, very careful, for from that day forward his juvenile adventures with dogs and cats were over. Nothing short of taking a human life could match the thrill he had experienced in his father's den.

Except possibly sex.

And for fifteen-year-old Erich Krüger, a young man just discovering the adult pleasures of life, the whole world suddenly blossomed.

As soon as he was old enough to obtain a driver's license, Erich convinced his mother that purchasing him a vehicle might be just the thing to ease the shock of losing his father. After a few interior modifications to a nondescript panel van that he eventually selected—modifications that included a bed, cargo fasteners bolted to the floor, and a locked storage box containing handcuffs, ropes, tarps, shovels, and an assortment of toys with which to continue his experiments—Erich began cruising teen hangouts and shopping malls, always making certain to do his hunting far from home. He preyed on the young castoffs of society—hitchhikers, runaways, flower children, and later even prostitutes—usually getting victims into his van with a just smile and the promise of a ride, or maybe some coke, weed, or a bottle of wine.

And it had been easy.

At first he had simply drugged his female victims and taken what he wanted, dumping their unconscious bodies after he was finished. Over time, however, he discovered that his most pleasurable experiences involved the ultimate demise of his partner. He particularly enjoyed dealing death with his hands, watching as the light in their eyes guttered and dimmed and flickered out forever.

And eventually, that was the only sex he wanted.

Later, concurrent with his college and postgraduate education, Erich extended his hunting grounds to the cities of Los Angeles, San Francisco, Portland, and Seattle. He routinely saved something from each of his unwilling partners—a ring, a lock of hair, an item of clothing—something to remind him. Later he began taking photos and videos, discovering that to be the most satisfying way of reliving his adventures. As always, he was careful to dispose of the bodies where they wouldn't be found until the elements had reduced them to little more than skeletons, forcing investigators to struggle simply to identify the remains.

It had amused Erich to employ his knowledge of forensics and police procedures to toy with authorities, always staying one step ahead. He even kept a scrapbook of the few times his activities had been chronicled in print. It was a pitifully incomplete record, and although his survival depended on secrecy, it had increasingly vexed him that the world was ignorant of the true scope of his activities.

And gradually, despite his better judgment, his desire for notoriety had grown. And in the end, during a paradoxical flash of insight that would forever change his life, Erich had realized his destiny.

The time had come to share his accomplishments.

Now, as Dr. Krüger entered his Rancho Bernardo neighborhood, he decided that additional research on Detective Daniel Kane would be necessary. Perhaps he had underestimated the rough-looking investigator. Nevertheless, although Kane's presence that morning added a new element of danger, Dr. Krüger was also intrigued by the prospect of challenging authorities on an increasingly *personal* level.

Reaching a cul-de-sac at the end of Lunada Point, Dr. Krüger turned into his driveway, admiring the sprawling residence he had built following his retirement from UCI. He pressed a remote control, waiting for his garage door to open. However it worked out, he decided as he drove inside and closed the garage door behind him, the game had just grown considerably more interesting.

Chapter 27
Necktie Cover-up

Working with Detective Aken over the next several days, Taylor, Deluca, and I continued chasing down cold-case murders that might have been connected to an earlier Magpie killing. Bureau agents did the same in Seattle, Portland, and San Francisco. To cover all bases, I asked that FBI investigators include unsolved strangulation murders in San Diego as well.

True to his word, Dr. Krüger sent us a list of students he had taught over the years, both at Cal State and UCI, anonymously transmitting the document via a FedEx fax machine. Krüger's forensic-student names were subsequently added to our database of textbook purchasers. Unfortunately, none of the added names popped up on our other lists, and by Wednesday, when I took a few hours off to drive Nate to his appointment with Dr. Berns, nothing new had shaken loose.

Later that Friday I got an unexpected call from Aken. "You have something?" I asked, hoping for good news.

"Dan, I know we've been looking at manual strangulations, but I just recalled a ligature strangulation I think we should consider," he said. "The victim was a graduate student studying forensics. I remember your mentioning forensics on that first day we spoke."

Aside from being a friend, Aken was also a relentless investigator, and I trusted his instincts. "I'm all ears, Jerry."

"There's a problem. The case is closed, with the boyfriend serving twenty-five to life at San Quentin."

"Then what—"

"Hear me out, Dan. Years back I was lead investigator on this one, and it's been bugging me ever since. The victim, a young woman named Darlene Mayfield, was found with her hands and feet bound to her bed and a necktie garrote around her neck—although the coroner's report also indicated the presence of deep tissue bruising consistent with manual strangulation. The necktie could have been window dressing."

"Go on," I said, starting to get interested. "Except for the ligature, this sounds like our killer's M.O."

"Right. Anyway, at trial the most damming piece of evidence against the boyfriend, aside from the presence of his DNA inside Ms. Mayfield, was a 911 call," Aken continued. "A woman reported hearing shouts coming from Darlene's Venice Beach cottage that night. The boyfriend, Brian Shea, was actually named in the call. The caller claimed she heard a woman scream, 'No, Brian! Don't!' The thing is, we never located the caller. And later, it turned out that the call had been made from an untraceable cellphone."

"Huh. If that's all you had, the case against the boyfriend sounds weak."

"It was. As a result, the ADA offered boyfriend Brian a second-degree murder plea. Brian refused, maintaining his innocence. And he maintained that innocence all the way to a first-degree murder conviction."

"They got first-degree on that?"

"Yep. You know juries. Brian didn't have an alibi, his prints were all over Darlene's condo, his tie was found around her neck, and Brian's public defender was new on the job."

"Any other inconsistencies?"

"One," Aken replied. "Along with Brian's semen, traces of a prophylactic lubricant were found in the victim's vagina. Darlene was taking birth control pills. Why the condom?"

"Could you send me the coroner's report?"

"Sure. Got it right here."

All physical evidence in a California murder trial is retained for the length of a convicted prisoner's incarceration, and indefinitely as long as the case remains open. Either way, I knew the 911 tape would also be available. "I'd like a copy of the 911 recording as well," I added.

"That might take a little longer, but consider it done."

"Thanks." I thought a moment to make certain I hadn't overlooked anything. "Was the body buried?" I asked, considering a possible exhumation.

"Cremated."

"Any unidentified prints in the bedroom?"

"Nope."

"You said Darlene was a forensics student. Where was she enrolled?"

Aken took a moment to reply. I heard a rustle of papers. Then, "California State University, Los Angeles."

After receiving the coroner's report from Aken, I placed a call to Dr. Ryder Songes, the forensic pathologist who had performed the postmortem examination on Darlene Mayfield. Fortunately, Dr. Songes was still employed at the Los Angeles Department of Medical Examiner-Coroner, and he was working that day. Although busy, he agreed to give me a few minutes later that morning.

An hour later I climbed a long flight of steps to the front door of the Los Angeles County Coroner's office. As I entered the understaffed, timeworn building, I detected a hint of ammonia and the lingering odor of death. Glancing around, I wondered how it could have been only weeks since I had last visited to attend the postmortem examination of Sandy Stafford.

It seemed more like a lifetime.

Dr. Songes, a short, trim man with snow-white hair and an easy smile, met me in a gurney-choked hallway near one of the autopsy bays. Songes was wearing a protective necropsy suit—cap, gloves, face shield, mask, a full-length scrub gown, and a rubberized apron that reached the top of his waterproof boots. "Kane," he said, flipping up his face shield and pulling down his mask. "Been a while."

I knew that the coroner's office was overworked. Nevertheless, although it wasn't yet noon, Dr. Songes already looked exhausted. "Too long, Ryder," I agreed, deciding not to shake his hand. "Good to see you."

"What do you need?" he asked, removing his gloves and checking his watch. "I don't mean to rush you, but I have another post scheduled in a few minutes. You mentioned a postmortem exam I performed some time back?"

"Correct," I said, passing him the autopsy report that Aken had faxed. "And it was a *long* time back."

"Nevertheless, I remember this one," said Songes, flipping through a few pages. "You don't forget posts like this. Ligature strangulation that probably wasn't."

"It probably wasn't ligature strangulation? Why do you say that?"

Dr. Songes checked something on an earlier page. "Okay, you need a little background here," he said, finding what he wanted. "In a strangulation homicide, as opposed to a *choking* incident in which food or a foreign object obstructs the trachea, death can occur for a number of reasons. For one, pressure on a specific area of the neck called the carotid nerve ganglion can cause a reflex arrhythmia and cardiac arrest, although that's uncommon. For another, pressure obstruction of the larynx during a hanging or some other ligature-type strangulation can prevent airflow to the lungs, resulting in death by asphyxiation—with the hyoid bone often being fractured in the process. "

"I didn't notice anything about a broken hyoid in your report."

"No, which brings us to a third and more common type of strangulation death. Relatively gentle pressure on the jugular veins can prevent venous blood from *returning* from the brain. Jugular obstruction causes passive congestion in the cranial vessels, a situation in which we routinely see petechiae on the face and conjunctivae of the eyes—pinpoint bleeding caused by the blockage of one or both jugulars. That particular condition *was* present in Ms. Mayfield's case," Dr. Songes noted, again referencing the report.

"And the petechiae on Darlene Mayfield's face and eyes could have been caused by the ligature strangulation?" I broke in, attempting to keep Songes on track.

Dr. Songes nodded. "That, or via prolonged and repeated manual pressure on the jugulars. But here's the thing. During neck dissection, I also found significant bruising over the carotid arteries, deep tissue trauma indicative of substantial thumb pressure having been placed on those anatomical structures—preventing arterial blood flow *to* the brain. It takes a lot of hand strength to do that, and the only way for that to have occurred was via *manual* strangulation, not ligature."

"So Darlene may have died of manual strangulation, with the ligature being placed afterward to throw off investigators?"

Again, Dr. Songes nodded. "At minimum, it's safe to conclude that before she died, Darlene Mayfield suffered repeated and prolonged manual strangulation."

On the drive back to West L.A., I thought about what I had learned. The similarity between Darlene Mayfield's murder and the current Magpie killings was undeniable. After binding her hands and feet to the bedposts, Darlene's killer had manually strangled her for some period of time, then ended her life with a garrote. Or maybe she had already been dead by then, and he had placed the necktie to divert attention from his manual strangulation. Given the inconsistencies in the case, was boyfriend Brian Shea even the killer? Either way, I knew how to find out.

But for that I needed to visit San Quentin.

Next I considered a possible connection between Darlene Mayfield and Dr. Erich Krüger, Cal State University professor. I thought back, mentally checking the dates and confirming that Darlene had been a Cal State graduate student during the same time Dr. Krüger had taught there.

Coincidence?

Maybe.

But I didn't believe in coincidence . . . at least not as a general rule.

On the other hand, Cal State offered one of the top forensic programs in the country. It was a huge university with nearly thirty thousand total students. Darlene had been enrolled in a graduate program, so it was conceivable that during her time there she had experienced no contact with Dr. Krüger and his undergraduate curriculum. At minimum, however, she must have been exposed to his textbook.

Thinking back, I reviewed Krüger's list of students. Although I had only glanced at it briefly, I was almost positive that Darlene Mayfield's name hadn't been on it.

Granted, that absence could be explained by her graduate status.

Still . . .

I decided another visit to Dr. Krüger was in order.

Coming to a second decision, I placed a call to Aken. "Jerry, I need something from you," I said as soon as he picked up.

"No problem. By the way, I sent over the 911 tape. You take a listen yet?"

"I've been out, but I will."

"Let me know what you think. In the meantime, what do you need?"

"I talked with the pathologist who performed the postmortem on Ms. Mayfield. He says manual strangulation was a factor in her death. I'm thinking maybe it was the *only* factor, and the necktie was meant to throw us off. Were any DNA tests run?"

"Just on the recovered semen, which turned out to be from Brian."

"Nothing on the tie?"

"Nope. That was way back before PCR," Aken replied, referring to a molecular-biology technique in which a polymerase chain reaction could amplify a few segments of DNA into millions of copies—making the identification of minute genetic traces, or touch DNA, possible.

"We need to test the tie," I said.

"You think there might be touch DNA on it?"

"Maybe, especially on portions of fabric that were pressed tight against her skin. I would expect Brian's DNA to be present, of course. But maybe someone else's DNA is there, too—"

"—transferred from the killer's hands being on Darlene's throat," Aken finished.

It was a long shot, but given the forensic-student angle, the strangulation murder that matched The Magpie's M.O., and an unexpected connection to Dr. Erich Krüger, my gut said we were on the right track.

"Good work, Kane. I'll get a DNA test on the tie underway."

"And make sure they test for male DNA only, okay?" I suggested, referring to a microdissection technique that could isolate a relevant target cell from an overwhelming mix of other cell types. With it, one could separate a male cell from a larger population of female cells, for instance—creating a clear DNA profile that would otherwise be swamped by the major sampling component.

"I'm on it," Aken assured me.

Next, instead of heading back to West L.A., I remained on the Santa Monica Freeway. There was one final piece of business I wanted to address before returning to the station. It was something that had been bothering me for some time, and right then seemed as good an opportunity as any to deal with it.

After exiting in the freeway in Santa Monica and taking Lincoln Boulevard crosstown, I parked in front of a steel-and-glass office building on Montana Boulevard. Stepping from my car, I checked the name out front: Donovan, Taylor, and Kerr, Attorneys at Law.

Inside, a friendly receptionist smiled as I entered, asking whether I had an appointment.

"Nope," I answered pleasantly. "I'm an old friend of Mark's. Thought I'd drop by and say hi. He around?"

"Mr. Taylor is with clients," the receptionist replied. "They're having lunch up the street, so he should be back soon. Would you like to wait?"

"No, thanks," I said. "Maybe I'll go find him. Is he at that upscale place with the brick patio, just past Pavilions?" I asked, familiar with restaurants in the area from years of Santa Monica lunches.

She nodded. "That's the one."

I walked a short distance to the restaurant. Over the past week I had done some research on Mr. Mark Taylor, Esq., and I recognized him from his DMV photo when I saw him on the terrace, dining with two other men in suits. The three of them appeared to have just finished a late lunch and had now progressed to dessert and another round of drinks.

"Mark Taylor," I said, pulling up a chair and wedging myself in beside him.

Mark, a thick-necked, muscular individual in his mid-thirties, struck me as a gym rat who probably spent a little too much time in front of a mirror. "Do I know you?" he demanded, clearly irritated by my presence and making no effort to hide it.

"No, but I know you. You like to beat up women, right?"

"I don't know what you're talking about," Mark replied, staring at me coldly.

"Really? Does, 'I'll hurt you in every way possible' ring a bell?"

One of the suits with Mark withdrew a cellphone. "I'm calling the police," he announced.

I flashed my shield. "I am the police. Both of you guys take a hike."

As the two men quickly stood to leave, Mark began rising as well. Placing a hand on his chest, I shoved him back into his seat.

"Not you, pal," I said. "You and I are going to have a nice, long talk."

Chapter 28
Leftovers

I spent the rest of Friday at the station, working well into the evening. Along with conferring with Deluca and updating various threads of the investigation, he and I repeatedly listened to Aken's 911 recording. On it, as described, a woman's voice reported hearing shouts coming from Darlene Mayfield's Venice Beach cottage, including the words, "No, Brian! Don't!"

To my mind, something about the call seemed staged. On a hunch, I sent the recording to my electronics friend Hank, asking him to examine it. I also sent the recording to Taylor, requesting that she forward it to her Bureau technicians and have them do the same.

Before the end of my shift, I also placed a call to the warden's office at San Quentin State Penitentiary, the California Department of Corrections and Rehabilitation prison where Brian Shea was incarcerated. After identifying myself, I requested a private visitation booking with Darlene's boyfriend. Instead of making it a compulsory prisoner interrogation, I asked that Brian simply be told I was investigating a case that might dovetail with his, and there might be something in it for him. I added that if he wanted, his attorney could be present as well.

Later, on my drive home, I received a call from Allison. Without saying why, she told me she had something important to discuss, adding that she would see me at the beach later that evening.

Following a solitary dinner of leftover pizza Dorothy had kept warm for me in the oven, I retired downstairs to the swing. By then both Dorothy and Nate had gone to bed, but Callie joined me on our lower deck, eventually assuming a full canine-curl on the planks when she discovered we weren't going for a walk.

Twenty minutes later Allison thumped down the staircase. "Hey, Pop," she said, easing in beside me on the swing.

"Hi, Ali," I replied. Although curious about her presence, I decided to let her get to things in her own time. "You bring Katie?"

Allison shook her head. "She's home with Mike. I assume you heard what happened."

"Did something happen to Katie?"

For a long moment Allison didn't reply. "Do you ever feel like you don't know what you're doing with your life?" she asked at last.

"All the time. What's wrong?"

"What's wrong is, while I was busy with my so-called career, Katie came down with a fever. Her temperature spiked over 102. Grandma rushed her to an urgent care center in Santa Monica."

"Is she all right?"

"She'll be fine—no thanks to me. The doctors think she might have a virus. They ran some tests and gave her Tylenol. We're making sure to keep her hydrated."

"I'm sorry, Ali. I'm sure Katie will be okay. It wasn't your fault."

"Maybe, but I wasn't there when she needed me. I feel so damn guilty . . ."

"Your mother faced this same issue," I pointed out, realizing what was bothering her. "Kids versus career. I'm ashamed to say, I interfered with your mom's decision on that, not that she wasn't happy being a full-time mother. But when you kids were older and she resumed her music career, I don't think I had ever seen her more fulfilled."

"What are you saying, Dad?"

"I'm saying that balancing a career with being a mother is something you have to figure out on your own. Sure, a lot of people are involved—Mike, Katie, Grandma Dorothy—all of us, actually, but it's your decision. And whatever you decide, I'm sure it will be the right choice, and I'll support it."

"Thanks," Allison replied. "I . . . I guess I have some thinking to do."

Allison gave the swing a push with her foot. Rocking gently, we both fell silent, gazing out at the ocean. "I talked with Trav today," Ali finally continued. "He and McKenzie just got a new place in Manhattan, closer to Mac's agency. I'm sure Grandma Dorothy won't be too pleased about that."

"Well, I like Trav and McKenzie being together, married or not. Speaking of which, do you think that's a possibility?"

"Their getting married? I hope so, if only to put Grandma's mind at rest."

"I hear you," I laughed.

"I also talked with Nate. Sounds like he plans to follow in your size-fourteen footsteps."

"How so?" I asked, sensing we still hadn't addressed the reason Allison was there.

"After finishing high school, he plans to take some time off and then apply to the LAPD Police Academy."

"Is that so? Well, your younger brother and I will be having a serious discussion about that."

"No police career for Nate, Pop? Why? I thought you liked being a cop."

"I like parts of it, Ali. Actually, I like most of it. Plus it's the only thing I've ever been good at, aside from playing college football. If Nate wants a career in law enforcement, I'm all for it, but he needs to get an education first."

"He says he can take extension courses while he's on the job."

"Like I said, Nate and I will be having a discussion about that," I repeated, thinking that few things in life turned out as planned. "Is this what you wanted to talk about? Nate's coming up with some harebrained scheme to torpedo his future?"

"Actually, no. I want to run an idea by you regarding The Magpie case."

I groaned. Since the "Blood Moon" murders in Trabuco Canyon, media scrutiny of the investigation had gone through the roof. Although hard to imagine, news coverage had grown even more critical of authorities, with reporters now accusing investigators of incompetence and worse. And to some extent, I had to agree. Time was running out for Snead's daughter—as "countdown clocks" on numerous media sites reminded watchers daily—and despite an immense expenditure of money and resources by both LAPD and the FBI, we were still coming up empty.

It had been twenty-two days since Ella's abduction. To date, Allison had been respectful in asking me for information. Although I generally tried to avoid watching news coverage on any case I was investigating, I also knew that Ali was one of the few reporters who were presenting a fair picture of the men and women working the case. Nevertheless, I had nothing to give her. I shook my head. "Ali, you know I can't—"

"Just hear me out, okay? It isn't what you think."

"All right," I reluctantly agreed.

"The memorial for your SWAT officers is this Sunday, right?"

"Correct. Crenshaw Christian FaithDome."

"The last time a service was held for an LAPD SWAT member killed in the line of duty, over ten thousand people attended. It was the largest police-officer funeral in United States history."

"That's also correct," I said, wondering where she was going.

"The memorial this Sunday promises to be even bigger. Televised coverage will be colossal. Millions will be watching—including The Magpie. He might even be present."

"The thought had occurred to me," I said. At my suggestion, along with photos and videos of every memorial attendee, the plates of all vehicles entering FaithDome parking lots would be recorded and their owners compared with our other databases, hoping for a correlation. Granted, following the Trabuco Canyon murders, the authenticity of some of those lists was now in question, but it had to be done.

"So during the memorial would be an ideal time for Captain Snead to make a direct appeal to the killer, asking for Ella's release," Allison continued.

"Excuse me?"

"Think about it, Dad. What better way for the killer to get recognition than by showing he can be merciful? It's worth a shot."

I shrugged. "Maybe, but—"

"I've already run it by Lauren," Allison rushed on. "She thinks it's a good idea. Channel 2 and CBS Evening News would cooperate with LAPD and the Bureau concerning call-tracing equipment and so on. Whatever you need."

"Sounds like you already have everything all figured out. What do you want from me?"

"We sent a request to LAPD. So far we haven't heard back. I'm not even sure Captain Snead was notified of our proposal."

"Probably not."

"Look, Dad, at this point how could it possibly hurt? And if Captain Snead does it right, he might even save his daughter."

"You want me to relay your proposal to Snead?"

Allison nodded. "Will you?"

I thought a moment. As Allison had said, broadcasting Snead's appeal for his daughter's life probably couldn't make things any worse, and we were desperate.

"Okay," I sighed. "I'll pass on your proposal to Snead. I don't think he'll go for it, but I'll ask."

Chapter 29
San Quentin

I arose early the next morning. Grabbing a Starbucks Venti on the drive to LAX, I caught a Saturday commuter flight to San Francisco, arriving at SFO around 8:00 a.m. After renting a car at an Enterprise kiosk, I drove to San Quentin State Prison in Marin County, crossing the Golden Gate Bridge on the way. Although the prison facility was only thirty miles from the airport, the drive took almost an hour, and I arrived with only minutes to spare before my 9:30 a.m. booking with Brian Shea.

San Quentin is the oldest prison in California and the state's only death-row facility for male inmates. I had visited the crowded, sprawling facility in the past, so I knew the drill. As such, I had requested a private visitation with Shea, realizing that for an inmate to receive a police visit could result in his being suspected by other inmates of being an informant—a potentially lethal situation for Shea.

After checking in with a guard at the main gate and parking in a visitors' lot near the central twin towers, I walked a short distance to the prison's processing center. There, my position as an LAPD detective allowed me to sidestep some of the prison's security procedures, but not all. After identifying myself and showing the Visiting Lieutenant my shield and ID, I surrendered my service weapon, filled out some paperwork, received a pass, and was driven by van to a secluded conference room in the East Block—a section of prison that housed a majority of San Quentin's condemned inmates.

Once there I waited in a windowless cubicle, sitting in one of the room's sturdy metal chairs. About fifteen minutes later Brian Shea was led in, accompanied by two burly correctional officers. One of the officers looked at me and lifted an eyebrow. I nodded, signaling for him to remove Shea's handcuffs.

Once his restraints were off, Brian sat across from me at a bolted-down table, the cubicle's only other furnishing. As the correctional officers departed, one pointedly advised me that if I needed assistance, they would both be right outside the door.

"I don't think that will be necessary. Do you, Brian?" I asked pleasantly.

"Uh, yeah," Brian replied, massaging his wrists. "I mean, no. You won't need them guards."

Brian, a tall, heavyset individual, might have been considered good-looking in his twenties. Unfortunately, his years in prison had not been kind. Now, along with several prison tats, his face displayed a broken nose and a droopy left eyelid—disfiguring additions that had undoubtedly been acquired since entering lockup.

"Didn't bring your lawyer today?" I noted.

Brian shook his head. "That dickwad is the reason I'm here. Why would I want to bring him?"

"Good point," I said, relieved not to be dealing with Brian's attorney. In the end, however, a lawyer's presence wouldn't have made any difference. I wanted one thing from Brian, and he was going to give it to me, whether he intended to or not.

"You told the warden you're here to help?" said Brian, unable to hide the bitterness in his voice.

"That depends," I replied, letting the silence between us grow.

"On what?" Brian finally asked.

"On how things go. I'm going to level with you, Brian. I think you killed your girlfriend, but there are some discrepancies in your case that are lining up with an investigation I'm currently working on. Maybe I can help you; maybe not. Either way, this isn't an interrogation. I'm not Mirandizing you, so nothing you say can be held against you, and you're free to leave anytime you want. Understand?"

"Yeah, I understand."

"Another thing. If you lie to me, I'll know."

"Whatever, cop. Let's get to the part where you're gonna help."

"No guarantees on that. But like I said, there *are* some things about your conviction that raise a couple of questions."

"Oh, really? You think?"

"Lose the attitude, Brian."

"Why should I?"

I glanced around the cubicle. "What have you got to lose?"

At that, Brian's shoulders slumped. "What do you want?" he asked, finally dropping his prison bravado.

"I want you to tell me your story. And don't leave anything out."

Brian lowered his gaze. "Okay, here's my story: I'm innocent. I know every buttplug in here says that, but I am."

"What about the evidence presented at your trial?"

"What evidence? My sperm being inside Darlene? She was my girlfriend, for chrissake," said Brian, beginning to open up. "We screwed that morning. No big mystery there. Same with my prints being all over her bedroom."

"And the necktie?"

"I slept over some nights. I kept a change of clothes in her closet. My pants, shoes, and a couple shirts were in there, too."

"But they weren't around her neck."

"I didn't do that."

"Okay. Go on."

Brian hesitated, then continued. "Look, Darlene and I got into an argument that morning, right before she left for class. She said she was sick of the drive to East LA, and she was going to move closer to school. My video editing job was in Santa Monica."

"And you didn't want to move."

"Hell, no. East L.A. sucks."

"No argument there. Then what?"

"Like I said, we got into a fight. She was unreasonable, as usual. I stomped out. We had fought like that before, and I figured we needed a few days for things to settle down. I drove to work, after which I went home, ate dinner, got stoned, watched some TV, and woke up with cops pounding on my door."

"What about the 911 call?"

"I can't explain that. I wasn't anywhere near Darlene's that night."

"That's it? That's your story?"

Brian nodded.

I stared at him. "I told you not to lie, Brian."

"I'm not! Everything I said is the truth."

"Maybe. But my gut's telling me you're leaving something out. What is it?"

Brian glanced away.

"What aren't you telling me?"

"Just that . . . I loved her," Brian said softly. "I could never have hurt her like that."

I felt a chill. I had what I'd come for.

"And?" I pushed, sensing there was more.

"And that morning, her moving to East L.A. wasn't the only thing we fought about. I think she was seeing another guy."

"Someone at school?"

Brian shrugged. "I don't know."

I thought a moment. "She was a grad student at Cal State. Maybe someone in one of her classes?"

"I suggested that to my lawyer, but her graduate advisor, who probably knew her as well as anyone at the school, couldn't come up with a likely candidate."

"Who was her advisor?" I asked, my pulse quickening.

"It's been a long time. Some German-sounding name."

"Krüger?"

"That's him," said Brian. "Dr. Erich Krüger."

Chapter 30
Touch DNA

Saturday afternoon, upon returning to Los Angeles, I drove directly to the West L.A. station. At my request, Lieutenant Long, Taylor, and Deluca were waiting there when I arrived. Though it was the weekend, time was running out for Ella, and everyone involved in the investigation was clocking overtime, hoping for something to break.

At last, it looked like something had.

Maybe.

All three of them listened as I ran down what I had learned at San Quentin. Even before I finished, I could tell they all saw the problem. Several problems, actually—the worst being that when it came to procuring a search warrant, reasonable explanations existed for everything I had said.

Aken had called earlier that morning, leaving a message that the touch DNA test on Darlene Mayfield's ligature had come back. Along with Brian Shea's markers, the profile of an unknown male had been present on the inside surface of the necktie. Aken had run the unknown DNA through CODIS, the Bureau's Combined DNA Index System containing a database of convicted felons.

No hits.

After hearing that, I had phoned Hank Dexter on my drive back from the airport. According to Hank, the 911 recording I had sent him showed clear signs that voice-altering software had been used to make a male voice sound female. In addition, the frequency-altering algorithms matched an earlier version of the Ircam Flux digital tool currently being used by the killer. Nevertheless, without knowing the exact Ircam Flux settings used in the transformation, there was still no way of reversing the process to obtain the original male voice.

"So bottom line, we have what looks like an earlier Magpie murder," I finished. "With the exception of the necktie ligature, which I think was added to throw off investigators, Darlene

Mayfield was tied to her bed, manually strangled, and raped during or after her death. Or both. Along with matching our killer's M.O., the use of Flux voice-altering software to incriminate boyfriend Brian ties Darlene's murder to our present investigation. Plus, the presence of an unknown male's DNA on Darlene's throat supports Brian's claim that he didn't do it."

"And you believe him?" asked Taylor.

I nodded. "He's telling the truth."

"You're sure?"

"I'm sure."

"This may get Brian a new trial," Long interjected. "But with the exception of pinning another murder on The Magpie, I don't see how any of this helps."

"I have several ideas on that," I said. "For one, we've been looking for someone who's familiar with Krüger's textbook. I think it's more than mere coincidence that Dr. Krüger was Darlene Mayfield's advisor."

"You think Dr. Krüger is The Magpie?" said Taylor, looking doubtful. "Granted, the guy is a narcissistic jerk, but a serial killer?"

"Either that, or someone is setting him up," I reasoned. "Considering the false trails the killer left earlier, I'm not ruling anything out. Remember, it was the supposed 'niggling' and 'paltry' slip that led us to Krüger's textbook in the first place. Maybe that lead was intentionally left as well."

We all fell silent, remembering the disastrous result of our previous rush to judgment.

"So how do we determine which is the case?" asked Deluca. "Is Krüger the killer, or is someone setting him up?"

"If it's the latter, it has to be someone who knew both Dr. Krüger and Darlene Mayfield, probably at Cal State," I replied. "Maybe a classmate, or another teacher? Someone Darlene was dating? We have a list of Krüger's students. We could start with that."

"And if it's Krüger?" asked Taylor.

I thought a moment. "Has anyone touched your ID since we visited Krüger's office?"

"Just me," Taylor replied, looking puzzled. Then, realizing my reason for asking, "Krüger handled my credentials. We have his DNA."

"Right," I said, withdrawing a paper evidence bag from a desk drawer. "He looked at mine, but he touched yours. Since then, have your creds been in your possession at all times?"

Taylor pulled out her ID. "They have," she said, dropping her leather credential folder into the evidence bag.

I sealed the bag with tape and handed it to her. "Fill out the Chain-of-Custody section on the front and have the Bureau run an expedited touch DNA test," I said. "We'll send the results to SID for comparison with the DNA found on the necktie. Oh, and make certain your techs run a microdissection male profile, in case Krüger's not much of a shedder. Don't want his DNA getting swamped by yours."

"I *have* done this type of work before," Taylor noted irritably.

Ever since arriving, I had been getting a strange vibe from Taylor. Wondering what was up, I glanced at Deluca. He shrugged and grinned.

"What?" I said.

"Nothing," he chuckled. "Just admiring your amazing touch with the ladies. Maybe I should take notes."

"Screw you, Deluca," said Taylor, scowling.

I laughed, at which Taylor glared at me, too. "That goes double for you," she added.

"Jeez, Taylor, what's bugging you?"

"Nothing."

I had been around women long enough to know that "nothing" meant "something," and I was just too dense to realize it.

"Let's get back on track," Long intervened. "Kane, you said you had several ideas on this?"

"Just one more. When we interviewed Krüger, he said he had been out of town providing expert-witness testimony at a trial in Arizona. The killer's 'Blood Moon' video was uploaded in Arizona, right?"

"At a Starbucks in Phoenix, to be exact," said Taylor.

I glanced at Deluca.

"I'm on it," he said.

Within minutes, following an online check of Maricopa County Courthouse records and a call to an off-duty assistant district attorney, Deluca confirmed that Dr. Erich Krüger had indeed testified at a murder trial there the previous week.

We listened as Deluca concluded his inquiry by asking, "And Maricopa County Courthouse is where, exactly?"

A pause, and then, "Phoenix? On West Washington? Thanks. You've been a big help."

After Deluca had disconnected, I said, "Looks bad for Dr. Krüger. But if someone *is* setting him up, whoever it is could have followed Krüger to Phoenix and uploaded the 'Blood Moon' video from there."

"For that matter, even if we do match Krüger's DNA to the necktie, his attorney will argue contamination if we ever get the case to court," Taylor pointed out. "Dr. Krüger was Darlene's graduate advisor. She often visited his office, where the two of them passed books and papers back and forth, after which she could have touched her neck, and so on."

"Bottom line, we might be on the right track, but we're not getting a search warrant based on anything we have so far," Long concluded.

I knew Long was right. Probable cause to issue a search warrant requires just that—probable cause. Krüger was in Phoenix when the "Blood Moon" video was uploaded. So were a million other people. Exotic voice-changing software? What did that have to do with Dr. Krüger? Dr. Krüger's name came up in an unrelated case from decades back? So what? For that matter, regardless of whether Dr. Krüger's DNA was present on the necktie, *any* connection between Darlene Mayfield's death and The Magpie investigation was as yet unproved—not to mention that a jury had already found Brian Shea guilty of Darlene's murder.

Nevertheless, we knew we were on to something.

"So what do we do next?" asked Deluca. "Is it time to bring in Snead and the Bureau?"

I glanced at Long. As ranking officer, he had the final say.

"The SWAT memorial is tomorrow, so not much will be happening until after that," he said. "By then we should have the comparison result on Krüger's DNA. How about if we wait until then?"

"Okay by me," said Deluca.

I nodded. "Me, too. You good with that, Taylor?"

Taylor hesitated, then shrugged. "Okay, fine. In any case, we won't actually know what we have until the DNA comparison comes back."

"Then it's settled," I said. "We take our findings to LAPD and the Bureau tomorrow, one way or the other. And if we do get a DNA match on Krüger, we stick to the basics. We sidestep any connection to our current investigation and simply have Aken apply for a cold-case warrant based on new evidence in Darlene Mayfield's murder. Touch DNA from Dr. Erich Krüger, Darlene's graduate-student advisor, was found on the murder weapon, and additional evidence has come to light indicating that voice-altering software was used to distort a key piece of evidence presented at trial—bringing into question the original conviction of Brian Shea."

"That might actually fly," mused Long.

"Speaking of which, if Krüger *is* our guy, then he has Ella," said Deluca, "We can't just sit around waiting for the DNA comparison to come back."

"I agree, Paul," I said. "Let's put a tail on Krüger right now. I'll call Lieutenant Huff in Orange County. I'm sure he has contacts in the San Diego Sheriff's Department who can set up some informal surveillance on short notice."

"That's all good, but what if we don't get a positive match on Dr. Krüger?" asked Taylor.

"If we strike out on Krüger, then we concentrate on anyone who might have come in contact with Darlene at Cal State—especially anyone who knew both her and Dr. Krüger back then," I said. "Teachers, classmates, maybe a boyfriend."

"If it's not Krüger, we should also take a look at any SID personnel who were working at Hertzberg-Davis at the time,"

Deluca suggested again. "Nobody downtown is going to like that, but it has to be done."

Long nodded. "Agreed."

Taylor, who had been sitting on the edge of a desk across from Deluca, rose to her feet. "I'm going to take this to the Bureau," she said, retrieving the evidence bag containing her ID. "We're meeting here tomorrow to carpool to the memorial, right?"

"Nine a.m.," said Deluca.

"Okay, see you then. Kane, walk me out?"

"Sure," I said, suspecting that Taylor had something to say.

I was right. As soon as we hit the street, she pulled out her cellphone.

"What's up?" I asked.

"This," she said, launching a voice message on her phone.

A moment later, a drunken male voice slurred, "Your cop boyfriend won't be around forever, bitch."

"Mark?" I guessed, recognizing the voice.

Taylor scowled. "God damn it, Kane. You promised not to interfere."

"I didn't exactly promise."

"I don't need you to fight my battles," Taylor continued fiercely. "I told you I needed to handle this on my own."

"And have you?"

Taylor looked away. "Again, none of your business."

"Taylor, this is serious," I said, turning her to face me. "I've seen more than one situation like yours end up at the morgue. I apologize for interfering. I do. I'm sorry. I know it's important for you to take care of this yourself. I just need to know what you plan to do so I can sleep at night."

"You don't understand, Kane," Taylor replied, abruptly seeming close to tears. "Anything I do just makes him angrier."

"I understand just fine," I said, realizing that Taylor was still terrified of her ex-husband, probably with a good measure of PTSD thrown in as well. "I've seen mutts like Mark Taylor before," I added. "There's only one way to handle guys like him."

"I know," Taylor sniffed.

"So what are you going to do?"

Taylor took a deep breath, struggling to get herself under control. When she finally spoke, she appeared to have come to a decision. "On Monday, I'm filing for a new restraining order," she said, squaring her shoulders. "And this time I'm going to request that it be permanent."

"And if he ever hits you again?"

Taylor hesitated. Then, straightening even more, "If he ever comes at me again," she said quietly, "I'm going to put him in the ground."

I smiled. "Good answer. Let me know if you need a shovel."

Chapter 31
Busy Evening

Ever since Detective Kane's visit earlier in the week, Dr. Krüger had been waiting for the other shoe to drop. Staring out a window near his front door, he realized that the time had finally come . . . with a vengeance.

At the end of his block, partly concealed behind a stand of oleander, a surveillance vehicle had taken up watch. Though the car was unmarked, Dr. Krüger knew from experience that the hard-eyed man behind the wheel was a cop. Although Dr. Krüger couldn't spot others, he suspected there might be additional units guarding the mouth of his dead-end street.

Now what?

Fighting a blinding headache, Dr. Krüger poured himself a large glass of Scotch. Drink in hand, he retired to his den.

Somehow he had been discovered.

That much was clear.

But as with Kane's earlier visit, the authorities couldn't know for certain. Not yet, anyway. Nevertheless, they suspected.

Or to put it more accurately, Kane suspected.

Probably.

No, definitely, Dr. Krüger decided.

This was no time for wishful thinking. Although Kane might not be able to prove anything yet, he wasn't going to give up until he could.

Dr. Krüger still hadn't determined how Kane had tied the forensic textbook to The Magpie murders. Agent Taylor's flattery about the killer having read his book hadn't rung true, so there had to be something more.

Think!

What had led Kane to his doorstep?

Could it have been the bank account in Newport Beach? he wondered again. *The private mailbox? The firetrap in Trabuco Canyon?*

No.

If they had breached his security on any of those, he wouldn't simply be under surveillance.

Every way he looked at it, Dr. Krüger arrived at the same conclusion: The police might suspect, but they didn't know.

Still, he felt the noose tightening.

Coming to a decision, Dr. Krüger strode to his kitchen and poured the remainder of his drink down the sink. It was time to take corrective measures.

And for that, he would need all his faculties.

Dr. Krüger had planned to wait several more days before disposing of Ella and acquiring a new calendar girl, but accelerating his schedule a bit wouldn't matter. Plus, unless he did something stupid, what better way to throw off authorities than by having another Magpie abduction occur while he was under police surveillance, safely ensconced at home?

Dr. Krüger checked the time. Less than an hour remained before sunset, and there was much to do before then. Later, when darkness fell, he would descend unseen into the canyon behind his house. From there, a short hike through brush and live oak would bring him to his killing van, concealed in a shed off Highland Valley Road.

Then a final visit with Ella; a trip to Del Mar; and back before dawn.

It concerned Dr. Krüger to be conducting his latest activities so close to home. Everything in the past had been done far from San Diego. Nevertheless, might not that very absence draw attention to his home turf—simply by a conspicuous lack of activity? In any case, the constraints of time left him no choice. Everything had to be completed by dawn.

Considering carefully, Dr. Krüger reviewed his plan one more time, deciding that if he acted decisively, it would work. And later, he might even find the means to settle the score with Detective Kane.

In the meantime, it was going to be a busy evening.

Chapter 32
Final Thoughts

As soon as the man entered the chamber outside her cell, Ella sensed something had changed.

He hadn't visited in days, but even then his appearances had become almost perfunctory, as if he had lost interest. No longer did he want to delve into her past, which was a relief. All she had to do was cooperate and take his pills. But now, peering at the man's face, Ella suddenly realized what was different. She saw it in his eyes, as clearly as if he had spoken aloud.

He was going to kill her.

It had been twenty-three days since Ella had last seen the sun. For much of her captivity she had been in near total darkness, and sometimes, in her despair, she had almost convinced herself that dying would be a blessing. Now that the time had come, she discovered she wanted to live.

The man strode to his cabinet and shook several tablets into a paper cup. Then, without speaking, he walked to her cell door and thrust the cup through the bars.

Heart pounding, Ella lowered her gaze. "No questions today?"

"Shut up," the man ordered. "Take your pills."

Over the past weeks, Ella had grown addicted to her captor's drugs, experiencing the nauseating symptoms of withdrawal each time he hadn't arrived. Her physical hunger for his pills seemed to amuse the man, who smiled knowingly each time she had snatched the cup from his hand. But along with Ella's addiction, she had also developed a measure of tolerance, enabling her to remain at least partially conscious during his photo sessions. During that time she had learned the man's routine, as well as what he did while she was drugged. And afterward, during her long hours spent in darkness, she had decided when it would be best to strike.

Now, gazing at the paper cup, Ella felt a craving she had to ignore. If she swallowed those pills, she would never awaken.

219

"I . . . I need to use the bathroom," she stammered.

"Hurry up."

Trembling, Ella shuffled to the toilet. Hands shaking, she drew the curtain.

Oh, God, she thought, *I can't do this.*

Yes, you can, came a voice from another part of her mind. *And you will.*

As she lifted the toilet lid, Ella reached down and slid open the drawer at the bottom of the unit. With trembling fingers, she retrieved her weapon from the compost. She had completed the dagger days earlier, honing the toothbrush handle to a point and thickening the other end with strips of cloth. Against the man it seemed pitifully inadequate, but it was all she had.

Ella tucked the weapon into the front of her jeans and pulled her loose-fitting shirt over it.

She had practiced for this moment, running over the sequence in her mind. But before she pulled back the curtain, she reviewed her moves one last time.

Wait till he leans down to remove my collar.

Right hand to my waist.

Pull the dagger from my jeans.

Stab him in the throat.

And keep stabbing.

"Get out here," the man commanded.

"I . . . I'm coming."

Taking one final breath, Ella slid back the curtain and stepped out to her cell.

Does he know? she wondered, avoiding his gaze as she took his cup of pills.

Without waiting for water, Ella tipped back her head and shook the pills into her mouth. Turning, she hurried to the sink and filled the cup with water, at the same time tonguing the pills high in her cheek.

Turning again to face the man, she drained the cup. She refilled the cup and drained it a second time, opening her mouth to show she had followed orders.

Seeming satisfied, the man retired to his armchair, watching through the bars.

As she had in the past, Ella returned to her bed. Trying to quiet her breathing, she lay on her side and pulled the sheet up to her waist. After a while she closed her eyes, watching the man through slitted lids. When he stood and walked to his cabinet, she spit out his pills and covered them with her pillow.

The man rummaged through a drawer, withdrawing several items. Then, humming, he pulled the key from beneath his shirt and moved to her prison door.

Ella's heart fell when she saw the plastic restraints in his hand.

He's going to tie me up!

In the past, after assembling his camera gear, the man had removed Ella's collar. The plastic handcuffs were new.

Will he still bend down to take off my collar?

Ella's plan depended on it. If he saw her weapon before she struck, her life was over. Fighting panic, Ella gripped her weapon beneath the sheet, forcing herself to remain still.

Still humming, the man dropped several handcuff ties onto her bed. Next he began transporting his camera equipment into the cell. Occasionally he glanced in her direction, but for the most part he ignored her.

Feigning a drugged stupor, Ella waited, her heart hammering in her chest like a cold medallion. Rivulets of sweat gathered under her arms, trickling down her side. And still he hummed, adjusting his equipment.

At last he moved to her bed.

He stood over her.

"It's time, tough little Ella," she heard him say. Leaning down, he picked up one of the restraints. Then, placing a knee on the edge of the mattress, he grabbed her left wrist and jerked it over her head.

Ella opened her eyes. The man was fumbling with the plastic tie, binding her wrist to the corner of the bed.

She gathered her strength.

Now or never.

Pulling her weapon from beneath the sheet, Ella struck.

Her shank penetrated the thick muscle at the side of the man's neck.

The dagger went in deep, but not deep enough.

Again!

Ella struck once more, aiming for the corner of the man's jaw where the big vessels ran.

Her weapon glanced off bone.

"You filthy bitch!" the man screamed, knocking the dagger from her hand.

His face filled with rage, the man doubled his fist.

His first blow struck Ella above her left eye, driving her head into the bed. The second broke her nose, sending a gush of blood streaming down her face.

At first Ella felt only a monstrous, inexplicable numbness, followed by a kaleidoscopic burst of light as the man struck her again. Choking on her own blood, she shook her head, trying to clear her vision.

"Please," she begged, tears mixing with blood on her cheeks.

The man struck her again.

Dazed and disoriented, Ella lay stunned. Floating in a netherworld of shock, she felt her clothes being ripped away, her wrists and ankles being tied to the bed.

She tried to struggle.

The man hit her again.

Mercifully, she lost consciousness.

When she awoke, she saw the man staring down, his face filled with bottomless cruelty. With a small sense of satisfaction, she noticed that a bloody gauze dressing was now taped to his neck, another covering his jaw.

At least she had hurt him.

Ella once more struggled to free herself, straining at her bonds.

The ties held fast.

Through tears of helplessness, she watched as the man stepped away to remove his clothes. Next he walked to his tripod and adjusted the camera, moving it to a slightly new position. A red light came on over the lens.

When he returned to the bed, the man paused briefly to examine her bonds. Then, grunting, he lay on top of her, his breath hot and fetid, his monstrous weight crushing her to the mattress.

Once more Ella struggled to free herself. And again she failed. Sobbing with exhaustion, she finally lay still.

And then it began.

Hands on her throat, the man started slowly, gradually tightening his grip. Blood pounding in her temples, her vision dimming, Ella repeatedly lost consciousness, only to be brought back again, and again . . . and again. And always when she returned, she saw his merciless eyes hovering above, malignant in her vision.

For what seemed forever, Ella suffered a nightmare of horror and pain, an eternity of torture during which time lost all meaning. Often she thought she could endure no more, only to discover that she could. Occasionally he would stop for a few minutes—time during which Ella prayed her torment was at an end.

But always, he returned.

And again, it began.

Hours later, when death came at last to Ella Snead, forever ending her tears and anguish and agony and despair, her final thoughts were of her family.

Chapter 33
FaithDome

I had previously visited the Crenshaw Christian Center FaithDome only once. On that occasion, it had also been to attend a memorial for a SWAT member killed in the line of duty. Back then the gigantic dome had been filled to capacity, but attendance for our fallen officers that day promised to be even larger. Law enforcement personnel and citizens alike had flown in from all over the country to pay their respects, with a huge screen being set up outside the FaithDome sanctuary to accommodate the overflow.

Officers from the West L.A. division had met earlier that morning, gathering outside the station in Class A dress blues. Those not on duty had carpooled across town, with Long, Deluca, and Taylor riding with me in my Suburban. On the drive, Taylor informed me that she'd heard from the FBI lab, and that the profile of Dr. Krüger's DNA recovered from her credentials would be available later that morning. When the results were in, she had arranged for them to be sent directly to LAPD's serology/DNA unit for comparison with the unidentified male DNA on Darlene Mayfield's necktie garrote.

Before leaving the station, I had made a few calls myself. One was to Aken, suggesting that he have his cold-case search-warrant affidavit drawn up and ready to submit—assuming our DNA comparison came back positive. He assured me it was already done, and that a San Diego County magistrate was standing by to issue the warrant, avoiding any venue concerns.

After talking with Aken, I made a second call—this one to Chief Ingram. Regardless of the outcome of Krüger's DNA comparison, we had made significant progress on the case, and it was time to bring in LAPD. On the drive, with Lieutenant Long's approval, I suggested that Taylor notify the Bureau as well. However things turned out, the investigation was coming to a head, and no one wanted last-minute surprises.

Although it was a beautiful Southern California morning, the mood on our crosstown trek was glum. Aside from exchanging a few pleasantries, none of us felt like talking. Forty minutes later, upon arriving at the Christian Center's thirty-two acre campus on South Vermont Avenue, we were flagged into one of several huge parking lots flanking the church. From there we walked to the FaithDome, a geodesic structure built to accommodate thousands. From the crowd already present, it looked like even that space would be insufficient.

As the memorial was being televised, our approach to the FaithDome was jammed with news vans, reporters, and journalists. For once, the atmosphere in the media ranks seemed respectful and subdued. For once it seemed the city had set aside its differences and come together to honor the slain men who had served it, joining hands across race and religion in a way I had never experienced.

Although hundreds of dignitaries and law enforcement personnel were in attendance, the blue-uniformed officers of the LAPD proved the predominant presence. Silent and somber, we stood at attention as four flag-shrouded caskets containing the bodies of our men were carried inside by fellow officers. At that moment, I don't think I have ever been more proud of the men and women with whom I served.

In the wake of a heartbreaking presentation by the Christian Center pastor, Mayor Fitzpatrick spoke, followed by Chief Ingram, Assistant Chief Strickland, several fellow officers, and members of the stricken families—mothers and fathers, wives and daughters, brothers and sisters and sons. And as the lives of our slain men were remembered by witness after witness, as our leaders spoke for once with frank, heartfelt eloquence, as the city joined together to hold hands and smile and sing and laugh and cry, the true magnitude of our wound became apparent for all to see. And, if only for a day, Los Angeles presented itself to the world as a city with dignity, as a city that cared.

To my surprise, toward the end of the tribute Captain Snead stepped to the podium. I had texted him regarding Allison's proposal, then promptly forgotten about it, certain he would refuse. As Snead hadn't known any of the murdered officers, I wondered what he was going to say.

I was sitting in the sanctuary with Deluca, Taylor, and Long, situated about halfway back. For a better view, I turned to watch Snead's image on one of the large screens circling the assembly.

Snead looked exhausted. Without it being voiced, everyone knew who he was, and that time was running out for his daughter.

After clearing his throat, Snead adjusted the microphone and began. "We have lost police members in the past," he said, struggling to steady his voice. "And it is always a tragedy. Always. I didn't personally know the SWAT officers who gave their lives in service to our city, and that is my great loss. I do know that these four individuals personified what is best in the LAPD—not the mistakes of MacArthur Park, or of Rodney King, or of police misconduct routinely fictionalized by Hollywood. Instead, those four officers embodied the spirit of the thousands of women and men of the LAPD who work together for a common purpose: 'To Protect and Serve.'"

Snead lowered his head, then looked up and continued. "But these four men were not just cops. They were heroes, yes. They were proud to be among those who protect our city, but they were also husbands, and fathers, and brothers, and neighbors, and friends. I can only imagine the void their deaths have left in the lives of those they loved, and in the lives of those who loved them."

Snead paused again, seeming to shift gears. "For a brief moment I would like to address the person who killed our men," he said quietly. "Those officers died trying to rescue my daughter. You have Ella now, and you alone have the power to save her. Please let her go. Only you can do that. Her name is Ella."

Snead glanced at one of the screens on the walls. As he did, his image was replaced by a black-and-white clip showing a toddler playing on a swing. "This is Ella when she was a child," he said. "Please release Ella and show the entire world that you can be merciful, that you can treat others better than they have treated you."

The image shifted again to Snead. "You are in control," he said. "Please release Ella. You alone have the power to do that."

With that, Snead stepped from the microphone and turned, not looking back.

"Pretty smart," I said. "I probably would have done the same."

"Why did he keep mentioning her name?" Deluca asked from his seat beside me.

"He was trying to get the monster who's holding her to see Ella as a human being, not as some depersonalized object," I replied. "Snead undoubtedly talked with one of the department's shrinks on that."

"Think it will work?" asked Taylor, who was sitting between Lieutenant Long and me on the other side.

"Unfortunately, no."

"Too bad."

"It was a good try, though. Maybe it will buy Ella some time."

"Maybe," said Taylor. "I hope so."

Just then my cellphone vibrated. I checked the screen.

It was Aken.

"Hey," I said, accepting his call. "Where are you?"

"Down in front. Where are you?"

"About halfway back, near the entrance," I answered, unsuccessfully trying to spot my cold-case friend. "What's up?"

"I just got a call from the Hertzberg lab. The comparison just came back on Krüger's DNA."

"And?"

"It's a match."

Chapter 34
Search Warrant

After Aken's call, I immediately left for San Diego, departing from the FaithDome with Taylor and Deluca in tow. Lieutenant Long said he would catch a ride back to the station with Banowski, advising us to keep him posted.

On the drive to Rancho Bernardo, I contacted the Sheriff's unit currently watching Dr. Krüger's residence—eventually getting transferred to the surveillance vehicle via the 4S Ranch Substation switchboard. After setting my cellphone to speaker mode and identifying myself, I asked, "Anything going on?"

"Nope," came the bored reply from one of the stakeout deputies. "He hasn't gone anywhere since Saturday morning. Up half the night, though—lights on, lights off, stepping out at dawn to bring in his newspaper—like that. "

"You're sure he's been there the whole time?"

"Absolutely. His house is on a dead-end street. One way in; one way out—and we're on it."

"What about his office?" asked Taylor, who was beside me riding shotgun.

"We have a second unit at the business park," the deputy answered. "No action there, either."

"Good. I'm calling to let you know we'll be executing a search warrant on Krüger's residence later today, as well as his office," I informed him. "Until then, LAPD will be joining the Lunada Point surveillance."

"The more, the merrier. You think this Dr. Krüger is your Magpie?"

"We'll find out."

After hanging up, I glanced at Deluca, who was sitting in the rear. "How about pulling up a shot of Krüger's neighborhood on Google?" I suggested.

"Sure," said Deluca. After checking his notes for Krüger's street address, he booted up his laptop.

"What are we looking for?" he asked.

"The stakeout deputy claims there's only one way in. I'd like to make certain he's right."

"Here it is," said Deluca. "Yeah, Lunada Point dead ends, like he said. Lemme get the satellite view." Then, a moment later, "The rear of Krüger's property descends to a canyon out back. Nothing much down there but trees and brush."

"What's on the other side?"

"Wall-to-wall houses. Looks like about a quarter mile across to the opposite ridge. Maybe we can find someplace over there to watch the rear of Krüger's residence—make sure he doesn't rabbit when our guys arrive with a warrant."

"My thoughts exactly."

"Binoculars?" said Taylor.

I nodded. "Glove box."

She smiled. "You're quite the boy scout."

"Yep, that's me," I laughed.

Just then I received another call from Aken. "Talk to me," I said.

"We have the warrant," he said. "We're on our way."

"Who's 'we'?"

"Captain Snead and several HSS detectives, a couple SAs from the Bureau, and me. San Diego Sheriff's deputies will be assisting. Metro wanted a presence, but tenth floor decided that might not be such a hot idea."

"Roger that," I agreed. Following the loss of our SWAT members, anger was running high in the entire department. If Krüger turned out to be responsible, having Metro there would be asking for trouble. "Can you email me the warrant?" I asked. "I'll text you my address."

"No problem. Anything else?"

"Let me know when you're getting close. We'll meet you out front."

Aken's email came in on my cellphone a few minutes later. I handed my phone to Taylor, asking her to check the warrant.

Within minutes, she handed back my phone. "Detective Aken stuck to the cold-case approach, as you suggested," she said. "He also had the affidavit portion of the warrant sealed, but he included it in his email. In the sealed affidavit he cites new touch DNA results surfacing in the murder of Darlene Mayfield, the use of voice-changing software to alter critical evidence presented at trial, and so on. We have the right to search Krüger's residence, office, property, and all vehicles present for any material related to the Mayfield strangulation—photos, videos, recordings, murder souvenirs, women's clothing, biological material, etc. We're also looking for voice-altering software. As such, we're seizing Krüger's computers, electronic storage equipment, and any computer passwords, if found. Bottom line, Aken's affidavit is in order, the description of Krüger's property is accurate and exact, and the list of items to be seized is particular, comprehensive, and related by probable cause. We're good to go."

"Damn, Taylor," said Deluca. "I almost forgot you were a lawyer."

Taylor shrugged. "Another lifetime."

"I have to admit, your legalese kinda turns me on."

Taylor smiled. "At the risk of repeating myself . . ."

"You don't have to say it," Deluca laughed. "Screw me. Seriously though, when we toss Krüger's house, I hope we find what we're looking for."

"Meaning Ella."

Deluca nodded. "Meaning Ella."

Twenty minutes later, upon arriving at Rancho Bernardo, we checked in with the Sheriff's unit guarding the mouth of Lunada Point. A deputy there pointed out Krüger's house—a rambling, ranch-style residence at the end of the cul-de-sac. After studying the structure's red-tiled roof and stone wainscoting, I informed the Sheriff's officer that we intended to watch the rear of Krüger's property from across the canyon, but that we would be returning to join the search once the warrant had been served.

After rechecking the satellite map, we drove to a vacant lot on the other side of the canyon, almost directly across from Krüger's estate. From the elevated vantage, I could make out what appeared to be a dirt road running the length of the canyon below. Overhanging trees concealed much of the washed-out roadway, and in places it appeared to be little more than a trail.

Still . . .

Leaving Deluca and Taylor with the Suburban, I walked back along the ridge. A quarter-mile down on St. Etienne Lane, I found a metal gate blocking access to the wooded canyon beyond. Numerical keypads, mounted on posts, had been installed on either side of the barrier.

I was about to climb the gate when I noticed an elderly woman watching me from a neighboring property. "Excuse me, ma'am," I called, displaying my shield. "A couple questions?"

Regarding me curiously, the woman moved to a fence guarding her property.

I walked over to join her.

"Yes, young man. How can I help you?" she asked when I arrived.

"Been a while since anyone's called me that," I said with a smile.

The woman shrugged. "Everything's relative."

"I hear you," I agreed. Then, glancing at the barrier, "What can you tell me about that gate?"

"I can tell you that in the opinion of an old lady trying to walk her dog, it's a damn nuisance," she replied. "The association put it in after the 2007 fire—supposedly to keep nonresidents from using the dirt road as a shortcut. You know, when traffic backs up on Highland Valley."

"How's that working out?"

"It's not. Everyone knows the code, including people who don't even live here."

"Highland Valley. That's where the dirt road comes out? Is there a gate there, too?"

The woman shook her head. "That's the problem. If there were, we wouldn't need this one."

"Can people still drive the road? Looks pretty rough."

"Sometimes. Mostly it's used by folks on foot, out to enjoy a little nature. The road has deteriorated some, but a car can still get through.

"What's the code?"

The woman hesitated.

"Ma'am, I'm working an official investigation. Are you really going to make me climb that gate?"

"I guess not," the woman replied. "Three, five, seven, nine."

"Thanks," I said, starting back toward to the barrier. "I appreciate your help."

"No problem. You take care, officer."

After thumbing in the code, I waited as the gate slid back on a track. When the barrier had opened enough for me to pass, I squeezed through and headed up the dirt road. Minutes later, after repeatedly fording a shallow creek, I arrived at the base of Dr. Krüger's property. Several hundred feet up the steep slope, partially hidden in palms and live oaks, I could make out Krüger's red-tiled roof and portions of his rock-wainscoted walls.

I also noticed a faint trail in the brush leading down from above.

My cellphone rang.

"What are you doing, Kane?" Taylor asked as soon as I picked up.

I squinted at the ridge behind me. Although I couldn't pick her out, I knew she was up there, with binoculars trained on me. "We may have a problem," I said.

"What?"

"There's a path leading down here from Krüger's house."

"Hmm. Where does that road you're on wind up?"

"Highland Valley. Easy walking distance. Same for the way I came in."

"Damn."

"Wait a sec. I have another call." I put Taylor on hold and answered an incoming call from Aken. "Where are you, Jerry?" I asked.

"Exiting the Fifteen Freeway. We'll be there in a few. By the way, I brought a copy of Dr. Krüger's building plans. Turns out he added a concrete wine cellar a few years back."

"Interesting. See you there." I clicked off and returned to Taylor. "That was Aken. Things are about to get started. I'm heading back."

Shortly after returning to the Suburban, I rephoned Aken. "You on site?" I asked.

"We are. Snead and the Sheriff's deputies just served the warrant. We're about to start tossing the place. Same for his office. Dr. Krüger is not a happy camper."

"Tough."

When Taylor, Deluca, and I arrived at Krüger's residence, we found a thicket of Sheriff's black-and-whites blocking the driveway, with San Diego deputies lending street assistance during the search. Inside, Dr. Krüger was sitting on a bench just off the entry. He glanced up from his perusal of the search warrant as we entered, glaring directly at me.

"Detective Kane. I might have known," he said.

Ignoring Krüger, I pulled on a pair of latex gloves and followed Taylor and Deluca into the house. Then, noticing a bandage on Dr. Krüger's neck, I turned. "Cut yourself shaving?"

He glanced away. "Something like that," he muttered, raising a hand to his throat. As he did, I noticed that his knuckles were scabbed as well.

I found Captain Snead in Krüger's dining room, just off a large kitchen with a south-facing breakfast nook. A half-dozen officers, some of whom I recognized from Robbery-Homicide, were searching the main floor of the house. "Any sign of Ella?" I asked.

Snead looked drained. Wearily, he shook his head.

"Nothing in the wine cellar?"

"Just wine."

"The Chevy Astro van?"

"Not here."

And in the end—following painstaking hours during which Snead and his HSS detectives, Aken and another officer from CCSS, two Bureau SAs, Taylor, Deluca, and I turned Dr. Krüger's house upside-down—that's exactly what we found.

Nothing.

The team searching Krüger's office reported the same.

Krüger's computers were encrypted. If we were ever able to defeat his security measures, we *might* find incriminating evidence on his hard drives.

Otherwise, we had nothing.

As we were beginning to wrap up, I got a call from Long. "Is Captain Snead still there?" he asked.

I glanced over at Snead. He was talking with Detective Aken—all hope of finding his daughter gone, disappointment and frustration written on his face. "He's here," I said.

"We found Ella. Her photo turned up this morning on the internet."

"Oh, God. Is she . . .?"

"Yeah. Same as the others."

"Where?"

"A park in Del Mar. North Bluff Preserve. She was beaten pretty bad."

"The Magpie?"

"Looks like it. Another woman was abducted from a nearby theater."

I fell silent, not knowing what to say.

"You have to tell Snead," said Long.

"Damn," I said quietly.

"You have to tell him, Dan. He needs to know."

"Yeah, he does," I agreed, noticing that Dr. Krüger was staring at me from the entry. "I'll take care of it."

Krüger's eyes followed me as I crossed the room to Snead. "Captain, could I have a word?" I asked quietly.

"Not now, Kane," he mumbled. "Unless it's important, I—"

"It's important," I said. Taking his arm, I guided him into the breakfast nook, shielding him from the others.

"What is it?" he asked nervously, seeing something in my expression.

"It's Ella. She was found in Del Mar."

I watched as his face began to crumple. He opened his mouth to protest. Nothing came out. His eyes filled with shock. "Are you . . . are you sure it's her?"

"Yes, sir. It's her," I said, placing a hand on his shoulder. "I'm sorry, Bill. I'm so sorry."

Tears shone in his eyes, but he held them back. "Thanks for telling me," he said, his voice trembling. "Could you take over here for me?"

"Of course. You want someone to drive you home?"

He shook his head. "No. I . . . I need to be alone."

I accompanied Snead to the front door. As I did, I noticed that Dr. Krüger was still watching. He caught my eye as we passed.

And he smiled.

It wasn't a grin. It was more of a smirk. And in retrospect, I don't think it was intentional. I think it was just something he couldn't help.

And at that moment, I knew.

I walked Snead to his car. A mobile news van was setting up at the end of the street, just past the sheriff's barricade. Although I wondered who had leaked, I wasn't surprised to see the media. Too many people knew about our search to keep it quiet for long.

As Snead opened his car door, he asked, "Where is she?"

I shook my head. "You don't want to go there."

Snead slid behind the wheel and looked up at me, his eyes filled with anguish. "Where is Ella?" he repeated.

"Del Mar. North Bluff Preserve. But—"

"I have to see her," he said, cutting me off.

I nodded. "I understand."

And I did, for I had once done the same for a child of my own.

After watching Snead drive past the news van, I returned to the house. Upon stepping inside, I grabbed Dr. Krüger by his shirt and jerked him to his feet. "You piece of shit," I growled.

He tried to squirm free.

I held him fast.

We stood for a moment, face to face. And in that brief instant, I realized that evil truly did exist in our world, and it was staring at me without a trace of fear.

Still holding Krüger by his shirt, I circled his neck with my other hand. Thumb on the gauze bandage, I pressed down hard on his wound. "Ella gave you this, didn't she?" I said, speaking quietly so only he could hear.

Krüger screamed, struggling to pull free.

"Good for her," I whispered, pressing down even harder.

"Jesus, Kane! What are you doing?" yelled one of Snead's detectives. He grabbed at my hand, trying to pull it from Krüger's throat.

Krüger continued screaming, his fingers scrabbling at my hand. "Get him off me! Get him off!"

Another HSS detective joined in, trying to pry Krüger from my grasp.

Ignoring them, I dragged Krüger even closer, nearly lifting him from the floor. "I know it's you," I said.

Then, with a snarl of disgust, I shoved him away.

Krüger stumbled. The rear of his legs hit the entry bench, sending him sprawling to the floor.

Rising to his knees, Krüger glared up at me. "This isn't over," he hissed.

Shaking off Snead's detectives, I stared back. "You're right about that, pal," I replied. "This is *definitely* not over."

Chapter 35
Drastic Measures

Dr. Krüger was stunned.

His house had been searched!

How had the authorities managed to get so close?

Sitting at his oak bar, Krüger took a long pull on his drink. Fighting another crippling headache, he studied the search warrant one more time.

The affidavit portion of the document, the section listing probable-cause issues, had been sealed by the judge, with the affiant—supposedly a Detective Jeroen Aken, although Dr. Krüger knew better—claiming that forthcoming search warrants might be compromised if the contents of this one were made public. Nevertheless, from studying the warrant's list of property to be seized, Dr. Krüger had arrived at several conclusions.

For one, although the document granted police the right to search for voice-altering software employed in the commission of a crime, nowhere had it specified the hidden-service protocol he was using to post his "calendar girl" photos. Dr. Krüger was certain the authorities knew he was using TOR software to evade detection. Why hadn't that been listed in the warrant?

For another, the right to seize video games and gaming equipment was also conspicuously absent. By now, the entire world knew that the dissonant music accompanying the fiery deaths of the SWAT officers had been lifted from *The Legend of Zelda: Breath of the Wild.* Why hadn't that video game been listed in the warrant as well?

There was only one explanation that fit: Lacking evidence in the current Magpie murders, the police had resorted to investigating one of his earlier killings. Dr. Krüger still wasn't certain how he had drawn Kane's attention in the first place, but only once before had he used voice-altering software in the commission of a murder.

Darlene Mayfield.

Dr. Krüger took another gulp of Scotch, unnerved that investigators had searched so far in the past to find him. And to be accurate, this was the work of one investigator in particular: Detective Daniel Kane.

After Kane's first visit, Dr. Krüger had expanded his research on the vexing detective. The second time through, the results of Dr. Krüger's online inquiry had proved even more disturbing. In almost every newspaper account, Kane had been portrayed as a ruthless investigator, with reports of several fatal shootings, numerous scrapes with LAPD's Internal Affairs Group, two gunshot wounds suffered in the line of duty, and an unparalleled reputation for closing cases. Kane was also described as a maverick, and an unpredictable one at that.

Initially, Dr. Krüger had recognized a dangerous adversary in Detective Kane. In the course of studying the police accounts, Dr. Krüger sensed something else as well.

Kane was willing to play outside the rules.

Dr. Krüger tossed aside the warrant and poured himself an additional three fingers of Scotch. Drink in hand, he retired to his den. Following the discovery of Ella's body, media coverage had reignited, with ripples of horror reaching every corner of the world. As such, Dr. Krüger decided that viewing the news might be just the thing to revive his spirits.

Settling into his leather armchair, Dr. Krüger flipped through the channels, as usual selecting CBS Evening News. On the screen, anchor Brent Preston was recapping the day's events.

" . . . in the wake of an emotional plea made earlier today at the Crenshaw Christian FaithDome by LAPD Captain William Snead," said the foppish blond anchor. "Captain Snead's appeal was later rebroadcast throughout the day in an exclusive interview with CBS correspondent Allison Kane. Ella Snead's badly beaten body was subsequently discovered in the seaside town of Del Mar, California. Ms. Snead has been missing for the past twenty-three days, purportedly abducted by a serial killer known as The Magpie. Following this morning's gruesome discovery, another woman was reported missing from the nearby city of Encinitas. The woman, Ms. Lisa Brady, is assumed to be The Magpie's latest victim.

"In a related story, today police raided the home of Dr. Erich Krüger, prominent author, teacher, and expert witness in the field of criminalistics and forensic science. Sources inside LAPD revealed that Dr. Krüger is currently considered a person of interest in The Magpie murders. The result of their search is still pending."

With a practiced turn to a new camera angle, the self-absorbed correspondent replaced his somber expression with a banal smile. "In other news today—"

Dr. Krüger thumbed the screen to darkness.

The police had discovered nothing in his home, his vehicle, or at his office that could link him to his recent murders—or *any* crime, for that matter.

How could they? Everything that could incriminate him was elsewhere.

The authorities had nothing.

Now that a new Magpie murder and abduction had turned up, the weekend surveillance of his home provided unassailable proof of his innocence. The authorities knew that—yet still they called him a person of interest?

Dr. Krüger decided that someone would pay. Tomorrow morning he would file a multi-million dollar defamation lawsuit, in the action naming the San Diego Sheriff's Department, the Los Angeles Police Department, and in particular, Detective Daniel Kane. Better still, he would file a second complaint citing police misconduct and the use of undue force, naming Detective Kane in that action as well.

Still, Dr. Krüger's reputation had been sullied. Money wasn't enough.

Pressing his palms to his temples, Dr. Krüger fought to control his anger. He couldn't afford to succumb to it. Not now. Later, maybe . . . not now.

Now, he had to think.

How had they found him?

With a shrug, Dr. Krüger decided for the moment to put aside that particular question. In time, the answer would come. For the present it was enough to know that it wasn't a faceless organization that was tracking him. It wasn't "they" who had found him.

It was Kane.

And somehow, Kane *knew*.

Dr. Krüger returned to the bar and freshened his drink. Then, after turning off the house lights, he stepped outside to a large terrace overlooking the canyon. Sitting in the darkness, he thought long into the night, using a cold, detached logic that had served him well in times of crisis. And in the end, abandoning all pretense, delusion, and wishful thinking, he arrived at two pivotal realizations.

The first was accompanied by the admission of an error. It had been a mistake for him to take a new victim. To establish his innocence, dumping Ella's body during the period he was supposedly under surveillance would have been adequate. Abducting another woman had been unnecessary, and now she presented a problem: With the possibility of further surveillance, how to get rid of her?

Before doing anything, of course, he needed to ensure he was no longer being watched.

With any luck, his lawsuits would accomplish that.

Nevertheless, Dr. Krüger realized he was now at risk. Kane knew. He might not be able to prove it, but he wasn't going to give up, either. Despite Dr. Krüger's triumph earlier that day, the time was quickly approaching when he would have to take corrective measures, and there was little time in which to decide what to do.

A few days at most.

Dr. Krüger's second realization of the evening was of a considerably more pleasurable nature. Over the past hours, as he sat alone in the darkness, one thing had become increasingly clear: Kane was the source of his problems—all of them.

And for that, Detective Kane would pay.

Not right away. No, for now Dr. Krüger would have to satisfy himself with legal action. That, and disgracing Kane in the media.

But later, when the dust had settled . . .

And with that thought, Dr. Krüger felt the throbbing in his temples beginning to abate.

But was killing Kane enough?

Weeks ago Dr. Krüger had seen Kane's news-correspondent daughter on television, and again today when she was interviewing Captain Snead.

What was her name?

Allison?

That was it.

Allison Kane.

Dr. Krüger suddenly realized how best to extract his revenge.

Chapter 36
Finish It

Dorothy turned to me from the kitchen sink, where she was busy rinsing our dinner dishes. "So what are you going to do?" she asked.

I was sitting at our kitchen table, staring glumly out the window. For the first time in recent memory, I wished I still drank. "I honestly don't know," I sighed.

After the discovery of Ella's body, the next morning had begun badly, starting with an emergency meeting at PAB. With the exception of Captain Snead, everyone involved in the investigation and the ill-fated search of Dr. Krüger's residence had been present in Chief Ingram's office. The meeting started promptly at 8:00 a.m., after which it had quickly degenerated into a free-for-all of accusation and finger-pointing.

Needless to say, many of those fingers were pointed at me.

Ella's nude corpse had been discovered in the oceanside city of Del Mar, her arms and legs wired to a nature-sanctuary fence. Earlier, a photo of Ella had been posted on the web, uploaded from an internet hotspot in nearby Encinitas. Across the bottom of the picture, the killer had added the words, "Miss July." Although the photo hadn't shown Ella's badly beaten face, her body was displayed overlooking a well-known section of beach in North Bluff Preserve, which had eventually led to her discovery.

In addition, following a midnight screening of *The Rocky Horror Picture Show* at the La Paloma Theater in Encinitas, a young woman working there as an usher had gone missing. Unfortunately, the police surveillance of Dr. Krüger, the estimated time of Ella's death, and the early-morning posting of the internet photo in Encinitas provided the good doctor with an unassailable alibi.

Nevertheless, I knew that wasn't the case.

About halfway through the PAB meeting, Strickland turned to me and demanded, "Kane, what the hell were you thinking?

You were supposed to be investigating *cold case* strangulations, not a homicide that was closed decades ago—a murder for which someone had already been convicted and is now serving time. Care to explain yourself?"

"Yes, sir," I began. "Working under the assumption that the killer might have left evidence in an earlier murder, I contacted Detective Aken and began examining previous strangulation cases that might be related. Even though the murder of Darlene Mayfield was closed years back, Dr. Krüger's DNA turned up on the necktie garrote found around Darlene's throat."

"He was her graduate advisor, Kane. They passed papers back and forth, she touched the doorknob to his office, and so on. She could have transferred traces of his DNA to her own throat in a hundred different ways. That evidence would never stand up in court."

"But coupled with the connection to Krüger's textbook—"

"Bullshit. The killer could have intentionally left the textbook trail for us to follow, just like the voice-changer lead that drew us into a firetrap at Trabuco Canyon. Plus, do I really need to point out that Dr. Krüger was under airtight surveillance for the entire time the real killer was dumping Ella's body and abducting another victim?" Strickland glared at Aken, then back at me. "It's clear where your off-the-reservation thinking got us. Both of you. And to top things off, Kane—you *assaulted* Dr. Krüger. Jesus."

Earlier that morning, Krüger's attorney had called a press conference, announcing that Dr. Krüger was filing a multi-million dollar defamation and unreasonable search-and-seizure lawsuit against the LAPD, the San Diego County Sheriff's Department, and in particular, Detective Daniel Kane. The attorney had added that Dr. Krüger would also be filing a criminal complaint against the same Detective Kane, citing police brutality and the use of excessive force.

"That dirtbag is our guy," I muttered.

"And you're basing that on what? Your gut, again?"

"Sir, Dr. Krüger could have slipped the Sheriff's surveillance. There's a trail—"

"—down the back of Krüger's residence and into the canyon below," Strickland scoffed. "Then what? Krüger hitchhiked to his next murder?"

"Maybe he has the van stashed nearby."

"But he *doesn't*, does he? DMV records show that Dr. Krüger owns only *one* vehicle, and it isn't an Astro van."

"Yes, but—"

"Another thing. If Krüger is 'our guy,' as you claim, where was he holding Ella? It sure as hell wasn't in his house. Your search there and at his office didn't turn up one piece of usable evidence, did it?"

I didn't have an answer for that, at least not one I liked.

At that point I noticed Strickland glance toward Chief Ingram. Tipping his head, Ingram nodded. I would like to think that he did so reluctantly. Either way, the result was the same.

"Detective Kane," Strickland continued, "pending the outcome of an Internal Affairs investigation into the excessive-force complaint filed by Dr. Krüger, you are confined to desk duty until further notice. Also effective immediately, your participation in The Magpie investigation is terminated. RHD will assume responsibility for your involvement in the case."

"But—"

"Kane, shut the hell up and consider yourself fortunate not to be on disciplinary suspension as well. That goes for you too, Detective Aken."

"Sir, can we at least maintain surveillance on Krüger?" I suggested. "Maybe another week? I'm telling you, that mutt is our guy."

Strickland shook his head. "And have the highly respected Dr. Krüger file an additional lawsuit for police harassment? Not going to happen."

And from there, although I didn't think it possible, things at the meeting got worse.

Later, upon exiting PAB, I was confronted by a horde of reporters yelling questions I couldn't answer. "How do you respond to the charge of police brutality, Detective Kane?" yelled one. "When will LAPD find the real Magpie, Detective Kane?"

called another. "Detective Kane, as lead detective on the UCLA murder, did your errors on the case contribute to the death of Ella Snead?"

To all, I gave the same response: "No comment."

But now, as I thought back over the day, it was the final question that had bothered me the most. If I'd acted sooner, maybe Snead's daughter would still be alive.

"Is there anything I can do to help?" asked Nate, regarding me from across the kitchen table.

"Thanks, kid," I said, attempting a smile. "I wish there were, but I have to handle this on my own."

"You're not, uh . . ."

I shook my head. "I'll be fine, Nate. Don't worry, I'm not going to do anything stupid."

"Good. One emotionally disturbed family member is enough," said Nate. Although he smiled when he said it, I knew he sensed how far I had slipped.

"Speaking of which, don't forget our appointment with Dr. Berns on Wednesday. Maybe we can get a two-for-one," I suggested, trying to lighten the mood.

"Maybe," Nate chuckled. Then, yawning, "Well, time for me to hit the sack. Hang in there, Dad, okay?"

"I will. 'Night, Nate."

"Goodnight, Dad. 'Night, Grandma."

After he had left, Dorothy said, "Nate is certainly becoming a fine young man."

"He is," I agreed.

"Catheryn would be proud of him."

"She would. By the way, has he said anything to you about skipping college?"

"And applying to the police academy? Yes, he has."

"What did you tell him?"

"I told him that if he were serious about a career in law-enforcement, he would be better served by first getting a college education. I also told him he needed to discuss it with you."

"Good. I'll straighten him out on that."

"Remember it's his decision, Dan."

"I'll try to keep that in mind."

Dorothy paused. Then, "Even with all that's going on, Catheryn would be proud of you, too," she said. "You know that, right?"

I felt a lump rise in my throat. I looked away, not trusting myself to speak.

"You were mentioned in the news today," Dorothy pushed on. "Regarding your involvement in the investigation."

I looked away. "Grim."

"It wasn't fair of your superiors to throw you under the bus like that."

"The brass will always do what's best for the department. Always have, always will."

"I suppose," said Dorothy. "Nevertheless, it's surprising how quickly things can turn. Two months ago you were a hero."

"Those days seem to be gone. Now I have an appointment to appear with my Police Protective League attorney at an Internal Affairs inquiry."

"Is that what has you down?"

"Not really. I can handle Internal Affairs. I just keep thinking about Ella Snead and what she went through."

"That poor girl. I can't imagine what this must be doing to her family."

I stared at my hands. "If I had acted sooner, she might still be alive."

"You can't think that way, Dan."

"I can't help it. Making things worse, I know who killed her—and I can't do a damn thing about it."

"Why?"

"I'm off the case and riding a desk. Maybe the time has finally come for me to turn in my shield."

"After more than twenty years on the force, would you really just quit?"

"I've thought about it, Dorothy. I have. But the truth is, I'm not certain I could."

"Because this is more than just a job for you, isn't it?"

"Yeah, it is," I admitted. "I can't let this thing with Ella stand. What that monster is doing, all the people he's hurt . . . I can't just walk away."

For a long moment, Dorothy remained silent. Then, "Have you thought about your promise to me?"

"About what to do with my life?" I shook my head. "Sorry. I've been kinda busy."

"Then tell me this. What are you going to do *now*?"

I hesitated. "I already told you. I'm not sure."

Dorothy regarded me closely. "When you started this investigation, you committed to finishing it, didn't you?"

I nodded.

"No matter the cost?"

I nodded again. "No matter the cost."

"Even if it meant ending your career?"

"That, too."

"Then finish it."

Chapter 37
War Council

The next morning, upon arriving at the station, I found Taylor, Deluca, and Lieutenant Long already present in the squad room. "Rough night?" asked Taylor as I dropped into a chair at my desk.

"Didn't get much sleep," I admitted wearily, running my fingers through my hair. "Is it that obvious?"

"Stay away from mirrors, *paisano*," advised Deluca. "Actually, you might want to avoid watching the news, too."

On the drive in from Malibu, I had caught some of the latest coverage on the radio. My name had been prominently mentioned, and not in a good way. Worse, a knot of reporters had been camped out in front of the station when I arrived— undoubtedly bursting with questions designed to add to my disgrace. Cursing under my breath, I had dodged them by parking in a gated lot behind the building.

"We need to talk," said Long. "Let's take it someplace private."

We followed Long into his office. After he had closed the door, I sat at a table opposite his desk. Taylor and Deluca joined me. Dropping into a swivel chair behind his workstation, Long regarded me for several seconds. "I know you, Kane," he said. "You're not going to let this go, are you?"

"Krüger killed Ella Snead. He's not going to get away with it."

"You're sure it's Krüger?"

"I am. I'm not certain how he pulled it off, but Ella's blood is on his hands, along with the blood of a lot of others, including our SWAT officers. I'm absolutely sure of it."

Long hesitated another moment. Then, seeming to come to a decision, "Dan, I trust your instincts. Where do we go from here?"

"Thanks, Lieutenant, but there's no 'we' in this. Just me."

"Wrong, partner," said Deluca. "I'm in."

"Paul, running a parallel investigation on RHD's case is grounds for censure, maybe even dismissal. I have to do this on my own."

"Wrong," said Taylor. "I'm in, too."

"Taylor, you don't want to screw up a promising Bureau career by—"

"We talked about this before you arrived," Long broke in. "Like I said, I trust your instincts. We all do, and we all want the man who killed our officers and murdered Snead's daughter as much as you do. The way things are looking, I don't think our guys downtown are going to get him."

"No argument there."

"So we're in."

I glanced and Taylor and Long, then at Deluca.

"I'm in," Deluca repeated.

"I still have some vacation days left," added Taylor. "Besides, right now the Bureau would be more than happy to distance itself from me."

"I'll run interference, cover for working the case out of West L.A., and provide any necessary investigative authorization," Long added. "As long as no one looks at this too hard, we'll be okay."

"I . . . well, thanks, all of you," I said, grateful not to be quite so alone.

"Now that *that's* settled," Long continued, "and unless someone wants to indulge in a group hug, what do we do next?"

"We're missing two things," I said, smiling at Long's suggestion. "Krüger's van, and wherever he's holding his victims."

"Both have to be close to Rancho Bernardo," Deluca reasoned.

"Right. When Krüger spotted our surveillance, he waited till dark, then hiked down into the canyon behind his house. From there he proceeded on foot to wherever he was holding Ella. Or maybe he has his van stashed someplace nearby, and he drove."

"Either way, the timeline suggests that wherever he was holding Ella, it has to be relatively close," Taylor added.

"Otherwise he wouldn't have had time to get everything done and still return home before dawn."

"And the Astro van?" said Long. "Why doesn't DMV list his ownership?"

"I've seen that before," I explained. "For one, he could have bought the van from a private party, paid cash, and never reregistered it."

"What about the plates and title?"

"He steals new plates whenever he uses the van. And if he were to get stopped with a body in the back, having current registration papers would be the least of his worries."

"So in addition to the van, we're looking for a second residence, or a warehouse, or someplace similar where Krüger is holding his victims," said Deluca. "Property records only show him owning the house on Lunada Point."

"Maybe we could place a GPS tracker on that Mercedes he parks in front of his office," suggested Taylor. "See where he goes. Maybe he'll lead us to his alternate site."

We all knew that placing a tracker on Krüger's vehicle required a warrant, a warrant we weren't going to get. Still, Taylor had suggested it. "Taylor, I'm corrupting you," I laughed. "Good idea, though," I went on. "I'll make an unofficial call and see whether I can get that done. In the meantime, any other ideas on how to proceed?"

"We begin with Rancho Bernardo as ground zero and work our way out," suggested Deluca.

"He has to be holding his victims someplace secluded, someplace where screaming wouldn't be a problem," reasoned Taylor. "Like a house with a basement."

"Right. Along those lines, we could survey building permits in the area for recent additions that could be converted to, say, a soundproof prison," I added, recalling Krüger's construction of a wine cellar. "We could also look for a storage garage within walking distance—someplace he could be stashing the van. Another thing: It's time we found out everything we can about Dr. Krüger."

"That's enough to get us started for now," said Long. "Unless anything else comes to mind?"

After a long moment, Deluca spoke up. "There is one thing," he said, turning to me. "I saw the way that hump looked at you on Sunday, *paisano*. Dr. Krüger has a hard-on for you. Until this is over, watch your back."

Chapter 38
Forest Lawn

Following our meeting with Lieutenant Long, Taylor, Deluca, and I divided up the work.

Reasoning that Dr. Krüger must have another site somewhere close to his house, we elected to limit our search to residential areas in Rancho Bernardo and surrounding neighborhoods. Deluca made a call to San Diego County Planning and Development Services, starting the task of locating Krüger's alternate location. Short of turning up Krüger's name on a deed, we realized that our odds of success were low, but the effort had to be made. On the upside, we had the building permit angle to narrow our search, and if I were able to get a tracking device on Krüger's car, there was a chance he would lead us to his alternate location himself.

Using Google Maps as a reference, Taylor started searching for a nearby storage unit where Krüger could be stashing the van. We set an arbitrary two-mile radius on that, reasoning that on the night of Ella's murder, anything farther away wouldn't have given Krüger time to do what he did and still walk back before dawn.

I had previously done some research on Dr. Krüger, but the time had come to broaden our inquiry past simply searching the criminal databases. We needed to know everything we could about Krüger, and that task fell to me.

The three of us worked together through Tuesday and all of Wednesday morning, by which time it had become obvious that our job was just beginning. Deluca had convinced a helpful secretary at Planning and Development Services to assist him with our San Diego property search, but nothing had turned up so far. Taylor had located a number of possible garage sites for the van, but confirmation was going to require feet on the ground. And despite turning up additional information on Dr. Krüger, including that his wealthy family had originally resided in San Diego, I had yet to make a breakthrough. Last, although I managed to get a warrantless tracking device on Krüger's car, placed there by an accommodating Sheriff's deputy, it had shown only trips between Krüger's home and his office, a visit to a mall, and several aimless hours spent driving around San Diego.

On Wednesday afternoon, with nothing definite accomplished, I took a few hours off to drive Nate to his appointment with Dr. Berns. In my absence, I suggested to Taylor that she continue my research on Krüger, as she seemed to have hit a roadblock finding a storage site for the van.

Later that afternoon, following Nate's counseling session, Dr. Berns stepped out to greet me in the reception area. After shaking my hand, he handed me a new prescription slip for Nate. "It's time to start tapering Nate's meds," he informed me with a smile.

"That's great," I said. "Anything we should know?"

"Just that we will be decreasing his dosage in increments, with several weeks or so between reductions. There aren't any hard-and-fast rules here, except that the decrease depends on the person. We'll see how it goes."

"Thanks, Sid. I'm really happy that things are going so well. And relieved, too," I added, glancing at Nate. Then, "Could you give us a minute, kid? I have something to run by Dr. Berns—not about you."

"About your case?"

"Right. I'll see you outside, okay?"

"Sure. Meet you at the car."

After Nate had departed, I turned to Berns, not certain where to begin.

"I've been following your investigation in the news," said Berns, sensing my indecision. "I feel terrible for Captain's Snead's family, especially after his televised plea to the killer. And although I hate to admit it, the media reports of your targeting Dr. Krüger as the killer are making it sound, uh . . ."

"I know how the media are making things sound," I said. "But between you and me, Dr. Krüger is our guy. I just can't prove it."

"Dr. Krüger? That's hard to believe. But if it's true . . ."

"It's true."

"And at this point he knows you're on to him, I assume."

"You assume correctly."

Berns rubbed his chin. "That's a dangerous situation for you to be in, Dan. Whenever a psychopath feels threatened, he *will* strike back—doing whatever he considers necessary to remove the threat."

"Which is me. How about someone close to me?"

Berns thought a moment. "Good question. That's hard to say, but one thing is for certain: When backed into a corner, a psychopath will turn and fight. In addition to feeling no guilt or remorse, Dr. Krüger probably doesn't fear you, either—making him doubly dangerous."

"He's not afraid?"

"Not the way you or I would be. He undoubtedly views you as a malevolent presence, someone who is attacking him. In a situation like that, a psychopath will typically resort to a purposeful use of violence to end the attack."

"Purposeful, huh? So for him it's a logical decision. No anger involved?"

"Oh, he's angry," Berns corrected. "His retaliation may be cold and logical, but inside he's raging. He blames you for his troubles, and although his primary goal will be to remove you as a threat, it could also include humiliating and degrading you, maybe even inflicting as much pain as possible."

"And to do that, he might target people close to me?"

"It's possible. If he did, he would need to factor in your response. That could make a difference, but I wouldn't rule it out. Be careful, Dan."

"You're the second person who's told me that. Anything else?"

"One more thing. Your killer, like most dangerous psychopaths, will undoubtedly have contingency plans. If he feels authorities closing in, he may proceed to Plan B, or initiate some endgame tactic, or whatever. Again, be careful."

"Thanks, Sid. I appreciate your input. I'll see you next week."

On the drive back from Orange County, I mulled over Berns's words. If my family were in danger from Dr. Krüger, as Berns had suggested, I saw three possible options. One was to remove my loved ones from harm's way, which I had done in the past. Another was to have security units in place for my family's protection, to which I had also resorted in the past. A final possibility was to eliminate the threat.

As far as I was concerned, all three were on the table.

After taking the 405 Freeway interchange toward West L.A., I glanced at Nate, who, for a change, was awake beside me in the front seat. "What would you think about spending some time with Grandma Dorothy at her place in Santa Barbara?" I suggested. "Just till this case is over."

"I can take care of myself, Dad."

"I know you can, kid. I just don't want to worry about you."

"You think the guy you're looking for might come after us? Like before?"

"I don't know. I can't take that chance."

"Trav is safe in New York, but what about Ali and Katie and Mike?"

"I'll be talking with your sister next."

"She won't want to leave."

"I know," I agreed. "I'll deal with it."

Nate was silent for a moment. "Can I take Callie?"

"Sure. Callie would love a nice little dog-vacation."

"Okay, it's a deal," said Nate. Then, "Could we visit Mom?"

"Now?"

"I know it's not exactly on the way home, but I would like to stop by . . . if it's okay with you."

I checked my watch. There wasn't much of the workday left, and we hadn't been to Catheryn's grave in a while. "All right," I agreed. "We'll pick up some flowers on the way."

Ninety minutes later, following a stop at a market in Burbank for a bouquet of yellow trumpet daffodils, we exited the Ventura Freeway on Forest Lawn Drive. After climbing a long driveway into the cemetery grounds, I pulled to a stop below a rolling, grassy knoll where we had buried Catheryn.

By then the sun had begun its descent into a layer of smog to the west, lighting the towers of Burbank in the valley below and the mountains to the east with a soft, reddish glow. I twisted off the ignition. Except for a distant rush of freeway noise and an occasional gust of wind, all was still. For a moment neither of us moved. Finally I opened my door and climbed out. "C'mon, Nate," I said. "Let's go visit your mom."

Heading up the slope, I noticed the smell of newly cut grass. With Nate following a few steps behind, we made our way across a seemingly endless array of brass plaques set into the ground, curving like contour lines in the close-cropped lawn. When we finally arrived at Catheryn's marker, I noticed that it had tarnished since our last visit, blackening to look more like my lost son Tommy's plaque a few spaces distant.

Nate withdrew a yellow flower from his bouquet. Kneeling, he set the bloom on his older brother's marker. Then, moving to Catheryn's grave, he set the remainder of the bouquet atop her plaque.

I felt I should say something, but as usual when visiting the cemetery, I found myself unable to express my emotions. Instead, filled with a sense of futility and sorrow, I sat on the lawn and stared out over the valley below.

And as I sat, my thoughts turned to other visits I had made to Forest Lawn. Sometimes I had come with family, sometimes alone, but over the years my trips had often been linked with turning points in my life. It was here that Catheryn and I had buried Tommy, accepting that the world could be unimaginably cruel. Later, upon discovering that my children were harboring a secret that had nearly destroyed our family, it was here I had realized my failings as a father. And it was here that I had said a final farewell to Catheryn, who had died because of me.

And here I was once again.

I had promised Dorothy to take a long, hard look at my life, and to decide what was truly important. When it came down to it, that really didn't take much thought. My family was the lynchpin of my existence—Trav, Allison, Nate, Dorothy, Katie—and all the people I loved. The problem that this entailed was simple: At times, my job put them in danger.

Not always, not even sometimes, but once was too often.

But as I had told Dorothy, there were things like Ella Snead's murder that I couldn't let stand, even if I tried. And worse, if I stopped being a cop, if I just walked away, would I be forfeiting any chance I might have to make up for past mistakes, any chance I might have for redemption—if such a thing were possible?

"Deep thoughts?" asked Nate, easing down on the grass beside me.

"Yeah," I admitted. "Sad ones, too."

"I miss Mom."

"I do, too," I sighed. "I miss her so much. Tommy, too."

We both fell silent. Finally I spoke again, changing the subject. "Grandma Dorothy says you're thinking of skipping college and applying to the Academy instead."

"I was going to talk to you about that."

"You know you have to be twenty-one to apply."

"I know. I thought I'd take a few years off after high school, maybe work for the police department as a civilian employee, then—"

"We'll talk about it later," I interrupted. "I have an opinion on that harebrained idea, but now isn't the time."

"Okay."

"Dorothy also said something about your mom," I went on, softening my tone. "She thinks Catheryn would have been proud of the young man you've become."

"Grandma said that?"

I nodded. "And I agree."

Nate smiled. "Thanks, Dad. Even with all that's happened, Mom would be proud of you, too."

I thought back, once more shamed by a lifetime of broken promises: My marriage vows. My commitment to be the best father possible. My pledge never again to disappoint my family. And worst of all, Catheryn—lost because of me. I wished with all my heart there were some way to tell her how sorry I was for my failures, but that was not to be.

"Proud? I'm not so sure about that, Nate," I said. "I've made a lot of mistakes, mistakes for which other people have had to pay the price."

"That may be, Dad. But everyone makes mistakes. Like you've always told us, it's what you do afterward that counts."

"Maybe. I hope that's true."

"It is."

I hesitated, surprised to be receiving reassurance from my youngest. Nate was growing up. I paused a moment more, then came to a decision. "Grandma Dorothy also told me something else," I said.

"What?"

I thought back, recalling her words. "She said that pain and loss are part of being alive, and that the important thing is to find hope and meaning and possibly even joy in life, even when things go wrong."

Nate remained silent.

"What do you think about that?"

"I think . . . I would like to believe it."

"I would, too."

Nate looked at me curiously. "It sounded like you just recited Grandma's advice word-for-word. Did you?"

"Pretty much."

"Do you remember *exactly* what she said?"

"I do, Nate. For better or worse, I remember everything I hear, everything I read, everything I see."

"Must be cool."

"Sometimes," I admitted. "Sometimes it's not."

"Do you remember what Mom told me in her letter?"

I looked away, caught off-guard by his question. A year prior to her death, on an evening before Catheryn was about to undergo a dangerous surgical procedure, she had written a farewell missive to each member of our family—just in case. Following her recovery, I had saved her letters unopened. It was only after

Catheryn's murder, on a dismal fall morning beside her grave, that Allison had read them to us aloud.

Turning back, I found Nate regarding me intently. "I remember," I said.

"Could you repeat it for me?"

"If you want. Your mom started off by saying she didn't think of you as the baby of the family anymore, but that—"

"Not that way, Dad. Say it the way Mom wrote it."

"Nate . . ."

"Please, Dad."

"Okay." I took a deep breath. Once again hearing Allison's words sounding in my mind as she read Catheryn's letters to us on that cold November morning, I began anew, fighting to steady my voice.

"My dearest Nate, my youngest. Although I don't think of you as the baby of the family anymore, you aren't a man yet, either. You have yet to spread your wings, and I am heartbroken that I won't be there to watch you learn to fly. Listen to your heart, Nate. And listen to your father. He loves you as much as I do, and he will guide you the rest of the way."

I paused, not trusting myself to go on. "Nate, I . . . I can't do this."

"Please, Dad. Finish."

Seeing the need in his eyes, I took a moment to compose myself. Then, again hearing Allison's voice in my mind, I began anew.

"I know you have doubts about yourself, places inside where you're afraid to look. Don't be. You have so much love inside; all you have to do is let it out. Decide what kind of man you want to be, and be it. It's all up to you."

"Thanks," Nate said softly.

"You're going to be okay, Nate."

"I know, Dad. So are you."

After that, Nate and I sat for a long time, neither of us speaking. And as we sat, gazing down at the monolithic towers and film studios and business parks of Burbank, their glass and steel steeples marching unabated to the distant mountains, Catheryn's final letter sounded in my mind as well. But this time it was Catheryn I heard, speaking to me across a gulf neither of us could cross.

"Please try to find joy in your life," Catheryn's voice murmured in my mind. *"Don't be alone. Open up to the people around you. They love you, too, and they can help. And please don't remember me with sadness. Focus on our good times together—our marriage, the love we shared, the birth of our children, our parties at the beach, our laughter, our friends, all of it—and remember me with a smile. Please take care of our family. And remember that I loved you with all my heart."*

Finally, as the sun neared the horizon, I pushed to my feet. "Let's go home," I said.

Nate rose to join me.

As we started down the slope, my phone rang.

It was Deluca.

With a dark premonition, I answered his call.

"We need you back to the station," he said. "Taylor just found something that changes everything."

Chapter 39
Surprise Visit

I made several hurried calls on the drive back to West L.A., the first to Dorothy—once more asking her to pick up Nate at the station. Whatever Deluca and Taylor had to tell me, I had the feeling it was going to take some time. While I had Dorothy on the line, I also asked that instead of remaining at the beach house that night, she drive Nate and Callie to her home in Santa Barbara and stay there until further notice. Although disturbed by my request, she agreed without asking too many questions.

As expected, my second call wasn't as successful. "No way, Pop," Allison replied stubbornly after I had explained the situation. "I told you before, I'm not packing up my family and sneaking out of town every time you piss off some creep."

"This isn't just 'some creep' we're talking about, Ali."

"Who, then?" A moment, then, "Oh, my God. The Magpie? I thought your search in San Diego was a bust."

"Things aren't always what they seem."

"All the more reason for me to stick around," Allison maintained. "Look, Dad, I'll lock our doors, set the security system, and have someone walk me to and from my car at work. Mike is home now, too. He has a handgun, and I know how to use it."

"I know, Ali. I taught you, remember?" I said, deciding I was fighting a losing battle.

"So it's settled. I'm staying. On another subject, thanks for forwarding my request to Captain Snead. It was a good interview. I'm just sorry that things worked out the way they did."

"Me, too."

"Will you keep me in the loop if something breaks?"

"I'm off the case now, riding a desk."

"When did that ever stop you?"

"Good point. Take care of yourself, Ali."

"You, too, Dad."

Twenty minutes later, after handing off Nate to Dorothy in front of the West L.A. station, I climbed the stairs to the second-floor squad room. Deluca and Taylor were waiting impatiently when I arrived.

"What took you so long?" Taylor demanded.

"Traffic," I replied. "What did you turn up?"

"We found Krüger's second residence," Deluca explained. "Actually, Taylor found it. Along with being a kayak champ and a Bureau hottie, she might actually make a good investigator someday."

Taylor turned. Before she could speak, Deluca grinned and added, "Yeah, yeah, I know."

"Exactly," Taylor laughed.

"Talk to me, somebody," I said. "What's going on?"

Deluca glanced at Taylor. Despite routinely jerking her chain, I now saw a look of respect in his eyes as well. "You did the work, Taylor," he said. "You tell him."

Taylor turned toward me, a flush of pride coloring her cheeks. "Okay, after you left, I continued our research on Dr. Krüger," she said. "I wasn't getting anywhere with his academic life, so I went back and looked into his family history. Like you said, he was born to wealthy San Diego parents—Margaret Summers Krüger and Professor Adolph Krüger. Turns out the money came from the Summers' side of the family. Anyway, when Professor Krüger eventually took his own life, his wife remarried, becoming Margaret Summers McCoy."

"How old was Dr. Krüger when his father committed suicide?" I asked.

Taylor checked her notes. "He was a sophomore in high school. Probably around fifteen."

"Hmmm. Go on."

"Later, Krüger's mother placed her estate in a revocable trust—The Margaret Summers McCoy Family Trust—listing herself and her new husband, William McCoy, as joint trustees, with young Erich designated as successor trustee. Later, a few years after Erich graduated from Stanford, his parents died in a plane crash in South America."

"Could you cut to the chase, Taylor?"

"Okay, here's the thing," Taylor continued, ignoring my interruption. "Dr. Krüger never exercised his right as successor trustee. His mother's estate continues to be held in trust, with Margaret and William still listed as trustees."

"Even though they're dead?" I said, beginning to see where she was going.

"I did a property search using The Margaret Summers McCoy Family Trust as owner of record," Taylor continued, again checking her notes. "The trust holds title to a residence in the Santaluz subdivision of Black Mountain Ranch."

"Where is that?"

"Seven miles from Krüger's Rancho Bernardo home."

"I checked with DMV," Deluca jumped in. "The trust also holds title to a 2004 Chevy Astro cargo van. For the past number of years, the property taxes on the Black Mountain Ranch residence and the van registration fees have been paid by Krüger Criminalistics Consulting, Inc. And here's the clincher: Five years ago, the trust applied for a building permit, submitting plans to construct a photography darkroom in the basement of the Santaluz house."

We all fell silent.

We had found Dr. Krüger's kill site, and possibly where he was storing the van as well.

"Good work, both of you," I said, breaking the silence.

"Thanks," said Taylor. "Now what?"

"Paul, can you bring up the Black Mountain Ranch property on Google?" I asked, considering what to do next.

"No problem. Gimme a sec," said Deluca, heading back to his workstation.

"I meant what I said just now, Taylor," I continued after Paul had left. "You did good. Really good."

Taylor smiled. Then, with a glance at Deluca, she lowered her voice. "I realize that I said it was none of your business, but I want you to know I filed for a new domestic violence restraining order against Mark. A temporary restraining order is now in place, with a court hearing set for two weeks."

I nodded. "You're doing the right thing, Taylor. If you need anything—"

"I'm okay. But . . . thanks."

"Check it out," Deluca called from his desk. "Krüger's house in Black Mountain Ranch."

Taylor and I crossed to Deluca's desk, peering over his shoulder at a satellite image on his screen.

"Can you zoom in?" I asked.

"Some," said Deluca, increasing the magnification. "Jeez, the place is huge."

I stared at the sprawling, Spanish-style residence on Deluca's display. The huge, one-story structure sat on what appeared to be several landscaped acres. A wide, curving driveway accessed the house and garage, guarded by a security gate at the street. In the rear, an enormous swimming pool overlooked a golf fairway and a pond to the west. The nearest neighbor was hundreds of yards distant.

"Plenty of privacy," Taylor noted.

"Roger that," I agreed.

"What now?" asked Deluca.

"Still not enough for a warrant. Not even close," said Taylor.

"Especially with Krüger's pending lawsuits," added Deluca.

I thought for a moment. "Does Lieutenant Long know what you two turned up?"

Deluca shook his head. "He left early today."

"I'll call and fill him in," I said. "I'm going to be vague about what comes next, however—give him deniability if things go south."

"If *what* things go south?" asked Taylor.

"I'm going down there to take a look."

"Damn, Kane. Don't you think we should take this to the brass?" suggested Deluca.

"Not yet. For one, it's going to be tough explaining why we're still working the case. I was ordered not to, remember? Besides, this time we have to be absolutely certain before we move."

"Yes, but—"

"Look, we don't have enough for a warrant, as you both pointed out. What will the guys upstairs do besides chew us out and then screw things up? Which leaves us one option: Someone has to check out that house."

"And that someone is you."

I nodded. "Depending on what I find, we'll proceed from there."

"I'm going with you," said Deluca.

"Not necessary, Paul. Like I said, if this turns bad, it could be a career-ender."

"I'm going with you."

"Damn," said Taylor. "I suppose I am, too."

I regarded them both. "I'm not going to underestimate Krüger this time. We don't know for certain yet what's down there. If things go wrong, I'll take the heat. No sense in everyone getting screwed. Agreed?"

"I don't like it," Deluca replied. "But . . . yeah. If that's the way you want to play it."

"That's the way I want to play it. Taylor?"

Taylor hesitated, then nodded. "I don't like it either. But, okay."

"Good. Let's hit the road. We have a long drive ahead, and there's a stop I want to make on the way."

Twenty minutes later I pulled to the curb in front of a well maintained, colonial-style home in Hancock Park. I double-checked the address, then killed the engine.

"You sure you want to do this, *paisano*?" asked Deluca.

"I'm sure," I said.

"Then good luck," said Taylor.

After sliding from behind the wheel, I proceed up a flagstone walkway to the front door of the house. At the top of a brick landing, I rang the doorbell. A moment later a light came on.

"Can I help you?" asked a pretty young girl, peering through a sliver of doorway. I noticed that the security chain was still in place, and that the girl had been crying.

"Would you please tell your father that Detective Kane is here?" I said.

The girl closed the door. A full minute passed before the door reopened.

"What are you doing here?" Captain Snead demanded, glaring at me from the doorway, his eyes red-rimmed and swollen. Behind him stood a tall, attractive woman in her early forties. Clearly, she had been grieving as well.

"I'm sorry to intrude," I said. "Something has come up. May I speak with you in private, Captain?"

"God damn it, Kane. This is not the time."

"I know, and I'm truly sorry, but you'll want to hear what I have to say."

Snead turned to the woman. "Will you give us a minute, Beth?" Then, stepping to the landing, he closed the door behind him. I don't think I have ever seen anyone look so angry and so broken at the same time.

He regarded me for a long moment without speaking. Then something changed in his eyes. "You found him, didn't you?"

"We *already* found him. It's Krüger. But now we know where he's holding his victims."

"Bullshit, Kane. Krüger can't be the killer. The Sherriff's surveillance proved that. You were ordered not to pursue the case any further. Now you have the gall to show up here and—"

"It's Krüger," I interrupted.

Snead hesitated. "How can you—"

"Listen to me," I said, again cutting him off. "I'm here because you deserve to know."

"Know what?"

And so I told him.

And as I spoke, as I laid out everything we knew, I saw Snead's expression change from disbelief, to surprise, and finally to acceptance—hardening to a look of grim resolve.

"Despite all that, there's still not enough to proceed with a warrant," I finished. "And now with Krüger hiding behind his lawyers, there may never be."

"True," said Snead. "Worse, he's probably getting rid of evidence as we speak. And he's holding another woman."

"I'm going down there."

"I'm going with you."

"I thought you might say that. You realize this is completely off the grid?"

"I'm going with you."

"If anyone deserves to be present when this goes down, it's you," I agreed. "One condition, though. Two, actually."

"What?"

"Rank aside, you are not calling the shots tonight. Understood?"

Snead nodded. "And your second condition?"

"There's a chance this might backfire. That asshole has already cost everyone enough—especially you. When we get down there, I'm checking out that house alone."

Chapter 40
Endgame

O ver the past several days, Dr. Krüger had spent considerable time making certain he was no longer being watched. Meticulous perusals of his neighborhood, unexpected reversals while driving, and checks in his rearview mirror on the trip to and from his office had convinced him that the police presence was truly gone.

As an added precaution, however, upon returning from work on Tuesday he had searched his Mercedes for tracking devices, examining his vehicle from bumper to bumper. To his dismay, he had found a small GPS tracker hidden in the left rear tire well.

After careful consideration, Dr. Krüger left the tracking device in place.

The police presence was gone, but he was still being watched. With the discovery of the tracker, Dr. Krüger decided that the time had come to end his current game. Although he had never believed the necessity would actually arise, he had emergency plans for almost every conceivable situation. Tonight he would initiate the most encompassing of those strategies. He was disappointed to be terminating his latest game before its completion, and for that he blamed Kane. Nevertheless, all good things must come to an end, and later he would initiate a new game. He already had a few ideas on that—several of which involved Detective Kane.

In the meantime, on that very night, he would finish with his latest calendar girl, dispose of her body, and burn his parents' residence to the ground—an endgame tactic that in one bold stroke would eliminate all evidence against him. Everything, with the exception of a few items he would need to destroy by hand, would vanish in a cleansing fire—his precious photographs and videos, his exquisite souvenirs and mementos, his cameras and computers and surveillance equipment, even the van—leaving nothing to tie him to any of his recent kills.

But first Dr. Krüger had a few stops to make, and for that he needed the van.

Later that evening, after removing the GPS device from his Mercedes and leaving the tracker in his garage, Dr. Krüger exited the 15 Freeway on West Bernardo. From there he took Highland Valley east. Minutes later he pulled onto a dirt road, stopping in front of a metal storage shed. There, after opening a padlocked garage door, he exchanged his vehicle for the Chevy Astro van, leaving the Mercedes in its place. Before relocking the shed, he unpacked a number of gasoline containers he had stored inside, loading them into the van.

Next, a short drive to Home Depot in Poway for a few supplies, stops at several service stations to avoid drawing attention by filling all the gas containers at the same location, and a final trip to Black Mountain Ranch.

As he slid behind the wheel of the van, Dr. Krüger's thoughts turned to his newest acquisition. Although he hadn't visited her since the night of her abduction, the prospect of seeing her again was a bright spot in an otherwise unfortunate conclusion to his latest adventure.

Nevertheless, conclude it he must.

Dr. Krüger twisted the ignition and started the van.

Time was growing short, and there was much to do.

Chapter 41
Santaluz

After badging my way past a Black Mountain Ranch security gate, I drove into the Santaluz subdivision. Minutes later I cruised past Dr. Krüger's second residence. As were many homes in the area, Krüger's house was dark. After making a second pass, I pulled to a stop several blocks down on Sendero Angelica, parking in a secluded spot with a view of Krüger's property.

"Bigger than it looked on Google," said Deluca. "And it appears nobody's home."

"Maybe," I said. "Where's his Mercedes?"

Deluca opened a phone app and checked the location of Krüger's tracking device. "Still at his house in Rancho Bernardo," he said.

"Good."

"Now what?" asked Snead, who was sitting in the back seat with Deluca. "I assume you have a plan."

For the most part, Snead had remained silent on the ride to San Diego. I knew he was uncomfortable with what was about to go down. We all were. What I planned to do entailed serious risks, but they were risks that I felt were necessary. In addition to making absolutely certain of Krüger's guilt and possibly even freeing his latest victim, I hoped to find evidence that could surface in some other way, thereby providing grounds for a new search warrant.

On the downside, I also knew that anything I discovered in Krüger's house that night would be worthless in court. My warrantless entry, not to mention our having placed an illegal tracking device on his vehicle, could invalidate any evidence obtained later—possibly even poisoning the entire case. Nevertheless, another young woman's life hung in the balance. Given the situation, I didn't see any other way.

I thought a moment. Then, in reply to Snead's question, I said, "The plan is for all of you to remain here while I reconnoiter the property. I'm going to sniff around, maybe look in a few windows," I added, lying.

When it came to Taylor and Deluca, it wasn't an issue of trust. As I had with Lieutenant Long, I simply wanted to provide them with some measure of deniability, should things come to that. Trusting Snead, however, was another story. "I'll stay in contact, but I'm going to mute my phone, so you won't be able to talk to me," I went on. "Depending on what I find, we'll go from there."

"Great plan," Snead muttered.

"You sure about this, Kane?" asked Taylor.

I shrugged. "Anyone have a better idea?"

No one answered.

"Okay," I said. Then, leaning across the seat and rummaging through the contents of my glove compartment, I withdrew a flashlight, a pouch containing a lock pick set, and a pair of latex gloves.

Although Taylor noticed the pick set, she remained silent.

Upon pocketing the flashlight and pick set, I stepped to the pavement and pulled out my phone. After setting my ringer and speaker volume to mute, I called Deluca's cell. As he answered, I dropped my phone into a jacket pocket. "Hear me okay?" I asked, speaking in a normal voice.

Deluca gave a thumbs-up from the rear of the car.

"Good," I said. "I'll be in touch."

As I turned to go, Taylor rolled down her window. "Kane?"

I looked back.

"Be careful."

Walking briskly up the moonlit street, I approached Krüger's residence. Upon reaching his security gate, I again checked the house. It sat at the end of a long paver driveway, partly hidden in trees and shrubs. The lights were still out.

After snapping on my latex gloves and vaulting the six-foot gate, I paused on the other side. Reaching inside my jacket, I withdrew my service weapon. Easing the slide rearward, I checked the Glock to confirm the presence of a chambered round.

I had thirteen more in the Glock's magazine, and a pair of spare magazines in my shoulder rig as well.

Satisfied that I was ready, I started up the driveway, staying close to the trees along one side. When I reached the house, I looked through a window facing the street.

Nothing was moving inside.

Deciding to take a direct approach, I crossed to the front door, holding the Glock behind my back as I topped a short flight of stairs. Standing on the landing, I peered through a side window, spotting a security panel in the entry. Not surprisingly, the system was off. If Krüger were holding a hostage inside, the last thing he would want in his absence would be for the police to respond to an alarm.

I listened.

Nothing.

I tried the doorknob.

Locked.

Above the knob was a Kwikset SmartKey deadbolt, described by the manufacturer as "unpickable." Although no lock was impossible to pick, rake, or bump, I didn't have the time. Besides, I figured there had to be an easier way in.

I turned to leave, then hesitated. Although the house was dark, I wanted to make absolutely certain no one was present. If Krüger were inside, it would be better to know before attempting an illegal entry.

Holding the Glock ready at my side, I rapped on the door.

****

Dr. Krüger paused in the bedroom, resisting an impulse to turn on the lights. Over the past minutes his eyes had adjusted to the darkness, and besides, his preparations were nearly complete. With the final five-gallon gasoline container now in place, he was ready to tackle a far more enjoyable task in the basement.

Of course, fire investigators would detect the presence of the gasoline accelerant. There was no way around that. As a result, the conflagration would undoubtedly be ruled as arson, invalidating his insurance coverage. There was no way around that, either. Still, the property wouldn't be a total loss. He could still sell the lot, whose value had risen astronomically over the past several years.

As for who was responsible for the blaze—well, that would forever remain a mystery. The authorities, including Kane, might suspect, but they wouldn't know . . . not for certain.

After all, why would Dr. Krüger torch his deceased parents' residence?

Why, indeed?

Upon arriving at the Black Mountain property, Dr. Krüger had spent an amusing hour in the basement getting acquainted with his latest acquisition. Initially Ms. Brady had resisted, as had most of his young women. It was gratifying to see how quickly the lovely Lisa's attitude had changed after just a few jolts from her training collar.

Because anticipation always played an important part in the process, Dr. Krüger had delayed drugging his attractive visitor until completing his upstairs preparations. Now that a container of gasoline sat in nearly every room of the house, it was time to proceed to the evening's main event.

Once again, it pained Dr. Krüger to have so little time to enjoy his new guest, but short and sweet was better than none at all. And with that pleasant thought, he turned to make his way back through the darkened house, heading for the basement.

Suddenly, a sound.

Someone knocking?

Dr. Krüger froze.

Someone was at the door.

****

"I'm on the front landing," I said aloud, checking in with Deluca. "No movement inside. I'm heading around back."

Walking quickly, I made my way around the side of the house, looking in every window on the way. Upon reaching a terrace at the rear of the property, I found a door leading into the garage. Like the door at the front entry, it was protected by a "pickproof" SmartKey deadbolt.

Clearly, someone didn't want intruders.

Hands cupped to an adjacent window, I peered inside.

The dimly lit space beyond was empty, with the exception of a single vehicle.

In one of the four garage stalls, someone had parked a Chevrolet Astro van.

"White Chevy van in the garage," I said aloud.

Squinting through the glass, I also saw what appeared to be an entrance into the main house.

Coming to a decision, I removed my jacket and wadded it against the window. Using my elbow, I gave the glass a sharp rap. The pane shattered, clinking to the floor inside. After removing several remaining shards of glass, I reached through. Straining to extend my arm, I twisted a thumb latch on the entry door.

After redonning my jacket, I opened the door.

I listened.

No alarm.

I slipped inside.

Except for the van, a mountain bike, and several cardboard boxes stacked in one corner, the garage was empty.

I felt the hood of the van.

Cold.

Quietly, I moved to the door leading into the house.

I tried the knob.

Again, locked.

This time the deadbolt was a Baldwin.

With a smile, I pulled out my pick set. Working quickly, I inserted a tension wrench into the deadbolt's keyway and twisted, maintaining slight pressure with my left hand. With my right, I scrubbed with a pick, raking the Baldwin's pins. One by one, all five clicked into place. Thirty seconds from starting, I rotated the cylinder.

I was in.

Chapter 42
Forever Blind

Before moving into the house, I stopped in a mudroom just off the garage, giving my eyes a few minutes to adjust to the darkness. Although I had my flashlight tucked in a jacket pocket, I could already see fairly well in the moonlight filtering in from outside, and I decided not to use it.

While I waited, I listened. With the exception of an appliance hum from somewhere close and the ticking of a clock from farther inside the house, I heard nothing. Nevertheless, before locating Krüger's basement, I decided to search the main floor to confirm that the residence was unoccupied.

"Back door was unlocked. Taking a look inside," I said aloud, starting to move.

The first room I entered was a kitchen: central island, eight-burner stove, double oven, an eating counter with stools, and a breakfast nook to one side. At the far end was an alcove containing a washer/dryer combo and small desk. I also noticed a door with a self-closing arm at the top.

The basement?

I crossed the kitchen and cracked the door. A stairway led down, accessing a pitch-black space below.

Check it out?

Not yet.

Clear the ground floor first.

I retraced my steps, easing back through the kitchen.

Glock extended in a two-handed grip, I crept deeper into the house.

****

From his hiding place in the pantry, Dr. Krüger listened as the intruder moved past. Moments later he heard the man pause in the dining room. "Gas cans everywhere," the man said aloud, undoubtedly communicating with someone outside.

Dr. Krüger recognized the voice.

Kane.

This can't be happening.

But against all reason, it was.

There has to be a way out.

Dr. Krüger regretted not having one of his handguns. Several were stashed in the Rancho Bernardo house, but it had never seemed necessary to keep a weapon in his parents' residence. He had a pistol concealed in the van, of course—in case he were ever stopped at an inconvenient moment.

Could he sneak to the van and get it?

Too risky.

Besides, a gunfight with Kane would probably end badly.

Examine the facts.

Kane had broken into the house, which meant he didn't have a warrant. Again, Kane was playing outside the rules. At some point he would descend to the basement, which presented possibilities. After careful consideration, Dr. Krüger decided that with an adjustment to his endgame plan, things might still work out.

Clearly, he would be unable to dispose of his latest victim before starting the fire. She and Kane must die together, leaving their bodies for investigators to discover in the ashes. Nevertheless, with a little luck, nothing that happened there that night could be tied to him.

With the gas accelerants in place, the fire would spread so quickly that Kane's associates, wherever they were, would have little time to react. In the confusion sparked by the blaze, Dr. Krüger could slip unnoticed out the back. Upon retrieving his bike and traversing the golf fairway, it was a short ride to an unguarded residents' gate to the south.

And from there, to freedom.

Granted, the presence of the bodies and the circumstance of the fire would put Dr. Krüger under considerable suspicion. Nevertheless, once he had returned to his own residence, there would be nothing to actually *prove* any of this was his doing. The authorities might suspect, but they would have no physical evidence to support that suspicion. Otherwise, why had Kane undertaken an illegal search in the first place? In fact, Kane's breaking into the Black Mountain property made anything discovered there inadmissible in court.

For that matter, who was to say that someone other than Dr. Krüger—the real Magpie, for instance— hadn't been using Krüger's parents' vacant house for his own purposes, setting up poor Dr. Krüger to take the blame? What's more, hadn't Dr. Krüger already been proved innocent by the earlier surveillance?

With a sense of renewed confidence, Dr. Krüger decided that in the unlikely event he were ever to face charges, with a smart lawyer and a sympathetic jury, he would never be convicted.

****

After checking the kitchen and dining room, I moved quietly through the rest of Krüger's house—clearing bedrooms, bathrooms, closets, a gigantic living room, an office filled with servers and computer equipment, and a den. With the exception of the living room and den, all lacked even the barest of furnishings. On the other hand, almost all contained a five-gallon jug of gasoline.

As a precaution on my way back to the kitchen, I unlocked the front door, leaving it ajar. "Front door's open," I said quietly.

Upon returning to the kitchen, I grabbed a stool from the counter and crossed to the alcove. "Main floor is deserted," I said aloud. "Checking the basement."

I opened the self-closing door and jammed the stool in the doorway, making certain it stayed open. Stepping through, I paused on the top landing.

Darkness below.

I listened.

A hushed roar, like a furnace.

Otherwise, nothing.

I withdrew my flashlight and turned it on. Gun atop my opposite wrist, Glock and flashlight now joined as one, I eased down the stairs.

Along one side of the staircase, someone had installed a ramp.

Something to help transport victims?

I stopped at the bottom. A passage led off into the darkness. I shined my light down the narrow hallway.

To the left, a door with an observation slit.

Farther down, two additional doors and a furnace at the end.

Gun out front, I eased forward.

I stopped at the door with the observation slit and shined my light through the glass. On the other side I saw what looked like a prison gate, with vertical iron bars running floor to ceiling.

Heart pounding, I tried the door.

It was unlocked.

I stepped through, swinging my light over the windowless room beyond.

I heard a sound.

I froze.

"Don't move," I ordered, stabbing my light into the darkness.

Caught in my beam, a young woman crouched beside a small bed, cowering in her underwear.

"Please don't hurt me any more," she begged, her long, dark hair falling in her face. I felt a chill, noticing a dog-training collar circling her throat.

"I'm not going to hurt you," I said. "I'm a cop."

The young woman squinted into my light. Lowering the beam, I swung it over the rest of the room. Against one wall, a cabinet and shower. Nearby, what looked like a chemical toilet. On the ceiling, an industrial light, like something you might see on a ship. And a webcam.

"Get me out of here," the woman sobbed, close to hysteria.

I lifted the light to my face and brought my finger to my lips, signaling her to be quiet.

"Don't leave me," she pleaded.

I checked the iron gate.

Locked.

"I don't have the key," I whispered.

"He wears it around his neck. Please, please, get me out."

"I'll come back," I promised. "I have two other places to check." Then, seeing something in her face, "Is he still here?"

"Oh, God," she said. "You don't have him?"

Suddenly I heard a door slam.

I rushed back into the hallway.

"Don't leave me, you bastard!" the young woman screamed. "Get me out of here!"

I bolted up the stairs, taking them three at a time.

The door at the top was locked.

With a sinking feeling, I smelled gasoline.

****

"Maybe we should go in," said Deluca.

Snead glared. "And compound Kane's illegal entry by adding more bodies to the mix? That's your idea of fixing things?"

"Actually, it is," Deluca replied. "What do you think, Taylor?"

Taylor hesitated. "Kane told us to wait, but we haven't heard anything from him since he entered the basement. He might need help."

"God damn it, it sounds like you two knew he was going to enter that house," said Snead.

"Krüger may be holding another victim in there," Taylor replied. "What exactly did you expect Kane to do?"

Just then a woman's voice sounded from Deluca's cellphone. "Don't leave me, you bastard," she screamed. "Get me out of here!"

A moment later came the unmistakable sound of gunfire.

****

I glanced down. Gasoline was flooding down the stairs, pouring in from beneath the door.

Krüger.

I didn't want to touch off the gas, but I had to back him off. Eyes stinging from the fumes, I pulled off my jacket and wrapped it around the muzzle of my Glock. Firing through several layers of fabric, I sent a half-dozen man-height rounds through the thick wooden door. A moment later the flow of gasoline lessened to a trickle.

"Deluca, Taylor," I yelled, yanking my cellphone from my pocket. "I'm in the basement, through a door off the kitchen. He's going to torch the place. The front door's open."

I turned up my phone volume in time to hear Deluca respond, ". . . on our way."

"I smell gas," the girl screamed from below, her voice now filled with panic. "Oh, Jesus, he's going to burn us like he did those cops. Get me out!"

Hoping one of my bullets had connected, I turned my aim to the lock. I blew through the remainder of my magazine, firing into the doorknob and jamb. Although the .45-caliber slugs made a mess of the wood, the door didn't budge. Apparently things didn't work like in the movies.

As I was inserting another magazine, I heard Deluca yell from the other side. "Kane! Stop firing!"

"I'm stopping."

"Where is he?" shouted Snead, also calling from the other side.

"I don't know," I called back. "Be careful. He may be armed. And get this door open."

Unfortunately, all that my shooting had accomplished was to jam the door. Even with Deluca and Snead shoving on one side and me pulling on the other, it still took some time to pry open.

Finally pushing aside the shattered portal, I stepped into the alcove. The reek of gasoline was overpowering. Several tipped-over five-gallon gas cans lay nearby—one in the kitchen, another in the dining room. At the top of the stairs, another partially filled container sat in a puddle of gas.

"What kept you?" I asked.

"Krüger must have relocked the front door," Deluca replied. "Had to bust in. Sorry about your car, by the way. Didn't bother to climb the gate."

"Where is he?"

"He was gone when we got here," Snead replied.

"Well, now he's back," Taylor's voice came from behind us.

I turned to see Taylor making her way into the kitchen, Dr. Krüger out front. Krüger's hands were cuffed behind him. I also noticed blood running from his nose and dripping onto his shirt.

"I caught him on the terrace, heading out for a midnight bike ride," Taylor explained. "We had a disagreement about his coming back. He wound up taking a spill."

"You bitch," Krüger spat, his face mottled with fury. "You are going to regret this. All of you."

"I doubt that," I said, grabbing Krüger by his bloodstained shirt. Popping a few buttons, I jerked a keychain from his neck. Then, glancing at the gas cans, "You set a timer to start your little bonfire here?"

Krüger glared. "I want my lawyer."

I turned to Deluca. "Find his igniter before this place goes up in flames. And don't turn on any lights. Fumes."

"On it," said Deluca, heading into the house.

"Watch him," I said to Snead. "Taylor, you're with me."

Accompanied by Taylor, I rushed back down the stairs, returning to Krüger's basement prison. This time I noticed a light switch beside the door. Afraid of sparking the fumes, I didn't flip it on, using my flashlight instead.

The young woman began crying again when she saw the key in my hand. "Oh, thank God, thank God," she whispered, tears running down her face. "I don't want to die."

"Nobody's going to die," I assured her, swinging open the iron door. "C'mon, let's get you out of here," I added, placing an arm around her shoulders.

With Taylor and me assisting the young woman, we retreated up the stairs. Snead and Deluca were on the landing when we arrived. Both had their weapons trained on Krüger, who was kneeling in a puddle of gas.

I tipped my head at Taylor, signaling her to take the young woman out through the garage. Then, to Deluca, "You find his igniter?"

"Yeah, in the den. Lit cigarette and a pack of matches."

"Any other incendiary devices?"

"I didn't see any. I didn't have time to search the entire house, but I think we're good, unless something accidentally sparks the gas. Either way, we should get out of here."

"I hear you. Let's go."

"I need a minute," said Snead.

"What for?" asked Deluca.

I looked at Snead, then back at Deluca. "Paul, I'll see you outside. Start getting a statement from the young woman. And get that collar off her neck."

"Right," said Deluca. Then, heading for the mudroom, "Don't be too long, *paisano*."

Still holding his weapon on Krüger, Snead glanced at me. "You, too, Kane. Out."

"I'm not going anywhere."

"Okay, then this is on you." Leaning down, Snead grabbed the partially filled gas can at his feet. Before I could stop him, he dumped the contents on Krüger, drenching him with gasoline.

"Jesus, Snead! What are you doing?"

"This piece of filth likes to burn people," Snead snarled. "Just giving him a taste of his own medicine."

Sputtering, Krüger stared up at Snead. "You're conducting an illegal search. Nothing you find here will hold up in court."

"You're not going to walk on this, pal," I said. "That is not going to happen."

"We'll see," Krüger shot back. "In the meantime, I want to speak with my lawyer."

"That's not going to happen, either," Snead said quietly. Stepping closer, he placed the muzzle of his pistol against Krüger's forehead.

"Snead . . ."

"Get out of here, Kane."

"I can't do that."

"After what this monster did to Ella, I can't let him go. You lost a child, Kane. You, of all people, should understand."

"I do. But . . . that isn't the way."

Oddly, Dr. Krüger seemed unafraid. Cocking his head to one side, he squinted into the glare of our flashlights. His tongue flicked across his lips. "You don't have the stones," he said to Snead.

Gun pressed to Krüger's forehead, Snead's eyes welled with tears of rage and frustration and utter, ineffable loss. Taking a breath to steady himself, he struggled to pull the trigger.

Krüger regarded Snead with cold, emotionless eyes.

"Bill, don't," I said. "Killing him won't bring her back."

Tears coursing down his cheeks, his finger trembling on the trigger, Snead screamed—venting his anger in one long, pitiful, heartrending cry.

Then, hand shaking, he lowered his weapon.

I moved in, deciding to get Krüger out of there before Snead changed his mind.

Suddenly I smelled smoke.

I turned.

Fire was flickering in the basement, probably ignited by the furnace. An instant later the flames began climbing the stairway. I rushed to the door, hoping to contain the blaze. The gunfire-shattered portal refused to close.

Soaked in gasoline, Krüger realized the danger. "No!" he screamed, struggling to rise. Hands cuffed behind his back, he lost his balance, lurching to one side.

The fire raced toward us. Heart pounding, I stepped away from the puddled gasoline. Snead did the same.

Krüger wasn't as fortunate. Squealing in horror, he again tried to rise.

And again he failed.

Like a hungry beast, the flames engulfed Dr. Krüger, devouring him in a fireball. Screaming, he attempted to quench the blaze by rolling on the gas-puddled floor, making matters worse.

Smoke was rapidly filling the room. Fire had spread to the kitchen. I could also hear a roar from other parts of the house, concluding that Krüger must have set more than one igniter.

Bare seconds remained before the entire structure went up in flames. I grabbed one of Krüger's ankles. Backing toward the kitchen, I began dragging him with me.

I glanced at Snead. "Help me," I yelled.

To his credit, Snead only hesitated a moment.

More quickly than I could have imagined, the inferno in the house took hold. Flames erupting on all sides, Snead and I retreated through the kitchen, hindered by a blazing, writhing, screeching Dr. Krüger.

My plan was to make it to the mudroom and from there to the garage. By then the flames consuming Dr. Krüger were searing my hands and forearms. I could barely breathe. A dark, oily layer of smoke was roiling overhead, lowering rapidly.

"Shit," Snead yelled. "Where are we?"

I glanced around, my flashlight barely penetrating the smoke-filled room.

Nothing looked familiar.

"Which way?" Snead yelled again, a note of panic rising in his voice.

"I'm not sure," I answered.

"Kane!" came a voice from the blackness, barely audible above the roar of the fire.

Taylor.

"Dan, where are you?" another voice called.

Deluca.

"Over here," I called back.

"Crawl toward us," Taylor yelled.

Nearly blinded by smoke, I squinted into the darkness. To the left, I saw Taylor squirming toward us on her stomach and elbows. Deluca was right behind her, barely visible beneath the lowering ceiling of smoke.

Changing direction, Snead and I started toward them, still dragging Dr. Krüger.

Taylor grabbed my coat. Deluca did the same for Snead. Together we scrambled to the garage. And from there, to the lawn outside.

A blast of flame followed us out.

Dr. Krüger was still on fire. While Snead ran to the front of the house to back my Suburban from the inferno, I blanketed Krüger with my coat—doing my best to smother the flames. Deluca stripped off his jacket and helped. By then Krüger's clothes were little more than blackened rags. Scorched by the heat, the skin on his chest and arms had begun to split—exposing a bubbling layer of fat below, further feeding the flames.

Although we worked quickly, by the time we finally extinguished Dr. Krüger, most of his handsome face had been obliterated—nose, eyelids, lips, hair, and ears completely gone, his fingers reduced to grotesque, charred stubs. The fire had even taken his vision.

Once we had done all we could for Krüger, I turned to Deluca, flinching as another gasoline container exploded inside the house.

"That was cutting it a little close in there, partner," said Deluca, clearly shaken.

"I hear you," I agreed.

Taylor, who had been standing on the grass with her arm around the young woman, removed her jacket, draped it over the girl's shoulders, and came over to join us. "You okay?" she asked, inspecting me closely, her face close to mine.

I took a deep breath, then let it out. "Yeah, I'm fine," I said.

"And you were just starting to regrow those lashes and eyebrows," she noted. "And your hair. Guess we'll have to shelve your modeling career for a while."

I smiled. "That was off the table a long time ago."

"With good reason. Not that you don't have your charms."

I held her eyes with mine. "Seriously, Sara, thank you. I'm not certain we were going to make it out of there. That's the second time you've saved my life."

Taylor smiled. "That's what partners do, right?"

I nodded. "That's what partners do."

"Hey, I went back in there for you, too," Deluca broke in, feigning insult.

"I know you did, Paul. Thank you as well," I replied with a grin. "But actually, I think you should take credit for saving Captain Snead."

"Probably never live that one down," Deluca grumbled.

Snead, who had been staring at the fire, turned. "I also appreciate what you two did in there," he said, addressing Deluca and Taylor. "I know you both went back for Kane, but . . . thank you anyway. As for credit, I'm not certain how much of that will be getting passed around."

"Speaking of which, we need to get straight about what happened here tonight," I said.

"What do you mean?" asked Snead.

I thought for a moment. "Okay, be quiet and listen," I replied, withdrawing my cellphone. Fumbling with my burned fingers, I dialed from memory, phoning Allison at home.

"Little late to be calling, Pop," said Allison upon picking up. "Some of us working people with kids go to bed early."

"Ali, you're on speaker with Special Agent Sara Taylor, Detective Paul Deluca, Captain William Sneed, and me," I informed her, skipping the pleasantries.

"Hey, Paul. Hi, Sara," said Allison. "Hello, Captain Snead. What's up, Dad?"

"First, you need to forget the names I just mentioned."

"What names?"

"Good girl," I said. Then, "I'm about to give you an exclusive on The Magpie investigation. One condition. What I'm about to say has to be attributed to 'sources inside the department.'"

"I don't have a problem with that," Allison replied, suddenly sounding excited. "Hold on, lemme get a pen." Then, "Okay, shoot."

"I'll keep it simple," I began. "This evening, acting on confidential information, members of an LAPD/FBI interagency task force investigating The Magpie murders arrested Dr. Erich Krüger. Krüger, who was critically injured during the arrest, will be charged with the murders of Ella Snead and others. Dr. Krüger was apprehended at a residence in San Diego where he was holding his latest victim, Ms. Lisa Brady. Ms. Brady was successfully rescued and is expected to make a full recovery."

"Sounds like there's more to *that* story," Allison observed.

I glanced at Snead. "There is, but I'm going to let LAPD fill in the details. You understand what I'm saying here, Ali?"

"I do. Thanks, Dad. Love you."

"Love you, too."

"It'll fly," said Snead after I hung up. "Once that version is out there, everyone will have to fall in line."

"That's how I have it figured," I said. "We all onboard?"

Everyone nodded.

Snead stepped closer, his scorched hands loose at his sides. He had been burned in our effort to save Krüger, but not as badly as I. "Thanks, Kane," he said, not offering to shake. "I appreciate what you did for me in there. I just . . . well, you know."

"You're welcome," I replied.

Snead looked away, then turned back to me. "I still don't like you," he said.

I smiled. "That's okay, Bill. I still don't like you much, either."

Coming from somewhere in the distance, I heard the wail of sirens.

"I called 911," said Taylor.

By then flames had engulfed a major portion of Krüger's house. One wing had started to collapse, settling to a pile of embers. Behind me on the ground, as the sirens grew nearer, I heard Dr. Krüger sobbing in anguish.

I turned to regard the monster who had caused the deaths of so many. He lay curled on his side—hideously disfigured, forever blind. Recalling the suffering he had inflicted, and all the innocents he had murdered, and the SWAT officers he had burned alive, I couldn't work up much sympathy. With a feeling of disgust, I turned my back on what remained of Dr. Krüger, closing my ears to his cries.

Epilogue
Birthday

Summer days in Southern California are generally hot, dry, and sunny, and Saturday, August 11th—the anniversary of Allison's twenty-third birthday—proved no exception, with the temperature on the sand soaring into the nineties. Cooling things a bit, an offshore breeze picked up around noon, holding back the waves and carrying down the sweet smell of sage from the hills behind our house.

All in all, a perfect day for a party.

One of the perks of living on the beach, aside from enjoying the sometimes breathtaking, often dangerous, forever changing beauty of the ocean, is having the ability to invite as many people as you want to an outdoor celebration. As a family, we Kanes had thrown many boisterous beach bashes, although with the exception of Allison's wedding reception, none since Catheryn's death. As such, I was looking forward to Allison's party, along with a belated nod to Nate's June birthday as well.

In the past, attendance at similar gatherings had numbered in the hundreds, and I estimated our turnout that day would probably total the same, possibly more. Also, as in the past when guests had brought a favorite entrée, side dish, or dessert, I had put out the word that for Allison's birthday we would be revisiting our potluck tradition as well.

Later that day, under a cloudless blue sky, I stood on our deck surveying party preparations with a practiced eye. Making certain nothing had been overlooked, I reviewed a mental checklist: Two Porta Potties, a precaution to avoid overstressing our septic system, had been delivered and were stationed on the street above. Beer kegs and soft drinks were cooling in ice tubs on our shaded deck. Barbeques were stocked with charcoal and ready to light. 40-gallon trashcans lined with a black plastic garbage bags had been strategically placed near the serving tables. Waiting on the food counters were paper plates and cups, plastic flatware, and an assortment of appetizers, side dishes, and cold casseroles that early-arriving guests had brought. Salads and other perishables were upstairs in the fridge, along with ice cream, melons, and a huge chocolate cake. Last, per the tide tables, the ocean was receding as predicted, providing plenty of sand for an armada of dinner tables rented from a local caterer.

Everything seemed ready. Most invited guests had indicated they wouldn't be arriving until later, but over fifty partygoers had already shown up, and like a runaway freight train, the party was gathering momentum and rapidly approaching the point of no return. With a shrug, I decided that if anything had been overlooked, it was too late to correct the omission.

Although the bandages on my hands and forearms had come off earlier in the week, I had yet to return to work—still remaining on a medical leave-of-absence imposed by Chief Ingram. Also as ordered, I had kept my head down and unavailable for comment, staying out of the media spotlight as worldwide print, radio, and television coverage on the investigation again took center stage.

During a contentious, high-level meeting following Dr. Krüger's arrest, the brass at PAB had agonized over what version of events to present. There were some, including Assistant Chief Strickland, who wanted to put a different spin on things than reported by CBS correspondent Allison Kane. Not for the first time, Strickland accused me of leaking to the press, which of course I had. In response, also not for the first time, I suggested to Strickland that he go pound sand. Finally, presented with little other option, the powers-that-be eventually decided their best course lay in elaborating on Allison's account of the story.

Afterward, during a news briefing attended by hundreds of clamoring correspondents, Chief Ingram, Mayor Fitzpatrick, Assistant Director Shepherd, and Captain Snead's task-force detectives had shared credit for bringing The Magpie investigation to a successful conclusion. Pending further investigation, the names of the officers participating in the actual arrest were being withheld.

The official PAB accounting of the case was as follows: On the previous evening, an interagency surveillance team had followed Dr. Erich Krüger—chief suspect in The Magpie investigation—to a second residence in San Diego, where it was determined he had imprisoned Ms. Lisa Brady. In the course of resisting arrest, Dr. Krüger had ignited a gasoline fire and been critically injured in the blaze. Following his capture, he was transported to the UCI Regional Burn Center. In a statement made at the scene, Ms. Brady identified Dr. Krüger as her captor, adding that at the time of her abduction, Dr. Krüger had been transporting the body of a young woman in his van—a body Ms. Brady later confirmed from photographs as being the corpse of Ella Snead.

In passing, it was noted that Detective Daniel Kane had been cleared of any wrongdoing, and that Internal Affairs Group was dropping its inquiry into his alleged use of excessive force.

Although I subsequently learned that my unauthorized investigation of Dr. Krüger had been retroactively "approved" by Chief Ingram, I was still uncertain what the long-term result of my insubordination would be. In the meantime, I had received heartfelt messages of appreciation from the families and teammates of the murdered SWAT officers.

And for me, that was enough.

For their work on the case, Lieutenant Nelson Long and Detective Paul Deluca received Meritorious Service Medals. Special Agent Sara Taylor was honored by the Bureau for outstanding initiative displayed during the course of the investigation, along with a bump in pay.

And I was good with that, too.

On another positive note, I had heard that Brian Shea would be petitioning for a retrial in the murder of Darlene Mayfield. Detective Aken and I assured Brian's new attorney that we were both more than willing to testify on Brian's behalf.

"You okay, Dad?"

I turned, finding Allison regarding me with a look of concern.

"I'm fine," I replied. "Just thinking . . ."

"Thinking, huh? By now you should have learned your lesson on that," Allison joked, shifting Katie in her arms. "Here, take your granddaughter."

"With pleasure," I replied. "Hey, you gorgeous little bundle of joy," I murmured, smiling as Allison handed Katie to me. "Are you going to give your mom as much grief as she gave me?"

Though Katie was barely months old, I swear she smiled back.

"Let's hope not," Allison laughed. Then, glancing around at the party preparations, "Thanks again for all this. It's been a while."

"You're welcome, Ali. And yeah, it has," I agreed, returning my gaze to the beach.

Travis, who had been invited to conduct a performance of the LA Phil's Youth Orchestra the following week, had flown in early with McKenzie for Ali's party. Wearing swimsuits, they were down by the water sailing a Frisbee back and forth with Nate and McKenzie's younger sister, Nancy, and Christy White, my son Tommy's girlfriend at the time of his death. Callie, racing along the ocean's edge, was retrieving missed tosses and doing her canine best to join in.

"I also appreciate your giving me that Magpie exclusive," Allison continued. "It put me on the media map. Permanently."

"I'm glad, Ali. You deserve it."

"You heard about Krüger, right?"

"I did," I said, having listened to a news report that morning stating that Dr. Krüger had died the previous evening, succumbing to sepsis and multi-organ failure at the UCI Burn Center. "Nice of him to save us the cost of a trial."

"He won't be missed," Allison agreed. "All the people he hurt, all the people he killed . . ."

"Roger that."

Not all of Krüger's Black Mountain Ranch property had been destroyed in the blaze. A number of items had eventually been recovered, including a computer server that fire crews managed to save. Bureau techs eventually broke Krüger's security protocols, and the material contained on the hard drive proved both heartbreaking and chilling. In addition to chronicling the deaths of the seven "calendar girl" women who had died in Krüger's basement since January, other videos detailed the torture and demise of thirty-one additional young women—all perishing at Krüger's hand. Though there may have been more, it was hoped their identification would bring the associated families some sort of closure, as painful as it might be.

"I don't know whether I told you, but Network offered me the New York anchor position—again," Allison went on.

"Huh. What did you tell them this time?"

Allison smiled. "I told them I was perfectly happy being a working mom right here in L.A. Which I am."

"I'm sure that decision went over well with Mike."

"It did," Allison replied. "Moving would be a mistake for him. His career in L.A. is really taking off. He's going to be the director of photography on Tom Grant's next feature," she added proudly, referring to an Academy Award winning actor who was also a family friend.

"That's wonderful, Ali. I can't tell you how happy I am that you and Mike and Katie will be sticking around. I'd have missed you if you left."

"Me, too."

Again glancing at the beach, I watched as McKenzie snagged a wild toss by Nate, diving to grab the Frisbee just before it disappeared in waist-deep water. Laughing, McKenzie backhanded the Frisbee to Travis, ducked under an approaching wave, swept back her hair upon resurfacing, and waded to shore.

"Anything new on your novel?" I asked, gently rocking Katie in my arms.

Allison brightened. "Mac sold it to one of the major houses. I'm going to be swamped with rewrites for the next few months. The publisher wants it out by Christmas, hoping to piggyback the book launch on my Magpie notoriety."

"Got a title yet?"

"Nope."

"Well, good luck on that," I said, noticing Taylor—who was carrying a towel, a large glass dish, and a beach chair—making her way down our side stairway. Smiling, I returned Katie to Allison, placing her back in my daughter's arms. "See you in a bit. There's someone I want to talk to."

Allison, who had also spotted Taylor, smiled back. "Say hi for me. Tell her I'll look her up after I feed Katie."

"I will."

Wearing dark glasses, sandals, and a sundress that showed off her tanned legs, Taylor paused at the bottom of the stairs. Then, threading her way across the crowded deck, she began making her way toward the beach, turning male heads all the way to the seawall.

Wading through a knot of LAPD officers struggling to tap one of the beer kegs, I intercepted her near the food tables.

"Hey, Kane," she said with a grin. "Glad to see the bandages are off."

"Me, too. Damn, Taylor, I almost didn't recognize you in street clothes," I noted as she raised on her toes to kiss my cheek. "You look like a movie star."

"High praise," Taylor laughed, executing a coquettish twirl that exposed a brief flash of thigh.

"Bring a swimsuit?"

She nodded, adding her potluck offering to the dishes already present on the food tables. "Have it on underneath. Potato salad," she continued, noticing my glance at her casserole. "My mom's recipe."

"I'll be sure to give it a try."

"You'll love it, I guarantee." Turning, Taylor surveyed the throng of partygoers already on the beach. "I didn't realize the celebration was going to be this big," she said, seeming surprised.

I laughed. "Hell, this thing is just getting started."

Past the seawall, several of Trav's friends were erecting our volleyball court—setting the posts deep in the sand and chaining down the corners of the boundary ropes—a summer task I had neglected during the investigation. Closer to the water, other celebrants were lounging on towels and beach chairs, while in a bid to escape the sizzling sand, a number of the younger attendees had swum to the raft. At least a dozen were crowded atop the ten-by-ten deck, with a half-dozen more hanging onto the sides, waiting their turn to board.

"Volleyball, huh?" said Taylor, eyeing the court.

"You play?"

Taylor nodded. "A little."

"Good. See you out there later on the sand," I said, noticing that the LAPD beer-tapping project was about to go terribly awry. "Right now I have a problem to attend to."

"A quick question before you go."

I turned back.

"I have some time off next week, and I'm heading up to the Kern River with a few dirtbag friends," said Taylor. "Get out of town, do some kayaking, camping, hanging out. Should be fun."

"Dirtbag friends?"

Taylor smiled. "If you're a kayaker, that's a good thing. Anyway, I thought Nate might want to get in a little more boating before school starts. There are several sections of whitewater I could guide him down, but I wanted to check with you before asking."

"If Nate wants to go, I'm all for it. Invite him."

"I will. Want to join us?" Sensing my hesitation, Taylor added, "No strings, Kane. If you want, I could find you a boat and some gear, maybe show you a few things on the river. Think about it."

"Thanks, Sara. I will."

Hours later, thanks to a steadily falling tide, a broad expanse of sand now extended to the water's edge, and Ali's party shifted into full swing. By then nearly two hundred additional guests had swelled our ranks, with a river of people still making their way down the outside stairway.

Taylor's claim that she played "a little" volleyball proved an understatement. It turned out she had competed in high school for the state-ranked Salmon River Savages, and together she and I held winners on the v-ball court for over an hour—finally getting knocked off by Travis and McKenzie.

As shadows lengthened, Travis, Ali's husband Mike, my cold-case pal Jerry Aken, and Jerry's daughter Madison started tending the barbeques—grilling a savory assortment of chops, ribs, steaks, burgers, and chicken. Meanwhile, upstairs in the kitchen, Dorothy, Allison, and Taylor began overseeing the heating of enough casseroles to feed an army. In addition, the serving tables on our deck were overflowing with salads, fruits, melons, corn on the cob, and a selection of cheesecakes, pies, brownies, and tarts.

At that point most of my LAPD associates had shown up, including Deluca, Banowski, and Lieutenant Long—the only member of the brass who had been invited. My ex-partner Arnie and his longtime girlfriend, Stacy, also joined our ranks. Even Lou Barrello, a retired detective friend from Orange County, motored down in his charter boat from Oxnard, tying up to the raft and swimming ashore to join the festivities. With considerable effort, I dragged several of the rowdy police group away from the beer kegs long enough to have them assist in setting up the tables and folding chairs on the sand.

Many of Catheryn's LA Phil associates, among them fellow cellist Adele Washington and family, Trav's first piano teacher Alexander Petrinski, and a score of Philharmonic musicians joined the party as well, gathering in sedate groups beneath the upper balcony. Mike's L.A. film crew, including cinematographer friend Don Sturgess and actors Tom and Rita Grant, laid claim to a spot near the sea wall, joined there by Roger Zemo, who would be directing Tom's next movie. Also adding to our group as dinner hour approached, a number of Allison's CBS associates, including bureau chief Lauren Van Owen and others, assumed a strategic section of deck near the bar. And finally, near the water's edge, a troop of youngsters—their tireless ranks accompanied by a sandy, scruffy, joyous Callie—still splashed in the shallows.

As I stood surveying the party, I spotted Taylor across a throng of partiers crowding the deck. Holding Katie in her arms, she was standing with Dorothy and Allison, laughing at something Ali had just said. I caught Taylor's eye and smiled. Raising a hand to her hair, she lifted her head and smiled back. And as she did, I was struck by the unexpected thought that I was intimately connected, in some way or another, with almost everyone present that day. They were an important, integral part of my life, as I was of theirs.

Nevertheless, until then the celebration had seemed a bit fragmented, with various groups sequestered in separate enclaves here and there. With a late-hour influx of neighbors from the beach suddenly ballooning our ranks, the party abruptly coalesced, with celebrants now jammed shoulder-to-shoulder into one huge, homogenous organism. And that organism was hungry.

It was time to eat.

Later, with dessert and the appearance of Allison's birthday cake, came an endless round of toasts. I stood on an ice chest and added to them, wishing both Nate and Allison happy a birthday and many more to come, as well as thanking Ali for giving our family a grandchild. Last, Coke in hand, I asked everyone to raise a glass with me to the next generation, expressing the hope that we might turn over the world to them in better shape than we had found it.

Afterward, as was usual for me at parties like that, the remainder of the evening flew past in a blur, with there never seeming to be enough time to talk with everyone.

Our last guest departed around 1:00 a.m. Dorothy and I were the last ones up. Leftovers stowed in the fridge, we were spending a final few minutes picking up trash on the beach before the dogs and birds could spread it around the following morning.

With the final garbage bag filled, I took a break before going to bed. To the east, rising above the glow of Santa Monica, a waning moon was illuminating the ocean in shimmering flashes of silver. Sitting on the seawall, I stared into the coals of a fire guttering in a pit several yards distant. I had purposely skipped building a bonfire for the celebration, having experienced enough blazes over the past month to last a lifetime. Nevertheless, following dessert Travis and several of his friends had gathered driftwood and built one anyway—claiming that a beach party without a bonfire was just plain wrong.

"Great celebration, Dan," said Dorothy, joining me on the seawall.

"It was. I think Ali really enjoyed it," I replied. "Nate, too."

Dorothy kicked off her sandals, digging her toes into the cool sand at the base of the wall. "I know they did. We all did."

With the setting of the sun, the offshore breeze had died. The air was now still, with the lapping of waves against the shore the only sound in the night. "I don't think I'll ever eat again," Dorothy continued with a grin.

"I hear you," I laughed, once again struck by how much Dorothy reminded me of Catheryn, especially when she smiled.

"That was a nice toast you made to Ali."

"A little more upbeat than the one I gave at her wedding."

"Yes, it was."

"Times have changed."

Dorothy turned toward me. "For the better?"

I hesitated, realizing that for the first time since Catheryn's death, I felt at peace. "For the better," I said.

"Good." Dorothy paused. Then, "Dan, the last time we talked seriously, I pushed you pretty hard. I did it for a reason."

"I know."

"You were choked with guilt over what happened to Catheryn. I told you it wasn't your fault, remember?"

"I do. And I said that that if it hadn't been for me, she would still be alive."

"You did. I let that go because at the time I didn't think you were ready to hear what I had to say."

"And now?"

"Now I think you are." Dorothy found my eyes with hers. "Of course Catheryn's death was because of you—at least to some extent. It was a result of your job. You didn't pull the trigger, but you inadvertently put Catheryn in the line of fire. There's no getting around that. But that is something for which everyone has forgiven you, if they ever blamed you at all. Now you need to forgive yourself."

"I'm not sure I can."

"You have to, Dan. Otherwise it will consume you."

"What about you, Dorothy? Do you forgive me?"

"There is nothing to forgive. It was just life. And if Catheryn were here, she wouldn't blame you, either, not even a little—nor would she change one minute of her time spent with you. What's more, now that she's gone, she wouldn't want you to be so alone. That's the truth in all this."

I looked away, gazing out over the moonlit beach. "So where do I go from here?"

"I told you earlier, but you couldn't hear me then," Dorothy replied. "Maybe now you can. Your guilt over Catheryn's death will never go away. Never. Nor will the pain of losing Tommy. Those feelings will always be with you, Dan. In time, they will simply become a part of who you are."

I nodded, remembering that at Catheryn's grave, I had once said something similar to my children.

"I also told you that the important thing for you now is to find hope and meaning and possibly even joy in life, even when things go wrong," Dorothy continued. "Can you do that?"

"I want to," I said.

"Then that's a start," said Dorothy, again finding my eyes with hers. "While we're on the subject, you made me a promise."

"I know."

"Do you remember what it was?"

"I promised to take a long look at my life, decide what was truly important, and commit to it."

"And have you?"

Again I nodded, realizing that during my last visit to Catheryn's grave, I had.

Dorothy smiled. "Good," she said. Then, placing her arms around my neck, she gave me a hug.

"Aren't you going to ask?"

"About how you're going to go on with your life, and what you plan to do concerning your career, and how you're going make everything all right?" Dorothy shook her head. "No, Dan, I'm not. After all these years, I don't need to ask."

"Why not?"

Still holding my eyes with hers, Dorothy smiled. "Because after all these years," she said gently, "I already know."

Acknowledgments

I would like to give thanks to a number of people who provided their assistance while I was writing *Kane: Blood Moon*.

To Detective Lee Kingsford (LAPD, retired), and to Henry "Bud" Johnson (Redondo Beach PD, retired), I owe my deep appreciation. Their gift of time, knowledge, and friendship proved invaluable during the preparation of the manuscript. Any inaccuracies, omissions, or just plain bending of facts to suit the story are attributable to me alone.

To Susan Gannon, my wife and trusted muse with a sharp eye for detail, to friends and family for their encouragement and support, to my eBook editor Karen Oswalt, to Karen Waters for her work on the cover, and to my core group of preview readers—many of whom made valuable suggestions for improvements—my sincere thanks.

If you enjoyed *Kane: Blood Moon*, please leave a reader review on Amazon or your favorite retail site. A word-of-mouth recommendation is the best endorsement possible. As such, your review would be sincerely appreciated and will help others like you search for books. Thanks for reading!   ~ Steve Gannon

About the Author

STEVE GANNON is the author of the bestselling Kane Novel series, which began with *A Song for the Asking*, first published by Bantam Books. Gannon divides his time between Italy and Idaho, living in two of the most beautiful places on earth. In Idaho he spends his days skiing, whitewater kayaking, and writing. In Italy Gannon also continues to write, while enjoying the Italian people, food, history, and culture, and learning the Italian language. He is married to concert pianist Susan Spelius Gannon.

To contact Steve Gannon, purchase books, check out his blog, or to receive updates on new releases, visit Steve's website at: stevegannonauthor.com

Made in the USA
Coppell, TX
03 June 2020

26948638R00166